DEEP IMPACT

MIKE SEARES

By Mike Seares

John McCready Series

Deep Steal

Deep Impact

Deep Hostage

Deep Control

Vinci Books

<u>vinci-books.com</u>

Published by Vinci Books Ltd in 2025

1

Copyright © Mike Seares 2019

The author has asserted their moral right to be identified as the author of this work in accordance with the Copyright, Designs and Patents Act 1988. This work is a work of fiction. Names, characters, places and incidents are the product of the author's imagination or are used fictitiously. Any resemblance to actual persons, living or dead, places and incidents is entirely coincidental.

All rights reserved. No part of this publication may be copied, reproduced, distributed, stored in any retrieval system, or transmitted in any form or by any means, including photocopying, recording, or other electronic or mechanical methods, nor used as a source for any form of machine learning including AI datasets, without the prior written permission of the publisher.

The publisher and the author have made every effort to obtain permissions for any third party material used in this book and to comply with copyright law. Any queries in this respect should be brought to the attention of the publisher and any omissions will be corrected in future editions.

A CIP catalogue record for this book is available from the British Library.

Paperback ISBN: 9781036703998

Printed and bound in Great Britain by Clays Ltd, Elcograf S.p.A.

Chapter One

Six weeks ago

From a height of a thousand feet the two coal-black eyes gazed down imperiously on the endless ocean below. On any other creature they might have appeared evil, menacing, but set back from the pale pink beak of the wandering albatross, they instilled calm, as though a window on the world from a wise and purposeful brain.

The albatross banked slowly to the right, the increasing breeze from the south sending ripples along the row of densely packed feathers that made up the giant wings and kept it in the air. Its wingspan was around twelve feet, the largest of any bird, and allowed the magnificent creature to soar on the strength of the wind for weeks at a time, covering thousands of miles in a single flight.

As it glided effortlessly across the sky it was difficult to tell whether it was thinking of its partner, many miles to the south on Macquarie Island, or if it was solely concerned with the task at hand—gathering food for its chick for what was turning out to be a harsh winter.

It had completed the turn and was about to head back in a grid-like search pattern looking for the telltale signs of where it might find its next meal, when it spotted a large cargo ship plowing through the waves. It adjusted its course, heading toward the vessel that was making heavy going of it through the ever-increasing swell.

In the vast expanse of the ocean, ships made good substitute feeding grounds. There was an almost continuous trail of scraps and detritus thrown overboard, so finding this one would save a time-consuming search for the squid and small fish that were the usual makeup of its diet.

But as it headed for the vessel, a sound on the air made it look up. It wasn't something to be afraid of, not an 'alert' kind of sound, more a far-off rumbling.

But it was growing louder by the second—which meant that whatever it was, it was coming closer.

The *Lady Christa* was not the most obvious name for a twenty-thousand-ton container ship whose sole purpose was to carry the products of the world across the oceans of the planet, but the owner was a sentimental type and had named her after a horse he had won his first bet on at Ascot when he was eighteen.

She had a blue hull and a pale green deck, though this was currently obscured by over five hundred large shipping containers. They were arranged five high and ten wide and took up the full length of the ship, all the way from the bow to the small white bridge at the stern, which just managed to peek its head above the cargo.

The containers were filled with everything from shiny new BMWs to jars of marmalade. Much of her superstructure was grimy and in need of a clean, and although the deck machinery, made up of winches, capstans and chains, had a fine coating of rust and had seen better days, she was still seaworthy.

She was one of a modest fleet of five, and right now she was heading down through the Coral Sea, way off the east coast of Australia, en route to Auckland in New Zealand, before the long trip back to Shanghai, which she had left twelve days earlier.

Her captain, Juan Rodriguez, was a small, overweight Mexican in his mid-fifties. He had black curly hair and a permanently scowling expression. He was currently peering out through the front windows of the bridge.

Every twenty seconds or so the bow heaved up and then crashed down through the next rolling mound of water, the wind whipping the spray across the tops of the containers to smash against the glass, briefly obscuring the view ahead.

He wiped a handkerchief across his brow, not from the heat, the air conditioning saw to that, but more from the sweat caused by the loss of time the waves were causing him. At this rate, it was unlikely he would be receiving any bonus when they arrived back in Shanghai, behind schedule, to load up the next consignment.

He glanced around the bridge to see if there was anyone he could berate about the lack of progress, but the only person on duty was the first officer, Sven Johansen, who was checking the navigation display. While he would dearly love to unload on the guy, he'd been on four voyages with Johansen and the man knew what he was doing. He'd leave him alone for now.

He needed some air.

Captain Rodriguez crossed over to the door on the starboard side of the ship and walked out onto the small flying bridge. He stared in frustration at the mountains of waves that were ranged against him. It was a conspiracy, he was sure of it. He was just about to turn away when something caught his attention high up in the sky.

He shielded his eyes from the glare of the sun. Way off on the starboard beam there was movement. As he looked up, he could make out a lone albatross curl in to track behind the ship and follow the wake, but it wasn't this that had caught his attention. It was far beyond the albatross, higher up. As he watched, he saw it again, a fiery trail, like a comet. But this was daytime. He had never seen a comet in daylight hours before.

As he continued to stare, it became brighter, then faded, ducking behind one of the sporadic bands of high cirrus clouds that filled the sky. When it emerged from the other side, it was larger—far larger. In fact, rather than a graceful arc across the sky you might expect from a comet, the angle of the trail, of what was almost certainly fire, indicated the object was coming straight toward him.

And there was something else.

He could now make out a loud roaring that had nothing to do with the agonized churning of pistons in the heat and sweat of the engine room thirty feet below. It was a sound that made the hairs on the back of his neck stand on end.

Right now, any thought of a lost bonus was furthest from his mind.

Right now, Captain Juan Rodriguez was more concerned about staying alive.

The thin sliver of gas that makes up Earth's atmosphere stretches from the surface of the planet up to a height of just over six thousand miles. It's made up of a series of layers. The lowest, known as the troposphere, reaches up to about seven miles and is the limit for commercial airliners. The stratosphere, mesosphere and thermosphere take things up to about three hundred and seventy miles, and the final layer, the exosphere, tops things off at a height of six thousand, two hundred miles. This is the domain of satellites and spacecraft.

This fragile, protective blanket is what makes life on Earth possible. It absorbs and deflects dangerous radiation from the sun. It keeps the surface at a habitable temperature, and it provides pressure to ensure water can exist in liquid form and not evaporate away into space.

Without it we could not survive.

Right now, at a point above the eastern seaboard of Australia, the mesosphere was being ripped apart.

It had started innocently enough, half an hour earlier, when the Cormorant B satellite had undergone a routine orbital correction maneuver. The technicians at the European Space Agency space operations center in Darmstadt, Germany, had made the correction to ensure the slight drop in altitude was reversed and the satellite was sent back into a more stable orbit—but something had gone wrong.

As soon as the technicians had made the adjustment they seemed to lose control of the satellite. It was as though a Wi-Fi connection had been dropped—reconnected—but they now had no control. They could still press their buttons, they could still see the displays change in front of them, but there was no confirmation message from

Cormorant B to verify the action had been successful—and more alarmingly, the radar tracking stations around the globe showed the satellite's orbit was decaying further, and was accelerating.

Messages had been sent, and the heartbeats of men and women with higher pay grades than the technicians at the ESA started beating that little bit faster.

The effect on a four-ton satellite re-entering Earth's atmosphere at over seventeen thousand miles per hour was catastrophic.

The delicate fifty-foot solar panels that stretched either side of the main core were the first to go, ripped clean from their mountings as though they were wings from a fly. Next, as the descent became steeper and the friction of the air increased, any external antennae and communications dishes dissolved into plasma as temperatures rose to an astounding five thousand degrees Fahrenheit.

Nothing could survive.

But something did.

At the heart of the satellite, where the computer control systems and other sophisticated hardware were located, the heat had done its worst, reducing them to no more than molten metal and plastic. But one area maintained an integrity and functionality that should not have been possible.

Hidden deep inside a box of thermal resistance material comparable to the underside of the Space Shuttle, a small computer hummed away as though sitting on a desk back at the Jet Propulsion Laboratory in California where it had been designed.

Deep Impact

The box contained a solid-state computer drive, and nothing on Earth could destroy the protective container in which it was housed.

It had been designed this way because the security of a nation depended on what was contained within the inner blocks of the drive's memory.

To Captain Rodriguez, the significance of the contents of the object hurtling toward him was academic. As he continued to stare up at the sky, he was transfixed by his approaching doom.

The crackling roar was now so intense that Johansen had joined him on the flying bridge to watch. They stood as one, fear masking their otherwise grim expressions.

"What do you think it is?" Johansen said in his distinctive clipped Scandinavian accent.

Rodriguez paused for a moment. "Looks like a meteor… but to be honest, I have no idea."

Johansen continued to stare. "Could be a plane."

Rodriguez glanced at him sharply. "Dear God, I hope not," he said, crossing himself quickly.

The ball of fire was now massive. It left a trail of smoke and ash across the sky, and there was no mistake—it was coming straight for them.

Then, as if broken from a trance, Captain Rodriguez turned and ran into the bridge. He made straight for the main steering control; not a large wheel as most might imagine, but small, like a family car. He spun it to the left for all he was worth, at the same time engaging full power.

While the wheel might be the size of a family car's, the ship certainly didn't respond like one. The lumbering hulk started to turn, but slowly—inch by inch, foot by foot. The odds of a six-hundred-foot cargo ship out maneuvering a fireball from the sky was not lost on the captain, but he had to do something, and this was the only option.

He went back outside with growing dread, but also with a certain fascination—few people had advance warning of the moment of their death.

The ship continued to turn, the twin screws almost tearing themselves from their mountings in a vain attempt to move the vessel out of the path of inevitable destruction.

But was it enough?

As the raging fireball grew ever closer, the two men ducked behind the side of the flying bridge—as if it would make a difference.

And then the matter was out of their hands.

The satellite hit the Earth…

…half a mile away.

The approaching roar was replaced by a massive explosion as the hurtling metal struck the ocean.

The surface of the water for a quarter of a mile around was vaporized. What was left filled the air with boiling droplets and a haze that obliterated any view. A burning seared their nostrils. Furnace-like heat scorched their airways. They gasped for breath…

…and then the blast wave hit, moving outward at multiple times the speed of sound. The captain flung his hands to his ears, crying out as his eardrums burst with the pressure of the shockwave racing through him on its ever-widening circle.

Captain and first officer sat there cowering behind the small metal side of the flying bridge—dazed, but alive.

After a nervous glance at each other, they pulled themselves slowly to their feet. But there was no time to recover.

Out of the haze, they watched in fear as the sea rose up in an ever-steepening wall that rushed toward them at terrifying speed.

It was now that the captain realized he may well have sealed their fate. The maneuver he had attempted earlier, which had ultimately served no purpose, now worked against him. The ship was sideways on to the approaching wave — the worst possible angle to be hit from. He ran to the wheel, desperately spinning it to try and bring the bow forward to meet the wave at ninety degrees.

But it was too late.

He had barely touched the controls when the vertical wall of water was upon them. The bow lurched upward, rolling the ship over to its side. A moment later water crashed across the deck. The top layer of containers was the first to go, flung aside like a child's toy boxes, dragging the second layer with them into the sea.

And the wave continued on.

Two further layers were swept away before what remained of the multimillion-dollar cargo was shunted back toward the superstructure. The huge containers piled up, metal grinding on metal. One smashed through the windows of the bridge, sending splinters of glass flying like transparent daggers. Water surged in, rising quickly. It pushed Captain Rodriguez back against the rear wall. He clung desperately to a supporting column, trying to hold on against the flow that now nearly filled the entire space.

Before the water covered him completely he watched in horror as Johansen was swept from the flying bridge. And then he managed a final breath as the water closed over him.

Later, the captain could not have told you how long he had been underwater. It could have been ten seconds; it could have been a minute. But after what seemed like an eternity, the water flowed from the bridge and he could slowly release his deathlike grip on the column.

He lay there for several minutes, gasping for air, and then slowly picked himself up. Once on his feet, he stood for a moment, regaining his senses. He glanced around at the devastation that surrounded him.

The rolling wall of death was gone, as though it had never been. The *Lady Christa* started to right herself. Gradually the oscillation slowed and she came to rest on an even keel.

Once the captain had taken it all in, he walked shakily out onto the flying bridge. He looked desperately around, scanning the water, but there was no sign of his first officer. He breathed a heavy sigh. It was one of sadness; Sven Johansen had been a good man; but it was also one of relief.

He had his bonus for the trip—he was alive.

From a height of a thousand feet the albatross had watched the drama unfold below. It had seen the satellite impact the water. The blast wave had sent it tumbling through the air —all rules of the physics of flight rewritten for several seconds. But then the shockwave had passed and as the giant bird had regained its composure it had stared down on a changed world. If it could have smiled, a broad grin would have spread across its face.

For as far as the albatross could see, the ocean was littered with detritus and flotsam from the spilled containers that had been ripped open by the force of the impact.

While his family wouldn't have much use for the numerous BMWs that floated with their trunks in the air, like the tails of metallic ducks foraging for food, one thing was for sure, they wouldn't be going hungry this winter.

Half a mile from the *Lady Christa* the water had started to calm.

Bubbles still rose from the depths, causing a froth on the surface. Ripples still radiated out from the point of impact. But these were insignificant compared to the tidal wave that had swept all before it only minutes earlier.

Aside from this disturbance there was little evidence of the massive event that had just taken place—but deep below, things were different. A tangle of twisted metal headed for the seabed.

The remaining pieces of the satellite, those that had survived the impact, plunged deep into the abyss in a tight spiral, heading away from the warmth and light above.

They had passed the hundred-foot mark after only a few seconds, then shortly after, three hundred feet. Five minutes later they were still heading deeper into the pitch-black of the Coral Sea.

After ten minutes they finally came to rest on a desolate alien landscape at a depth of sixteen thousand feet. The ragged mass of metal impacted the deep-sea sediment, sending a cloud of fine silt up into the water above.

Here, the pressure was over seven thousand pounds per square inch and the temperature thirty-five degrees Fahrenheit, but there was also now something else, something this distant part of the world had never seen before.

Light.

As the cloud of silt slowly dissipated, moved away by a gentle deep-sea current, the phenomenon of light entered the world for the first time since the oceans had covered the planet. It took the form of a small red flashing panel on the side of a sealed box.

And along with the light, other radiation was also emitted. But this was on an entirely different wavelength, one that, for those who had the ability to detect it, could reach all the way to the surface and many miles in all directions.

It basically said, *I'm here, come and get me.*

The only question was, who would get there first?

Chapter Two

Today

The electronic digits on the alarm clock clicked over to show a five followed by a couple of vertical dots and then a three and a zero. At the same time an urgent beeping aggressively interrupted the still and quiet of the room.

John McCready eased an arm out from under the thick duvet and pressed the small black button that would return calm to the room. Once all was silent, he rolled over, opened his piercing blue eyes and stared up at the ceiling. He paused for a second, as if reluctant to move, and for good reason. Once he made the decision to engage with the day and climb out of bed, he knew things would be changed forever.

He stood up, wrapped a thick toweling robe around his lean, muscular body, and walked downstairs to make a cup of coffee. He gently worked his shoulder, which still ached from an incident with a helicopter and the River Thames coming together more than a month previously, and sipped the coffee, letting the warmth flow through him and relax his tense and tired muscles.

He smiled ruefully at the business card of the *Sunday Times* journalist Tania Briscoe, who had been so instrumental in bringing down his former boss Malcolm Mercer, and that was propped casually against a packet of biscuits. He then took the coffee through the open-plan, split-level layout of his house to the lower living area. He picked up a small remote and clicked a button marked OPEN. Immediately there was a low humming and the seven-foot-high drapes pulled back from the thirty feet of paneled glass that stretched across the entire rear of the house. They moved smoothly aside, revealing a panoramic view across a wild and isolated bay on the west coast of Scotland.

It was still black outside, and as he slid open the central glass panel, the wind swept in. He quickly closed it behind him and walked out to the edge of the raised deck to stare out across the bay. The clouds that had been approaching earlier now covered the entire sky, and the winds that had brought them were gusting across the bay in occasionally violent bursts. There was no precipitation yet, but the temperature felt right for snow.

On the far side of the curved bay he could make out the dying embers of a fire that he knew came from a derelict building. The events of the previous evening were forever etched on his mind, but they had been necessary to right a wrong, or at least partially right it.

As he had walked back from the building earlier that night he had glanced at the small grave of the otter pup at the end of his garden. He had expected it to be just a glance, but he had been brought up short by seeing Mira, the pup's mother, lying on the small mound of earth looking at him. His breath had caught in his throat and they had stared at each other for several long seconds. It couldn't have been, but it was almost as though she knew what he had done. He had lingered a second longer and then carried on back to the house. Actions had consequences, and sometimes the *right* thing and the *correct* thing to do, were, in McCready's mind, not always aligned.

Looking down now from the deck, he tore his eyes away from the grave and stared out over the waves that were crashing against the shoreline with ever-increasing ferocity.

His life had changed with a brief phone call the previous day.

The consequences of that call and the subsequent ramifications he was soon to experience; suffice to say, he knew that his previous actions had come back to haunt him in a way he could not have imagined. He was only now beginning to find out what those might be.

He allowed himself one last glimpse across the bay as a 'free' man and turned and headed inside. As he pulled the glass panel to behind him, the first flakes of snow started to fall. They were large and fluffy, and the frozen water tumbling from the sky would soon become thick and all-enveloping.

McCready spent the next half hour showering and preparing for he knew not what. The instructions he had been given were very specific. He should pack for several weeks' duration and he should make sure no one would question where he was or what he was doing, which wasn't exactly difficult given he didn't exactly know where he was going or what he was going to be doing.

Once he was sure he had everything, he took a final look around the house. His gaze lingered on one end of the living room. Hanging on the wall were three items from his life that he always wanted close to him.

One was a spear from a Maasai tribal chief in Kenya, whose daughter's life he had saved and whose tribe had made him an honoree warrior, complete with his own personal spear.

The second was a poncho from Peru, given to him by a girl he'd fallen totally and hopelessly in love with when he had been backpacking shortly after leaving school. Due to events beyond his control it had never been able to go anywhere, a regret he would carry for the rest of his life.

The third item he kept almost as a punishment to himself, and if not that, then as a warning. In fact, it was not one but two items.

The first was a set of matching gold antique pistols given to him by a Saudi prince when McCready had helped him out of a particularly difficult situation during a salvage operation in the Red Sea. It had resulted in the prince saving face on a monumental level. The man had been eternally grateful, and had said that if there was ever anything McCready wanted he only had to ask. The circumstances in question were not, in McCready's view, his finest hour, and he had wanted to extricate himself from the prince's debt as soon as possible. It was all he could do to say he would never contact the prince again, at which the prince had laughed uproariously. A month later the pistols had arrived by special courier to show his gratitude. McCready kept them on the wall as a reminder to never trust anyone and also of the true value of things. But with his current situation he looked long and hard at them, and then with a heavy sigh and a shake of his head he did something he had promised himself he would never do; he went to a drawer in a wide desk below the pistols, and from the back, pulled out a small black box. This contained the second gift the prince had given him. He opened the box and stared at the object inside. He unfolded the small card that had accompanied it —*This is for you, John. Know that I am truly in your debt.* It was followed by: *If you ever need help, I will be there. A debt is always paid. Your friend, Khalid.*

Despite himself, he almost managed a smile as he pulled the Breitling diver's watch out of the box. It was a hefty design and something McCready would not normally have worn as it was so ostentatious, but part of the heft was due to a thicker than normal body form that housed something very special, something McCready just might need as he journeyed into the unknown. Surprisingly, for his Arab friend, it was not gold-plated. He had probably thought McCready would never have put it on if it had been.

He had been right.

He slipped the watch over his wrist, almost shuddering at its touch, and then slid his sleeve over it, as if out of sight was out of mind. But he could feel its grip beneath the cotton sweatshirt. He would just have to get used to it.

Five minutes later, he lugged a large kitbag out of the front door. He pulled the old oak door closed behind him and then took out his iPhone. He checked that the app displaying the security cameras that surrounded the house was working, and then, after tapping ALL LOCK, he pressed his thumb onto the fingerprint recognition button and heard the reassuring clunks of locks around the house slamming to, protecting the building. They were accompanied by a ten-second series of beeps as the alarm armed itself inside. He was now as sure as he ever could be that the labor of love he had toiled for five years to build would be as safe as possible. What he couldn't protect as thoroughly, though, was the wall at the end of the half-built games room beyond the patio at the side of the house, a wall that was probably worth more than any other on the planet—but then there were only a handful of people who knew it was there—and one of them, whom he was yet to meet, had given him an ultimatum he couldn't refuse.

That was something he would never forget, and someday there was going to be a reckoning.

McCready threw the kitbag into the rear of his Corris Gray Range Rover Sport and climbed into the driver's seat. With the ignition started, he turned up the automatic climate control to full heat and let it do its thing. The car informed him the outside temperature was twenty-three degrees Fahrenheit. He kept the Berghaus climbing jacket tightly zipped around him.

The wipers shoveled away the snow that covered the windshield as he slipped the car into gear and pulled away up the dirt track that led to the main road half a mile away.

The instructions had been clear.

Be at Ocean Oil, the company he co-owned, by midday. Since the company was in Aberdeen, that meant a four-plus hour drive in normal conditions. The conditions were far from normal so McCready had given himself extra time. Even so, with the way the snow was mounting up, he would be lucky if he made it at all.

By the time the car reached the main road the snow was falling in ever-increasing amounts. It almost completely obscured his view. The wind swirled in unpredictable gusts, creating large drifts at the side of the road, and McCready could see that the grit lorries had already been out. The snow, though, was quickly covering the thin layer of salt that lay on the surface of the tarmac, making the process of little real use.

He glanced down at the terrain setting dial, just to the rear of the gear lever, and rotated it to SNOW. And with that he turned left onto the A816 and headed off into the blizzard.

There were few cars on the road, but occasionally the white barrier twenty yards ahead, which was the limit of visibility, would brighten as headlights came toward him. They would intensify, almost dazzling for a moment, and then a vehicle would emerge from the gloom and shoot past. He had to grimace. The speed some of them were going would mean there would be plenty of work for the breakdown services by the time it was light.

He had been traveling for about twenty minutes, and the snow actually seemed to be easing, when, through the flakes, another light could be seen illuminating the shifting patterns of white in the darkness ahead.

The spinning blue lights of a police car shone out, making the snow glow and pulse like some sort of frozen discotheque.

McCready slowed, and as the lights grew in intensity he could also make out the red brake lights of a couple of cars stopped just before the stationary police Land Rover that was parked in a large lay-by fifty yards ahead. In the summer months a mobile kitchen used the lay-by. It made amazingly good bacon sandwiches, which McCready had taken advantage of on numerous occasions, but now it looked cold and uninviting, lit by the strobing blue lights.

A police officer was leaning down to the first car in the queue talking to the driver. There was what appeared to be a brief conversation and the officer waved the car on. The car in front of McCready slowly crunched forward on the impacted snow. The officer again leaned down.

A minute later the car drove off.

Then it was McCready's turn.

He drove forward slowly. He could see the policeman

was wearing a high-vis jacket over a black all-weather uniform beneath. As McCready approached, the cop swung the beam of a torch onto the Range Rover's license plate.

It looked like he was looking for someone in particular.

McCready glanced ahead. There was a second man standing by a black Range Rover just beyond the police car. But this guy was no regular cop. He was wearing full body armor, a black balaclava and cradled a Heckler & Koch submachine gun in his hands. He was also actively scanning the area with an almost terminator-like intensity. Beyond him, further up the road, another man, similarly armed, was watching for traffic coming the other way.

Clearly, whoever they were looking for, it was serious.

As McCready pulled to a halt, the policeman in the high-vis jacket walked over. He again shone his torch on the license plate. He glanced in at McCready. The garbled noise of an unintelligible message crackled over his two-way radio. He lifted the mike that was attached to the front of his jacket and spoke quickly. As he did so, McCready noticed the two armed men further up the road turn to look in his direction.

He started to feel extremely uneasy.

Chapter Three

As the policeman walked around to the driver's side, McCready could see the armed officer further up the road flag a car to a halt and speak briefly to the occupants. Two more cars drew up and stopped.

The cop was now outside the window indicating for him to lower the glass. McCready obliged. Immediately the warmth of the interior was sucked out into the freezing night. Flurries of snow swept into the car.

The cop glanced around the interior. He was about forty years old and had a friendly but no-nonsense demeanor.

"Evening, sir. Could I ask your name, please?" As he spoke, his breath formed a mist that seemed to hang in the frozen air between them.

"What's this all about, officer? Bad night to be out."

"It is indeed. Just your name, sir, if you wouldn't mind."

There was no point in being obstructive. "John McCready."

"Do you have any ID on you?"

McCready reached across to the glove compartment and pulled out his driver's license. He showed it to the man. After a brief inspection he handed it back. "If you could just hang on here Mr. McCready. This won't take long."

Before McCready could say anything, the policeman had stepped back and again spoken into his radio. He then clipped the mike to his chest before walking off to check around the car. McCready raised the window to keep out the biting wind and snow.

Ahead, the two armed men now coordinated to seal off the road completely. The one at the top stood in front of the oncoming stationary cars. The one closest to him lifted what looked like a bulky satellite phone and spoke briefly into it. At the same time, he looked further up the road, beyond his companion, to where there was a gentle incline leading to the brow of a hill about four hundred yards further on. As he did so, a car came into view, its headlights momentarily pointing high into the sky as it surmounted the rise, before falling back down to light the road in front of it. It too came to a stop at the end of the rapidly growing queue.

McCready checked his mirrors. He could see the cop looking at the rear of the Range Rover. He suddenly remembered something and gave a slight groan. That was all he needed. If he was delayed much longer he wouldn't make it to Aberdeen for midday.

A second later there was a knock on the glass. He lowered the window.

"You know one of your taillights is out, there, Mr. McCready?"

"Yeah, sorry. I've been meaning to get it fixed. Not going to be a problem, is it? I really have to get to Aberdeen. It's very important."

The cop looked at him with an inscrutable expression

before answering. "Be more than my job's worth to give you a ticket tonight, sir. Probably end up directing sheep in the Orkneys for the rest of my career... And as for getting to Aberdeen, I don't think you need worry about that."

McCready looked at him with a puzzled expression, but before he could answer, there was a noise like an approaching freight train coming from up the road. Both men turned to stare in that direction.

Beyond the rise there was a bright light approaching. Along with it came a growing rumble and a deep THUMP, THUMP sound that vibrated through to your very soul. Suddenly, two lights appeared over the brow. McCready's immediate thought was that it was a massive truck with lights on the top of the cab, but they kept on rising.

A second later and McCready realized it was no truck.

As the lights rose ever higher, a massive Chinook helicopter soared overhead with a deafening roar. He could make out the twin rotors spinning in the night air. It circled around behind them and came in to hover above the road in front of the Range Rover, its nose facing away.

The two armed men stood their ground. The policeman held onto his hat as the banshee wail accompanied a hurricane of wind created by the downwash. The Range Rover shook and vibrated. Any loose snow on the ground was immediately whisked into the air in a white tornado. Within seconds the tarmac was free of the white stuff as the four sets of wheels touched down.

It seemed like the fuselage had barely settled on the ground when the rear loading ramp started to lower. McCready watched in stunned amazement as the ramp hit the tarmac. Immediately two spotlights shone out from inside. The policeman leaned down, shouting above the roar.

"Have a good flight, sir."

McCready just stared at him as he indicated for him to drive forward. McCready glanced around, raised the window and then started to head slowly toward the chopper. As he did so he saw a figure walk to the mouth of the cavernous interior and stand at the top of the ramp. McCready couldn't make out any of the figure's features, as the spotlights threw it into a stark silhouette, making the scene look like something out of a Spielberg movie, but by the way the man stood, McCready could tell he had a confidence and assuredness unlike most men.

He also knew exactly who it was.

He drove carefully up the ramp. As soon as the rear wheels were inside, the ramp started to lift. Immediately, two men in army issue overalls started to secure the Range Rover to the floor with wide tensioned straps.

The man McCready had seen from the car had moved to the back of the cargo bay and stood watching him.

McCready climbed out of the Range Rover and walked slowly over.

The two men stared at each other for several seconds.

The man in front of him was of average build, about five foot seven, and had a hard, weather-beaten face with medium-length, but well-groomed, dark hair. He was dressed in casual slacks and a black turtleneck sweater. He was late forties and his eyes were gray. At this moment he wore a friendly but inscrutable expression.

He offered his hand.

"John, nice to meet you. Martin Steel. Thanks for coming."

McCready didn't initially take the hand. "I didn't think I actually had a choice."

Steel watched him closely. The hint of a smile crossed

his lips. His eyes turned briefly to flint. "Ah, come on, now. You made your choice when you decided to go into those tunnels… taking the law into your own hands." He raised his eyebrows slightly.

McCready knew he was right. He slowly took his hand and Steel's grip was as strong as his own.

"Follow me. It's somewhat noisy in here."

He led McCready out of the cargo section into a small sealed-off area close to the cockpit. The space was cramped. The walls and ceiling were quilted with thick insulation. On each side were two high-backed aircraft-style seats. In the corner a small desk was fixed to the floor. There was a laptop on the desk. Files and papers stood upright in neat divided racks on the wall. Steel closed the door behind them. Immediately the noise quietened.

"Better buckle up," said Steel. "It can get a little bumpy."

As McCready sat down and strapped a seatbelt securely around his waist, Steel spoke into a walkie-talkie. "Ok, Gary, take us up."

With that, McCready could hear the engine pitch increase in tone and volume. Slowly the large helicopter lifted off from the road. As he glanced out of the small round window to his left, he saw the two armed men climb into the black Range Rover and drive away. A few moments later the Chinook smoothly changed from vertical to horizontal flight.

Steel turned to McCready.

"Firstly, apologies for all this." He indicated the surroundings with a wave of his hand. "But the road is blocked further north and you wouldn't have made it to Aberdeen this side of a couple of days. And I do need you there today."

He paused for a few seconds before continuing.

"I guess you're wondering what this is all about."

"It had crossed my mind."

"You're here because I need your help. It involves your expertise, as well as that of your company and its equipment. And time is of the essence."

McCready decided not to reply; to let Steel explain himself.

The man opposite him picked up a file from the desk and scanned through it. "You have an interesting background, John. Somewhat colorful if I may say so." He spoke with a distinctly British, but definitely not posh, voice. It oozed high education, but there was also a strength to it that hinted at experience in the field. A man of the world. A smart man. Martin Steel had definitely been there and done it.

But done what exactly?

That was the question.

He continued scanning the file. "Learned to dive at an early age. Worked in dive schools around the world as an instructor. Proficient in subsea surveys, salvage, explosives, saturation techniques. Seven years with Deep Sea Explorations in the States, then ten years with Global Salvage until fired two months ago—which we all know about. While at Global Salvage was a main shareholder and initial investor in Ocean Oil Exploration; founded with Craig Richards, ex sub pilot, brilliant engineer. Company handles maintenance contracts for the North Sea oil industry, as well as cutting-edge design work for underwater vehicles and other related tech. One thing of interest—involved in near diplomatic incident in the Red Sea that almost resulted in a standoff between Egyptian and Saudi governments, over, and I quote 'the saving of face of Prince Khalid Amir Yassin.'" At this he looked up. "Care to elaborate?"

"Not really."

Steel put down the file and looked straight at McCready.

"Okay, let's get to it." He paused. "Something's come up in the Western Pacific. Something that could have serious implications for British national security. You're here to help serve your country."

McCready was intrigued, but confused and somewhat skeptical. "Couldn't you have just asked? Why all the threats back at the house with the drone?"

Steel almost made it to half a smile. "Sometimes it's better to leave people without an option. Sometimes you have to focus the mind."

"Personally, I find cooperation through mutual needs and goals to be better than fear and coercion—but maybe that's just me." He paused, as though wondering whether to ask the next question.

But he did.

"Would you have done it?"

"Fired the drone?"

"I have to know."

Steel picked up the walkie-talkie. "I guess we'll never know." He pushed the transmit button. "Gary. ETA Aberdeen?"

A crackle came over the speaker.

"In this weather, should be wheels down around nine hundred."

Steel put the radio down. He glanced at his watch—eight hundred.

"Ahead of schedule. You'd better call Richards. Tell him

to be early. We have no time to lose. I'll go over the specifics when we get there."

He was about to turn to the laptop on the table.

"There is just one thing," said McCready.

Steel stopped what he was doing and glanced at him.

McCready was hesitant. "What about the gold?"

Steel looked him straight in the eye. "What gold?"

...which was the one answer McCready had not been expecting. He was ready with all these options, ideas, scenarios, but "What gold?" had not been one of them.

Steel put it simply. "You help me. I help you. Use it in that company of yours. Build some more toys we can use in the future. This may not be the only time we work together, John." It was a statement, not a request. "Anyway, it would only go back to the Russians, and with the way those bastards play games these days, we can't really be having that now, can we?"

McCready looked at him with genuine astonishment, but his mind had already started ticking over. Then he looked up.

"One more thing."

Steel watched him closely.

"Just who the hell are you?"

Chapter Four

Six weeks ago

The Kamchatka Peninsular in far-eastern Russia is a remote, largely uninhabited region, covering an area of over a hundred thousand square miles. Large parts are covered in forest, out of which numerous volcanic peaks jut arrogantly into the sky, some of which are still active. There are a number of sizable lakes and rivers, and the tip of the peninsula on the eastern side is made up of high cliffs and fjord-like inlets, which is fully exposed to the harsh elements that could sweep in off the northern Pacific Ocean. It is the perfect location for a military base that wanted to stay hidden from prying eyes.

Situated on one of the furthest outposts of the Russian state, the base was home to the Russian Navy's special forces and submarine warfare facility, and right now its clandestine capability was concealed even more by the storm force winds that were blowing drifts of snow across the region with ever-increasing ferocity, causing an almost complete whiteout.

About a mile north of the base, on a deserted single-track road, Irina Lazarev turned the heating control up on her forty-year-old Lada as far as it would go. The fan made a loud clattering noise, stuttered for a second, and then settled back into a low drone that was nowhere near full speed. She cursed, muttering to herself. It was fourteen degrees Fahrenheit outside, and even in her thick woolen coat, scarf, mittens and hat, she was still freezing. At least there were only ten more minutes before she could escape the car. But even then it wouldn't be easy. There were twenty yards of open ground to cross from the carpark to the rear entrance of her workplace. At sixty-eight years old, with arthritis in both knees, she was not looking forward to the journey.

She had taken over cleaning duties at the base since her husband had come down with chronic bronchitis, and the twelve-hour shifts were starting to get to her. She never seemed to have any energy. She was constantly exhausted, but they had to put food on the table somehow.

She leaned forward to wipe the condensation that had built up on the windshield. As she did so, she knocked the small wooden crucifix that dangled from the rearview mirror. She apologized under her breath, crossing herself quickly. She was sure before the day was out she was going to need his help.

The car moved slowly on, the tires crunching along the two indents in the snow-covered road. She peered out through the windshield as the wipers desperately tried to clear a view through the driving flakes that were coming down even faster now. They piled up on the screen almost as quickly as the wipers could sweep them away, but then finally she breathed a sigh of relief as the vague outline of the guardhouse at the entrance to the base came into view through the snow.

She stopped at the small window and waited.

No one came.

She cursed again, under her breath, and gave a sharp jab on the horn. A second later a face appeared. The window slid aside. The man who looked out did not look pleased. He was in his fifties, had a bloated, ruddy face and wore a disheveled naval uniform. He stared down at her with a condescending expression as his eyes swept contemptuously over her and the car. He continued to stare with a disinterested look until she wound down her window and produced a well-worn and creased security pass, even though he knew her from going through the same ritual every day. He didn't even glance at the pass, keeping his eyes fixed on her. But after a minute, when all the heat from the car had been drawn out into the freezing air, he slid his window closed without a word. A second later a section of the chain-link fence rolled aside to let her pass.

Irina pressed her foot carefully on the accelerator and the old car moved off through the snow.

Ahead, she could only see about twenty yards. She edged forward slowly.

She had driven for around five minutes when there was a cough and a splutter from the engine and the motor died.

She sat there, immobile.

She was completely disoriented. She had no idea how far away the car park was—or even in which direction. She cursed again, glancing quickly at the crucifix and shut her eyes. There was no way she would be able to walk from here and survive. The heater had gone off with the engine, and now, with the complete lack of car noise, the sound of the wind enveloped the vehicle, as though it would carry it away into the ether at any moment, for her never to be seen again.

She tried the engine.

There was a strangled whine from the starter motor that continued until she finally turned back the key. It was as if the car was crying out in agony. She couldn't let that continue. She waited for a minute then tried again—but nothing.

The snow started to pile up around the tires. Soon it would be up to the doors.

She had to do something. She glanced at the crucifix. There was nothing to lose. She shut her eyes and reached into the depths of her soul and back to all the beliefs that had been instilled in her as a little girl growing up in Saint Petersburg, and she prayed for the engine to start.

But when she opened her eyes, her mouth dropped open and fear crawled up her spine.

Beyond the crucifix, beyond the windshield, out there in the howling gale, the snow swirled around a figure hanging in the air—in the shape of a cross.

It was the figure of a man.

Something covered his lower body, but his torso and shoulders were bare. His head was slumped forward, long, raggedy hair obscuring his face.

He must be dead.

She glanced back at the crucifix. Dead? He could never have been alive out there…

…unless.

She stared back at the image, but the snow had closed in again and it was gone.

Irina crossed herself several times in quick succession. She was a deeply religious woman. She needed to be. If you didn't have religion working here, you had nothing. But then she pulled herself together. She must have imagined it. But a second later the wind briefly blew the snow away, and for an instant she saw the figure again, only this time the face lifted to stare at her.

She gasped.

It was covered by a rough, scraggy beard, but behind it the expression showed such agony, such pain—more than any mortal man could endure. She could come to only one conclusion.

She was staring at the face of Jesus Christ.

She looked away and turned the key again.

There was an initial whine, then a cough and splutter and the engine fired. She closed her eyes and prayed under her breath. She glanced up at the figure, but it was gone. The snow had closed in. She kissed the crucifix and thanked God.

Her prayers had been answered.

She had seen his son.

There could be no other explanation.

But what was he doing here, in such a godless place?

Irina Lazarev had definitely not seen God, or indeed any relation. What she had seen was the closest thing to the devil ever to have walked the Earth.

The crucifix, or iron cross, is the hardest position to maintain for any gymnast. The official world record is slightly under forty seconds. The thought of one minute would be superhuman; two minutes would not be possible. Major Yuri Ivanov had been holding the position for two and a half minutes. The agony coursing through his body was extreme, but Major Ivanov thrived on extreme.

With a final scream of anguish, he unwound his hands from the white bands that were secured to the metal frame he had been suspended from and dropped to the ground. He fell into a crouch position, leaning forward, letting his body relax from the pain and stress it had endured.

His legs and lower torso were covered with a tight, thin neoprene suit, while his upper body was naked to the snow that swirled around him.

After a minute he slowly stood up. His body was lean but with an overdeveloped muscle structure that would not look out of place on any world champion bodybuilder. But where a bodybuilder's shape was all about power and bulk, here there was an elegance, an athleticism, that suggested speed as well as stamina. His neck was also not thick like a weightlifter's, almost delicate in its form, but the veins that could be seen wending their way up beneath the hair at the side of his head also suggested that this too was powerful.

The face itself was an enigma. Brutal, while at the same time intelligent. You got a sense that a throat could be cut in an instant with no remorse, but that this man could also calculate, speculate and improvise in a split second. There was also something behind the eyes that suggested any affection and empathy would be for inanimate objects only—nothing living.

This was a man you would not wish to cross at any cost.

In fact, you would not just cross a road to avoid him—you would move to another city.

Once Ivanov had calmed his breathing he looked around into the falling snow. He stored a complete map of the base in his memory and could run the area blindfold if necessary. He was a man of many talents; talents that had been honed by the Russian special forces until he was more of a weapon than a man—but that was how he liked it. He was under no one's control. He wanted to impress his superiors. He wanted to do the things they asked of him, whatever they may be—he enjoyed it.

With a final deep breath, he started running.

His bare feet crushed the newly fallen snow into telltale footprints that marked his path. They would soon be gone, swallowed up by the ever-falling flakes.

Within a few seconds he was on a track he knew well. The visibility ahead was around ten feet, but he speeded up. He felt none of the cold as his feet pounded the ground. As he ran, what little sweat that formed on his body froze instantly, leaving a sheen of ice that covered his skin and gave him a certain artificial, almost android-like, appearance.

After five minutes of hard running, Ivanov arrived at the top of a long, gentle slope. He ran down to the bottom. Once there, he walked forward about ten yards and stopped. The snow was as thick as ever. He could barely make out the ground beneath his feet.

He advanced a further five yards and stopped.

As he looked down he could see the texture of the ground change in front of him. Under his feet it was white, with a solid feel. Two yards ahead it was equally white, but the feel was more gaseous, ethereal.

He stood, regaining his breath, and as the freezing wind swirled around him it briefly drew back the cloud and mist to reveal the edge of a vertical, hundred-foot cliff. As he stared down, he could see the crashing waves on the rocks below. For a moment he thought about what it would be like to let his body fall. What the impact would be like, and what his existence, if indeed there was one, would be like after.

But then the thought was gone.

He knew he was beyond saving for any world beyond

this one. He was better off staying where he was for as long as possible. As they said, life was just passing time until you died; it was how you passed the time that counted—and by any account, Ivanov had passed his time in the extremes of human experience—and none of it had been good.

He stepped back from the edge as the cloud and mist closed in again.

He took a deep breath, turned to his left, and ran across the hard ground. As he did, he started breathing heavily. Slow, deep breaths. Anyone watching would have thought he was out of breath, but far from it. Even though he was now sprinting, his breath was slow, deep and completely under control. He needed to saturate his bloodstream with oxygen. He was going to need every molecule he could cram into his body.

After a minute of sprinting, a small wall appeared from out of the snow ahead. He sped up, knowing exactly what was on the other side.

As he reached it he channeled all his raw power into his legs, and at the final moment he sprung up and dived over the wall.

His body soared in a graceful arc. As he crossed the five-foot obstruction he brought his arms forward, hands clasped together, palms out.

The drop was around twenty feet.

He plummeted headfirst.

A second later a wide flat white expanse came into view in front of him. He was heading straight for it as fast as gravity could pull him down.

And then he hit—hard.

He knew from past experience that at this temperature the ice should only be half an inch thick.

It wasn't—it was an inch.

But the surrounding surface must have been thinner, as it shattered and he plunged through into the freezing water below, small jagged strips of ice splintering up around him.

The cold hit like a million needles stabbing into every square inch of his body.

But he was prepared for it.

For any normal human being the cold water shock would have made them gasp uncontrollably, but Ivanov had trained to ignore it. He wouldn't say he was impervious to pain, just that he could function through pain where most human beings would curl up and die.

As his feet disappeared below the surface, he pulled himself deeper with his arms. Once he was five feet below the ice he swam with powerful strokes away from the side of the massive enclosed area of water he was now swimming in. He calmed his heart rate and concentrated on each stroke. Each individual movement was the only consideration in his mind. He didn't feel the water across his body; he didn't feel the intense cold that permeated his soul; it was just one stroke, then the next one, then the next one—a constant rhythm that he knew after two minutes would take him to the far side of the most secret submarine base in the world.

Precisely two minutes later he turned onto his back and, for the first time, opened his eyes. The dull, flat surface above was only marginally lighter than the water around him. He felt his feet scrub against the sloping ground beneath. He crouched down, and then with an explosive burst of energy that used up nearly all the remaining oxygen in his body, he thrust upwards, smashing against the thick frozen surface above.

And nothing happened.

For a second his body lay close up against the ice. He

could make out features through the surface—trees, the sloping ground at the side of the water.

And then his whole instinct was about survival.

He turned upside down.

Scrabbling around, he found a tree root sticking out from the shallow slope. He grabbed hold of it and swung his legs vertically above him. Using all his strength he pushed his feet upward in an explosive action that if it didn't work would have expended the last remaining oxygen and seen his body recovered when the ice melted sometime in the spring.

But it did work.

The layer of ice shattered. In a second, he rotated himself, pushing his head above the surface. He gulped in the life-giving air and crawled out onto the side of the slope.

A few seconds later he was in a crouched position on the ground, resting on his hands, his whole body racked with explosive breaths as he replaced the precious oxygen he desperately needed.

It took only a minute to steady and lower his breathing rate to what would be considered normal.

He looked around.

A small kitbag lay on the ground twenty feet away. Ivanov glanced at the bag and the place where he had emerged from the water. He frowned. He would have to do better next time. He crossed over to the bag, extracted a thick black tracksuit top and a pair of well-used trainers. He quickly pulled them on.

The snow was still falling, but not so intensely now, allowing visibility to increase to around fifty feet. He slung the bag over his shoulder and then set off, jogging along the side of the massive tank he had swum across. The edges had been made to look entirely natural, with grass and a sprinkling of trees along the side, so from afar, or above, the tank would look like a large lake.

He headed for a building further along the water. It butted up against a vertical cliff wall that disappeared up into the snow above. To the left of the building the water continued on under the rock for the full width of the tank, with a clearance of about twenty feet.

He made his way to a door at the end of the building. As he approached he noticed an old woman struggling up a set of steps from the car park below. She carried a box of cleaning materials. He arrived ahead of her. She was stooped over, clearly having difficulty with the steps. He glanced at her for a second, then opened the door and walked through, letting it close behind him.

Irina Lazarev stared at the door.

Before it had banged to behind the man, she had caught a glimpse of his face. Her mouth had dropped open and she had stood rooted to the spot.

Jesus Christ had entered the building.

Chapter Five

Today

The sunlight threatened to break through the rapidly thinning clouds as the Chinook continued north-east toward Aberdeen. The mountains, rivers and lochs of central Scotland passed below like a beautiful geographic tableau.

Inside the Chinook, Martin Steel stood up, stretched and looked closely at McCready.

"You wanted to know who I am."

He paused before continuing.

"To put it in its simplest terms, I work for the British government in what could best be described as an overwatch capacity. I head up a think tank that has access to the resources of the state to use without condition to achieve the security of the nation—*carte-blanche*—win at all costs."

McCready looked at him, genuinely impressed, but with a question. "That's some responsibility. So who oversees you?"

"I coordinate closely with the Prime Minister. That's all you need to know."

"But surely you can't mean *at any cost?*—there are rules, conventions you have to abide by," said McCready.

"The world is changing, John. There are no more rules. I wish there were. In the past you could expect things to be done in a certain way. Sometimes it got dirty, but there was always a framework as to how you behaved with other nations. That's all gone now. The internet, fake news, hacking, AI—everything is up for grabs. There are no borders anymore. Even in the face of definitive proof, certain nations think a public denial is all that's required, and they can get away with—quite literally—murder. They think they're above international law, that there will be no consequences. Well, I'm here to say there will be."

"What about the UN, the Security Council?"

"The UN was always powerless when it came down to it. Never had any real teeth. It's just a sham; a hollow shell existing to make the masses feel there is some sense of law and order out there. As for the Security Council, whenever anything constructive can be achieved, the Russians just go and veto it if it isn't in their interest. It's powerless. No, the security of nations is now carried out more and more in the shadows, subverting the norm, taking any angle that will give them an edge, covering up that underneath, it's just the wild west, a constant battle to maintain the status quo. Sometimes we win. Sometimes we lose."

McCready thought for a moment. "So, what, you're Ministry of Defense, MI6?"

"You mean, does my car have a center console full of buttons and switches? Not quite. In my experience it's more important to have somewhere to put your coffee than revolving number-plates."

McCready couldn't tell if he was being serious. "Okay, so why me? Why Ocean Oil?"

"All in good time."

McCready turned to look out of the window. Many things were racing through his mind. He watched as the hills and valleys gave way to a patchwork of snow-covered fields and rural properties as they approached the run-in to Aberdeen. It wouldn't be long before they were there.

He checked his watch.

Eight forty-five.

Not long after, they flew over the outskirts of the city.

McCready looked down at the streets he knew so well. Seen from the perspective of a thousand feet they had a completely different feel to them. Everything seemed so much closer together—like looking at a real-life, real-time, Google Earth. The traffic was busy coming into the city and he could make out queues on the High Street.

Soon they were over the docks. He could see a severe chop on the water, even in the shelter of the harbor, caused by the strong wind blowing in off the North Sea. A moment later the pilot swung the large machine round in a wide arc to run in on a compact industrial complex. It covered an area of about ten acres and was dominated by two huge buildings. As well as a large car park, various offices and a security gate were located at the main entrance. At the rear, a large, open backlot butted up against the back of the two massive buildings. There was a dry dock with a large tower crane on one side that led out to the sea beyond.

This was Ocean Oil.

As they approached, McCready could make out a massive oil rig leg standing guard in the dry dock.

The helicopter started to descend toward the backlot.

The surrounds of the open area were piled high with scrap metal from long-dead equipment, vessels and oil industry paraphernalia.

But in the middle stood a lone figure.

As McCready watched the ground approach, he could see the man walk to one side, out of the way. He was dressed for the cold with a thick blue Parka jacket and black woolen hat. He was stockily built and in his early fifties. He was currently staring up, trying to shield himself from the vicious downwash from the helicopter.

When McCready had spoken to him earlier, he had not been happy to be woken at an "ungodly hour" and had grumbled that he still had a hangover from the previous evening, but Craig Richards was professional to the core and McCready had always known he would be there.

Ten years earlier, McCready had given him the start-up cash for the company. The two had worked together ever since to build up the business. There was no one in this world he trusted more.

The Chinook settled onto its wheels and the pilot shut down the engine. The massive twin rotors gradually spun to a halt, their long blades drooping from the weight. Once they had stopped, the rear ramp was lowered.

In the small onboard office, Steel packed his laptop into a bag, pulled on a thick jacket and turned to McCready. "Okay, let's go."

McCready climbed into the Range Rover and carefully reversed out of the cargo bay. Once on the tarmac he swung round and parked at the rear of one of the buildings that bordered the backlot. As he opened the door and climbed out he saw Richards crossing over to him.

"I have to drive through blizzards and drifts to get here

and you bloody well fly in!" McCready could see his friend was not best pleased. "What's this all about, John?" asked Richards, but there was curiosity, not anger, in his voice.

McCready walked forward. They shook hands. "Thanks, Craig. Something's come up. I'll explain when we're inside." McCready turned and indicated Steel, who was giving instructions to one of the army personnel at the top of the ramp. "This guy needs to have a word with us, and we need to listen."

Steel walked toward them.

Richards looked at the chopper, turning his back to the biting wind. "Well, if he can command this sort of kit, I guess I can give him five minutes of my time. Hope he can afford the parking fees. We charge by the hour now, you know."

McCready grinned. At least he hadn't lost his sense of humor.

As Steel approached, they walked over to meet him.

"Craig, this is Martin Steel. He needs our help," said McCready.

The two men looked each other up and down and shook hands.

"Does he now?" said Richards. "Okay then, I guess you'd better come with me. You can drive, John."

They climbed into the Range Rover and McCready drove down the side of the building. Once they were past it they headed round to the front of the second large building. It was two hundred feet long and forty feet high. On the facing wall a metal stairway led up the outside to a door at a first-floor level. McCready parked the car and they climbed out. Richards led them up the stairway and held the door for them at the top.

McCready and Steel walked inside.

Deep Impact

They were in a design studio with a low ceiling and multiple workstations with high-back chairs spread around the room. On the far side was a set of windows that looked out onto the inside of the building, which housed a massive wave simulation tank. Richards led them to a door halfway along the left-hand wall. They went through and found themselves in a conference room. It had a large rectangular table in the middle that could seat ten in formal, but comfortable, chairs. At one end was a screen. Along one wall was a worktop with a small sink, kettle and a pile of mugs and cups stacked neatly by.

"Have a seat," said Richards. "Coffee anyone?"

"Thanks," said Steel. "Black, no sugar."

"Usual," said McCready.

Richards crossed over to the kettle and flicked it on. McCready joined him while Steel unpacked his bag and pulled out his laptop.

"Who the hell is this guy?" said Richards under his breath. McCready watched as Steel removed a small oblong device about the size of a deck of cards with SONY written on the top. He plugged it into the laptop with an HDMI cable and oriented it so it was pointing at the screen.

"He's from the government. Not quite sure which department. He was a little vague about that, but he's not playing around, I can tell you that much."

"What does he want?"

"I'm not sure, but he needs the expertise of the company and he mentioned you."

Richards dumped a spoonful of coffee into each of the mugs and grabbed the just-boiled kettle.

"So what if we don't like what he says?" asked Richards, still in a low voice.

"That could be a problem."

"Why?"

"I'll tell you later. Just take it from me, we have to do this... whatever it is."

McCready went to sit at the table as Steel fired up the laptop. Immediately, the desktop was mirrored on the screen on the wall via the small portable projector he'd plugged in. Steel typed on the keyboard. The screen changed to a black backdrop with a government logo and the words "EYES ONLY" in large white letters below.

After Richards placed the mugs on the table he sat and looked at the screen, then glanced at Steel. "Okay, over to you."

Steel stood to the side of the screen. He watched the two men closely.

"What I'm going to show you is classified at the highest level. This conversation is being recorded and will be admissible as evidence if required. Before I continue, I need you to confirm that what we discuss will remain confidential."

They both replied that it would.

"Okay," he continued. He hit a key and a map of the Western Pacific and the Coral Sea appeared on the wall. "Six weeks ago, a satellite monitored by the European Space Agency, but under our control, malfunctioned. It reentered the Earth's atmosphere and landed around here." He tapped the trackpad. A small red circle appeared on the map to the east of Australia.

McCready leaned in closer. "Yeah, I think I saw something about that on the news. Almost hit a container ship."

"That's right," continued Steel. "She was lucky to survive. The information put out was that it was a weather satellite that had passed its sell-by date. That wasn't entirely accurate."

He had their attention.

"I won't go into detail, but there's something on board that survived the impact that is of vital importance to British national security."

Richards and McCready glanced at each other.

Steel continued. "We sent one of our nuclear submarines, HMS *Resilient*, to retrieve the item…"

"Wait a minute," interrupted Richards. "By the position on the map, that's over fifteen thousand feet of water out there. No nuclear sub I know can go down that deep, certainly not one with any lockout capabilities to retrieve anything."

Steel half smiled. "Right on both counts. It's actually just over sixteen thousand feet, and no, you won't know of any nuclear sub that can go down to those depths… but that doesn't mean one doesn't exist."

Richards looked duly chastised.

"The sub was successful in retrieving the item. It was heading north to rendezvous with a carrier group conducting exercises near the Philippines so the device could be brought back to the UK. We didn't want to put into port anywhere as the whole operation was so sensitive. Unfortunately, she ran into difficulties around here." Another circle appeared on the map to the east of the Philippines. "She's now lying on the bottom at an angle of around ninety degrees, which means our standard rescue sub can't mate with the escape hatch. That's why we need you guys. You have the gear to lock onto the sub, gain entry, retrieve the device and assist the crew in any way you can."

He stopped and looked straight at them. "And we need to do this, like, tomorrow."

For a moment there was silence.

Richards looked at McCready, and then Steel, with an incredulous expression.

"Okay, first off, no idea where you got the idea we have any gear that can do that—we do not. Second, the depth of water out there is thousands of feet deep. There's no way we could get down there."

A flick of concern crossed Steel's face. "But your recent exploits under London required a rotatable lockout hatch on your sub. I understand that was a mark 2 design and you have another sub right here."

"While your information is disturbingly accurate, it fails to recognize one thing—there's a reason for the mark 2: the mark 1 didn't work. At least, the pressure seals weren't secure on the collar. We had leakage seventy percent of the time at sixty percent of the angles when rotated. It wasn't fit for purpose. There's no way I'm putting that sub anywhere near the water, let alone take it down to depths a prototype was never designed for."

He looked at Steel with a that's-the-end-of-that expression.

Steel took a second to think. "Okay, first off, she's lying on a ridge to the south of the Palau archipelago at a depth of around eight hundred feet. From the information I have there are strong currents and she could topple off into deeper water at any moment, hence the urgency. Secondly, I'll take a thirty/forty percent chance of your sub working any day. I normally operate with far worse odds."

"You can't be serious?" said Richards.

Steel started to pack up his laptop.

"I suggest you talk to John about just how serious. I have to be at a Cobra meeting this afternoon in London. I'll leave you two gentlemen to work out how you're going to do this. But whatever you come up with, we need to leave tomorrow. They don't have much time down there."

With that he headed for the door. "I'll see myself out."

Richards was about to protest when McCready interjected. "Even if we can sort the sub, how the heck are we going to get on site in that time frame?"

Steel turned. "Let me worry about that. Just get the thing ready. Lives depend on it." And with that he exited the door, pulling it closed behind him.

When he had gone, Richards turned to McCready. "Okay, just how serious is this guy?"

McCready drained the last of his coffee and then looked straight at Richards.

"He knows about the gold."

Chapter Six

Six weeks ago

Two hours after Major Ivanov had entered the base he stood in a large ornate bathroom looking straight into a rectangular mirror that stretched from the rear of the basin up to the ceiling four feet above. To the side, a series of round, flat lights shone out with a soft glow that illuminated his face, which right now was half covered with shaving foam. He had a towel around his waist and his hair had been cut short to an almost crew cut. Half of his beard was gone, and as he pulled the razor across his left cheek, plowing the foam away, it revealed a rough, weather-beaten skin that added to the menace of the character that was starting to be revealed.

It was a ritual he went through before every important mission. When training, the focus was solely on raw physical fitness and peak performance, but for the job itself he needed to adjust: a reset of his body and mind. A change in his appearance aided in this transformation.

After another line of foam was scraped away, he paused, staring at the man in the mirror. It was someone he had to live with every day—but someone, who on occasion, he wondered where had come from.

Major Yuri Ivanov was thirty-four.

He had been born in Moscow on the rough side of town. His mother had died giving birth to him; at least that was what he had been told. Later he would learn she had died as a result of one too many beatings from his father. This was something he should have guessed, given the number of times he had suffered at his father's hand himself. Either way, he had never known his mother.

Life as a child had been hard. His father had laid down the law. Any divergence had been met with physical punishment. These had been Yuri's formative years; they were where he had learned about life, and the lessons could not have been harsher.

His father had a disdain for women. He used them, abused them and then threw them out when he'd had enough; more often than not when they left it was in the back of an ambulance. It had taught Yuri that women were there to be used and tolerated. They were disposable. They existed for sex and for looking after a man—nothing more. He never felt any empathy for them.

He never cared for any.

He never saw the point.

Except once.

At age eighteen he had been fleeing from the police. It followed a break-in at a jeweler's in central Moscow. They had been gaining on him. He had been running out of options.

He had suddenly found himself in a dead-end street. Looking desperately around, he had managed to force open the fire exit of a converted warehouse. Once inside, he had walked up the old wooden stairs and pushed open a door at the top.

He had found himself in another world.

The massive space that had greeted him was dark, apart from a brightly lit area at the far end. Loud rock music pumped out, filling the warehouse.

As he had moved closer, he had seen that it was a photo shoot of some description. About twenty people were clustered around the lights. Some were watching; others were busy moving backdrops and equipment around.

No one seemed to take any notice of him.

As he approached, he saw a photographer moving in and out with his camera. He had been talking all the time, encouraging, chastising, laughing. And when Ivanov had seen the focus of his attention, he had stopped dead, rooted to the spot.

She was the most beautiful woman he had ever laid eyes on, an exotic creature he had never known could exist. Of mixed race, her strong, high Russian cheekbones, blended with the soft exotic delicacy of Asian eyes to produce an intoxicating mix of extraordinary beauty. The provocative poses she held and the alluring expressions she wore could be described in only one way…

Perfection.

Yuri had stood, unable to move—mesmerized. Something deep inside of him had stirred, and for that moment he wasn't the kid from the Moscow slums, the one who robbed people and beat them when they protested. He knew in that moment he wanted this woman more than anything he had ever wanted in his life.

When she had come off the set for a break, she had brushed past him, glancing straight into his eyes for a moment longer than was necessary.

For the rest of the day he had helped out, making coffees, moving props around, basically doing anything to avert any question as to his presence on the set.

When the shoot was finally over it had been nearly 1am. He had waited for her at the exit of the studio. A limousine had been there to pick her up. As she had walked to the car she had noticed him again and beckoned him to enter the car.

What had followed had been indescribable. He had never known pleasure like it.

He had seen her regularly for two weeks, but one day she had said she had to go out of town. He felt as though he was breaking inside.

He had gone to her apartment just to be close to her presence.

While he had been pacing around outside, he had seen a car draw up. A man had climbed out and greeted her on the steps of the block. He was much older than her, dressed in a dinner jacket and bow tie. They had shared a long, passionate kiss before he had held the door open for her to climb into the car.

Yuri had confronted her, yelling and screaming.

The man had intervened. Yuri had knocked him unconscious. He would have killed him if the woman hadn't tried to drag him away. In his rage he had lashed out, cutting her face. Drawing blood. When he had seen what he had done; when he had seen the look of total disgust and contempt on her face, he knew it had all been a fantasy. People like her, people like him—it was never going to happen. Nothing that good could ever be a part of his life. He had turned and run and never looked back. There were no tears, just a hardened realization of the world as it was—and Yuri Ivanov was never going to let the world beat him again.

Never again would he let anyone have control over him.

The next few weeks had been hell on Earth. He had felt like he was imploding inside. He had left home after a fight where he had finally stood up to his father and beaten him to the floor. He had almost died from not eating, dissolving into a world of drugs and crime. He had become involved with one of the most notorious gangs in Moscow. Over the following years he had grown to be one of their most feared enforcers, enacting punishments and beatings even hardened gang members disapproved of. But everything had been about revenge for that night he had seen her with the man.

He would never trust a woman again for as long as he lived.

His father had been right.

He also learned that through violence you earned fear, not respect. But all he was concerned about was compliance. Respect he didn't care about, unless it was from those closest to him: other gang members. If people did what he wanted them to do through fear, that was fine. It was never about being the all-powerful leader—it was about getting done what he wanted to get done. The power and backup a gang gave you was the key to that goal.

It didn't take long for him to come to the attention of the authorities. He had often been on jobs and occasionally noticed someone had been watching him, but he had never known who, or what, they were. Once, when he had approached a man he had seen on several occasions, the man had vanished into the city. After a particularly brutal murder of a high-ranking official he had upset the wrong people one too many times. He had been arrested and convicted. The punishment was life without parole.

They were going to throw away the key.

He had been led out of the court, heading for a black van with blacked-out windows, when a man in a leather jacket, short-cropped hair, and a small goatee beard had shown an identity card to the guard who had been escorting him. Immediately, the guard had become incredibly submissive and let go of the firm grip he'd had on Yuri's arm.

From that moment on he'd been with one of the most terrifying gangs on the planet—the Russian state security system.

And he'd never looked back.

Ivanov snapped out of the reverie.

The hot water had been running and steam had risen to cover the mirror with condensation. He turned off the tap, dragged the razor across the final foam-covered area under his chin, then used his hand to wipe away a strip of condensation from the glass.

The face that stared back at him was a different man.

He was ready.

He walked out of the bathroom into what looked for all the world like a suite in an expensive hotel. It was lit with strategically placed lamps around the side of the room rather than a harsh central light, which created a certain ambience. The decorations were tasteful, if minimalist in style. A large king-sized bed was on one side of the room, while a dressing area and a worktop took up the opposite side. A large rectangular mirror was in the center of the wall above the worktop. On a swivel stand on the wall beside the mirror was a fifty-five-inch 4K OLED TV. It was currently showing a news channel from the UK. The only unusual thing about the room was that there were no windows.

He pulled the towel from around his waist and dried off the final areas of moisture from his body.

He dressed in a pair of dark slacks and a thin black rollover jumper, watching the screen as he did so. He was waiting for a report he knew was coming. He liked the channel. It had a fiery redheaded news anchor he would very much like to meet one day. The language was no problem for him as he was fluent in over six, making his job easier as he traveled the world at the behest of the Russian state.

At the moment, the woman was interviewing a bank manager about a private bank in London where some recovered gold was going to be stored. He took a mild interest as the gold had been Russian, stolen by the Nazis in World War Two, but quickly the report was over and the picture changed to an aerial shot from a helicopter of a patch of ocean strewn with floating debris as far as the eye could see. Sitting to one side of the picture was a large container ship that had clearly lost its cargo.

Ivanov flicked up the volume.

"And now an update on our top story," the anchor started. "The *Lady Christa* had been sailing for Auckland in New Zealand when it was almost hit by a rogue satellite that had fallen out of orbit."

The screen changed to show a map of the Coral Sea with the position of the impact shown in graphical form as a dramatic explosion of water. Ivanov took a particular interest in the map. The position was pretty much five thousand miles due south of his current location.

The anchor continued to speak over the image. "The satellite, known as Cormorant B, was controlled by the

European Space Agency. We're still waiting for a comment from the organization as to what went wrong. One crew member from the *Lady Christa*, First Officer Sven Johansen, was killed when the wave generated by the impact hit the ship. *Lady Christa's* captain, Juan Rodriguez, had this to say."

The shot changed to a shaky image of the captain on the flying bridge of the *Lady Christa* with the debris field behind.

"It came out of nowhere. And the noise. You never heard anything like it—like a train roaring toward you. There was nothing we could do. I'm lucky to be alive."

The screen changed back to the anchor in the studio. She looked out of the TV with a relieved expression on her face. "That's one lucky captain. Now, something else that's lucky—a cat and her kittens were rescued from a storm drain in Mexico. More after the break."

The screen flipped to ads and Ivanov clicked off the TV. He crossed to the worktop. He was about to open a laptop when there was a knock at the door. He hesitated, but then a thin smile spread across his lips.

He moved to the door and opened it.

Standing there was a naval lieutenant who was about thirty-five years old. He stood rigidly to attention. His uniform was of regular navy issue. There was nothing else about him that Ivanov even registered. What he was interested in was what the lieutcnant was holding with his right hand. She was about four foot six, around sixteen years old and was clearly of Asian descent. She was dressed in a pale green sweatshirt and denim jeans. Her small face looked at the ground. She was clearly terrified.

Ivanov moved his hand to her face and raised her chin. He caressed her soft skin as the girl glanced up at the lieutenant with pleading in her eyes. He risked a look down at her.

"Eyes straight!" commanded Ivanov. The man's gaze snapped forward. "What is your name?"

"Lieutenant Pasha Sokolov, sir."

"Well, Sokolov, make sure you do as you are told."

"Yes, sir."

"Come!" ordered Ivanov to the girl.

She clung to Sokolov's hand as though her life depended on it.

It did.

"Come here now!" Ivanov's voice was raised a level.

The lieutenant was about to speak, but Ivanov shot him a glare that would turn most men to stone. He held his ground but said nothing. Very slowly he released the girl's grip. She looked up at him and tears started to fall.

Once her hand was free, Ivanov grabbed it, pulling her into the room. He looked Sokolov straight in the eyes, daring him to say something, then slammed the door in his face.

Sokolov knew his orders. He stood to attention, his back to the door.

But out of sight was not out of mind.

Nothing could put out of mind the screams that came from the room behind him.

He tried not to think of his own daughter, Dominika, who was only thirteen.

He tried not to think of what he would do to a man who did things like that to his daughter.

All he knew was that one day he would not remain silent.

Chapter Seven

Today

"How the hell does he know about the gold?"

Richards was staring at McCready incredulously.

"Long story," said McCready. "He'd been looking into Mercer's activities for a while. We came across on his radar. The guy has serious resources. And by the way, we can keep the gold if we do this."

Richards looked at him dubiously. "And you believe him?"

"I'm keeping an open mind. The man has lots of plates in the air. I think we could be an asset to him in the future."

"Yeah, but at what cost?"

McCready drained the last of his coffee. "Okay, so what's the condition of the sub?"

"You mean *Emily*?"

"You named this one as well? Didn't know you were married to an Emily."

"Well I wasn't. But we had six passionate months

together and then things became too much." He looked despondent.

"What things?" asked McCready.

Richards didn't reply.

"What things?"

"She was into cosplay," said Richards, as though that explained everything.

"Cos... what?"

"PLAY. You know, taking on the identity of film and TV characters and going to conventions."

McCready tried to stifle a laugh. "You're not serious?"

"Don't even go there! After three months of weekends dressed as a dwarf from *Game of Thrones*, that was it!"

He looked sheepishly at McCready, who couldn't contain himself any longer and laughed uncontrollably. "You do pick 'em!"

Richards started to laugh as well. When they'd calmed down, he turned serious. "Come on, I'll show you the problem."

They walked out of the conference room, across the design studio, and through a door to a set of metal stairs that led down to the floor of the main building.

McCready had always been impressed by the size of the place. It was like a small hangar—no, a large hangar. In the center of the floor was the massive tank that took up most of the area. It was a hundred feet long by fifty feet wide and twenty feet in depth. In the middle was a forty-foot-deep section. He had spent many hours in there testing submersibles and various forms of dive kit. There was also an underwater viewing window at one end, but for now, Richards led him over to a tarpaulin-covered structure that was sitting against the side wall of the building.

"Give me a hand."

McCready grabbed one corner of the scruffy, heavy-duty tarpaulin, and Richards another. They pulled together. As the large sheet fell to the ground it revealed a rather battered-looking submersible beneath. It had clearly seen better days.

At the front was the usual domed glass cockpit that provided a one-eighty-degree view for the pilot. Along the sides ran various pipes and tubes, but midway down its length was a collar that ran three-sixty around the hull. At the bottom of the collar was a lockout hatch.

Richards stepped back, as though seeing an old friend for the first time in a long time.

"So, bring back memories of the little people?" jousted McCready.

Richards just gave him a look, stooping down to peer at the collar beneath the main hull. He gripped a section of it and yanked.

Nothing happened.

He tried again. Still nothing.

"She's stuck fast."

He stepped back and suddenly looked serious. "I don't know if we can do this, John. And even if we can get her working, I wouldn't send anyone down in her. She'd be a death trap."

"Well, you wouldn't be going in her. I'll go with Logan. I'll explain everything to him. If he doesn't want to do it, you can show me the controls and talk me down over the comms."

"Well Logan's out for a start, and there's no way I'm letting you in there on your own. Why are you so fixated on doing this, anyway?"

McCready looked at him. "Because I made a deal."

"Under duress."

"Yes, but he knew what we'd done. The alternative isn't worth thinking about—locked up, no doubt for a considerable time at Her Majesty's pleasure. And that would have included you." He became thoughtful for a moment. "And I kind of get this guy. He thinks outside the box. No problem is insurmountable. Also, he seems to want to do the right thing—whatever the cost."

"Yeah, 'whatever the cost.'" Richards looked at his friend and shook his head wearily. "Okay, I'll see what I can do."

"So why is Logan out?" asked McCready. "I'm sure I could talk him round."

"From a hospital bed?"

"Huh?"

"You missed all the fun and games. He's in Aberdeen Royal Infirmary, along with Porter. Car crash around two this morning. The air ambulance had to airlift them out."

"What the hell happened?"

"Last night. Driving back after the party," explained Richards. "Never a good idea to have Logan and Porter in the same vehicle. There was an argument about who should drive before they left, which Logan apparently won, but it then carried on during the journey. They were both out of their skulls. Porter tried to grab the wheel. They hit a rock at the side of the road. Ended up upside down in a ditch. It's sent Anglo-Scottish relations back years. What's worse is they were causing such a disturbance in the main ward at the hospital they had to be moved to a private room. Trouble is, there was only one available and they're in there together. It's driving the nurses nuts."

"How do you know all this?"

"Because, John, Craig begins with a C and John begins with a J, and C comes before J in Porter's contacts app. So

I'm the one that gets called. One of the nurses overheard him telling me all about it, grabbed the phone and said that something needed to be done, else they'd call the police."

"They seemed to be getting on fine at the party," said McCready.

"Yeah, but that was before they were upside down in a ditch, pissed as newts. I guess circumstances bring out your baser instincts."

McCready sighed. "Okay, I'll go up there. See if I can sort it out."

"Either way, you're not going in that sub, and that's final!"

"We'll see," said McCready, heading for the door. "Just find out what it's going to take to get her in the water. I'll be back later."

Richards watched him go, and then turned to the sub. He checked McCready had left and said, almost in a whisper, "Now then, *Em*, me dear, be off to Winterfell, shall we?"

He triple-checked McCready wasn't there and then chuckled to himself.

The nurse carefully counted out the pile of pills onto a small tray.

She checked they were all in order and made her way down the busy hospital corridor. She'd been on duty all night and was covering for a colleague who had come down with the flu at the last minute. She was exhausted.

It was always busy over the winter months. People were falling and spraining ankles or breaking arms or legs in the snow and ice. But the two that had come in earlier that morning were another matter. They'd been a constant pain, arguing with each other from the moment they'd arrived. And while, admittedly, for the most part they'd been fine with the staff, it had got to the point where no one had wanted to go into their room because of the constant air of tension. It was the last thing she needed, but she had a job to do and whoever you were you were entitled to care and attention when injured or unwell.

She took a deep breath and pushed open the door to the private room that normally had only a single bed in it but now had two.

The room itself was fairly plain, with light blue walls and a window running the full length of one side. However, it was small. Even with the beds placed as far apart as possible, there was only just room for a narrow chest of drawers between them and the appropriate medical equipment required for monitoring. A hastily erected dividing curtain had been put in place to give the two occupants as great a concept of privacy and separation as possible, but it wasn't doing much good.

The first issue had been who had got the bed by the window. The large Scottish man had won this one, and the smaller but stocky English man had complained ever since. The no-nonsense matron on the ward had finally resorted to slipping a couple of relaxants into each of their pill concoctions, and it had, at least, kept things quiet for a while.

The larger man had cuts and abrasions and had suffered severe concussion. The smaller man had broken his leg. His case was more serious, and while the leg was in a cast for now, suspended from a traction device, they were waiting on further X-rays to see if any surgery would be needed. Even this, though, had provoked an argument, with the Englishman stating that if he had to have this done, why wasn't the Scotsman suffering equally? Numerous swear words and utterances of discrimination and lawsuits had been heard, but it was largely put down to the alcohol content that had been recorded in his bloodstream. To be honest, the doctors had been quite bewildered by the results, with one commenting that the Englishman's blood was a hundred percent proof.

The nurse paused for a moment in front of both the beds. From this angle you could hardly see the divide separating the two, but she was glad it was there. They were both sleeping peacefully at the moment, but that would end when she woke them up to give them their pills.

But who to start with?

She now had a major decision to make.

Left bed or right.

McCready drove through the streets of Aberdeen, heading for the Royal Infirmary. He had to go past the docks, through the center of the city, and up to the Foresterhill site where the hospital was located.

As he drove, he thought about the enormity of the changes in his life that had occurred in the past twenty-four hours.

The task Steel had given them was not trivial. While he didn't have any details on the item that was to be retrieved from the sub, it was clearly important. The thing that focused McCready's mind, though, was the crew, stranded hundreds of feet down on the seabed. He knew he would do whatever it took to help them and try and bring them back safely. How long they had was anyone's guess, but the longer it took, the less chance there was of success and of returning them to their families. He made up his mind that, whatever Craig said to him, it would not deflect him from this goal. The only problem was whether they could get the sub working in time, but McCready was reassured that if anyone could do it, it was his friend back at Ocean Oil.

He had never let him down before.

His thoughts turned to the two men he was going to see at the hospital—Eugene Porter and Mac Logan. He hadn't known either of them for that long, and while he could well believe the story Craig had told him about their behavior, there were no two people he would rather have on a job that required their particular skillsets.

Logan was a sub driver and expert technical diver, well used to using mixed gas and rebreathers to explore deep into treacherous cave systems. Porter, while certainly not a diver—he couldn't swim—not that helpful, was an expert in explosives and had turned the science into an art form. There was nothing this man couldn't make go bang in a precise and devastating way. He wouldn't be needed for now, but he would dearly love to have Logan along for the ride. He just hoped he was in a fit state. The last thing he wanted was a showdown with Craig about whether he would be able to go in the sub with him or not.

He turned into the hospital site off Foresterhill Road.

It was a large, modern facility, with over nine hundred beds, but the buildings were utilitarian and not particularly attractive.

It took him around fifteen minutes before he found a parking space. It took another twenty to establish where Porter and Logan were and for him to find his way through the maze of corridors to their room.

He knew he was getting close when he could hear raised voices. There were three of them. One had a broad Scottish accent that bellowed out every now and then. The second was loud and bullish and classic East End, while the third was a soft, almost timid yet harassed, Scottish female voice that seemed to be at its wits' end.

He pushed open the door and stood watching the scene playing out in front of him. The nurse was trying to pull the divide closed between the two beds. Porter on the left then grabbed it and pulled it back.

"Listen, love, I need to see the light. Since Scottie here gets the window seat, I want some light. That's not too much to ask, now, is it?"

Before she could answer, Logan had piped up. "Now listen, you daft plonker, she's just trying to do her job. We wouldn't even be here if you hadn't grabbed the wheel and put us in a ditch!" With that, he pulled the divide back across between them.

Porter immediately yanked it back again, knocking over a cup and saucer, which crashed to the floor. "If I hadn't done, you'd have hit the bloody lamppost!"

"We were in the middle of the sodding mountains. There were no lampposts!" shouted Logan.

"Gentlemen, please!" the nurse said, her voice sounding ever more desperate. "You need to take your pills."

McCready had seen enough.

"Hey guys," he said calmly.

Immediately there was silence. All three turned toward him. It was like a freeze-frame from a Road Runner cartoon. Everyone remained frozen to the spot.

The nurse was the first to speak. "Can I help you?"

McCready smiled at her. "Yes. First, I must apologize for these two idiots. I hope they're not causing you too much trouble."

The nurse was hesitant. "Well, they have been a bit of a handful."

McCready glared at Logan and Porter. "Guys, come on now, this nice young lady's only trying to do her job."

Porter and Logan glanced at each other. It was clear they both wanted to go off on one. Porter was the first to speak. He was all innocent and light. "Well, guv, you see, it was like this. Scottie here doesn't know how to drive…"

Logan couldn't not reply. "John, it wasn't like that," he said wearily.

"Guys. We need to talk." Again there was silence.

The nurse glanced at McCready, relieved he was getting involved. "Well then, I'll leave you to it. Just let me know if there's anything you need."

McCready nodded. When she'd left he looked at Porter and Logan. "What the hell happened? And I don't want an argument."

Five minutes later he had the whole story.

When they had finished, McCready sighed and turned to them. "Okay, but just remember, the staff are here to look after you, okay?"

"Yes, guv," said Porter meekly. "But it looks like I'm in here for the next few weeks."

McCready turned to Logan. "Mac, what do the doctors say?"

"Major concussion, but nothing that won't heal."

"When will they discharge you?" asked McCready.

"Probably a couple of days, maybe three. Need me in for observation. But I'm going to end up in a psych ward if I spend another day in here with him." He nodded at the other bed.

Porter was about to protest but McCready glanced at him sharply.

He paused for a moment then looked directly at Logan. "Something's come up. I need a sub pilot, but it has to be tomorrow. Can't say more than that right now. Do you think you can make it? It's dangerous and it's risky, but it's serious and important."

Logan didn't hesitate. "Of course. Just tell me where to be."

"What about me?" protested Porter.

"Sorry, Eugene, but there's a lot of water involved… and we don't need to blow anything up."

"Well, you know where I am," he said with a sulky expression.

At that moment a doctor entered. He saw McCready. "Nothing urgent. I can come back later."

"Doctor," said McCready, "how long till this guy is out of here?" He indicated Logan. The doctor glanced at Logan and then picked up his chart. He looked it over and then looked up.

"At least three days. We're worried about some swelling on the brain…"

At this, Porter spluttered, wearing a massive grin. "I think you'll find that's always been there!" Everyone glared at him.

The doctor continued. "Even then it's important he isn't put in any stressful situations for several weeks, after which we'll need to reevaluate things." He replaced the chart and headed for the door. "I'll be back shortly."

McCready looked at Logan. "Sorry, Mac. No way I can take you."

Logan protested. "But John, that's just doctors. You know how they are."

"I can't take the risk." Then he thought for a minute. "But there is something you can do."

McCready spent the next ten minutes talking to Logan. Throughout the conversation Logan's expression changed from concern, through incredulous, to firm commitment.

When McCready left, he knew he could count on Logan to do what he had asked, and he felt a whole lot better. Things had been happening fast, but not so fast he wasn't thinking clearly, and there was one thing that life had always taught him.

Always have a Plan B.

Chapter Eight

Six weeks ago

The Russian base was built on a number of levels deep inside the mountain, hence the lack of windows in Ivanov's quarters. It had taken two years to construct, but it had been worth it. While most people associated the city of Vladivostok with Russia's Pacific submarine fleet, that was what you were supposed to think. It took prying eyes away from Kamchatka, where more clandestine technology and equipment was developed and operated from.

Inside the mountain, the base was arranged over five levels.

Starting from the top...

Level 5 was the location of the technical labs for research and development.

Level 4 housed eating and recreational facilities, as well as the infirmary.

Level 3 was accommodation and general living quarters.

Level 2 was the operational part of the base, where

missions were planned and coordinated from in a communications and control center, as well as the location for the base commander's office. On the same level was the control room for the main tank and water facility.

Level 1, or Tank Level, was where the massive water tank was situated, along with the infrastructure required to ensure its smooth operation. The armory and vehicle garages were also located on this level.

Aside from the different levels within the mountain, there were also divisions between personnel. One section was for the baseline workers—cooks, administration staff, etc., and another was for the scientists, managers and elite special forces operatives, of which Major Yuri Ivanov was at the top of the tree. While there were many things in Russia that were run-down, cheap, in decline and, not to put too fine a point on it, broken, there was always money for those at the top of the food chain, particularly those who helped protect and secure the Motherland's future place in the world and its security. As Ivanov had come to experience and exploit, there was nothing he would be refused, however extreme, however depraved it might be. It was one of the reasons he lived this life—he was allowed to indulge his needs and cravings in ways that would not be tolerated in normal society.

This was forefront in his mind as he looked down at the naked body lying on the bed. He glanced dispassionately at the staring, unseeing eyes. He had almost smiled as she had cried out in pain and terror. He had enjoyed himself, but not that much. He had read once about serial killers who became immune to their actions and needed more subjects to fuel their addiction. He would never admit he was addicted to anything, but he was finding that the small pleasures he gained from his acts were diminishing. Still, there were plenty more where she came from.

He pulled on a jacket, crossed over to the door and walked out into the corridor. He didn't even glance at the lieutenant who had stepped aside as the door had opened.

"Clear that up!" was all Ivanov had said as he walked down the corridor.

Sokolov took one look inside the room and had to run into the bathroom to throw up in the toilet. When he could face walking back into the room, he stood there transfixed, tears welling in his eyes.

This was not why he had joined the Russian Navy—not in a million years.

When Ivanov reached the end of the corridor he turned left. He headed down another corridor to a small atrium with an elevator. Once inside, he pressed the button for Level 2—Control and Operations. The doors slid smoothly to, and the elevator descended one level down before the doors opened in a central hub area. From here, passages led off to the various facilities located on the level.

There was a constant background hum in the complex, like the noise of a ship's engines. Ivanov liked it—it felt as though something was happening, as though he was part of a greater machine, which indeed he was.

He walked across the hub and down a short corridor that led to the tank control room. He was heading for the operations center, but he always liked to take a detour. The control room had a view out onto the tank, which, after all, was the reason they were there in the first place.

As he entered the room, people glanced up. He noticed a slight stiffening of backs when they saw who it was. He had a reputation, and he wasn't going to be the one to change that in any way. As he had learned, fear produced results.

The room was about twenty feet wide and thirty feet long. There were four technicians working at panels that showed the position of equipment in the tank and controls for the machinery that serviced it. The most impressive aspect, though, was the glass that stretched the full length of the room and looked out on the water twenty feet below. From this height the window provided a view across the entire facility.

Ivanov walked over to the glass and looked down on the activity below.

The tank was housed in a massive cave hewn out of the rock. It was nearly three hundred and fifty feet wide and four hundred feet long. At the far end he could see the entrance, which stretched the full width of the tank. Beyond the cave the water extended for more than a quarter of a mile, forming an artificial lake.

The facility had a hardened concrete work area that surrounded the water. As he watched, he could see vehicles moving about carrying supplies and weapons. Above the tank, hoists, mounted on moving gantries, could access any position over the water to aid in the lifting and repositioning of heavy equipment. But the main focus was the four dry docks that split the width into separate sections and were located closest to him.

One of the docks was currently empty. It looked like a massive rectangular hole in the water. A second had been drained but was occupied by a prototype fast attack sub that was supported by a massive steel cradle on the floor of the dock. It was over two hundred feet long and was currently being fitted out with specialist equipment around the hull by engineers working on a mass of scaffolding that enveloped the sub like a wire cocoon. In the third dock, a small deep ocean submersible, with complex manipulators and a large bubble viewing dome on the front, floated on the surface. It was the final dock, on the far right-hand side, where Ivanov's main interest lay.

The dock was full of water. In it floated a submarine, but one of a design unlike the world had ever seen. It was just over two hundred feet long. At the front was a large bulbous bow that contained the latest in tracking and detection technology. As he looked back along the deck he could see the eight launch tubes. Underwater, they were sealed behind a cowl, but they were now open for servicing and loading. Each housed newly developed hypersonic missiles that had nuclear propulsion systems and could travel at over twenty times the speed of sound. They could deliver a nuclear, or conventional, payload anywhere in the world virtually without detection. Even if they were detected, they traveled at such speed and utilized such advanced avoidance capabilities that they were effectively invincible.

Past the launch tubes was an angular, streamlined conning tower. It stretched up from the smooth matte black deck toward the rear of the vessel. It was this feature that had led to the name of the sub—*Blackfin*.

Behind the conning tower was a large section that contained a sealed 'garage.' It housed a small submersible for covert operations, as well as two powerful surface craft for incursions into enemy territory. It also allowed divers access to the water and could be used to launch remotely operated vehicles.

Finally, at the rear, was the propulsion system. It was

housed in two pods that stretched out from either side and was the latest in stealth design, leaving no sound signature in the water, even when traveling at high speed. The exact top speed of the sub was classified, but Ivanov was reliably informed the propulsion system could move the vessel through the water at over a hundred miles per hour. The incredible speed was achieved by the use of a supercavitation drive. This created a layer of air over the surface of the sub, minimizing drag, allowing the machine to slip through the water smoothly and silently.

Another highly classified detail was the depth capability. While most nuclear submarines were normally restricted to a few hundred feet, the limits of *Blackfin* were measured in thousands, though even Ivanov had been unable to ascertain exactly how many.

For now, the sub floated calmly in the water. It represented the result of ten years of scientific research and breakthroughs in materials design and power source development. It was the most formidable vehicle ever to have traveled beneath the waves and would allow Ivanov and his men to reach all corners of the globe and inflict a devastating blow to any enemy on the face of the Earth.

He watched as the sub underwent preparations for the mission ahead. An array of small vehicles drove up and down the dockside in a continuous line, like worker bees attending to their queen. Numerous supplies were loaded on board. He saw the final hypersonic missile being carefully lowered into its launch tube from the gantry above.

He checked his watch and reluctantly drew himself away from the window. His task now was far less enjoyable, dealing with the commander of the base, Admiral Vladimir Cherenko.

As Ivanov entered the base commander's office,

Cherenko was on the phone. He was a rather rotund man, in his late sixties, with thinning gray hair. He wore his Russian naval uniform with pride, and Ivanov could tell it had probably been pressed earlier that day. Behind him a large screen covered the wall. It currently showed a map of the Western Pacific. Cherenko finished the call, put the phone down, and glanced at Ivanov. His expression immediately darkened.

"I was expecting you earlier, Major. You are an hour late."

Ivanov was unperturbed. He knew Cherenko liked to throw his weight around when he could, but masters way higher up the chain of command had his back, and Cherenko knew it.

Ivanov replied evenly, "I had things to attend to."

At this, Cherenko's expression turned to disgust. "Your predilections will not be tolerated much longer. Even Moscow is starting to talk."

"Somehow I doubt that." Ivanov's face was unreadable, but the tone said all that was necessary.

Cherenko considered a response but thought better of it.

"Okay, to business," he said, and turned to the screen. "As you know, the satellite landed in the Coral Sea around here." He indicated the position to the east of Northern Australia. "The information we have is very specific. There is something in the wreckage that is of vital importance to the British, which means, in turn, it will be important to the Americans. Your mission is to retrieve it before they do. That will mean the deployment of *Blackfin*. It will provide the perfect shakedown dive for her."

"I am looking forward to the mission, Admiral."

"I'm sure you are, Major, but there is a problem."

"What problem?"

"There is a fault in the cavitation drive. The engineers are working on the issue, but it may be a while before you can leave."

Ivanov smacked his hand down on the desk in fury. "That is unacceptable!"

"It's not ideal," said Cherenko. "But it's a fact."

"Why was I not told of this earlier?"

"It has only just come to my attention."

"How long is the delay?"

"Unknown. Days, maybe a couple of weeks."

Ivanov looked like he was about to throttle Cherenko.

"But the British will surely beat us to the location," he said.

"Clearly the British will send in assets. To counter this, and buy us some time, an Antonov will drop a circle of underwater drones to the seabed in a five-mile radius around the crash site. They will monitor and give us a three-dimensional picture of anything that enters the area. Should the British get there before you, and leave, the drones will follow them, keeping track of their position.

"The recovery of the object is paramount. It overrules every other mission parameter. In other words, when you get there you are to use any force necessary in the execution of your orders, but, and I cannot stress this strongly enough, you are only to engage if you come directly under attack. While Moscow does not want any interference with the recovery of the object, it also does not want to provoke an international incident."

Ivanov smiled. "Any force necessary."

"The key word is 'necessary.' As I said, do not involve yourself in any *un*necessary confrontation with external forces. Get in. Get the item. Get out. Preferably unseen. Is that clear?"

"Perfectly."

"You will be informed when the sub will be ready. In the meantime, stay prepared to leave at a moment's notice. Any questions?"

"Just one. What is it exactly that is so important to the British?"

Chapter Nine

Today

The white BAE 146 Royal Air Force jet banked round in the final turn for the runway at RAF Northolt a few miles west of London.

It was a medium-sized four-engine aircraft that had the engines mounted below a top wing that was arrayed over the fuselage. She was part of 32 Squadron, also known as the Royal Squadron, and was primarily used for shuttling cabinet ministers and Ministry of Defense (MOD) personnel around the country, and, as the name suggested, members of the royal family, when required.

The pilot had received priority clearance from air traffic control at the small tower in the largely unknown airfield that handled military aircraft in the London area, as well as an ever-increasing number of private flights.

In the plush interior Martin Steel closed his laptop and glanced out of the window as the jet prepared to land. The snow and wind of Scotland had gone, but in its place was a dull, dreary day with low cloud and light drizzle. He could make out the distinctive crossed runways in the shape of an X that had first been used by Spitfires and Hurricanes in the defense of the capital in the tense and vital days of the Battle of Britain. He could almost hear the Merlin engines scream up to full power to lift their brave pilots up into the sky to defend the country's freedom. He always loved flying into the airfield. It reminded him of why he was here—the job he had to do.

It had been an uneventful flight from Aberdeen, but his meeting with McCready and Richards had left him concerned. Things were on a tight schedule. It was critical, for a whole number of reasons, that Richards managed to get the sub working—and fast. They had to recover that very special item from *Resilient*. He would receive further updates at the meeting he was heading to, but the situation was fast becoming one that was spiraling out of control. One not helped in the slightest by certain 'external factors' that had come into play.

The wheels of the jet touched down with a screech of rubber and a light puff of smoke. As Steel looked across the tarmac, he could already see the high-performance steel-gray Jaguar XF waiting for him on the stand.

The jet pulled to a halt and the steward lowered the steps, which rolled out from the side of the plane like a large metallic tongue. They had barely been extended, when Steel, after a quick thank you to the pilots, hurried down the steps to the waiting car. He was met by his personal driver, Duffy Jenkins, an old colleague from the regiment. Jenkins was a stockily built man in his late forties, but it was all muscle. The man was someone Steel trusted with his life. The two nodded to each other and then Steel slid into the back seat and buckled his belt.

Jenkins pushed the door to and climbed into the driver's seat.

"Should be about thirty minutes to Whitehall, sir. Traffic's not great at the moment, but we have the lights."

"Thanks, Duffy. Need to make this quick."

"Yes, sir," Jenkins replied. And with that he flicked on the two strobing blue lights set behind the radiator grille, and sped out of the airport complex onto the crowded A40 Western Avenue.

The traffic was heavy but drivers soon pulled out of the way when they saw the aggressive grille of the Jag with the blue lights coming up behind them. Those that didn't were treated to a blast of the two-tone horn.

In the rear, Martin Steel stared out of the window, but he didn't take in the scenery as it sped past the bulletproof glass.

The situation they faced was far more complex than even most of the players who were actively involved in it actually knew. There were times when he wished he was back in a simpler life, when all that mattered was surviving the day in one piece and being able to go to bed, alive and kicking, all limbs intact. But those days were long gone for him.

He had agreed to his current position after a distinguished career in first the army and then the special forces, most noticeably the Special Air Service, known around the world as the SAS. Their reputation preceded them and it was well deserved. There was not a force on the planet that could match them for capability, experience, and their pretty much unchallenged success record.

He had risen as high as he could go, to commanding officer of the unit for five years. And then things had changed. The world order was turning itself inside out.

New threats were coming at the country from all quarters, and it was becoming more and more difficult to tell your friends from your enemies. It was getting to the stage where you could trust no one. The only way to maintain even the status quo was to play beyond the rules.

The opportunity to do something about this had presented itself when Dominic Carter had become Prime Minister. Steel had been at Oxford with Carter. The two had formed an immediate bond over their desire to do the right thing and for Britain to maintain its presence in the world order, despite its size. The morals and values of the country were without reproach, and although over the years these had been called into question—the acts that were so often criticized and reviled now had been a consequence of their times. People, particularly the media, seemed to make observations of historical events and take them out of context without the veil of time; judging decisions and actions taken many years previously on the way the world was today. These accusations and comments were lapped up on social media by those with an agenda. Soon you had chaos and mayhem based on fake news and misinformation. It was something that realistically could no longer be stopped or controlled due to the proliferation of the digital age. But someone, somehow had to make a stand. And since Dominic Carter had become PM, he had brought Steel in to do just that—no restraints, no boundaries, no accountability. Some might say that was a dangerous path to travel, but it was a dangerous world out there and it needed an equally radical response.

Martin Steel was prepared to provide that response right up to his dying breath.

The Jaguar had long since negotiated the traffic blackspots of Hanger Lane and Shepard's Bush and was now speeding along Bayswater Road, which bounded the north side of Hyde Park. Steel's attention was brought sharply back to the present as the car braked hard to avoid a white Transit van that pulled out from a side road without warning. A blare on the two-tone horn and a contemptuous "Wanker!" from Jenkins caused Steel to smile, and they were past.

Ten minutes later they drew up at number 70 Whitehall, an impressive white three-story building set back from the road. It was situated just north of Downing Street and housed the meeting rooms where the government's COBRA group met.

The world was full of acronyms, but COBRA, used for the emergency meeting group of the British government, was probably as good as they came. The name clearly indicated decisive and aggressive action, but it was actually convened in all times of crisis, from war and terrorist incidents to floods, fires and outbreaks of disease; basically, any time when action was required on a large scale to counter a threat to the nation. It had even been used during tanker strikes where the supply of fuel to the country's petrol stations had been in jeopardy. In fact, in spite of its fearsome name, the acronym was far more benign, dull even, simply standing for **C**abinet **O**ffice **B**riefing **R**ooms. The fact that briefing room **A** was normally the one used in times of extreme crisis simply added to the myth.

Steel stepped out of the car into the light London drizzle gripping his laptop bag. He thanked Duffy, who drove smoothly off. He then pulled his collar up and crossed over the wide sidewalk and up the three short steps to the innocuous black door at the front of the building.

Once inside, he was immediately greeted by an aide who stood up from a desk in a wide reception area.

"Is he here?" asked Steel.

"Yes, sir," the aide replied. "They're all here. They've been in session for thirty minutes."

Steel frowned, thanked the man, and then headed down the corridor. The walls were a pale yellow in color, and there were paintings from across the eras decorating them. He reached an elevator at the end. At the push of a button the doors slid smoothly open and he stepped inside. He pressed the button for Basement Level 2 and waited while the metal box made its short descent into the Earth. The room had previously been located on the entrance level, but to provide greater protection against electronic eavesdropping it now resided two floors below.

Once the doors had opened, he stepped out and walked down a corridor to a door with a large 'A' in its center. He pushed it open and walked in.

The room itself was small, cramped even. It was dominated by a large light pine-colored table that filled about eighty percent of the space. Around the table were twenty padded chairs that were less comfortable than they looked. On the table was a tray with a coffee percolator and a small plate with a dwindling pile of biscuits. Half-empty coffee cups sat in front of the occupants, as well as files and papers of varying sizes. One end of the room was covered by a large screen, which was currently split into eight smaller ones showing a variety of live camera feeds as well as maps and other data. It felt hot, almost stuffy, in the room, particularly after the cold of outside.

Five people were seated in the chairs. A face also stared out of one of the screens, clearly on a conference call.

They all turned as he entered.

At the head of the table was Dominic Carter. He

offered a quick smile to Steel. The two nodded at each other.

Carter was not someone you would immediately figure as the leader of a country. He was in his mid-forties and not particularly charismatic at first glance, but as they say, appearances can be deceptive. He had a lean but canny face, with thick, well-groomed dark hair. His eyes were gray, but focused and perceptive, and looked out on the world through a set of thin steel-framed glasses. On the face of it his demeanor was somewhat quiet. But beneath the calm exterior he was as hard as nails. He couldn't be persuaded to deviate from his course once he had made up his mind, whatever the obstacle. At the same time, he was more than happy to listen to advice, and he would act on it if he considered it was better than the action he had decided on. It was for these attributes, among many others, that he had won a landslide victory at the previous year's election.

To Carter's right was the chief of staff, Carol Baxter. She was a bright woman in her late forties, with short hair and a firm and severe expression. Steel had never really got on with her. She was good at her job, which was why she was where she was, and there was nothing he could put his finger on, but that was what bothered him; he could normally profile people after the briefest of time, but with Carol Baxter he had never been able to do that.

Next to Baxter was Robert Cooper, head of MI6, a tall, unflappable man in his late fifties. Calm under pressure and with an ironic sense of humor, who, while not overly enthusiastic about Steel's job description—effectively National Security Adviser—understood the Prime Minister's thinking and had always supported their actions in the past.

Opposite them sat Admiral Chris Buchanon from the Royal Navy, a trim man in his sixties but with a world of experience and a sharp eye and equally sharp tongue. He was an ex submariner and was in charge of naval warfare operations.

Next to him was Stephanie Caine, the Foreign Secretary. She was a tall, stylish, attractive black woman in her late thirties. Many had complained at her lack of experience when she had been appointed to the position, but she had quickly gained the respect of her peers with her uncompromising attitude, which had been instrumental in securing the release of a number of high-profile British citizens who had been imprisoned in Iran and Yemen over the previous two years. Steel had always got on with her, and there had at times been a certain frisson between them. It had even gone further than that, and Steel had often thought there could be even more. That was, at least, until after one Foreign Office function where the alcohol had flowed freely, and she had left him in no doubt she was merely playing with him and he should get over himself—but it was a game both of them seemed to enjoy and he wasn't going to be the one to put a stop to it.

There were a few pleasantries exchanged and then the Prime Minister spoke.

"Good to see you, Martin. I think you know everyone, except maybe Captain Hargreaves." He indicated the face staring out from the screen. "He's on the *Queen Elizabeth*. They're currently steaming south to offer any assistance they can."

"Good to see you, Captain," said Steel, looking at the screen.

"Likewise," replied Hargreaves.

"How's progress?"

"Not bad. There's a typhoon heading up from the south. It'll be over the Palau region in the next few days. We should be able to handle it, but it'll make the operation somewhat tricky."

"Thank you, Paul," said the Prime Minister. "Now, Martin, how did things go in Scotland?"

Steel sat down, at the same time placing his laptop on the desk. "Not as good as I'd hoped. It appears our information wasn't entirely correct. They have the equipment, but it's not in a go capability at the moment. They're working on it and I've made sure they're aware of the urgency. I should hear from them tomorrow."

Buchanon's expression was hard. "This is our last option, Martin. They have to come through."

"I have a feeling they will. This McCready guy wants to do the right thing. He'll move heaven and earth to make it happen. He knows lives are at stake."

The Prime Minister turned to the admiral.

"Chris, what's the latest from the sub?"

Buchanon replied, "It's not looking good. We've heard nothing since receiving information they'd made it to shallower water, were over at an angle and pretty much dead on the bottom. They were getting ready to blow the tanks and surface—but then, nothing. I think we can be pretty sure they've been attacked, and no guesses by whom."

Robert Cooper from MI6 continued the thought. "It's undoubtedly the Russians. The grapevine has been alive out of Moscow. The thing is, we don't know how they knew about the satellite or just how valuable the computer drive is."

Stephanie Caine interjected. "There's no other explanation. There must be a mole." Everyone looked particularly uncomfortable at this.

"Or," said Steel, "they have new technology we don't know about."

The comfort factor did not improve.

The Prime Minister was the next to speak. "Okay, Bob, what's MI6's damage assessment if the Russians get their hands on the drive?"

Cooper took a deep breath before answering. "It would be devastating. As you know, the cover of a weather satellite didn't last for long. In fact, it was part of the GPS system we put up to ensure we didn't need to rely on European satellites. While this is great for navigation applications, among others, it also allows us unfettered access to the airspace above foreign states and is doubling as an information-gathering tool of an unprecedented nature. The satellites are fitted with advanced laser technology that can eavesdrop on any citizen on the planet by firing the laser at windows of buildings, or even cars. It can also suck data from any hard drives present at those locations. It's technology that's been around for some time, but only at short range. Being able to do this from orbit is a game changer. Even the Americans haven't managed to crack it, and it's not something we're prepared to share with them at the moment."

"Which comes back," interjected the Foreign Secretary, "to just how the Russians have wind of this."

"Quite so," agreed Cooper. "The bottom line is, whoever has that drive will not only know of our capability, but also have access to the information and data that was backed up on it as a failsafe. I can assure you, that is something we do not want to happen."

"And if we can't get down to the sub, what then?" asked the Foreign Secretary.

"We have the carrier task force sailing south as Captain Hargreaves confirmed," replied Admiral Buchanon. "On board the *Queen Elizabeth* are her squadron of F-35 Lightning jets, so we will be able to confront any opposition on the surface. The problem is the worsening weather. Help from the surface may not be an option. The only factor we have in our favor is that as far as we know the Russians don't have the capability to lock onto the sub at the angle she's resting at. Only this team in Scotland can do that."

The Prime Minister looked at Steel. "So, Martin, looks like it's down to you. You need to ensure this McCready realizes the seriousness of the situation."

"Don't worry. He'll be left in no doubt."

Admiral Buchanon looked up. "What did he say when you mentioned the Russian involvement? He's a civilian after all. Going down there to save lives and bring back the drive is one thing. Having the Russian military in the area is something else entirely." He looked evenly at Steel.

Steel returned the stare. When he replied, his tone left everyone in no doubt of his intentions. "I think the full details of this operation are on a need-to-know basis." He paused. "And, right now, they don't need to know."

Everyone slowly looked up at Steel, shock written across their faces. Everyone, that was, except the Prime Minister. He locked eyes on Steel with a look that said, *I hope you know what you're doing*.

Steel's gaze didn't waver.

He could second that.

Chapter Ten

Two weeks ago

Major Yuri Ivanov walked down onto the tank surround, a kit bag over his shoulder. He was dressed in a tight-fitting black one-piece overall with numerous strategically placed pockets. It would be a long trip and he had no idea when he would return, or indeed, if he would return.

The kit bag contained no personal items. He didn't have any. It was just the equipment he needed to get the job done, including an array of close-quarter weapons, from a compact automatic to an assortment of knives. You never knew what you would encounter. He always liked to be prepared, even if the whole mission could very well be completed without ever leaving the inside of *Blackfin*.

The dark mood he had been in for the last few weeks was starting to lift now they were finally on their way. Someone would pay for the delay though. Heads would roll. If he had his way—quite literally.

Around him the last of the crew were making their way aboard.

As he approached the intimidating black hull, he felt a surge of adrenaline. Up close it looked like the deadly killing machine it was and he felt a certain kinship. It was as though the machine was a mechanical embodiment of himself. They were as one in their purpose, existence and goals.

Ivanov walked onto the metal ramp that led to the hatch. Once his feet left the hardened concrete surround, his mind was focused on only one thing—the mission. The next time he would think of the world as it was would be at the end—success or failure, his life now had only one objective.

From high up in the control room Cherenko watched the man in black walk onto the deck of the sub. As Ivanov did so, the colors seemed to merge and become one, and then he had disappeared down into the machine that would take him across the world in the service of the Russian state.

There was something at the back of Cherenko's mind that hoped Ivanov would not return. But to wish for that meant to wish for the probable failure of the mission, and that would look bad for himself, not to mention the embarrassment of his masters in Moscow.

No, failure was not an option.

Once the hatch had closed and he had confirmation the sub was secure from the captain, he turned to one of the technicians in the control room and gave the order.

"Send her to sea, and God protect them." Though he was sure that any god looking down would have far better things to be doing.

The technician looked out of the window at the vessel lying peacefully in the water. When he received a radio message from a worker on the side of the dock confirming all lines had been released, he leaned forward and pressed a button on the panel in front of him. This action started a series of events that showed the sheer ingenuity and clandestine nature of the base.

Twenty feet below the sub, a cradle on the bottom of the dock rose up until it was resting directly beneath the hull. It was shaped to perfectly fit *Blackfin*. The technician spoke into a mike. He received confirmation from the captain that they were ready.

A moment later, air erupted around the sub as the ballast tanks were blown. The huge machine settled onto the cradle. Once the technician saw the sub was stable, and the sensors indicated a secure lock, he pushed a lever forward.

Underwater, the cradle descended to the floor of the tank. It then moved smoothly forward on a track that stretched away from the dock and disappeared into the gloomy water beyond.

The track made a curve to the left to a position in the center of the tank. Here, it was joined by tracks from the other docks. It then extended out to a point in the middle of the man-made lake. Here, there was what looked like a U-shaped concrete island dock four hundred feet long and four feet high. The open part of the U faced the mountain. There was a small building on the left-hand side that handled the control systems for this stage of the operation.

The underwater track fed into the open part of the U on the bottom of the lake.

Here, the cradle moved into, and locked onto, a metal structure attached to two vertical rails tight against the dock walls. A deep water-filled shaft disappeared into the rock below.

In the control room on the island dock, a technician monitored the position of the sub through a series of underwater CCTV cameras. Once he was sure the cradle was secure in the metal structure, he clicked a mike button. "Lift contact secure. Prepare for descent."

"Roger that," came the reply over the speaker.

The technician flipped a switch and watched the monitors as the sub, still in the cradle, dropped out of frame at the bottom of the screen. He operated a joystick and panned the camera down to watch *Blackfin* descend vertically. It disappeared into the gloom below.

The sub continued its descent to a depth of a hundred feet. Once at the bottom, the cradle settled onto another track. The clamps from the lift system disengaged. The technician again confirmed the status with the sub's captain and flicked another switch. A massive door in front of the bow of the submarine opened, revealing a tunnel beyond.

At the press of a button, the cradle carrying *Blackfin* moved smoothly forward on the track, heading down the tunnel.

After twenty minutes the cradle stopped at what appeared to be a dead end. The technician clicked the mike again. "Final checks. Ready for cradle release and open door."

"Affirmative," came the reply. "All systems check. We're good to go."

"Roger that. Door opening."

In front of the sub the wall started to split in two. The top half moved up; the bottom half moved smoothly down into the rock. After two minutes, the large bulbous bow of *Blackfin* stared out at the ocean beyond.

Gently, the sub rose up out of the cradle.

After hanging perfectly suspended in the middle of the tunnel for around a minute, the thrusters on the rear pods started up and she moved forward.

There was no noise, no fuss. Russia's most feared agent of war slipped into the Pacific Ocean and disappeared into the murk.

Behind her, the door closed, concealing the entrance of the base to any who would dare to find her.

The next time the sub made its presence felt would be over three and a half thousand miles away.

Chapter Eleven

Today

When McCready arrived back at Ocean Oil he found a number of engineers crowded round *Emily*. One was lying underneath and was responsible for the loud clangs of metal striking metal as he assaulted a stubborn rusty bolt with a large wrench, which he was hitting with an equally large hammer. They were engrossed in their work, but they looked up when McCready asked where Richards was.

"Up in the studio," came the reply.

McCready walked across the concrete surround of the tank to the metal steps that led up to the first-floor studio. At least it looked as though there was a plan for fixing the sub. Now that Logan was out of the picture it would be down to Craig and himself to work out an operational strategy, should the hardware prove to be functional.

He pushed the door open and walked inside.

He had a quick scan and saw Richards leaning over one of the designers at a monitor. He was pointing animatedly at a schematic on the screen. Two other designers were working at their stations in the room.

"How's it going?" asked McCready as he approached.

Richards held up a hand briefly and continued his conversation. When he turned round he looked tired.

"We're getting there, John, but slowly. The guys are changing the seals as we speak. Then we have to get her in the water and check they work. Make sure there are no immediate leaks. With the mark 2 we engineered a completely different collar—think two seals as opposed to one. But even if this holds, there's no way we can pressure test her in the time we have. Whoever goes down is going to be taking a hell of a risk."

"I need to talk to you about that," said McCready.

"Okay, give me a second. I'll finish up with Stacey then we can talk in the conference room. Put the kettle on."

McCready headed for the conference room while Richards turned back to the screen.

Ten minutes later, the water had boiled, the coffee had been poured and Richards entered the room. He closed the door behind him and sat wearily down opposite McCready.

He took a gulp, savoring the warmth of the liquid.

"How did it go at the hospital?"

McCready shook his head. "Those two... Why can't they just get along?"

"But I was right, yeah, Logan's out of it?"

"Looks that way. So it's just us."

Richards took a deep breath and looked straight at McCready. "I know why you want to do this. I understand your reasons. Damnit, I should know you after all these years, and I don't expect to change your mind, but please think long and hard, John."

McCready was about to answer when his phone rang.

He glanced at the display, saw the caller ID, and let it ring. After a few seconds it clicked off. He took a second and then looked at Richards.

"Craig, what's the general state of the company?"

Richards looked at him curiously. He thought for a moment. "Well, we're at an advanced stage with the aerial delivery system - *Skyline*. You remember, air-launched from a plane with autonomous navigation to any GPS location. Capable of delivering supplies/rescue equipment to any water-based location in the world." He thought again. "Then there are the early designs for a deep-sea drone that's capable of scanning the deepest parts of the oceans, but that's still on the drawing board. Just looking for funds to take it to prototype."

"And the North Sea?"

Richards hesitated. "We're waiting for the contract to be renewed with BP and we have some Scandinavian companies potentially interested."

"But it's dying, right?" said McCready.

Richards took an even longer pause. "It's slowing, sure, but the world economy is in a pretty fragile state right now."

"Yeah, and as far as oil and other fossil fuels are concerned, pretty much on a death bed."

"And your point is?"

"We need to move the company away from the service and repair of rigs, and over to more technology design and development. Doing this for Steel will allow us to do that."

"Not if we don't come back alive."

"I know there are risks, but it's an opportunity. And think of the men and women on the sub. We could be their only hope."

Richards sighed. "As usual, you know I'm going to say

yes. But there are ground rules. Number one—I'm the only one going down initially. Until I'm sure she's sound. They have to give us time for a test dive and fix anything that comes out of that."

McCready was about to protest.

"That's non-negotiable."

McCready looked at him with a we'll-see-about-that expression.

"Number two. We have safety equipment on board in case it all hits the fan when we're down there. We have to have another way out. And I have the final say on any abort. If I'm not happy, we come up—whatever is happening. You ok with that?"

"Well, not exactly…"

"Those are the conditions."

McCready's phone rang again. He glanced at the caller ID and again let it time out. A few seconds later a 'ping' indicated he had a voicemail.

Richards glanced at the phone and then at McCready. "That's the third time you've done that today. Anyone I know?" he asked pointedly.

McCready glanced at him. "I can't deal with that now. Not with all this going on."

Richards sighed and leaned forward onto the table. "You talk to me about my screwed-up relationships—what about you, John? That girl's the best thing that ever happened to you. Jesus, you wouldn't even be here if it wasn't for her!"

"I know. Believe me, I know, but what can I do? We can't talk to anyone about this. We're going to be away for god knows how long. What do I tell her?"

"You tell her something. Anything that doesn't let her

think you don't care. I saw the way you two were at the party. She's good for you. Not that you deserve her."

"Maybe it's me. Maybe I'm better off alone. Carol left me…"

"But you guys were really young, and anyway, that was the job—not you."

"But she should have understood. You have to make the money somehow."

"Well, some people just can't take the length of time away. Look at military partners. Some can hack it, some can't. Then there was Sarah…"

"Sarah?" McCready looked sharply at Richards in shock. "What about Sarah?"

Richards looked at him with mild amusement. "Everyone knew, John. It was written all over your face."

Sarah had been married to McCready's brother, Sean. But McCready had met her first and had thought they could have had a future together until he'd seen how happy she was with his little brother, and he'd backed off. Now Sean was dead, following an incident on a salvage operation in the North Sea. But there could never be anything between them. She was like a sister to him now.

"Everyone?"

"Everyone, except Sean. He never knew. He was so wrapped up in her."

"Jesus!" exclaimed McCready. "I didn't know anyone knew."

"Which is why, me old tosser, that Clare is not one to let get away. She won't hang around forever you know."

"McCready glanced down at the now silent phone. "I know. But is this really what I want right now?" He looked up at his friend.

"Better make your mind up, else you'll end up like me, naming hulks of metal after your exes!"

They both grinned. Richards stood up. "I have to get back to the guys. Check on progress. I'll let you know how it goes."

"Cheers, Craig, and thanks."

"You're welcome. And don't be a stupid bastard!" With that, Richards walked over to the door and out of the room, shutting it behind him.

When he'd gone, McCready picked up the phone and clicked onto voicemail. There was a single message: CLARE CALLED AT 18:30.

He paused for a moment and hit PLAY, lifting the phone to his ear. When he heard her voice, something caught in his throat. For a second his mind hesitated about what he was doing, but it was only for a second.

"Hi, John, it's me. Not sure when you'll get this, but I really wanted to talk to you before I head back to the States. My flight's in a couple of hours so I guess that may be too late. It was great seeing you again yesterday. I wasn't sure how I'd feel. I was really happy you seemed to feel the same way. I was a bit puzzled how you left things though. You were very cryptic about what you were up to, saying you had to go away. I may be reading things wrong of course—hey we all do that—but I thought I detected a certain distance, as though you were having second thoughts? Could just be me of course. It is a while since we saw each other. Anyway, I have to head back to LA. Looks like there could be the possibility of a job at a new center that's been built just out of town. It's a bit of a left move for me, but it sounds exciting and somewhat challenging if I'm being honest. As you know, the events of a month ago meant there was no way I could continue at Pipe and Flow, and beggars can't be choosers. This came up and the

interview's been moved forward, hence the early flight." She paused. *"Anyway, if you get this, give me a call. If not, I'll try to reach you in a couple of days. Take care of yourself. You mean a lot to me. Bye."*

And with that the message ended.

McCready let out a long sigh.

His finger hovered over the RECALL button, but then he took a deep breath, pocketed the phone and stood up.

Chapter Twelve

One week ago

Ivanov sat on his bunk.

It was hot.

He was wearing only a pair of thin cotton shorts. Even so, his body was covered with perspiration. It appeared the air conditioning was another system on the state-of-the-art sub that was having technical difficulties.

He breathed in deeply, held his breath for a minute, and then let it expire slowly over the following thirty seconds until as much as possible was removed from his lungs.

Then he breathed in again.

He repeated the cycle for the next five minutes, all the time sitting in a perfect yoga lotus position while relaxing and tensing his muscles in a predetermined sequence. The process allowed him to sink to a place where he was in total control of his body. It helped fine tune his brain and prepare him for what was to come.

Once he was finished, he dressed quickly in a black navy

jumpsuit, splashed some water on his face in the small sink at the side of the cramped cabin and walked out, closing the door behind.

He was lucky to even have a cabin, as space was at a premium on the submarine. There were only two individual cabins on the boat: one for the captain and one usually reserved for visiting political dignitaries and other VIPs. Such was the esteem and importance accorded to Ivanov that he was installed in the second cabin for the mission. Even the other officers had to bunk at least two to a room, and most of the thirty other crew had to hot bunk in tiers of three.

As he walked down the narrow, clinical corridor of brushed steel, he had to marvel at the technology and engineering around him. He could feel no real movement that would indicate they were traveling at over fifty miles per hour, five hundred feet below the surface of the Pacific Ocean.

It was almost as though they were tied up at the dock.

After the problems with the propulsion system, the captain had been loath to fully open her up, but they had tested it up to eighty miles per hour and the promise was there. Now they were just cruising. The captain had varied the speed every few hours to monitor the sensors, but so far everything had looked good.

He was still annoyed at the time they had lost though. It could have a major bearing on the outcome of the mission.

He came to a bulkhead door, designed to seal off compartments if any section should become flooded. He pulled open the thick metal with a small round window at head height and walked into the vehicle access chamber. He was in an area half the width of the vessel where the final preparations for extra submersible activities took place.

Here was where any personnel would kit up before transferring to the equipment in the 'garage' above. At one side a ladder disappeared into the ceiling through a watertight lockout hatch. It led up to an area where three vehicles were housed under a protective watertight cowl that opened onto the ocean beyond.

Ivanov would be climbing the ladder very soon.

But first he had to check on the final status of the mission. A lot had happened since leaving the base.

He walked through another watertight door that led to the ops room. Once inside, he glanced at the two men standing at a large central table whose whole surface was an electronic touch-screen display. Beyond the table, on one wall, an equally large display showed information, data and video from numerous sources, all controlled by the electronic table in the middle.

Captain Demitri Caspanov nodded at Ivanov. He was a small man in his early fifties, but with years of experience in the Russian fleet, many of those as a submarine commander. The post to *Blackfin* had been a reward for outstanding service in the face of adversity and under extreme pressure. He had a small trimmed beard and short dark hair. His face also seemed to always have a permanent frown.

Next to Caspanov was Valeri Kozlov. He was a major in the feared Spetsnaz special forces, and although of similar rank to Ivanov, he was undeniably second in command on the mission. He was a hard man of around six feet, all muscle, and, as Ivanov knew from experience, someone you could count on in a fight. He was one of the most ruthless killers he had ever come across, and that included himself. The man never showed any mercy, a trait Ivanov considered a requirement in this line of work.

Ivanov crossed to the table.

"Do we have an update?"

Kozlov replied, "The status is unchanged. The British sub is still stationary on the bottom. We should be there within the hour."

Ivanov nodded with satisfaction.

While for most of the journey there had been little to do except go over any plans and stay fit, there had been constant updates from the drones dropped by the Antonov many miles to the south.

In all, four had been deployed, forming a perimeter five miles out from the crash site of the satellite. One had initially descended to the sixteen-thousand-foot depth of the wreckage to record video and provide an assessment of the site itself. This had then returned to the perimeter on a watching brief, looking for any approaching British submarines.

Two weeks later one had arrived. It had been detected by the drone in the north-west. The sub was homing in on the signal emitted from the small box on the seabed.

Over the following hours, the drones had provided ample coverage. Ivanov had watched as the sub had moved onto station over the wreckage and deployed an ROV. The small tethered machine had emerged from a hatch in the hull and searched through the wreckage of the satellite. At one stage it had cut away the central core of what was left of the damaged metal casing and taken it back to the mothership. The whole operation had taken five hours and left the Russians with a dilemma. Once the sub started moving, she would soon vanish into the ocean.

The drones were set to follow.

The British sub had set off in a northerly direction with the drones in pursuit. They had then received information, through intelligence sources, that the British sub had a problem. It wasn't known what it was but she certainly wasn't operating at full speed.

The drones had kept pace for the previous three weeks. She had finally come to rest just to the south of the Palau archipelago. She was currently straddling the ridge of a seamount at the edge of a wide, sloping plateau. Any strong current or even seismic activity in the area could send her toppling over the edge into the abyssal depths for good, from which there would be no recovering her, or the cargo she carried that was so important.

Once the sub had settled on the bottom, it had remained there. A large amount of signal traffic had been detected coming from the communication system, so it did indeed look as though she had serious issues. Maybe the propulsion system had failed; they couldn't be sure.

While the Russians couldn't decipher the communications, they knew that help would be called for. Their window of opportunity was closing fast. At the relatively shallow depth of eight hundred feet there was far less you could plausibly deny than at a depth of sixteen thousand feet.

So, here they were, with *Blackfin* arriving on site within the hour and Ivanov and an assault team preparing to board the British sub.

He lived for moments like this, never knowing if you were going to live or die, never knowing how the day would end.

He glanced at Kozlov.

"Okay, let's get ready."

An hour later Ivanov climbed the ladder, up through the hatch, into the vehicle garage followed by Kozlov.

They were joined by a second soldier and the pilot of the minisub. The soldiers were dressed in loose-fitting combat clothes, the upper body of which had a Kevlar skin that could withstand close-quarter bullets, while they wore neat Kevlar helmets that had full communications built in. All three carried the latest Kalashnikov submachine guns, which had been adapted for combat in confined spaces. Around their waists they carried a webbing belt with additional ammunition, as well as a large knife in a sheath. If all went as expected none of these would be needed, but Ivanov always planned for the unexpected. You never knew the outcome of any encounter until it was over. Even then there could always be an unexpected surprise.

There was one other piece of kit each of them carried, one they would definitely need—a state-of-the-art gas mask.

The garage area itself wasn't large. What space there was, was filled with three machines that could allow missions beyond the capability of the sub to be carried out. There were two surface assault craft, which to the casual onlooker looked just like standard rigid inflatable boats, but closer inspection would reveal something more special. For a start there was no outboard motor, as would be traditional. Instead, a cowl covered a rear engine compartment that fed to a water jet, the nozzle of which protruded out the back of the boat. In its present form the other curious thing was that there were no inflatable sides. Where the buoyancy tubes should have been, there was simply a metal cover, as though concealing a compartment. The boats were in fact capable of underwater, as well as surface, operation, being powered by electric motors while underwater and, when required, using a petrol engine on the surface. Once on the surface, the sides were inflated by compressed air contained in cylinders embedded in the hull. Above the water they were capable of speeds in excess of sixty miles per hour and were armored and protected against enemy attack, the inflatable sides being made of thin Kevlar.

The main area was taken up by a minisub. It wasn't large, around twenty feet long, and was completely encased in metal. There was no dome at the front to see out of, or any form of window. All view for the pilot was provided by an array of cameras around the outside of the hull, which fed into a virtual realty headset. This allowed the pilot to look in any direction as if the hull of the sub wasn't there. It also allowed the strength of the hull to be uniform all the way around, making it more impervious to any weapon or detonation it might encounter. In the center, beneath the hull, was a lockout hatch. This was where you entered and exited and also through which Ivanov would gain entrance to the British nuclear submarine, by locking onto their emergency escape hatch.

The outside of the sub was covered with pipes and valves, and for this mission, a set of cylinders had been attached to the side. Hoses from these ran to a central valve that fed into a single hose that was connected to a metal spike held by one of the two manipulator arms at the front.

The sub itself was suspended four feet off the floor in a metal cradle with remotely operated clamps holding it securely at each end.

The pilot climbed in through the hatch underneath. He was followed by Ivanov, Kozlov and the third soldier. Five minutes later they were securely in their places within the sub. The pilot turned to Ivanov.

"Ready?"

"Ready," came the simple reply.

The pilot pulled on the virtual headset and clicked the

mike button. "*Blackfin*, this is *Assault One*, we are clear for release."

"Roger that," came the reply. "Flooding and withdrawing cowl."

The pilot flicked some switches and glanced around him, being able to see in crystal clear vision everything that was happening outside the titanium hull of the sub. He watched as the garage slowly flooded and the water rose up to cover the sub and fill the space. There was a mechanical grinding sound. He could see the metal cowl protecting the garage retract to reveal the ocean beyond. He did a final systems check and then flicked the clamp release that secured the sub to the cradle. There was a distinctive metallic *clunk* and they were free.

He pulled back on the controls and the small sub rose up through the water.

Once clear of the chamber, the pilot clicked on the sonar visual display in his headset. Immediately the area around him appeared in computer-enhanced clarity. Although not photorealistic, he effectively had a clear view of the seabed and any terrain as far as five hundred yards away in any direction, all without the aid of lights, which for certain operations, was highly desirable.

After a quick check around for underwater obstructions, the pilot pushed the throttles forward, heading toward the large mass a hundred yards in front of him. It currently registered as a long cylindrical shape, but as they closed the distance, the distinctive, formidable outline of one of the deadliest machines on the planet became ever more clear.

The nuclear submarine was sitting upright on a steep slope at the edge of a large, flat underwater plain. As the pilot moved along the side of the hull, toward the stern, he could see that the rearmost fifty feet were hanging out over an abyss that disappeared into the depths.

It was possible the crew of the British sub were aware of his presence, but the minisub wasn't in any danger even if they were. While these terrifying machines of war were quite capable of taking out a city thousands of miles away or combating a large sub in open water with an array of highly sophisticated torpedoes, they could not counter a threat from a small, highly maneuverable machine close in, particularly when lying crippled on the seabed.

As the pilot moved around the sub, there was no obvious damage to be seen, but who knew what had happened inside.

He checked his position and then headed for the side of the curved hull closest to the control room, just forward of the conning tower.

He was carefully adjusting the controls to bring the sub up over the deck when he was suddenly pushed sideways in the water.

"Whoa! What was that?"

Ivanov and Kozlov glanced up. "Problem?" asked Ivanov.

The pilot checked his electronic display and made some adjustments. "Current. Must be coming up over the drop-off. It's erratic and could be a problem if we're not in the lee."

"Will it affect the mission?" asked Ivanov.

"Not if I'm careful," replied the pilot.

"You know what to do, then," said Ivanov curtly.

The pilot maneuvered the sub along the side of the hull to a position close to the conning tower.

He then clicked a button marked AUTO and the computer took over control of the thrusters, keeping the sub exactly in position, whatever the external factors on the hull. They could hear the independent electric motors firing up in turn as they spun the four maneuvering propellers to keep the sub on station.

The pilot grabbed a second control column at the side of his seat and pulled forward a wrist-mounted control device. Through his headset he could see the actions his hand movements had on the manipulator arms outside the sub. He skillfully maneuvered the left-hand arm to extend out to the hull of the British sub. The arm held a thermic lance. A second later, flame spewed from the end as the lance started to cut a neat two-inch hole deep into the metal of the hull.

After a minute, bubbles erupted from the hole, indicating the hull had been breached. The pilot withdrew the lance and brought the second manipulator arm into play. In its grip it held the metal spike that was attached to the hose, which in turn was attached to the long cylinders down the side of the minisub.

He twisted and rolled his hand to bring the device directly above the newly cut hole. Then, with a quick press of a red button on the top of the controls, there was a loud metallic *thunk* as the spike was driven into the hole, capping it off and sealing the leak of bubbles.

The pilot calmly turned and spoke to Ivanov.

"All yours."

Ivanov reached over to a control panel on the side of the sub. He grabbed a small lever that was positioned at ninety degrees to a thin pipe. Without further thought he turned it to line up with the pipe. Immediately there was the tinny sound of flowing gas.

All the men sat in subdued silence.

They knew what was happening.

After five minutes he twisted the lever to its original position. The pilot disconnected the hose from the metallic spike that was now firmly embedded in the hull of the British sub. He flicked off the AUTO mode and retook control.

He pulled back on the controls and started to head for the escape hatch that was located in the rear section of the sub. To do this he rose up above the hull and alongside the conning tower.

Suddenly, out of nowhere, the sub was hit from the side.

The pilot fought the controls, but the current and its ferocity had taken even him by surprise.

The sub was pushed hard against the conning tower, causing it to lean over.

The British sub was so precariously balanced on the edge of the drop-off that even this small movement caused some of the seabed to give way.

The massive machine started to roll.

A second later it began to slide down the slope.

Inside the minisub they could hear the movement—a slow grinding of metal against rock—and then it stopped.

The huge machine came to rest twenty feet further down the slope. There was now another ten feet of the hull sticking out over the drop-off.

It wouldn't take much for her to go over completely.

But what was more important, and something the pilot realized was catastrophic, was that she had rolled over to an angle of ninety degrees.

The pilot stared into the headset in shock.

"So, what happened?" asked Ivanov. "Are we ready to go?"

The pilot maneuvered the sub to a stable position, then lifted the VR headset.

He turned to Ivanov.

"No, we are not. The British sub has rotated ninety degrees. There's no way we can dock onto the hatch at that angle." He hesitated before continuing.

"The mission is over."

The look Ivanov gave the pilot sent ice-water through his veins. The pilot knew the man's reputation. He also knew that Ivanov didn't know how to pilot the sub. Even so, he feared for his life.

After a second, Ivanov shifted his gaze to the two men at his side. Then he stared purposefully at the wall of the sub, as though seeing through the metal surrounding him to his mission beyond.

He then turned back to the pilot and fixed him in his stare.

"Nothing is over until I say it is over."

Chapter Thirteen

Today

The wind was blowing down Whitehall in occasionally violent gusts and the light was fading as Martin Steel exited the door of number 70.

He liked this time of day. It was like the changing of the guard when daytime London became nighttime London. There was still some brightness in the sky, but the twinkling lights of the buildings were coming alive, making the city look like a bejeweled metropolis.

After the Prime Minister had left the Cobra meeting earlier that day, having requested Steel come and see him at Number 10 later, the other attendees had gathered their things and left for their respective departments. Carol Baxter, the chief of staff, had given him a particularly dirty look as she'd left, one that had not gone unnoticed by Stephanie Caine.

As Caine had packed up her papers she'd glanced at Steel, who had still been sitting in his chair looking at the displays on the screen and going over information on his laptop.

"You two still not seeing eye to eye?" Caine had asked.

Steel had come out of his thoughts and turned his gaze on her. "I don't get her. She's good at her job, but there's something there. Things don't all add up," he had replied.

"You and your conspiracy theories. Like what you think happened between us," she had said, almost with a twinkle in her eye.

"It did and you know it," Steel had replied emphatically.

"In your dreams!"

"Yeah, well, sometimes."

It was her turn to have shot him a dirty look. "Anyway, you have a reputation to uphold… If only people knew."

"What?"

"Man of steel, heart of gold! Doesn't suit you somehow."

Steel had rolled his eyes, then glanced at some files on the desk. He'd picked them up, offering them to her. "Could you drop these back at reception for the archives on your way out?"

She'd stared at him, shaking her head. "You know, you never did get my job description, did you?"

"Huh?"

"There's a 'foreign' before the 'secretary.' Do it yourself, you lazy bastard!" And with that she'd left, but there had been no malice in her words.

Steel had watched her go.

Stephanie Caine was a challenge, and he loved challenges, but right now the one he had to focus on was not so pleasurable.

The sharp blast of a bus horn snapped him out of his

reverie. He stepped back from the side of the road and waved an acknowledgment to the driver. The big red double-decker swooshed past, a massive poster for the latest *Mission Impossible* movie plastered across its side. His first thought was, *Jesus, doesn't that guy ever get any older*, and then, with a wry smile, that that was his life spread across the side of a bus.

He checked the street carefully and made his way between the queues of slow-moving rush-hour traffic to the far side. Once there, he grabbed a copy of the *Times* from a mobile vendor selling newspapers and magazines.

He then checked his watch.

He had some time before his meeting with Carter so he set off down Whitehall to stretch his legs. As he headed south toward the Houses of Parliament, he passed the Cenotaph to his right.

The old monument was positioned centrally in the middle of the wide street and was where the United Kingdom remembered its dead from the First and Second World Wars. It was thirty-five-feet high, made from Portland stone, and was a permanent memorial built in 1920 following a temporary structure erected following the First World War. It had a stone wreath at each end, as well as one on top, and was where the National Service of Remembrance Sunday was held each year.

Steel took a second to stare at the dignified pillar that represented such great loss and that reinforced the reason he got out of bed every day and went to work. As always, he dipped his head in acknowledgment before walking on further down Whitehall.

When he reached Parliament Square, he cast an appraising eye over the security teams he could see in place around the area. Some were obvious, some not so. He then turned around and headed back up, making his way through the throng of commuters hurrying home with their heads down, eyes glued to cell phones.

It gave him time to think through the strategy he was adopting.

He didn't like keeping the full truth from the other members of the Cobra committee, but sometimes you had no choice. You had to go on instinct for the greater good. And, aside from the Prime Minister, he wasn't completely sure who he could trust.

A few minutes later he arrived at the imposing black steel gates of Downing Street.

They had been erected in 1989 following an increase in Irish terrorism and were a mark of the times, providing an uncomfortable link to the Cenotaph in so much as they represented the new 'world war' of terror, while the old stone structure represented the horrors of the past.

After a nod to one of the armed security officers on duty, whom he knew, he walked down the famous street to one of the most well-known doors in the world. He didn't even need to knock, as the black door with the famous number was smoothly opened to let him enter as he approached. He nodded his thanks to the steward who told him the PM was expecting him in the small drawing room and to go straight up.

Number 10 Downing Street was a bit like the Tardis. It looked fairly small from the front, but it extended back a considerable distance. It provided an excellent base at the heart of the city from which the British Prime Minister could live, work and entertain visiting dignitaries from overseas.

Steel walked across the entry hall, down a short corridor to an anteroom, past a massive globe, given as a gift by President Mitterrand of France, and up the winding stairs to the first floor. Lining the walls of the staircase were portraits of past incumbents of the address.

Some he had ultimate respect for, others he did not.

Once at the top of the stairs he found himself on a narrow landing. He knocked on one of the wooden doors to the side and walked into a small drawing room. The ceiling was high, as with the rest of the rooms in the residence, and in the center of one of the walls was a fireplace with an impressive ornate surround. Three sofas were arranged around the fireplace with a small glass-topped table in the middle. Seated in the deep cushions on one of the sofas, studying some papers, was Dominic Carter. He was dressed casually in a checked shirt and gray V-neck pullover. There was a half-empty brandy glass on the table. He glanced up as Steel entered.

The two shared a grim smile. Carter was the first to speak.

"Grab a drink, Martin. I'm sure you need one."

Steel crossed over to an oak drinks cabinet at the side of the room. He poured himself a brandy, offering the decanter to Carter, who shook his head. He took his drink and sat in a sofa opposite the Prime Minister.

Carter took off his glasses, leaned back and looked directly at Steel.

"So, what's the situation?"

"It looks like the crew of *Resilient* are dead. We obviously can't confirm without eyes on the ground, but they've been out of contact for too long."

"And you want to send in this Scottish team without full knowledge. Is that wise? They won't be prepared."

Steel took a deep breath, but when he spoke there was no hesitation.

"We need to be inside the sub. They are the only guys who can do that. If we tell them the whole story they may balk at the mission. We can maybe drip feed some information nearer the time. Less chance of them backing out then."

"Will they be ready in time?"

"I'm flying back up first thing. There'll be a transport standing by to leave Aberdeen the moment they're good to go."

Carter looked up at the ceiling briefly. "I hope you know what you're doing, Martin. I'm pretty uncomfortable with the situation you're putting them in."

Steel shot back immediately. "I'm pretty uncomfortable with the whole situation. Sometimes there are limited options. This is one of those times. We're walking a tightrope here." He paused for a moment. "We both agreed that going in there would be times like this. We just have to stay steadfast. The needs of the many outweigh the needs of the few and all that."

The Prime Minister glanced at him. "They never put this on the job description. If they did, no one would be running the country."

Steel took another swig of the much-needed brandy.

He would have to agree with his boss.

Chapter Fourteen

It was half past ten in the morning when Steel arrived back at Ocean Oil.

He walked into the large test tank building to find a hive of activity.

The first thing he noticed was an open-backed truck parked just inside the wide roller doors through which he had entered. Behind it was a large articulated flatbed backed onto the concrete surround. Its carrying bed lay beneath the track for the overhead gantry.

All around, equipment was laid out on the floor.

He could make out a number of inflatable rafts, a row of gas cylinders, along with what looked like a couple of red spacesuits. On closer inspection he realized they were submarine escape suits. As he followed the track of the gantry over to the tank, he saw two engineers standing at the side. They were watching a diver attach a cable from a winch assembly on the gantry down to the top of the sub that was floating in the water.

To one side McCready was handing a cutting tool to

Richards, who was in the water in full scuba gear. Richards took the cutter and then noticed Steel approaching. He nodded at McCready.

"Your friend's back."

McCready turned to see Steel walking toward him.

"Good luck with that!" said Richards before disappearing below the surface and swimming over to the sub.

Steel took in the activity as he stood next to McCready.

"Looks like you're making progress."

"They were working all night. It's not perfect but we'll give it a go. It'll be a suck it and see process. Start shallow, attached to a support boat, then work up to depth. Any problems, we abort."

Steel glanced at him. *If only he knew.* "So, when can we load up?"

McCready indicated Richards in the water. "When Craig's finished trimming a stanchion we had to add and done a final check on the seal, we can start loading the gear. The flatbed can take the sub. The other truck is for all the support equipment. We've only got two life rafts that can be attached to the sub for anyone we bring out. If there are going to be large numbers we'll have to make multiple trips. Any support boats on the surface will have to take them on board as quickly as possible. I don't suppose you have any update on that?"

Steel shook his head, his expression neutral, giving nothing away.

"I assume you have some sort of air transport arranged?" said McCready.

"C-17 Globemaster. There's nothing smaller than can carry all the kit. Also, range is important. It's got an additional center wing fuel tank that should be good for just over three thousand miles. You'll have to refuel en route a couple of times, but we need to keep it to a minimum. Time's short."

"You're not coming with us?"

"I may come out later. For now I have to fight fires back here. There's a lot of political flak behind the scenes I need to take care of. Believe me, I'd far rather be out there with you."

"So where do we land? It'll need to be close to the site. We also need a vessel with a substantial A-frame and a crew experienced in the launch and recovery of submersibles." McCready looked at Steel.

For the first time Steel was hesitant.

"We're... er, still working on that. The weather down there is changing all the time. Pretty calm in the target zone at the moment, but there's a typhoon heading up from the south. It's going to be tight. Let's just say it's a work in progress."

McCready didn't look happy.

He turned back to the tank. A loud clanging of metal came from beneath the sub. A moment later and Richards appeared at the side. "Okay guys, take her up. She'll do."

A second later there was the whirring of machinery and the sub lifted up out of the water suspended from the gantry, droplets of water cascading from the hull. Richards finned over to the side of the tank. He looked up at McCready and Steel.

"She's not perfect, but then who is?" His expression was hard. "But we'll try, Mr. Steel. You'd just better pray luck is on our side. We're going to need every single drop of the damn stuff that's going around right now."

Steel smiled back grimly. "I always think people make their own luck. Just don't let me down."

McCready and Richards exchanged glances and then

McCready helped Richards out of the water and remove his gear.

An hour later the sub had been lowered onto the back of the flatbed and secured for the short journey to the airport.

Richards, now showered and changed, was going over a checklist of the other equipment. As he checked items off, they were loaded onto the second truck by members of his crew.

He came to the two submarine escape suits that lay there like bright red man-shaped balloons. They were in fact an advanced form of loose-fitting drysuit. They had two large waterproof zips up the front and a long oval transparent face visor and hood that was built into the suit. While you wouldn't win any fashion awards, they could save your life from tested depths of up to six hundred feet. He'd been lucky to get hold of these two at short notice, and only because a colleague in the Royal Navy had gone above and beyond the call of duty. He hoped they wouldn't have to be used, but it was always good to have an option.

He knelt down and rolled the first one up, sliding it into its protective bag. He started to roll the second, when, as he straightened out the external metal waterproof zip on the front, he stopped up short. He knelt there, unable to move for a moment, then closed his eyes and under his breath, said, "Oh no!"

The drive through Aberdeen to the airport was slow but steady.

The long flatbed had a police escort, but even so, negotiating the traffic and the streets was a laborious process. At one point a delivery lorry on the High Street held everything up as it blocked most of the road. A quick word from one of the accompanying police officers meant that Boots the Chemist wouldn't be getting its delivery as fast as they might have liked, and the small convoy moved on.

Richards rode in the cab of the second truck, along with Graham, one of the technicians who would help load the sub and the accompanying equipment onto the plane. McCready rode in Steel's car. It was tense as the two men sat on the rear seat.

"I'm sure you can do this, John. I have every confidence in you," said Steel.

McCready glanced at him. "I hope you're right. We'll do our best. Don't worry about that."

"By the way, can you call through Wi-Fi on your phone?"

McCready looked puzzled for a second and remembered it was included on his monthly plan. He'd had to turn on the setting, but it did at least mean he could call from anywhere in the world for no cost when on a Wi-Fi network. "Sure. Why?"

"The plane has a satellite connection. I may need to update you on the way. Send you some files. Some of the information will be highly classified, which I don't want going astray. Just check with the crew and log on when you get on board. Also, if you have the phone, I can contact you wherever you are. Keep it on you at all times."

"Sure."

Up ahead McCready could see they were approaching the airport.

After a brief stop at a security gate, where Steel showed an ID card, they were swiftly waved through. The car swept into the airport grounds.

Ahead of them were two large hangars. They drove round to the front. McCready could make out the main runway not far beyond. Parked outside the buildings were two aircraft. One was a white BAE 146 jet with RAF markings. It currently had a fuel tanker attached to it by a couple of thick black hoses. The other was one of the most impressive aircraft McCready had ever seen.

The Boeing C-17 Globemaster III was large. It was one of a fleet of eight operated by the RAF as its main transport capability. It was over 170 feet long and had a wingspan of just under 170 feet. It could carry a payload of over 170,000 lbs, and was powered by four Pratt and Whitney turbofan engines, which allowed a cruising speed of five hundred miles per hour. It was truly impressive, and while not as large as something like an Airbus A380, painted in the RAF's combat gray, it projected an image of power and menace parked on the tarmac.

The rear loading ramp was down, revealing a massive interior beyond. A large metal pallet lay on the tarmac at the base of the ramp. It was connected to the aircraft by a cable attached to a winch. McCready assumed the sub would be transferred to the pallet and then hauled back into the aircraft.

The car pulled up at the side of the Globemaster. The two men climbed out. A few moments later the open-backed truck drove up, and not long after that, the flatbed.

Over the next thirty minutes the RAF crew transferred the submersible from the truck to the metal cargo pallet using a small mobile crane. Under Graham's supervision, other members of the crew moved all the support equipment from the smaller truck and loaded it into the Globemaster.

McCready stood next to Richards and Steel watching proceedings.

Richards turned to Steel. "Still no update on our destination?"

"Not yet. It's weather dependent and we want to get you as close as possible to the site."

Richards looked at him dubiously. "You'll still need to get a ship ready. They're highly specialized. Not many of them around. You can't just order them up at the drop of a hat."

"I know. Don't worry, we'll get you there." Steel's expression gave nothing away. "I'll update John with more specifics in-flight. There are aspects of the mission I can only let you know nearer the time. As I said, I may well join you in a few days depending on how things pan out here. In the meantime, good luck. There are a lot of people counting on you. Just remember why you're doing this. Whatever happens, however things might change, the goal is the same."

With that, he shook their hands and walked toward the other jet that had just finished refueling.

Richards watched him go. "What the hell did he mean, 'however things might change?'"

"I don't know," said McCready.

Richards watched Steel climb aboard the jet and disappear inside. "I don't trust that guy. I've sorted something out, just in case."

McCready glanced at him. "In case of what?"

"I'll tell you when we're on board."

And with that they walked up and into the massive hold of the Globemaster.

From inside the cabin of the BAE 146 Steel watched the loading ramp of the Globemaster lift up to seal the cargo bay. He didn't feel bad not telling McCready and Richards the truth. They would have to confront it sooner or later and they were resourceful men. Also, if they weren't given any option to back out, they would have to deal with the situation as they found it and he would deal with the consequences later. That, he could live with. As he always told himself, the end justified the means.

He was sitting at the rear of the aircraft, as there were a couple of other passengers who would be joining the flight and would be sitting in the front section of the cabin. Steel never normally liked waiting, but for one of these passengers he was prepared to make an exception.

He watched the Globemaster taxi over to the runway, and then out of the small oval window he saw a black Rolls Royce pull up at the base of the steps of the BAE 146. There were a few moments when nothing happened, then a smartly dressed man in a suit and tie walked onto the plane. He glanced around, saw Steel and nodded.

He nodded back.

A few moments later, a small, elderly gray-haired lady walked into the cabin and straight to the seat indicated to her by the man in the suit. Once she had sat down one of the pilots came out and said a few words to her and then disappeared back into the cockpit.

Steel eased back into his seat, fully reclining it for the flight to London. He had met the elderly lady a few years previously when he had been involved with security arrangements for her grandson's wedding to some American actress.

As the engines started up and he closed his eyes, he

thought he could hear the faint barking of dogs coming from the hold.

They sounded a lot like Corgis.

He had one thought on his mind as he drifted off to sleep.

Don't worry, ma'am, I'll keep your country safe.

Chapter Fifteen

Miles Crabshaw watched the Victoria's Secret model pour baby oil from the small plastic bottle over her hands and let it dribble through her fingers and onto his chest.

Her tall, supple body was covered in a beautiful dark tan that was only broken in a couple of places by a bright orange thong that barely slipped its way between her legs, and two, small, seemingly postage stamp size pieces of material that barely covered her prominent nipples on her more than ample breasts. Her eyes gleamed with intrigue and her hair, braided into rows of ringlets that hung around her face, gave her an alluring, exotic look that made it very hard for him to contain himself where he lay.

She was simply stunning.

He couldn't quite believe he was here.

She started to rub her long slender fingers over his body. They were slick from the oil and transported him to a heaven he hadn't known existed.

He didn't feel he could hold on much longer.

This was not what usually happened to a balding, overweight, fifty-year-old lawyer from Ohio. But for the moment he really didn't want to think on things too much in case the angel in front of him disappeared.

Unfortunately, just as she was kneading the excess flesh below his belly button, and about to head further south, an insistent tinkling sounded in his head. He tried to make it go away, but it wouldn't. Instead, it seemed to grow louder and louder as though coming closer. Eventually it was like a chorus of church bells ringing between his ears. Then it stopped abruptly and was followed by a sharp knocking and the words "Dive briefing. Ten minutes."

Crabshaw didn't dare move.

The supermodel was fading from his sight.

His eyes were fuzzy.

With a massive effort he flicked his eyelids open and found himself staring at the bottom of the wooden frame of a bunk bed two feet in front of his face. The sound of the ringing bell disappeared further down the corridor outside his cabin.

He slumped back on the narrow mattress and sighed.

"Bollocks!"

Ten minutes later he was sitting on the blue canvas cushions on the rear seating area of the *Palau Explorer* liveaboard dive boat, along with the fifteen other guests who were avidly paying attention to the dive guide standing at a whiteboard hanging on the wall in front of them.

The seats were at the rear of the hundred-foot catamaran, which could carry sixteen guests in unabashed luxury and was arranged over three decks. The area was open to the sky, and right now a refreshing breeze flowed across the space, cooling the tropical temperatures that engulfed the islands. There had been talk of some bad weather coming, but for now the water was millpond flat, perfect conditions for exploring the ocean.

As Crabshaw glanced around, he could see many of the others sipping water from the provided refillable bottles to help them hydrate before the dive. They were all concentrating on the briefing.

The guide stood at the whiteboard wearing a black T-shirt with the words DIVE HARD scrawled across it in yellow. In his hand he held a green magic marker and was drawing out an image of the dive site they were about to go explore. It was quite a work of art, using various colors to showcase the different features of the site.

This particular one was called Siaes Tunnel and consisted of a large cathedral-like cave you could swim through, the entrance of which was at about eighty feet. There were smaller chimney-like side tunnels that led into the main one, but they were too narrow for a fully kitted diver to fit through. The plan was to swim the whole way through the large tunnel and out to the reef on the other side.

It was the third day of a seven-day trip and Crabshaw was already beginning to feel the strain. It was supposed to be a bloody holiday! But when the website had said he would be able to do thirty dives on the trip, he was damn well going to make sure he did thirty dives, even if it meant doing five a day. It was the reason he'd been asleep dreaming of supermodels at two o'clock in the afternoon. All you seemed to do was eat, sleep, dive, repeat. Factor in the time it took him to set up his underwater camera gear, and there were barely five minutes left in the day to have a crap.

He was almost cursing the fact he'd brought the camera

on the trip. But then the reports of Palau as a dive destination from his friends and online reviews had been so gushing he'd just had to struggle onto the plane with an excess baggage charge of two hundred dollars each way and a case that needed built-in rollers to be able to move because of its weight. Couple that with the fact that for some bizarre reason he'd had to change in Miami—the original lost-luggage destination—and he thought he might never see his gear again.

The reports had been right though.

From the air the archipelago of Palau was an amazing sight.

Stretching for a distance of around ninety miles in a vertical strip, north to south, it was situated in the Western Pacific, around six hundred miles to the east of the Philippines. It was made up of over three hundred individual islands and islets, and the capital, Koror, was located about a third of the way up from the southernmost tip.

What made the place so distinctive, though, was the group of rock islands in the lower region of the group. They were made up of small, round interconnecting pieces of rock, formed from porous limestone, and were covered in vegetation right down to the water's edge. From the air they looked like round green humps in a brilliant blue sea.

Like many places in the Pacific, the islands had a troubled past, having experienced particularly fierce fighting in the south during World War Two, when they had been occupied by the Japanese and then liberated by the Americans. They became an independent state in 1994. With a population of around twenty thousand, their main income centered around fishing and tourism, the latter to which Miles Crabshaw was currently contributing.

He tore himself away from watching some small

blacktip reef sharks that were swimming around the rear of the boat and listened to the dive guide wrap up the briefing, finishing with the instruction that they would be boarding the tender in fifteen minutes.

Crabshaw eased himself out of his spot on the bench seat and could tell by some of the other weary groans that the initial first few days' enthusiasm was rapidly wearing off for some of the other guests as well.

He made his way down to the camera room to make final preparations to his gear.

He stood in front of the large black metal housing with the white Nauticam logo across the front. It always amazed him how quickly the company managed to get housings out after the release of a camera. And given that the big brands were coming out with new cameras every year, that was an awful lot of housings to design and manufacture. He was a sucker for it, though, always having to have the latest kit. Yachtsmen moaned that if you wanted to pour money into the ocean you should buy a yacht.

You could also take up underwater photography.

He pushed the Nikon D850 into the housing, made a quick check that the O-ring was clear, and snapped the back shut. He then went through the pumping ritual to create a vacuum inside the housing. This would allow him to tell by a green light recognition system if there was a leak anywhere and hopefully save what had happened on his previous trip when several thousand dollars' worth of kit had gone swimming with the fishes.

Once satisfied, he picked up the huge rig with the scaffolding-like arms that held the two massive strobes, one either side, and made his way to the dive deck.

He handed it to one of the crew who would load it onto the tender, and then went to pull on his thin Lycra dive suit.

It would take off the chill, though with the water temperature up around the eighty-six degrees Fahrenheit mark, he would hardly need it. It did, at least, save him getting stung or scratched by any coral on the reef and also helped to hide his few extra pounds.

Once he had pulled it on, he grabbed his mask and fins from the green storage crate under his station on the dive deck and walked to the rear of the boat where the other divers were assembling to climb into the tender. His cylinder, regulator and weights were already on board, courtesy of the ever-attendant crew.

While on most liveaboards you had to climb into inflatables to take you out to the dive sites, here, the dive tender was a thirty-foot hard-sided boat that was raised and lowered by a lift system at the rear of the liveaboard. All you had to do was step into the boat at the dive deck level and when everyone was on board the lift lowered you onto the water and the boat was free to drive away.

As the lift descended, he felt like he was in the kid's TV show, *Thunderbirds*, though with the slow descent rate of around ten feet over five minutes, it wasn't quite like launching Thunderbird 4 from the pod of Thunderbird 2.

Once the boat was free of the lift, it pulled slowly away and then sped off across the flat calm water.

The *Palau Explorer* was currently moored a few miles south-west of Koror so the group could experience the impressive dives at the edge of the surrounding offshore reefs.

The ride in the fast tender would take about fifteen minutes to get to Siaes Tunnel.

Crabshaw enjoyed the trips in the boat. He was sitting at the rear, facing backward, and watched as the smooth wake, like a giant swan's wing, spread out over the calm ocean. He reluctantly tore himself away from the view and picked up the housing that had been placed at his feet by one of the crew.

He was just checking some of the settings on the back when he heard giggling coming from his left. He glanced over to see Yang, one of the two Chinese tourists on the trip, grinning at him. The man seemed very nice, but he didn't speak a word of English. On many of the other dives Crabshaw had noticed him flying around the reef as though he was on steroids. Definitely a case of not putting Duracell in that one. He now looked down at the diminutive guy who was grinning from ear to ear.

"What is it?" asked Crabshaw.

Yang didn't say anything but continued to grin, indicating the large housing and strobes Crabshaw was trying to balance on his knees.

"What about it?" asked Crabshaw.

Yang didn't reply, merely lifting up a small camera tray with handles at each end. Sitting in the middle of the tray was a GoPro camera about the size of a few sugar cubes. He continued to grin.

Crabshaw grimaced. The man's camera was a fraction of the size and weight of his and, as far as video was concerned, could probably take equally good footage. He nodded, smiled through clenched teeth, and turned back to fine tune the settings.

But he couldn't stop himself from muttering "bastard!" under his breath.

They arrived at the site five minutes later.

After a final brief from the dive guide they rolled over the side of the boat and into the clear blue water.

This was the time Crabshaw always enjoyed the most, when you returned to the underwater realm. The heat of the tropical air was gone, replaced by a refreshing coolness that spread across your body.

The cumbersome weight of the housing was also gone, and now his rig was as light as the infernal Yang's GoPro, and what was more, he could fly.

He was weightless.

It was the appeal of the sport, why he traveled halfway across the globe for amazing adventures in foreign climes.

He made some final adjustments to the camera through the housing and then looked around to get his bearings.

The rest of the group had already set off after the guide. The boat had dropped them about fifty feet from a sheer coral wall. All around there was deep blue water that stretched into the depths. He could see a whitetip shark meandering its way along the reef fifty feet below.

The main group were easy to see. They were following the guide toward the entrance of a large cavern in the reef wall about eighty feet down. He pressed the vent valve of his buoyancy compensator and sank slowly vertically down.

After reaching a depth of about ten feet and clearing his ears to ensure the pressure equalized in his middle ear, he moved into a prone position and followed the group of divers toward the entrance of the cave.

When he got there, it was a truly impressive sight.

The cave was like a massive arch extending into the rock. It was at least thirty feet in height. He couldn't see the far end, though there was light entering in the distance. The bottom was sandy gravel and there was plenty of marine life on the coral-encrusted walls to keep him busy with photographic subjects.

Although the cavern was large and would normally

require a wide-angle lens to do it justice, he was after the smaller creatures, those that lived in crevices and under ledges on the walls. To this end he had fitted a macro lens, which would mean he would have to get right up close and personal when he found them.

He glanced at the group. It was slowly making its way through the cave about twenty feet further along. He was used to the bane of the underwater photographer, always being left to his own devices as others lost patience with the time it took to set up shots and modify settings for that perfect image, but he didn't mind. The conditions were fine, the water was warm, and the visibility was great.

It didn't get much better than this.

As he made his way along the cave wall, close to the roof, he noticed some smaller side tunnels—more like shafts really—that let light in from the reef outside. He finned over in the hope of finding some juicy critters to fill up his memory card.

He was just focusing on a particularly spectacular nudibranch that was making its way slowly over a protruding piece of the rock wall when a shadow passed across the end of the side tunnel.

He glanced up, curious but not worried. It was probably one of the small sharks he had seen earlier cruising along the outside of the reef. He was more concerned that the change in light intensity might screw up his shot at the vital moment.

Whatever it was had disappeared. There was nothing there.

He steadied the camera on the coral. He knew he would be frowned upon for this, but there was no one to see him. Through the viewfinder he framed the nudibranch so the small cluster of gills on its back were silhouetted against the light from the side tunnel. He took a deep breath and held it to allow him to steady the shot.

He was just about to press the shutter release when everything suddenly went dark, and something very big and very fast rushed straight toward him.

Chapter Sixteen

Through the viewfinder it looked like the open jaws of a shark.

He had no time to react, except to try and back away, when something grabbed his mask.

It pulled it from his face.

Water flowed around his nose and eyes.

If he'd been a less experienced diver he might have snorted water up his nostrils, making him cough and gag. In a cave, that could have disastrous results, causing him to shoot up for air to a non-existent surface. But Crabshaw was an experienced diver and didn't panic. Even his heart rate didn't increase that much. What he did do, though, was instinctively let go of the camera to try to catch his mask, which was starting to sink in the water in front of him. As soon as he did so, the housing was whisked away.

As it was pulled from him, one of the strobe arms caught in his regulator hose, pulling his mouthpiece from his mouth.

He now had no mask on his face and no breathing supply in his mouth.

His heart rate did now start to increase.

Although he couldn't say for sure, he thought he had seen the darkness in front of him lighten, as though something was disappearing, but then darken again as though whatever it was had returned.

After that, he was preoccupied with retrieving his air supply and restoring his sight.

A few seconds later he had his mouthpiece back in his mouth. He exhaled to blow out the excess water and then looked around for his mask.

He saw it right in front of his face.

By some bizarre stroke of luck it had snagged on a piece of coral six inches in front of him. Once he'd pulled the strap over his head, he breathed out through his nose to clear the water and then looked up the side tunnel in front of him.

He thought he saw the flick of a fin from the entrance but couldn't be sure.

There was one thing he was sure about, though, and that was that his six-thousand-dollar camera rig was nowhere to be seen.

The outside of the reef was a sheer wall.

At sporadic places along the coral, small shafts fed into the large cave beyond. Out of one of these shot a creature at high speed. It was streamlined and seemed to flow as one with the water. It was covered in a multicolored skin that blended perfectly with its surrounds and seemed to sparkle in the sunlight like the scales of a fish. The only thing out of place was the large camera rig and strobes that seemed to be attached midway down its body.

It disappeared up the coral wall to surface next to a small floating object that, from beneath, looked to have the silhouette and profile of a surfboard.

Suki Tanaka hauled herself up onto the back of the Jet Ski that was floating next to the wall. She took in a series of deep, controlled breaths as she replaced the oxygen in her body that had been depleted over the five-minute free dive.

It had taken slightly longer than expected as she'd had to make sure the diver had managed to get his regulator back in his mouth after it had been knocked out when she'd grabbed the housing. She had also caught his mask and placed it on a piece of coral where he could easily find it.

But now she was back on the surface and all was well.

She wore a tight-fitting Lycra suit that covered a small, lithe body. The suit had been made specially for her by an American artist she had found online in Florida. The girl did amazing paintings of sea life and abstract patterns of the water, which could be put onto hats, T-shirts and leggings, and, as it turned out, Lycra suits. The work was impeccable and made Suki look like some sort of mythical sea creature when she moved through the water. The other specific thing she had asked for was the thin Lycra hood she now pulled from her face, revealing an ultra-low-profile dive mask behind. The hood was adorned with the artwork of the open jaws of a great white shark with two small holes she could see through.

As she pulled off the mask it revealed a face of extraordinary beauty…

… except for one thing.

Extending from her left eye, all the way down the side of her cheek, was an horrific scar. It was as though it had been put there as such perfection should not be allowed to exist. Her face was framed by short, dark hair that looked more like a boy's than of an eighteen-year-old young woman.

The precise, almost elfin-like, features clearly showed her Japanese heritage, but somewhere in there was the influence of Western genes, altering the full-on Asian look to a slightly softer image. Her large, almost doe-like eyes twinkled with life as she had come out of the water, but as she prepared the Jet Ski to leave, and untied the small line she had secured to the rock, the deep black pupils seemed to dull somewhat. They took on a haunted, almost harrowed expression, like those of a frightened deer. It was completely at odds with the rest of her.

Suki sat crouched on the back of the Jet Ski. She hauled the camera housing and strobes up onto the small area at the back, and then folded everything in carefully to make it as low profile as possible.

Once she was happy, she moved forward to sit on the seat and pressed the engine start. As she twisted the throttle, a powerful jet of water shot out of the rear of the craft propelling her forward. She headed away from the small island and back toward the mainland, a wide wake spreading out behind.

As she sped across the calm water she heard a far-off rumble of thunder. She looked south to the horizon. Storm clouds were approaching. This would have to be her last job for several days. It looked like all diving would be canceled by the operators due to the weather coming in. It would mean she would not be able to pay her masters the monthly tariff they'd imposed on her.

It meant her mother might no longer be safe.

She shuddered at the thought.

A deep sadness spread from her beautiful eyes across her

face, creating a small being of utter desolation in a surrounding world that was as close to paradise as it was possible to find.

Twenty minutes later, Suki rode the Jet Ski into a sheltered lagoon on a small island a couple of miles to the west of Koror. She was heading for Palau Watersport Adventures where she worked. The facility was a squat, low-rise facility that catered for all the watersports Palau had to offer, from diving and snorkeling to sailing and kayaking. It also had the Seabreacher experience, which allowed tourists to take a ride in the next generation watercraft.

As she rode in past the PWA jetty, she saw Matt, the golden-haired Australian manager, heading out in one of the machines. He had the cockpit canopy slid back. He gave her a wave.

"I need that outboard fixed by tomorrow! It's been two days!" he shouted.

She waved back and gave him a thumbs up, watching him head out.

The Seabreacher was an incredible machine. It had been designed in the States as an accessory to a multimillionaire's yacht. It was shaped like a dolphin—though there were other variants that looked like sharks, killer whales, even swordfish. A driver and passenger could travel in the two-seater variant and were enclosed behind a genuine F-16 fighter jet canopy. With the use of a water jet engine and variable angle fins, the Seabreacher could exceed speeds of fifty miles per hour and dive to a depth of ten feet. This would then allow it to fully leap out of the water and barrel roll through the air.

One of the things Suki enjoyed the most about working

at PWA was that she got to play with these amazing machines on downtime or whenever they had to be serviced and someone had to go out and check them over.

She gunned the Jet Ski engine.

With a spurt of speed she drove straight up the gently sloping beach to park on the sand next to four other machines waiting for tourists to take them out. She glanced around and then grabbed a towel from a nearby table. She quickly covered up the housing and walked as fast as she could, without arousing suspicion, to a shed at the back of the main office building.

Now came the part that had turned her life upside down and meant that the smile she had just given to Matt was short-lived.

Now she had to return to her world of torment and hell.

She pulled open the rickety wooden door of the shed. It was dark inside but she could tell he was there. The rank smell of stale cigarettes and unwashed clothes reeked throughout the enclosed space. She stood for a second adjusting to the darkness.

"You have something for me?" The words were in Japanese, and as they were spoken, a figure walked out from the shadows.

The man that stood before her filled her with fear and dread. He was around forty years old, but you would never have known it; he looked more like sixty. His body was thin and wiry and his face looked as though half the flesh had been sucked out of it. The skin that was stretched tight across what remained was a jaundiced yellow color. His eyes were small, almost like pinpricks, but they held a menace, particularly when he smiled, that sent shivers up her spine. It was as though all the pain of his condition was being projected on those he met. He ruled by ruthless power. He had no empathy or compassion. He had complete control over her.

"Yes, I have something, Mr. Saito," she said hesitantly.

"Let me see," ordered Saito.

Suki quickly unwrapped the housing from the towel and offered it to him. He took it, cast a quick gaze over it, and nodded.

That was all the approval she was going to get.

"I need more. Tomorrow."

"But the weather... I may not be..."

"You know the consequences!" he shot at her. "You know what will happen."

She said nothing.

He then moved toward her. She felt her skin crawl. He reached forward and touched her arm. She could hardly stand the feel of his flesh on her own. It was like being touched by a reptile. She started to hyperventilate. He knew the effect he had on her. A slight smile revealed a mouth of brown and disfigured teeth. As he breathed, a rasping came from his throat, as though even the air he exhaled was somehow infected when it left his lungs.

"Now," he said, "what else do you have for me?" The smile grew leery.

This was too much for Suki. Even with the hold he had over her, she could stand it no longer. She withdrew her hand sharply and ran for the door. His laughter followed her through the small wooden opening that transported her to another world, one of warmth and humanity.

Suki ran to the water's edge and dived below the surface, trying to rid her body of the vile touch she had just endured.

A minute later she surfaced and slowly swam back to the shore. She crouched there shivering, but not from the cold.

No one followed her from the shed. It was as though he had never existed.

But he did.

He had been in her life since he had killed her father when she was ten years old. She remembered the night as though it was yesterday. Her mother had put her to bed in the small town of Funai, around twenty miles from Kyoto in the Kansai region of Japan. Her father had worked as a mechanic in a small garage he owned. Suki had loved helping him out, learning anything she could about cars and how to fix them. It had been like a game to her, a challenge to get them going again. He was American and had been traveling in Japan before going to university. The result: he had met her mother, fallen hopelessly in love and never left.

While running the garage, her father had found himself in financial difficulties and, unbeknown to Suki's mother, had been doing jobs for individuals who turned out to be involved with the Yakuza. In other words, he had been working for organized crime. By the time he had realized this, it was too late.

He had unwittingly been transporting drugs when something had gone wrong. They had been seized by the police. He'd been arrested.

When the Yakuza had got him out of jail they'd come to ask for money to cover the cost of the drugs. Of course, her father had been unable to pay; he was just a mechanic.

They had killed him in front of Suki and her mother.

Her mother had then been forced into prostitution to pay off the debt and to keep her daughter alive. As her mother had grown older, the Yakuza's attention had turned to Suki.

That was when Mr. Saito had come to see her.

She had been taken away and forced to work in the brothels in Tokyo.

She had been popular. Her exquisite looks and demur manner made her a favorite at the high-class hotels in the city, particularly with foreigners in search of the exotic. All the time she had been told that if she didn't comply her mother would suffer the consequences.

Eventually, though, even that had not been enough. She decided she would rather kill herself than spend another day in the service of Mr. Saito. She had run away to the Philippines. She had been drawn to the water, always loving it as a child, and used it as an escape. She found she had a skill and trained herself to be able to free dive to extreme depths, holding her breath for over six minutes. It was another world down there; the only place she felt safe; somewhere they couldn't touch her.

But they had tracked her down. When they had tried to force her back into service she had cut herself, from her left eye, down the side of her cheek, in the hope she would no longer be attractive to customers.

It had worked.

She had been requested less and less. And despite constant beatings she could no longer earn the money they expected.

But then they had learned of her skills and had found a new use for her.

She had been moved to Palau.

There, under the guise of working as a mechanic at one of the watersports centers, she was made to steal from the well-healed tourists who flocked to the islands in their thousands. If she didn't furnish Saito with a regular supply of expensive camera gear, they would take it out on her mother back in Japan.

At least it was better than the brothels, but Suki hadn't been able to contact her mother for the past two months. She was fearful something had happened to her. She couldn't risk running away again, though, just in case.

She sat in the shallow water at the edge of the beach, clutching her knees to her body. Small wavelets broke over her feet. Further out, a gentle chop had started to form. The sun, that was usually a brilliant glowing orb as it sank below the horizon, was now hidden behind ever-darkening clouds.

The tears that she knew would come, now fell.

She was unable to stop them.

Moments later she saw the pebble-dashed surface of the water advancing toward her like a curtain, as the ever-increasing droplets of rain thundered down.

And then she was engulfed by the water falling from the sky. It was as though the heavens were crying in sympathy and she was sitting in an ocean of their tears.

Something cataclysmic was coming.

She could feel it.

Both from Mother Nature and in her life as well.

Chapter Seventeen

The taxi dropped Clare Kowalski at the base of a set of steps that led up to an apartment in a small block in Malibu Palisades around twenty miles west of Los Angeles.

She paid the driver. He unloaded her bags from the trunk, and she watched as he drove away past a black Kawasaki Ninja H2 Carbon motorbike that was parked in the middle of the parking area, blocking her Audi TT RS Roadster.

She was dressed in the comfortable open-necked cream cotton shirt and loose-fitting pants she'd worn for the flight from London. A quilted climbing jacket was slung over her shoulder, in acceptance of the warmth of Southern California after the cold of the UK. She was trying to grow out her glossy dark hair, which currently hung loose in a tousled tangle just south of her shoulders. Her usually smiling face, which accentuated her high cheekbones and mysterious green eyes, was currently in a non-committal scowl.

She was tired from the flight, annoyed she'd not heard back from McCready, and pissed off that her roommate,

Jade Mancini, had not been at the airport to meet her. She had promised she would be there.

Clare wearily started to climb the stairs with her computer bag across her shoulder and her case wheels bumping up the steps. But then she did finally smile. Her retriever puppy, Max, would be there to greet her. She couldn't wait to scoop him up in her arms and give him the hugest cuddle.

She reached the top of the stairs, fumbled for her key, and then backed the door open, still clutching her bags. Before she even turned round she shouted out.

"Max! Max, come here boy!"

Then she did turn round... and froze. A second later she dropped her bags, not quite knowing what to do.

"Who the hell are you?"

Standing in the middle of the room was a small woman... well, girl really. She must have been barely twenty years old. She was thin with an androgynous face that was somehow beautiful. But the most striking thing about her was the spiky black hair and the way she was dressed. She wore tight black leather pants, along with a black leather waistcoat that was currently hanging open. She wore nothing underneath. She had piercings that lined the outer rim of each ear and a large nose pin. Her eyes were coal black and they stared at Clare with an intensity that unnerved her.

Neither woman spoke.

Suddenly there was a voice from the open door of the bedroom beyond.

"Hey honey, do you really have to go?"

Both women turned to the door to see a half-naked black woman pulling on a pair of ripped faded jeans and wearing a small white tank top that left little to the imagination. When she saw Clare she stopped dead. She glanced between the two women, a surprised expression on her face. "Clare, what the hell are you doing back?"

Clare just stared at the two of them. "I thought you were going to pick me up at the airport?"

Jade glanced quickly at her watch. A pained expression crossed her face.

"Shit, I'm so sorry, but"—and she glanced at the other woman—"something came up." Her face crumpled into a guilty lovesick goo as she glanced at the leather-clad girl. "Clare, this is Georgie. Georgie, this is Clare."

Neither woman spoke.

Clare was too shocked to say anything.

Georgie just stared menacingly at her.

She then crossed over to Jade, pulled her face close to hers and they locked mouths with a passionate, almost cruel kiss that seemed to go on far longer than was necessary, but one that Jade didn't seem to mind in the slightest. Her eyes were closed but Georgie never took hers off Clare.

After what seemed like more than a minute, she broke the kiss, picked up a small black backpack from the floor and headed for the door.

Before she left she turned to Jade. "Ciao, babe." The accent was heavy East European.

Jade watched her go, her eyes a dreamy mush. "Bye, Georgie. It was great. It's always great."

Clare just watched as Georgie walked out of the door. She glanced back at Jade.

"Isn't she amazing," said Jade.

"She's 'something,'" said Clare, still stunned at what she'd seen. She crossed over to the door and watched as Georgie walked down the steps and over to the Kawasaki.

"What are you doing?" asked Jade.

Clare came back into the room as the quiet was shattered by the roar of the bike speeding off down the road.

"Just checking to see if she had a tattoo of a dragon on her back!"

Clare shut the door and crossed over to her friend. "How long have you known her?"

Jade was still in a slight trance. "A couple of weeks."

"Does she come round here often?"

"Oh yes!"

Clare looked at her friend to see if she meant what she thought she meant. The wicked expression said that she did.

"She doesn't talk much," said Clare.

"She's from Croatia. Doesn't speak a lot of English."

"So how do you guys converse?"

Jade had a sly glint in her eye. "There are other forms of communication, you know!"

Clare shook her head. She was about to say something when she realized there was something missing. She glanced around the room, starting to get anxious.

"Max! Max! Where are you, boy?"

Jade watched her with a puzzled expression. "Hey, what's wrong?"

Clare was becoming ever more frantic. "Where's Max?" She rushed around the room looking behind the sofa and chairs.

"Chill, girl," said Jade. "He's in your bedroom."

Clare hurried over to her bedroom and flung open the door. The small bundle of white fur was curled up in the middle of her bed fast asleep. She ran over and lifted him up. Max woofed with alarm, and then when he opened his eyes and saw Clare, he stretched with a wide yawn and barked excitedly, licking her face, his tail wagging ten to the dozen. Clare walked back into the main room to see a faintly amused Jade watching her.

"What was that all about?" asked Jade.

"Just making sure your friend wasn't into animal sacrifice!"

Jade let out a massive laugh. "No, but she does get jealous, so probably best not to be around her when she's near the kitchen…"

Clare looked at her, confused.

"Knives."

"But we're not…" blurted out Clare.

"I know, I know," said Jade, apologetically. "But you know, better safe than sorry. And probably the sooner you move into the new place the better." Her expression was pleading.

The two girls looked at each other, then Clare dropped Max onto the floor and crossed over to hug her oldest friend. They held the hug for a while and when they broke apart Jade looked at her.

"Hey, we good, girl?"

Clare smiled back. "Yeah, we're good, girl."

Half an hour later Clare emerged from the bathroom, showered and feeling far better than when she'd walked through the door. She pulled on some sweatpants and a T-shirt, and when she entered the living room Jade greeted her with a large glass of white wine.

The two of them went to sit on the small balcony that looked out over houses and scrubland to the sea in the distance beyond. It was a warm evening but a cool breeze was blowing in off the ocean making the temperature more tolerable than the recent heat of the day.

Max trotted out of the double glass doors and hopped up onto Clare's lap. She stroked his soft ears soothingly and he relaxed into his default position for the night.

Clare stretched out and took a long swig of the wine. "Ah, that's better."

Jade looked at her friend. "So, how was the trip? Things work out?"

Clare took a deep breath, swilled the wine around in the glass and took another swig. She let it slip down her throat. "It was interesting. The job's gone for good, but I was expecting that. They were happy to give me references. They had no problem with my work. It almost seemed like they wanted to keep me on."

"But..."

"But I guess the shareholders couldn't put up with someone working for the company who'd been involved in a multi-million-dollar heist, however innocently it seemed from the evidence."

Jade looked out to sea across the twinkling lights that were starting to light up the night sky.

"So what will you do now?"

"Well, I knew it was coming, so I have some interviews lined up. There's one a headhunter company in San Diego contacted me about. Don't know if it's my sort of thing, running a convention center. But maybe I need a new direction, a new start. The interview's later this week."

Jade took a swig of her own drink and looked straight at Clare.

"Okay, so what about the important stuff?"

"Huh?"

"Duh, the 'guy.'"

Clare smiled ruefully. "Ah, the 'guy.'" She scratched Max's ears. A contented sigh came from her lap.

"Jury's still out on that one."

Jade looked confused. "I thought you two were gonna be tight. I mean, you saved each other's lives an' all. How close do you need to be?"

"What's that about relationships forged under extreme circumstances…?"

"So, you're gonna take wisdom from a *Speed* movie and use that to run your life?"

Clare smiled. "I thought there was something. I was all for staying up there with him, but a couple of days ago something changed."

"Like what, he grow horns?"

"Something came up he wouldn't tell me about. Something he had to do. I've left a load of messages, but he hasn't got back." She paused. "I didn't think he was like that."

"He's a man, idiot! They're all like that. If you have to put up with them, you have to factor it in. Good job I don't have those problems."

Clare looked at her in disbelief. "Er, and what was it that walked out the door earlier? You can't exactly call that normal."

"That, my sweet girl, was heaven."

Clare suddenly focused. "You serious about me moving out soon?"

"Hell no! I was just kidding." But then, ever hopeful, "But you don't know when it might be, do you?"

Clare looked at Jade's expectant expression and smiled.

"Okay, I just have to sign the final papers and then I can move anytime. You want to come see it?"

"Yeah, sure. Always wanted to see how the rich and shameless live."

"Hey, come on. I'm getting a good severance pay and

the settlement with my cheating ex is almost final, so I'm gonna make the most of it. But I'll be moving back here if one of those jobs doesn't work out."

"Then I guess we have to hope you knock 'em dead!" said Jade. "You want a joint? I'm getting one."

Clare shook her head distractedly as Jade walked back into the apartment.

She was conflicted about so many things. Somehow, being back here, her home, thousands of miles from the UK, it almost seemed like the events of a month ago had never happened.

Had it all been an illusion?

Maybe Jade was right—the circumstances had been extreme. Maybe what she needed was a complete change. Some normality in her life.

But still, she couldn't help thinking about McCready.

Where he was, and just what the hell he was doing.

Chapter Eighteen

"Hey, you might want to come and watch this."

McCready looked up from the second most uncomfortable seat he'd ever sat in, and he'd been there for over nine hours. It was set back against the side of the front section of the Globemaster's hold and wasn't quite as bad as the one in the cramped interior of a diving bell, but it wasn't far off.

The smiling face of Corporal Colin Chivers stared down at him. He was one of the aircrew who had been looking after them on the flight.

McCready stretched, tried to stifle a yawn and failed, then checked his watch and sighed. "What is it, Colin?"

"Refueling. You were asleep for the last two. Thought you'd like to see what goes on."

McCready felt like he hadn't slept at all.

For the last hour the plane had been continually battered as it had flown through what appeared to be significant turbulence. Every now and then there would be a jolt and a bang as equipment in the cave-like hold jumped and then settled back against its restraints. At one point the submersible had slid three feet before one of the crew had run over and retightened the metal clamps on the webbing straps holding it secure.

McCready glanced at the seat next to him. He nudged a snoring Craig Richards in the ribs. "Oi, old man. Wake up!"

Richards groaned, tried to turn over as though he was in bed, and promptly fell out of his seat. McCready grabbed him before he could hit the hard metal floor. Richards glanced around, not knowing where he was for a moment, then focused on McCready.

"We there yet?"

"Still a way to go." McCready glanced at Chivers. "How long you reckon till we land?"

At this, the young airman seemed somewhat uncomfortable. "I'm, er, not too sure. I can check if you like. So, you want to come up to the cockpit?"

Chivers led them to the front of the plane and up the small flight of steps to the cockpit. McCready had been in a number of aircraft cockpits before but never one quite like this. It was currently lit up with an array of subdued, subtle lights and screens relaying information.

Outside the windows it was beginning to go dark.

The view was spectacular.

Above, the stars were starting to come out and twinkle. Over to the west there was a golden glow from the horizon, where the sun was rapidly disappearing, illuminating the end of the day. But looking ahead, all McCready could see was an impenetrable bank of black clouds, and they were flying straight toward them.

Of greater interest, though, just in front and slightly above the Globemaster, was the rear of a large aircraft far closer than one would normally hope to see another plane.

As McCready and Richards squeezed into the small cockpit the pilot acknowledged their presence before concentrating on the task ahead.

Mid-air refueling was a delicate operation.

There were two ways it could be carried out.

In the first, two aircraft flying thousands of feet above the Earth, at hundreds of miles per hour, had to come together so precisely that the aircraft being fueled could locate a metal probe that extended from the fuselage into a conical-shaped basket on the end of a hose trailing fifty feet behind a tanker aircraft.

In the second, as in the case of the Globemaster, the aircraft requiring fuel had to maneuver so that a small connection clamp on the top of the plane, just to the rear of the cockpit, could lock onto a solid probe extending down, near vertically, from the tanker.

In ideal conditions both techniques required expert flying, but with the buffeting the aircraft was currently receiving it would require supreme skill.

McCready and Richards watched in fascination as the plane inched forward and upward toward the probe in front of them. It seemed to dance around in the slipstream as the pilots threaded the needle. Then a few moments later it locked into the clamp on the Globemaster. A red light appeared on the cockpit display, accompanied by a loud beep.

"Capture. We have capture," said the pilot calmly into the radio.

Seconds later, a loud rushing noise could be heard above their heads as fuel started to transfer from the tanker into the Globemaster.

"This should be the last fill-up," said the pilot. "It'll take

Deep Impact

us all the way to where we drop you guys off, then we can head on home."

"Can't you refuel at the airport?" asked Richards.

The pilot looked at him curiously.

"I think you should talk to Lieutenant Freeman. He'll fill you in."

"Okay, will do," said McCready. "And thanks for the show."

They left the cockpit and went to find Freeman.

The lieutenant was in charge of the support crew on the plane. He was an easygoing, nothing-could-phase-him kind of guy in his late thirties, with a crown of fair hair and down-to-earth attitude. They found him watching some of the crew who were attaching metal hawsers to the pallet the sub was resting on. Lying on the floor close to the pallet were a number of large canvas bundles.

Richards was about to ask him what the crew were doing when McCready spoke.

"The pilot said you could let us know when and where we'll be landing."

Richards added, "We really need to be able to get in touch with the ship that's going to take us to the site. Make sure she has all the right kit." He was still watching the activity around the sub.

Freeman looked slightly uncomfortable for a moment and then looked straight at them.

"Well, the thing is guys, we're, er, not going to an airport."

McCready and Richards glanced at each other, confused.

"Yeah, it's like this," continued Freeman. "Given the time constraints and the seriousness of the situation, we didn't have time to arrange a ship with all the gear you need and get it on site. Soooo, what we *were* going to do was rendezvous with the *Queen Elizabeth* and off-load you onto her. She's steaming south as we speak at full speed." He was about to continue when Richards interrupted.

"Off-load? But at which port?"

"Ah, now that's the thing," continued Freeman. "No time to put into port. We were going to hot drop you onto the flight deck."

He looked at them as though it was the most natural thing in the world.

Richards was looking more confused. "Hot drop? What the hell is 'hot drop?'"

But McCready was way ahead of him, and his face showed real concern. "It's where a plane flies in low to the ground and the equipment is dropped out the back with a braking parachute to slow it down when it hits the ground."

Richards looked from one to the other. "But there wouldn't be any ground."

"He means the deck of the carrier," said McCready.

Richards looked incredulous. "You can't be serious?"

At this, Freeman's smile increased. "No, you're absolutely right. Bit of a crazy idea if you ask me. Actually, the carrier can't make it to position in time anyway. The typhoon has moved further north more quickly than expected and they're making heavy weather of it. Something like thirty-foot waves and that sort of malarky, so no worries, we won't be trying to drop you onto the carrier."

A look of relief crossed Richards' face. He glanced at McCready and shook his head.

"Crazy bastards! No wonder your friend didn't give us any details. He knew we'd never have gone along with it." But McCready didn't share his relief. He had a feeling about what was coming. He too had seen the men working around the sub.

"Okay then," said Richards, "so what's the plan now?"

Freeman glanced between the two of them.

"Now... now, it's far simpler. We're just going for a straight parachute drop into the water. Far less chance of damaging anything, or hitting the ship."

They just stared at him. Richards was the first to be able to speak.

"So hang on a minute. Let me get this straight. You want to fly into the middle of a typhoon and airdrop us in a submersible, miles from anywhere, straight into thirty-foot waves?" said Richards.

"Yeah, that's pretty much it," said the lieutenant cheerily. "Got it in one."

"No fucking way!"

It took Richards ten minutes to calm down, in which time Freeman had gone to check on the men working around the sub. Richards turned to McCready.

"John, this is insane. You do know the odds on us surviving this?"

McCready looked equally concerned. "Yeah... but it might just work. I guess it would depend on whether the sub's damaged hitting the water."

"Or whether we can free it from the harnesses. Or whether we can locate the stricken sub. Or whether *Emily*"—McCready glanced at him—"can even withstand the pressure. We have no time for a checkout dive. If something happens at depth—she springs a leak—there's no back up. No one to assist us."

"The lieutenant said the carrier was on its way."

"Yeah, but when the hell would she get here? And even if she did, how the hell would she find us in the middle of a typhoon? And she's not equipped to work with submersibles. No. No way, John. We can't do this!"

"We have to. We've come this far. What about the crew of the sub? What about retrieving this device? We have to try."

Richards looked at him wearily. "Well, you'll just have to work out what that's worth. Is it worth your life?"

McCready was quiet for moment, then looked up.

"Maybe."

Richards shook his head slowly. McCready continued. "You don't have to go, Craig. I got you into this. I know about submersibles. There'll be a signal to locate *Resilient*. Steel gave us the transponder and frequency. Just walk me through docking onto the escape hatch. I'll get it done."

Richards looked at him and shook his head. "You really think I'd let you take my *Emily* down there on your own, you've got another thing coming. No idea what you two might get up to. You don't know how to treat her. Her little ways. When she's going to throw a tantrum… and if she does, how to calm her down. No way, matey. You go, I go, and that's the end of it. In fact, I'll go one further. You're not going at all."

"What?"

"What about Clare? Whatever you say, you guys had something. What have I got? The odds are neither of us will come out of this alive. If you're up here, at least you can put pressure on Steel and whoever to get that carrier down here and help out. We'll need somewhere to off-load anyone we rescue, and I'd rather trust you than any of these guys. They may do a great job, but they've nothing invested. I trust you with my life, John. Let me do this."

Deep Impact

McCready looked at him and sighed. "No. We both go. And that really is the end of it."

He walked over to the sub to look at the parachutes the aircrew were fixing to the top of the steel hull.

Richards watched his old friend. *Okay, if that's the way you want it. But you're not dying down there. No way.* He knew the sub couldn't survive at depth, of that he was sure. When they had done the tests at Ocean Oil there were so many unreliable components he knew it would never work, but McCready had been so set on the mission Richards had gone along with it. He'd always thought they would have time for a checkout dive, where the problems would come up and the mission would be scrubbed. Now though, this was entirely different. It was a suicide mission, and there was no way he was letting his friend get killed.

A plan was formulating in his mind, and McCready was the last person he was going to tell.

Half an hour later Freeman walked over to the sub, where Richards and McCready were making last-minute preparations. The gear they would need had been loaded aboard, and two large life rafts were attached to the side, where the manipulator arms could release them when needed.

McCready had received a PDF to his phone from Steel that showed the layout of *Resilient* and the last-known position of where the hard drive was located. The message had also ominously said that it had been some time since anyone had heard from the crew inside. He should expect the worst. Steel had signed off with a simple GOOD LUCK. McCready had texted back a simple THANKS and then shown the sub layout to Richards. They estimated they would need about fifteen to twenty minutes to find the drive if all went well.

A sudden flash of lightening and a rip of thunder made them all jump.

A few seconds later the whole inside of the Globemaster lit up as another strike flashed close by. Even though there were only a few small windows down the fuselage, it was as though someone had set off a series of high-power flashguns.

"That was close," said Richards.

An announcement from the pilot came over a speaker. "Ten minutes to drop. Starting holding pattern."

Freeman turned to McCready and Richards. "That means we're over the location."

There was another massive crash of thunder.

"The pilot's circling, so anytime we go you should be on target."

"Like the way you put 'we' in that sentence," said Richards. "We're seriously going out in that?"

As the plane bucked from the raging storm outside, everyone held on to stop themselves being thrown across the hold.

"By the looks of things, you'll be better out than in," commented Freeman.

"Care to swap?" asked Richards.

"I'm going to open the tailgate. You'd better get ready," said Freeman. He crossed over to the controls and pressed the OPEN button. Immediately, the two-piece tailgate started to open. The top part raised itself up into the roof of the plane with a hydraulic whine, while the bottom half lowered to stick out horizontally into the night sky.

The full force of the storm made its way inside.

McCready and Richards looked out with horror.

There were now almost continuous flashes of lightning followed by massive explosions of thunder that seemed as though they were centered on the plane itself. As if in sympathy the aircraft bucked and shuddered as the airframe fought against the elements ranged against it.

Richards turned to McCready and shouted above the noise. "John, can you get me a wrench from the toolkit? Something I need to adjust."

"Sure."

McCready walked unsteadily toward the front of the plane to find the toolkit.

Richards took a deep breath.

It was now or never.

He crossed over to the main roller activation control that would start the rollers embedded in the titanium floor. These would propel the submersible on its pallet down tracks toward the rear and out of the tail ramp.

He glanced around.

No one was watching.

He set the rollers in motion. No one would hear a thing above the roar of the storm. He then quickly made his way to the hatch that was now in a vertical position at the top of the sub.

He climbed in.

Once inside, he clamped the hatch shut and waited.

Out of the dome at the front all he could see was blackness punctuated by the occasional flash of lightning that illuminated the void he was about to fall into.

He had never been so frightened in his entire life.

At the front of the cargo bay McCready grabbed the wrench from the toolbox and turned round. For a second, he couldn't process what he was seeing. It appeared the sub was moving toward the gaping hole at the back of the plane.

"Hey!" he shouted. "What's happening?"

Immediately, members of the crew looked around and, for a second, froze.

McCready started running for the tail ramp.

One of the crew headed for the roller control.

At that moment a massive flash lit up the sky. There was an explosion from above. The whole plane lurched on its side and started to fall out of the sky.

"We're hit," shouted Freeman as everyone was thrown to the floor, sliding uncontrollably to the port side.

Sparks flew from electrical outlets around the hold. The lights went out. All was dark for a moment, before dull red emergency lighting flickered on.

Further down the hold a cable had come loose. It thrashed and squirmed like a snake on steroids, smacking the side of the submersible, tearing at the parachute assembly on top.

In horror, McCready watched as one of the parachute harness attachments came loose from the pallet. It whipped around the air in a frenzy.

"We've got to stop it!" he cried.

But no one could hear him above the screaming of the wind.

He ran for the pallet.

An airman reached the controls and desperately tried to turn the system off, but it wasn't responding. He shouted at McCready.

"It won't stop!"

The lightning had blown the electrics.

The submersible was now ten feet from the end of the

hold. Any second now it would be beyond the point of no return. With the parachute harness unfastened it meant only one thing. When the chute opened it would be ripped from the pallet, sending it, and the sub, plummeting to the ocean, killing Richards inside.

McCready ran as fast has he had ever run in his life. On the floor was the winch cable that had pulled the pallet on board. He grabbed it and continued running. If he could attach it they might be able to stop the sub falling out of the plane.

But he was never going to make it.

Another violent lurch from the aircraft sent him skidding across the floor to smack hard against the inside of the fuselage. He picked himself up in time to see the pallet, with the sub on top, start its final descent down the ramp and into the unknown.

There was nothing anyone could do.

McCready ran for the ramp.

He was almost there…

…and then it was too late.

The sub went over the edge and disappeared.

For McCready, time seemed to stand still, and in a moment he could never quite explain, other than he knew his friend was in the sub, he knew what he had to do.

"Fuck it!"

And with that he ran for the end of the ramp and dived out into the blackness of the night.

Chapter Nineteen

McCready was normally pretty good at maintaining focus in stressful circumstances, but right now anybody would be able to focus.

Life and death situations had a habit of doing that to you.

As soon as he left the aircraft he started to tumble. The slipstream, coupled with the howling gale, tossed him around like a leaf. He had parachuted before, but it had been a long time ago and he was no expert. He spread his arms and legs and arched his back, which was supposed to turn you over into the classic free fall position.

But it didn't seem to be working.

He was still on his back.

Every now and then a dazzling lightning strike lit up the sky. He could see the Globemaster rapidly disappearing above him until it was merely a speck in the distance.

Suddenly, a massive, jagged bolt shot out of the clouds and hit the plane. It must have been the center of the fuselage, where the extended fuel tank was situated. There was a huge explosion. A fireball lit up the night sky for miles around.

Whether it was the force of the explosion or the fact that he was now falling at terminal velocity—a hundred and twenty miles per hour—but his body suddenly flipped over. Before he could focus, he was hit in the face by a small square piece of nylon around four feet in diameter. At first he couldn't think what it could be, but then he realized it was the drogue chute designed to stabilize the fall of the submersible before the main chutes deployed.

He grabbed hold, using it to guide his fall down to the sub. The glow from the explosion still lit up the sky, and through the clouds of moisture racing past him he could make out the amber color reflected off the white steel of the sub thirty feet below.

The wind buffeted him hard. It tried to tear him from the chute, but he held on.

Two people's lives depended on it.

A few seconds later he made it to the top of the sub.

He knew the parachutes would deploy automatically when they reached a height of a thousand feet, but he had no idea where they were now. All he knew was that a thousand feet would be along pretty soon.

With eyes streaming from the wind he managed to make out the loose strap. It was flapping crazily. Every other second it would whip toward him and back again. As he tried to grab it, it almost took his eye out. After a tense few seconds, where he threw all caution to the wind, he managed to get a firm grip and tame its violent action.

He now had to locate the metal ring on the pallet to attach it to.

He gripped the pipework on the outside of the sub and hauled himself down. He managed to reach out with his left hand and grab the ring. He was about to pull the strap down to clip it to the ring when a flash of lightning made him freeze. Beyond the sub he could see the raging ocean below.

It was coming up fast—very fast.

"Jesus!"

His focus was suddenly back. He strained with all his might to pull the strap down, but it wouldn't reach. He pulled the two entities together but it was no good—strap and clip were three inches apart.

It was impossible.

As he pulled, he felt pressure on his foot. He couldn't think what it could be. There were so many forces assaulting his body it was hard to differentiate what was what. And then it hit him. He pulled the strap again—still three inches away.

And he looked at his foot.

The strap was caught around his boot. He loosened his grip on the strap and pulled his foot free. Then, with a massive effort, he yanked the metal clip down to the ring and clipped it on.

Barely a second had passed before he saw the three parachutes start to deploy.

He was so caught up with relief at the sight that he almost forgot to hold on. But then the howling wind and rushing air forced him from his thoughts. He grabbed onto the side of the sub with all his strength.

A couple of seconds later there was a massive deceleration. It almost wrenched him from the sub. But then everything became calm...

...relatively speaking.

There was still the howling gale, the rapid swaying from

side to side, but gradually that too seemed to quieten and he felt a smoothness to the descent.

He glanced up. To his relief he could make out the three wide-open canopies above, jostling for space in the turbulent air. At least that had worked. He took stock for a moment and managed to get his breathing rate back under control.

And then he smiled.

Craig was going to have one hell of a shock when he knocked on the window.

Inside the sub, Richards was thinking his plan wasn't actually such a great idea after all.

After leaving the Globemaster the pallet and sub had rolled upside down. This hadn't been expected. He'd been thrown to the roof, banging his head. A few seconds later the whole thing had seemed to stabilize. The drogue chute must have deployed.

From then on it had been quite a surreal experience.

Inside the metal cocoon he was completely insulated from the raging storm and the near hundred and twenty mile per hour plummet to the ocean below.

He had sat in the pilot's seat, looking out through the glass dome at the front, almost as though he was watching some Discovery Channel program about inclement weather.

He'd been falling for about a minute when he heard a banging on the side of the hull. He had no idea what it was. Something must have come loose on the outside. It wasn't constant, but every now and then he felt the metal shudder as something made contact with it.

It was around about now that he had time to think

about what he had actually done. If the parachutes didn't open in the next few seconds he'd be dead several seconds later. His heart rate started to rise and he gripped the seat with a ferocity he didn't realize he was capable of.

Then, without warning, he felt a sharp, sudden jolt. The muscles in his neck twisted painfully with the whiplash.

The parachutes had opened.

A wave of relief swept over him. He didn't even think of the thirty-foot waves he would soon be making contact with. He relaxed right up to the point he saw someone move in front of the glass dome and knock on it.

He felt he must have blacked out or was dreaming.

He *was* dreaming.

McCready's smiling face looked in through the fishbowl-like dome. He pointed to the top of the sub and made an unscrewing motion. It took Richards several stunned seconds to realize what he wanted.

He moved back from his seat and hurried to open the hatch. He needed to get McCready inside before they hit the water. If the pallet and parachutes didn't detach, the sub would be dragged under. No problem if everyone was inside—not so good if there were freeloaders outside.

He spun the handle and pulled the hatch open. McCready climbed in. Richards shut the hatch and then sat down and just stared at him.

"What the hell are you doing?"

McCready was breathing heavily. He didn't immediately say anything but he looked slightly uncomfortable. He reached around to the source of discomfort—something in his back pocket—and pulled out the wrench Richards had asked him to fetch. He offered it to him.

"Here's your wrench."

Richards took it, still unable to believe McCready was here.

"The main parachute strap came unhooked," said McCready. "If I hadn't been able to get it back on, the chutes would have detached and you'd have hit the water at a fair old lick.

"You crazy bastard!" was all Richards could manage.

And then.

"You risked your life."

"Well, if I'd stayed on the plane, I'd be dead by now, so I guess I have you to thank for that."

"The plane's gone?" said Richards in shock.

"Lightning strike soon after I jumped. They didn't have a chance."

Richards shook his head slowly.

"I think we should get ready for the landing," said McCready. "It could be a little rough."

They positioned themselves in the rear of the sub with their legs braced against the sides.

All they could do now was hold on.

McCready was about to say something when they hit the water—hard.

In fact, they struck the side of a breaking thirty-foot wave.

The rolling wall of water picked them up, bundling them over, as they were caught in the rotating ball of kinetic energy that powered the wave as it swept across the ocean.

But then it was past and the sub began to right itself.

Inside, the two men had strained to keep their positions, but as the sub completed its third three-sixty they collapsed in a heap on the floor. Battered and bruised, the motion slowly subsided, but they could feel the swell beyond the metal hull and knew the pallet and parachutes had to be detached quickly.

"I'll go, said McCready."

Richards was all focus. He moved to the front of the sub and started the power-up procedures for the motors.

McCready unscrewed the hatch and climbed out.

Immediately he was hit by the strength of the wind and spray slamming into his face. The relative quiet of the interior of the sub was gone. He was experiencing the full force of a Category five typhoon. He struggled to hang on.

After pulling the hatch closed he crawled along the side to the first strap.

Thirty feet away the parachutes were lying on the surface of the water. McCready could see they were starting to go under. Soon their waterlogged weight would drag the pallet and sub down with them.

He reached the first clamp and undid it. The strap floated off on the surface of the water. He scrambled round to the second one, narrowly avoiding the propellers that had started up and were being tested by Richards inside.

The second one was done.

A quick glance to the rear. The chutes were completely underwater now. He scrambled further round and the third attachment was free.

Just one to go.

When he reached it, he could see it had become wedged under the forward manipulator arm of the sub. He could also see that the sub was nearly beneath the waves. He hammered on the glass dome, indicating for Richards to move the arm. It took him a few seconds to understand, but to his relief McCready saw the arm move out of the way.

He had access to the final clamp.

He reached down underwater but couldn't undo the

locking screw. It was too tight. He now had to keep lifting his head to get air.

It was no good.

He swam round the side and up to the hatch. He spun it open and yelled inside. "I need the wrench!"

A second later an arm thrust the wrench up to him. He turned away, assuming Richards would close the hatch behind him.

He took a deep breath and swam down to the attachment point on the pallet. He took the wrench, adjusted the claw end, and reached down to the bolt. He applied all the pressure he could, putting one foot against the side of the sub for purchase.

But it wouldn't budge.

He could see they were now ten feet underwater and only going deeper.

With a superhuman effort he tried again.

He could feel it move. He wasn't going to drown after everything they had been through.

With an explosive burst of energy, he pulled it one last time. The bolt turned. He spun it a couple of rotations and the strap came free. He swam it away from the sub and watched as the pallet disappeared down into the depths.

Now free of the pallet, *Emily* bobbed up to the surface. McCready climbed wearily on top. Richards opened the hatch and McCready almost fell in. With the hatch secure, he slumped down on the floor, exhausted, soaking.

Richards turned to him cheerily.

"Well, now comes the hard part."

McCready gave him a look that needed no interpretation.

Chapter Twenty

Ten minutes later they had returned some kind of order to the inside of the sub.

To avoid the movement from the incessant waves, Richards had taken them down to a depth of sixty feet, though, even at this depth there was an up and down motion that wouldn't completely disappear until they were deeper.

When Richards was happy the sub was operating as expected, and there were no leaks, he started to set up the receiver Steel had given them to lock onto the transmission coming from the emergency beacon of *Resilient*. They still didn't know how far away they were.

When he'd done this, he turned to McCready.

"Okay, we need to go through a few home truths," said Richards.

McCready looked up. "Go on."

"*Emily* isn't going to make it. When we did the tests in the tank we had two issues. One, the collar would only rotate one-eighty degrees, so we can only dock from one side. And two, at certain positions, for some reason, we had a greater chance of leakage through the seal. So again, if we are at the wrong angle the seal may not hold depending on the time the collar is in that position."

McCready thought. "Okay, how about hull integrity. Can she handle the depth?"

Richards didn't answer immediately. "She should do. But there are no guarantees. The hull hasn't been under any real pressure for over a year. We replaced all the O-rings we could in the time, but some of the other components... who can tell? The original design was sound, tried and tested on previous vehicles. But the collar, that was unique. That could cause problems."

"So the depth shouldn't be a problem. It's just docking we have to worry about?"

"Hopefully."

"All we can do is get down there and see what happens."

Richards blew out a long puff of air. "I just want you to know what you're getting yourself into."

McCready smiled at him. "Thanks, Craig. But what choice do we have?"

"Yeah, I know," said Richards. He took a deep breath.

"Okay, let's go." said McCready.

Richards turned to the receiver he had set up and switched it on. A small screen lit up. The words SCANNING FREQUENCIES appeared. It cycled through what seemed to be an endless range of numbers. It finally locked onto one. FREQUENCY FOUND was displayed, quickly followed by a simple graphic that showed their current position at the center and bottom of the screen. A flashing orange dot was also displayed near the top left of the screen, with the figures 270 DEGREES and 1,600 FEET.

"Right, we have a position fix. Here we go."

And with that, Richards rotated the control to release air from the ballast tanks and they started their descent. The depth of water below them, at their current position, was eight hundred feet. Rather than head straight for the target, Richards preferred to drop straight down, checking everything was working as expected as they slowly descended. When they reached the bottom, they could then head over the seabed to *Resilient*.

As they dropped into the depths, they kept an eye out for potential leaks and any unusual sounds coming from the hull.

A few minutes later a small beeping came from the control panel, along with a flashing red light.

"Coming up on the bottom," said Richards.

He grabbed the controls and steadied the descent, at the same time flicking on the external HMI lights. Immediately the surrounding water lit up as a quarter of a million lumens of light flooded into the ocean. Even with this power it only illuminated around thirty feet from the sub. McCready leaned forward to look out of the dome at the front.

A few seconds later he could see the bottom. It was pretty nondescript: a sandy substratum with the occasional rock and accompanying marine growth.

Richards brought the sub to a controlled stop. A puff of silt lifted up into the water where the skids touched down. A gentle current soon moved this away to reveal clear water that disappeared into blackness beyond the reach of the lights.

Richards checked the receiver. The display showed *Resilient* to be over two thousand feet from their position. They must have drifted with the current on the descent. He checked they were lined up on the target and then raised the sub to around ten feet off the seabed. He pushed on the joystick. They could hear the whirring of the electric motors as they propelled the machine forward. It would take around fifteen minutes to cover the distance depending on the strength of any current they might encounter.

Richards turned to McCready. "Okay, what's the plan?"

"We do an initial sweep of the hull to see if we can see any damage. Steel didn't say what had happened, just that things had gone wrong, they were down on the bottom, and they'd lost all contact.

"Assuming the hull looks sound—hasn't been breached—we locate the escape hatch and see if we can dock. Then we have to gain entry. If we can open the hatch, I'll check on the crew and try and find the drive." He pulled out his phone, bringing up the schematic Steel had sent him. "According to this, it was being checked over in the electronics bay, which is just aft of the main control room behind the conning tower. If I can find it, and depending on the state of the crew, we then hightail it out of there."

"Okay," said Richards. "Just remember, we're going to have very little time."

Both men remained quiet as the small sub made its way over the seabed. Neither of them knew what to expect when they reached *Resilient*, but neither was feeling good.

They had been traveling for about ten minutes when Richards gripped the controls harder. "Whoaa!"

"What is it?" asked McCready.

"Current's picked way up. At this rate we're going to have trouble holding station on the hatch."

McCready glanced out through the dome. He could see the seabed was moving slowly beneath the sub, but that particulate matter and plankton in the water was flying past.

A minute later their attention was taken by the view

twenty feet in front of them as the bow of *Resilient* loomed out of the blackness.

"Holy crap!" said Richards. "I knew they were big, but this is something else."

"She's over at almost ninety degrees," said McCready.

They watched in awe as the lights picked out the black outer casing of the submarine. They moved slowly up the front of the huge vessel and then headed over the top. The current was stronger there, and Richards had to apply more power to make headway. He dropped down into the lee created by the massive hull and headed for the stern.

They did a complete sweep of the sub. It looked perfectly intact.

"Okay, let's find the escape hatch. Get this done."

Richards turned back to the front and set about driving the sub forward.

The current became stronger as they moved further along the hull. They were passing close to the conning tower, which was now on its side, when McCready spotted what looked like a thin metal spike sticking up from the hull.

"What's that?" he said, pointing at it.

"No idea," said Richards.

McCready couldn't think what it could be, but there was an idea playing in his head that he didn't even want to contemplate.

They moved further along the hull.

"Coming up on the hatch," said Richards.

McCready looked out of the dome. He could see it just coming into view.

As it was normally positioned on top of the sub it was now at an angle of ninety degrees. McCready operated the collar rotation control to move the collar so the small submersible could mate with the larger sub.

"Careful, John. This position. The angle of the collar. Not good from our testing." McCready shot him a glance and checked the position.

They were about to move closer to lock on when there was a rumbling in the background.

"What the hell is that?" asked Richards.

McCready listened for a moment, looking out of the dome. A second later another rumble echoed out of the blackness. He noticed a few small rocks roll across the sloping seabed.

"Could be a small tremor. We're close to the Ring of Fire out here. All kinds of earthquakes and seismic activity happening all the time."

"Great! Just what we need!"

"Well, nothing we can do about it."

With the collar at the right angle, Richards edged the sub sideways until the connecting metal transfer skirt was hard up against the hull of *Resilient*. It was held in place by the external water pressure after pumping out the water from within.

When a contact recognition light started to flash, Richards flicked a switch. They could hear the sound of the pumps working to expel the water from inside the skirt. A minute later another light blinked to show a secure seal. The two machines became one.

Richards let out a sigh of relief. He could now relax, no longer having to fight the controls to stay in position in the current that had picked up even more since they'd arrived on site.

When he turned back to McCready, his friend was preparing the equipment he would need.

McCready pulled on a small respirator and tucked his phone into his pocket so he had the layout of *Resilient* with him. He then picked up a walkie-talkie and held it close to the respirator. He clicked the TRANSMIT button. "You hear ok?"

His voice echoed out of the speaker in the cockpit.

"Good luck, John. Be careful."

McCready nodded and pulled open the hatch. He looked over into the skirt and saw the top of the escape hatch on the glistening wet hull of *Resilient* a few feet away.

He crawled into the airspace. Once he was fully inside, he checked around the seal to make sure there were no leaks. Satisfied, he leaned forward and spun the large metal ring that opened the hatch on the massive sub.

After a glance back at Richards, and after taking a deep breath, he pulled open the hatch and looked across into the airlock beyond. Thankfully it was full of air, which at least meant there had been no flooding. But that didn't mean the rest of the sub was free of water. He was about to move into the space when he heard a violent hissing from behind.

"Oh shit!" cried Richards.

He looked back. "What is it?"

But he could see what it was.

Water was jetting in through the seal at the side of the collar. It wasn't a flood at the moment, but it could change at any moment.

He looked at Richards, who replied calmly.

"Go on. Let me handle this. But we don't have much time."

Without another word Richards pulled the hatch on *Emily* closed. McCready closed the outer hatch of *Resilient*, then opened the inner hatch and made his way down into the nuclear submarine.

He found himself in a small compartment that could be

Deep Impact

flooded if the crew had to make emergency ascents. He located the watertight door and opened it.

As everything was at ninety degrees, he had to crawl through into the main part of the sub.

When he stood up, he made sure his feet were secure on what was effectively the side wall of a corridor.

He looked around and froze.

A hundred feet away, the drama unfolding between the two subs, and the movement of McCready into *Resilient*, had been watched in exquisite detail in the control room of *Blackfin*. The images were coming from thermal cameras on a drone positioned around twenty feet from the escape hatch of *Resilient*.

Unseen in the blackness, it sat there and watched.

And waited.

A rueful smile crossed Ivanov's lips.

"Let the games begin."

Chapter Twenty-One

McCready's expression was grim.

All around him were members of *Resilient's* crew.

Dead.

The lights were still on, but dimmed. It seemed there hadn't been any major damage to the power system.

He moved forward, crouching down next to a woman in naval uniform. She looked like she was in her twenties. She had short blonde hair and was of medium build. But what was evident, was that she, along with the other members of the crew, had died horribly. Some of them had frothing at the mouth, others, tortured expressions on their faces. He thought back to the metal spike he'd seen on the outside of the sub. It could mean only one thing: *Resilient* had been attacked and the culprits had used poison gas.

He unconsciously pressed his respirator mask tighter onto his face. He lifted the radio. "Craig. This is bad. From what I can see, all the crew are dead in this section. It looks like gas."

Richards was quick to reply. "John, get out of there. It's not worth it. If your mask leaks…"

A million thoughts ran through McCready's mind, but the one foremost in his brain was what he was going to do when he saw Martin Steel again—IF he saw Martin Steel again.

"That bastard!" said McCready. "He must have known."

"Yeah," said Richards. "He must have known. So, what do we do now? This is something else. We've no idea what happened here. Who attacked them? And more seriously, when? They could still be down here."

McCready was thinking. "Okay, as I'm here, I have to find the drive. If Steel wasn't prepared to tell us about the crew, what else didn't he tell us? We have the drive, we have leverage. Agreed?"

"Agreed," said Richards.

Both men realized the game had changed.

Now it was every man for himself and hang the consequences.

"Give me ten minutes. If it's not where he said it should be, I'm coming back," said McCready.

"Okay, ten minutes. No more. The leak here isn't going away."

McCready flicked off the radio and pulled out his phone. He brought up the schematic and tried to orient his position. After a couple of minutes of working out where he was, he rotated the layout to the direction in which he was facing, pulled out a flashlight, and headed off.

The angle of everything made things difficult. He'd been inside many wrecks where they had been on their side, or even entirely upside down, but there you could at least swim in midwater through them. Here, you had to step over objects that had fallen from the sides onto the floor, not to mention avoid stepping on any of the bodies that were everywhere. Clearly, many had tried to make it to the escape hatch. An escape from this depth was on the edge of what was possible, but it was certainly feasible. The gas must have overcome them before even one could make it out.

He headed down a short companionway that led into the accommodation section of the sub. Further on, one deck down, he found what he was looking for, a small workshop next to a generator room.

Inside, it was a mess. Tools and equipment were strewn across what was now the floor. It looked like this was where equipment was brought from different departments for repair. There was everything from broken fan heaters to kitchen appliances to underwater housings for cameras. What he was looking for, though, was a small hard drive enclosed in an orange casing. Small, but distinctive. Steel had said it should be here. This was where they had been working on it. He must have been in constant contact with the sub. He probably knew everything that had happened. The fact he had given them no warning only added to the mounting number of questions he would have to answer the next time they met.

McCready was moving closer to one of the benches when there was another rumble from outside. This time he could feel the vibration through the hull. It was followed by a series of irregular bangs, as rocks hit the side of the sub.

Something was definitely happening outside.

It gave him even more incentive to move quickly. But where to start?

His radio crackled. "John, you feel that?"

"Yeah. I'm in the workshop, but it's a mess. I just have to find the drive."

"Hurry!"

Over the radio he could hear the sound of water jetting into the small sub. He started to sift methodically through the pile of technical equipment on the floor.

He had been at it for five minutes when a massive crash echoed around him. At the same time the whole structure seemed to roll slightly. Whatever had caused that had to be pretty substantial. To move something the size of *Resilient* would take a huge amount of energy.

His feeling of unease was growing.

As the sub had rocked it had disturbed a metal panel that had been leaning against a table. It had fallen over. McCready was about to move on when the beam of his torch picked out a flash of orange.

He moved closer, pulling away a series of broken circuit boards and coils of wire from the pile. There, underneath, was an orange box around six inches square. It was cracked across the top. One side had a massive split down it. But attached to one end by a small lead was what looked like an SSD drive. McCready pulled out his phone and flicked to a photo Steel had sent him.

It matched perfectly.

The problem was, its protective case was damaged. He had to find something to carry it in. Who knew what was going to happen over the next few hours. What he needed was something strong, water and pressure proof, and easy to carry. As his eyes scoped the room they fell onto one of the camera housings lying in a corner. He scrambled over to it, pulled it from the debris, and brushed off a layer of dust. It was for a DSLR and was easily big enough to take the drive. He opened up the clamps on each side, which applied pressure to the O-ring seal, and pulled out the tray the camera would normally be attached to. He then grabbed the drive, disconnected it from the orange box, and searched around for something to cushion it with. He found some discarded bubble wrap, folded it round the drive and placed it in the housing. When the rear was clamped shut it made a perfect seal. Nothing rattled when he shook it. He breathed a sigh of relief.

And then the radio crackled.

"John, you have to get out of there. Something's happening out here. It looks like the whole side of the slope's giving way. It's increased the leak. There's a foot of water in the bottom of the sub and it's only getting deeper!"

"Okay, heading back now."

He grabbed the housing, making his way back as fast as he could.

He was halfway there when he felt a primordial rumbling and vibration beneath his feet. This was followed by a dramatic movement of the sub. But this was not a small rocking motion. This was a strong, lateral movement.

And it wasn't stopping.

The whole sub was sliding sideways down the slope toward the edge of the abyss.

He ran for it.

The scraping noise beneath his feet intensified. He could feel more tremors.

He finally made it to the escape hatch.

His respiratory rate was increasing.

His face mask was misting over, but he had to climb up through the series of hatches to get back into the smaller sub. He made it through the first one and pulled the door closed behind him. Even though there was no water to flood into *Emily*, if the hatches weren't closed, the toxic air could follow him through.

He was about to reach for the handle to open *Resilient's* outer hatch when the radio crackled.

"Make it fast, John. The flow's increased. Not sure how much longer I can keep the collar at this angle."

"I'm at the hatch. Be with you in a second."

He grabbed the handle and turned it.

But it wouldn't move.

He gripped it for all it was worth, straining every muscle in his body, but it was stuck fast.

"Oh shit!"

He picked up the radio. "Craig, the hatch is jammed. Anything you can do from your end?"

There was silence for a second, then came a crackly reply, "Let me see." But from the tone of the voice he didn't hold out much hope.

At that point the massive hull of *Resilient*, along with the smaller sub it was mated to, tipped over the edge of the abyss and started its descent into the depths.

Chapter Twenty-Two

"That's really not good," said Ivanov watching the screen on *Blackfin*. "We lose them down there we lose the drive."

The image from the drone showed the massive nuclear sub and the parasitic-like smaller sub roll over the edge. They had been able to listen to the conversation between the two men when they had used the walkie-talkies. It was clear what had happened. Ivanov thought quickly, then turned to the drone operator sitting next to him.

"Target the hatch."

The operator turned to him as though he hadn't understood. "Target the…?"

"If you hit the hatch with low impact ordinance it'll blow it and separate the subs. The small one won't be dragged down."

"But what about the guy in the large one?"

Everyone in the room looked at Ivanov.

"It's the only chance. Right now we lose everything. We blow the hatch, maybe he gets out, maybe he makes it to the smaller sub. We do nothing, he's lost down in the trench.

There's one chance he doesn't get out, two he does and lives or dies. Two to one odds I'd take any day of the week. Do it!"

The operator glanced around the room at the captain, but nobody questioned Ivanov's order.

He turned to the controls and took a firmer grip of the joystick. He selected his weapon of choice and pushed the button that brought up a targeting crosshair on the camera display. Right now it showed the two subs in a vertical position starting the long fall down the wall into the deep.

"It's no good," said Richards through the metal hatch that separated the two submarines.

He had tried everything from grease and solvent to brute force and physical impact, but nothing would budge the stubborn hatch that prevented McCready from exiting *Resilient*.

He could feel them descending. He wondered at what point they would pass *Emily*'s crush depth. For one bizarre moment he thought he had let her down, bringing her to a place like this, but his thoughts were interrupted by a loud thud on the metal outside the hatch. It was followed by what sounded like an explosion.

The whole sub shook with the impact. Noise rang in his ears. He fell back into the smaller sub, banging his head. Pain rushed through it.

It was followed by a massive flood of water.

Not only was she flooding from the collar seal; now water rushed in from the joint between the two submarines.

A second later *Resilient's* hatch flew open and McCready's head appeared.

He struggled through the inflow of water. As he made it

across to *Emily's* hatch, it looked like the whole metal dome was going to crack.

The sound was terrifying.

Then as McCready pulled himself through, the subs split apart.

Water thundered in.

Both men threw themselves at the hatch to try and close it, but the pressure was immense. It surged against them. It took all their strength to finally force it shut.

Exhausted, they both fell down into the sub, panting heavily, their ears ringing.

Richards had the foresight to operate the collar control, bringing the hatch down into a vertical position at the bottom. It helped with the leak but hadn't stopped it. He then leaped into the cockpit to bring the sinking sub back under control.

A couple of moments later he stabilized the descent.

They were level.

The depth read twelve hundred feet.

They'd been there barely a second when a groan came from the metal around them. It was followed by a splintering sound from the dome at the front…

…but it didn't break.

Richards glanced around nervously as *Emily's* hull creaked with the strain of the pressure. "Sorry about that, luv," he whispered. "Have you up in a jiffy."

He pulled back on the controls and they rose slowly up the wall. A minute later they cleared the edge of the drop-off. He moved away from the edge and smoothly brought the sub safely to rest on the seabed.

Looking out of the dome they could see the massive graunch marks where *Resilient* had slid across the seabed. It looked like a plowed field in an otherwise pristine, baron wilderness.

Richards turned to McCready. He was sitting in two feet of water. "What the hell was that?" he asked.

"No idea," replied McCready, "but whatever it was, it saved our lives."

"You got the drive?"

"Yeah. It's in here for safekeeping." He indicated the housing which now bobbed in the rising water.

"Okay then…" said Richards, "guess now would be a good time to get the hell out of here."

McCready was about to say something when his eyes widened. He pointed out the front of the dome.

"We might have a problem."

Richards turned around. Through the dome he saw a small remotely operated vehicle about six feet from the sub. It had an array of cameras on the front. At the sides were two manipulator arms. On the top was what looked like some sort of pod that could fire projectiles. There were four tubes. One of them was empty.

"Well, I guess now we know what caused the explosion," said Richards.

"Where did it come from?" asked McCready.

Richards peered closer, realizing that whoever was controlling it could see every move he made. "Well, by the looks of the engineering, it's Russian. It's also likely to be controlled by a mother sub somewhere close by. Conditions on the surface are too bad for anyone to be up there."

"Could it be long distance?"

"Unlikely. Comms over long range are not always reliable. I'd definitely go for another sub."

"Okay, so what do we do?"

"Depends on their agenda. Let's assume they're after

the drive. Do they know you have it, or are they just guessing?"

"With *Resilient* over the edge, I guess they think we have it."

"Question is, what's their next move?"

Richards received his answer within a couple of seconds, as the drone moved forward, the claws on its manipulator arms starting to attack the control systems of the sub.

Richards turned to the front. "Well that's not nice. How dare you hurt my *Emily*."

He brought his own mechanical arms into play. They fended off the initial attack, but then the drone moved around the side and Richards lost it from view. He pulled back on the controls. The sub turned. They heard a mechanical sawing sound from the rear. He looked at McCready. "That's not good."

"What's there?"

"Thruster controls and life support." A second later the power failed on the thrusters. The sub settled onto its skids on the seabed.

It was dead in the water.

Richards thought for a moment.

They were running out of options.

"Okay, I'll see what I can do here, but this isn't going to end well. Get into an escape suit, John. I'll follow when I've done this."

McCready looked unsure. He'd done a practice escape at HMS *Dolphin* in Gosport in the hundred-foot training tank, but here they were at eight hundred feet, a totally different ball game. He started to feel apprehensive as he reached for the pack that held the suit.

"They have done escapes from this depth before, right?"

Richards glanced at him. "Yeah, course they have."

"But I heard six hundred was the limit."

"Don't be crazy, John. They're not going to publicize what they can really do."

McCready could see the logic, but he didn't believe his friend for a minute.

He unbundled the suit, trying to keep it above the rapidly rising water. It was bright red and unrolled like an oversized dry suit. He climbed into it and pulled it up halfway around his waist.

But then he stopped and glanced around.

"Where's yours?"

Richards continued to check the gauges and controls in the cockpit. He didn't look at McCready. "Er, it's behind some of the gear at the back."

McCready looked at the gear at the back, but there wasn't another suit.

"There's only one suit, isn't there?"

Richards stopped what he was doing. He turned to McCready. "The other one was damaged when I checked them at Ocean Oil. There was no time to get a replacement."

And then he said simply, "Put it on, John."

"No way."

McCready started to pull it off.

Richards crossed over and stopped him. "Put it on, John. We talked about this. You've more to lose than I do. Only one of us can go. It's that simple. There will be no argument."

McCready sat motionless, looking at Richards. He didn't know what to say. There was nothing he could say, but he did know that if it descended into an argument they'd both die. His friend's logic was sound, but it made no difference to him. He would gladly give up the suit if it meant Richards would live, but there wasn't time. He said nothing, but he looked Richards straight in the eyes as he pulled the top over his head and zipped up the waterproof zip. There was just one section to go, the full visor that was built into a second top section of the suit and would allow him to breathe during the ascent.

Before he pulled it on, he looked at Richards, a thought coming to him. "Doesn't the sub have drop weights you can jettison to bring her up?"

Richards smiled ruefully. "We never fitted them. She was a prototype. Never designed to go down to these depths."

McCready was trying to think. Anything to reassure his friend. "I'll bring someone back. Do what you can to keep life support going. Maybe the Russians will follow me. All they want is the drive. It would be logical for the guy heading for the surface to have the drive."

Richards smiled. "Good try, John. How the hell are you going to find someone to get back down here? There's a typhoon up there. We both know what this is. Now go before you use up any more of my air."

And with that, McCready pulled the visor over his head. He zipped up the final section and stepped into the hatch. He stood there for a second in the water, then looked at Richards one final time.

An unspoken understanding passed between them. He then grabbed the housing with the drive inside, along with a small one-man Survival Equipment Services life raft he clipped to the suit.

He then ducked down into the water and opened the hatch. He could breathe normally from the air inside the suit, which would expand on the way up, but it wouldn't last for long.

Once outside, he immediately kicked for the surface. As he did so he saw the drone detach itself from the rear of the sub and move toward him. There was no way it could catch him, but he did see the cameras turn in his direction and follow his ascent as he disappeared up into the blackness above.

Inside *Emily*, Richards sat there for a second, contemplating his situation. He then moved back to the cockpit and looked out into the water beyond.

As he watched, he saw the drone return to look in through the dome. A few seconds later it disappeared.

He glanced around and sighed, resigned to his fate. If he'd had a cigar he'd have lit one. There was no way out of this.

The sub was dead on the bottom.

Help wasn't coming.

There was nothing he could do.

"Well, *Em*," he said wearily. "Looks like it's just you and me then."

And he leaned back and closed his eyes.

In the control room of *Blackfin* Ivanov had a dilemma.

He'd seen the escape suit race for the surface and berated the drone operator for not catching it or at least firing something at it. He had assumed the drive was with the man in the suit and that the man in the sub was now surplus to requirements. He had recalled the drone to *Blackfin*.

Now, though, he had to make a decision.

"Okay, we leave him there," he said eventually.

The captain looked at him incredulously. "You're going to let him slowly suffocate?"

When Ivanov looked the captain straight in the eyes, the man was left in no doubt where his reputation came from.

"We need to be up there." He indicated above him. "That's where the drive is."

And with that he strode from the control room.

When McCready broke through the surface he found himself in an aquatic vision of hell.

Rain fell from the sky as though pouring from a tap.

Waves crested at over forty feet, while the winds, which were blowing at over two hundred miles per hour, whipped the tops into a cauldron of foam and spray.

There was no direction.

No order.

Simply chaos, revealed by the regular flashes of lightning in a pitch-black world.

And the noise…

It took him a few moments to gather his thoughts, but he didn't have long as a wave crashed over his head, submerging him for thirty seconds before rolling on across the ocean.

He reached down to his waist and grabbed the life raft that was attached to the end of four feet of line. He pulled it to him, searching for the inflator toggle. Finally he found it and pulled hard. Immediately the small raft inflated in front of him. It was tiny. Literally, large enough for one man.

The two buoyancy tubes sat on the water with a material cowl over the top that would completely cover the occupant in a sitting position. There was a clear plastic visor on the front to look out of.

McCready unclipped the housing from his waist and threw it into the raft. He then tried to haul himself in, but the waves kept pushing him back, making progress almost impossible.

Ten minutes later he made it.

He was still in the cumbersome escape suit, but it provided warmth and kept him dry, so there was no point in taking it off.

Once inside, he zipped the cowl securely closed to keep out the screaming wind and driving rain.

When he had finally managed to get his breath back, he slumped against the side, exhausted, and thanked his lucky stars he was alive.

He'd thought he had run out of air at about a hundred feet, but as the air had expanded in the small life-support bubble surrounding him he'd managed to get enough to sustain him until he hit the surface. He had remembered to make sure he never held his breath, preventing any possible lung damage. What he didn't know was whether he had suffered any other pressure-related injury. Even as he lay there, he could have micro, and some not so micro, bubbles of nitrogen charging around his body, ready to strike at any moment—the bends.

There was nothing he could do about that now, though.

He had no idea where he was and no means of going anywhere even if he had known. He would just have to ride out the storm and hope someone found him when the weather calmed down. He didn't even have the strength or wherewithal to look for an emergency beacon.

He slumped back into the raft, overcome by exhaustion.

He felt desolate about Craig, but there had been

nothing he could have done. The practical side of him realized there had been no choice. The emotional side knew he would never forgive himself for as long as he lived. He tried to force his thoughts away from that undeniable truth, but he couldn't.

Sometimes there were impossible decisions to make. Sometimes there was no way out. He lay there in a world of grief, sadness and frustration, but he knew now he had to try and survive. And to do that, he had to find a thought he could cling onto. One good thing in his life. Something to live for.

He had almost drifted off to sleep when he found it.

And her name was Clare.

Chapter Twenty-Three

It was around seven thirty in the morning when Clare drove the Glacier White Audi TT RS Roadster off the Santa Monica Freeway and onto the I-405 San Diego Freeway.

She pulled smoothly out of the inside lane and accelerated across into the fast lane, heading south-east. Traffic was heavy, but it kept moving. The car was through the main built-up part of Los Angeles in about half an hour.

Progress was slowed by an accident just east of Laguna Woods, where the I-405 joined the I-5, which brought all lanes to a standstill. While stationary, she took the opportunity to lower the car's soft top. It folded smoothly back to align flush with the body just behind the two leather-clad Super Sport seats, restoring the sleek lines of the roadster.

Above, the skies were blue and clear. It was going to be hot.

She pulled on her Wayfarer shades, clicked on Rod Stewart's latest album through the Apple CarPlay system, and relished the thought of the three-hour drive down to San Diego.

She wore a simple but stylish black trouser suit and her hair was pulled back into a neat ponytail. She would normally have flown, but the drive would give her time to think and prepare herself mentally for the meeting she had at the other end. It had been many years since she'd been for a job interview and she was well out of practice.

When she had finally accepted the fact that her days at International Pipe and Flow were numbered, she had thought about what came next.

The company had been understanding, given the circumstances, and she realized the reasons for her dismissal, but she'd been put in an impossible situation. Having said that, she had made decisions based on emotion rather than responsibility, and that had been a mistake.

One she was determined not to repeat.

She was headed for a recruitment agency on the far side of San Diego that had apparently been aware of her situation and had actually sought her out. The job they'd put to her was one she had initially been reluctant to consider, but after a few days to mull over it, it had actually seemed somewhat appealing, particularly once she dug down into the detail and realized the full scope of the position and the opportunity to advance within the company.

It was a managerial role at a new convention center located in Los Angeles. Where the interest lay though, and what made it special, was that it was designed to hold conferences and meetings between high-up movers and shakers from across the globe. It was even hinted that world leaders might make use of it shortly for an upcoming summit to thrash out global issues in a secure and relaxed atmosphere. She hadn't been given all the details, but the security aspect was one of the highlights of the complex and something she hoped to learn more about today.

Two hours, forty-five minutes later, she pulled into the parking space at West Coast Recruitment. She'd been directed there by a charming young man on the security gate at the side of the modern six-story building. He hadn't seemed more than about twenty years old, but he'd been polite, professional and had even managed to make her blush.

She stopped the car, still smiling, and glanced at her watch.

Ten forty-five.

Her appointment was at eleven and she was glad she'd allowed herself the extra time. When she had reached San Diego there had been a major hold-up driving past the exit to North Island. Only single-line traffic allowed through. She hadn't been able to learn much from the motorcycle cop who had chatted to her in the queue, other than it was connected to a major security incident at the naval base.

She clicked the button to raise the roof of the Audi, grabbed her bag from the passenger seat, then climbed out and blipped the electronic locking.

A few minutes later she'd found her way to the front desk and told one of the three receptionists she was there to see Mr. Williams. The girl checked through her system and smiled.

"Yes, Miss Kowalski. Would you take a seat? I'll let him know you're here."

Clare thanked her and walked over to a comfy L-shaped sofa that looked out onto a small garden with a water feature in the middle.

She'd been watching a small bird flit in and out of one of the pools when she was approached by a short, balding man in his fifties. He wore a smart suit, but one that looked as though it had seen many late nights. He looked slightly harassed. As he approached, he offered his hand.

"Miss Kowalski, sorry to keep you waiting, I'm Owen Williams. Let me take you through."

Clare stood and shook his hand. "Nice to meet you, Mr. Williams. Great place you have here."

Williams glanced around as though noticing it for the first time. "Yes, yes, I suppose it is. One forgets after a while." He smiled briefly before leading her over to the elevators. He called one, and when the doors opened he let Clare walk in first.

As they ascended, and the floors flicked past, Clare was curious. "I was just wondering how you came to pick me out of all the options out there. I mean, my CV doesn't exactly scream out 'convention center manager.'" She regretted the question as soon as she'd asked it—*why be so negative?*

Williams looked at her briefly as though his mind had been elsewhere. "I'm afraid I couldn't really tell you. I'm not the one who'll be conducting the interview."

Clare frowned. Williams had always been who she'd been told was her contact with regard to the position.

"So who will be interviewing me?"

Williams looked at her. "The client. Highly unusual, you understand. We normally like to vet applicants before they see anyone. But he insisted."

She was about to say something when the elevator made a loud 'bing' sound and the doors opened smoothly on the top floor. She decided to stay quiet and see what happened.

Williams led her down through an open-plan office area to a closed-off room at the far end. Clare couldn't help but admire the view across some marsh land to the ocean beyond. She could see the crashing surf and a few surfers enjoying the waves.

"Here we are," said Williams. He opened a door for her to walk through. He then closed it behind her and left.

Clare was standing in a plushly decorated corner office with even more magnificent views. There was a wide glass table with a computer screen on it facing a tall black leather chair on the far side. A smaller, but still comfortable, chair was on her side of the table. Two of the walls had files and books on shelves that stretched to the ceiling, while the other two sides were floor-to-ceiling plate glass windows that provided the spectacular views.

A man was currently standing, looking out of one of the windows. From behind, he looked tall and muscular and his striped shirt was stretched taut across his back. His butt didn't look too bad either, she noticed. He had a mass of flaxen hair that just nudged down below his collar. Clare was about to speak, when he turned around and smiled at her.

She froze, rooted to the spot.

"Hi, Clare," he said with a grin. "It's been a long time."

She was speechless.

"Brad? Brad Walker?"

"The very same."

"My God! What are you doing here?"

"Well, er, I'm the one who's interviewing you actually," he said almost sheepishly.

And in that moment all the memories came flooding back.

It had been her last year at college. She'd been running the sub-aqua club for students to learn how to scuba dive. This tall guy with film star looks had walked in and immediately made a beeline for her. She'd been wary of him at first, but they had started to date. It soon became clear he was besotted with her. He had been the perfect gentleman, completely unlike what she had expected. All her friends had told her to stay away from *Brad the Impaler*. But as time had worn on, she realized he had wanted too much from her. She'd had to break it off. She had been truly sorry and knew she had broken his heart. She'd agonized over the decision, but she was just starting out in life. The last thing she'd needed was to be tied down in a serious relationship; there was just too much to do in the world. It had been a case of bad timing. She had never heard from him since but had often thought about him when she'd been going through rough times, wondering what it would have been like if they'd stayed together.

This was all on her mind as she walked toward him and gave him a massive hug.

He looked at her slightly uncomfortably, returning the hug, but more out of politeness.

She suddenly realized where she was and how inappropriate her actions were. She hadn't seen the guy for god knows how long, and here she was in a job interview, throwing her arms around him. For all she knew he was happily married and had never wanted to see her again.

She hastily backed away, straightening her jacket. She looked at him apologetically.

"Brad, I'm so sorry. It's just been so long. You look great by the way."

"Thanks, Clare. Don't worry." And then he added, "You look very smart too. Very professional. You were always the one who was going off to change the world."

She laughed, glad he hadn't taken her actions the wrong way. But she was still slightly confused.

"So, how come you're here? This is such a coincidence."

Now it was his turn to look slightly uncomfortable. "Well, er... not entirely."

She looked at him curiously.

"Sit down, please. Would you like some coffee?"

"Yes, that would be great. White, no sugar, thanks."

Walker hit an intercom on the desk. "Paul, could you bring in two white coffees." He received an acknowledgment and then sat down opposite Clare.

"Okay," he said. "I have a confession."

Clare looked intrigued.

"This isn't quite a coincidence."

Now she was curious.

"After you broke my heart..."

She rolled her eyes, but he was smiling.

"I always kept an eye on what you were doing. Checked in on your Facebook page now and then." A slight frown crossed her face and he continued quickly. "Not in some creepy, stalker-like way. God no. More..." He thought for a moment. "More to check you were okay. Make sure you weren't in any trouble." With any other guy, Clare would have taken this as a line, but with Brad, she knew it was true, and something melted inside her.

He continued. "I saw how successful you were in your job... Saw you got married..." A slightly pained expression crossed her face, understanding what this must have done to him. "And then..." He looked slightly embarrassed. "All the recent headlines. I can't believe they're true." He paused. "And then your name came up on our database with the agency and I just had to see if there was any way I could help..." He shrugged. "And here we are."

Clare thought for a moment. "But what about Mr. Williams? I thought he was handling my case?"

At this, Walker looked slightly uncomfortable. "Ah, well,

yes. I thought that if you saw my name you might not apply or even get back. I just wanted the chance to see you again. Make sure you're okay." There was such pleading in his eyes that she could only feel affection for him.

"I don't know what to say. That's so sweet."

"It's not meant as anything else. This is all about the job, which I guess we should probably talk about."

Clare was sure that while on the surface Brad would be professional and honest with her, she was in no doubt whatsoever that, underneath, this was about more than just the job. The thing was, rather than be offended, or freaked out, she felt a warm feeling inside. Maybe this was all part of her new life.

Her new start.

"Okay," she said, looking straight into his eyes.

"Tell me about the job."

An hour later, the coffee had come and gone and Brad had been through the details of the position.

It was as assistant manager at a new facility called the *Omega Complex*. Being in LA, it wouldn't be far for her to commute, and it was for a trial period of a year to see if she fitted in and had the commitment to stay for the long term. It was one of those positions where you were on call twenty-four seven, so it wasn't for everyone, but, as Brad had said, she had always been going for it twenty-four seven. She would be reporting directly to him, as he was the manager of the complex, but she would have freedom to bring her own ideas, energy, and style to the position.

She had smiled and said she would take all the documents away and look through the details over the coming week. In fact, she'd become so comfortable in his presence and he'd seemed so easygoing, carrying no baggage from the past, other than seeming to really care for her, that when he'd asked her to have dinner with him that evening, she'd barely hesitated.

She had said that if she did she'd have to stay in San Diego overnight. He'd recommended the Hotel del Coronado, which was right on the beach. The manager, Philip, was a good friend and would look after her.

Once she'd checked she would actually be able to get to the hotel, as it was on North Island where the problems at the naval base had occurred, she'd agreed to meet him there at eight that evening.

It was now seven-thirty.

She was staring into a full-length mirror in her room, checking that the skirt and blouse she'd hastily bought that afternoon fitted okay, and thinking that the day had turned out unexpectedly well.

A TV was playing in the corner. The weatherman on CNN was currently telling her the next few days would be fine and dry.

His tone then changed.

She glanced at the screen.

"And now to the typhoon in the Western Pacific, which has been wreaking havoc across the region." The screen was filled with images of storm force winds ripping palm trees from their roots and tearing roofs from houses. It was followed by crying children being comforted by their mothers. "It's currently tracking north across the Philippines, where over a thousand people are feared dead. In its wake it's left much of the island nation of Palau in ruins and is expected to head further north toward the Chinese mainland in the coming days."

She shuddered and flicked off the screen. She couldn't imagine what it would be like to experience something like that.

After a final check on her makeup and hair in the mirror, she walked out onto the balcony and looked out across the flat sea to the setting sun. The surfers had given up as the waves had calmed. There were a few couples walking hand in hand at the edge of the water, taking advantage of the last of the rays.

For a moment she felt a pang of guilt.

McCready.

But then she scolded herself. They had no commitment to each other. He hadn't even called her back from wherever he was.

She was going to enjoy herself, but somewhere in the back of her mind a little voice said, *here you go again, Clare*.

The food had been excellent and the company charming.

The restaurant was outdoor and overlooked the ocean, and a pleasant breeze had drifted across the tables.

Clare had started with a California wedge salad and followed it with a delicious Pacific halibut with saffron broth, little neck clams and Spanish chorizo. For desert she'd enjoyed a mango lime cheesecake with a splash of cream. It had all been washed down with a smooth Chardonnay from the Napa Valley, of which she'd had most of one of the bottles.

She was feeling exhilarated, if not a little woozy.

They had been joined for the first half hour by Walker's manager friend, Philip, a charming, erudite Englishman who was immaculately dressed and had that smooth, confident assurance you want in a hotel manager. He had regaled them with tales from his experiences in the business over the years, which had left them in fits of laughter at the demands of some of the guests and the antics of certain celebrities.

When he had left them on their own, Clare and Walker had talked long into the night. She felt comfortable with him—a closeness, one that had come out of their previous friendship. It was also, though, tinged with a pang of guilt on her part for leaving him the way she had.

But now was a different time, a different place.

They were all grown up.

They could see the past for what it had been, an interaction of two people at that stage of their lives—but this was a different stage. And neither seemed to make a judgment on what had gone before.

Walker lifted the wine bottle. He poured the last few drops into Clare's glass. "Wooow, you did pretty well there," he said, laughing.

"You can talk," she said, smiling. "At least I didn't have the two whiskies before."

"Oh, I see, gin and tonic doesn't count then?"

She looked slightly confused for a minute. "I had a gin and tonic?" The words were slightly slurred.

"A large one."

"Blimey, it must have been a good night."

They both laughed long and hard.

Clare downed the last few drops of wine and then checked her watch.

One o'clock.

"I really have to get to bed. Long drive back tomorrow... er, today."

Walker looked at her. He seemed to be hesitating, but then he managed to pluck up the courage.

"Would you like me to walk you to your room?"

She smiled at him, her bright green eyes shining. She looked down at the table for a moment, as though deciding, then looked straight at him.

"Yes, that would be lovely."

Chapter Twenty-Four

The typhoon had swept across the Palau islands with an unrestrained fury.

It had ripped palm trees from the ground, torn the simple corrugated roofs from many of the houses, and left a trail of devastation in its wake. The only saving grace was that it had moved quickly and had not left behind a flood disaster, as so often caused by slow-moving storm systems dumping millions of gallons of water on a small area over a long period of time.

As if in a last defiant blast of its power, a massive crack of thunder had ripped through the night, shaking structures across the region. And then it was gone, as though it had never been, off to wreak its terrible wrath to the north-west as it headed toward the Philippines.

It was this final violent outburst that was the last straw for Suki.

She had been trembling for several hours beneath the thin sheet on her bed, curled up in a fetal position, hugging her knees to her chest in a pathetic defense against the elements.

Thunder had always terrified her.

She could trace it back to the time when she was five years old. It wasn't just the storm, though, that had led to her terror, more where she had been on the day the weather had hit, and more importantly, what she had seen.

As the memory came flooding back, her eyes grew moist and her body shuddered at the thought of what she had witnessed all those years ago.

The day had started sunny and bright, and little Suki, aged five, was dressed up for a day out.

Her mother had bought her a new dress. It was pale pink with patterns of cherry blossom winding around it. She had been in awe of the blossom when she had traveled to Tokyo the year before on her birthday. She always smiled when she saw the beautiful colors and the mass of petals—and now she could wear them all the time. Her hair was long and straight and black, and stretched halfway down her back, of which she was very proud. At the front was a fringe that she loved, and on her feet she had on short white socks that peeked above bright red sandals.

They lived in the Kansai region of Japan. The day out was a treat to the coast. There was a small town called Taiji that had a harbor and walks along the cliffs overlooking the water. She had seen the sea once before and had marveled at the flat blue expanse that seemed to carry on forever. She had imagined strange and wonderful lands over the horizon and was determined to travel to them one day.

She had an inquisitive and curious mind and always saw the good in everyone. She thought bad things only happened because of mistakes and errors, and that some people just needed help occasionally.

The day had been great fun so far. After an exhausting time traipsing around the town, they had stopped for a picnic on a gently rising slope that overlooked the sea. It was still sunny but there were some ominous clouds heading their way from the horizon. Earlier, they had walked around the small town of Taiji and seen all the shops selling dolphin stickers and toys. Suki had been filled with joy. She had fallen in love with a dolphin she had seen on the television at a friend's house. They always seemed so happy—always smiling, always playing. She also liked the idea they lived in close family groups. It seemed to be an idyllic life.

When she grew up, she wanted to be a dolphin.

She took a gulp of orange juice from the small plastic bottle that was her personal drinks container and looked around her. Her father was asleep on a rug on the ground. An occasional snort-like snore came from his mouth, which made Suki giggle. Her mother was reading a novel of some sort.

Suki stood up and looked across the grass slope they were sitting on to a section of low trees that led up to the top of a rise.

"Mamma, can I go for a walk?" she asked.

Her mother glanced up briefly and checked around. Everything seemed safe, but the dark clouds were far closer now and Suki had thought she had felt a spit of rain a few minutes earlier. "Don't go too far now, petals, it might start raining," she said, and then returned to her book.

Suki was pleased and thought about which way to go. She had always loved looking down on things. She liked the perspective it gave her, as though she was above everything else, somehow more important. So she headed up the slope toward the trees.

As she got closer, she noticed the wind had picked up a little, and with it came a noise she couldn't quite place. But it was coming from up the hill. It came and went with the wind. It sounded like shouting and whistling of some sort— maybe a carnival of some description.

She walked further into the trees. The branches were thin and she could easily see through them. The ground, though, was gravelly. It had small rocks embedded in it and was quite hard going for her little feet.

A couple of minutes later she came to a wire mesh fence that was a barrier blocking her way. It seemed a strange place for a fence, so she walked along it until she found a split where an animal of some kind had wormed its way through. She got down on her knees and pushed through, tearing her dress slightly on a loose piece of wire.

She stood up. The noise was louder now, shrill even.

The wind had strengthened into a stronger, more consistent force, rather than the intermittent gusts of earlier. She glanced up. The sky was black. A few drops of rain fell onto her head, but the noise was definitely louder. She couldn't pinpoint what it was, and there seemed to be something else about it, something she had never heard before. It made her uneasy, like something was wrong.

But still she was drawn forward.

Up ahead, the trees stopped. There was a small open area of ground before a cliff edge. She walked up to the edge and looked down into a small cove below.

What she saw changed her life forever.

The cove itself was secluded. It was elongated in shape, with a small shelving beach at one end. There were two high cliff buttresses at its entrance, one of which she was standing on.

As she looked down, she could see the top of a long net stretched across the entrance. But the strange thing was that the whole bay was red, not the blue of the ocean only a few feet from the entrance. Inside the net there were men standing in the water. All around them the water was being thrashed by something within it.

And then she realized.

As she stood there, her brain had a hard time catching up with her body. Before she knew why, she started to tremble, then shake uncontrollably. The tears poured down her face. She tried to scream but her vocal cords wouldn't work.

She knew what the sound was now.

It was cries of terror and pain from the slaughter of hundreds of dolphins.

She watched transfixed as the men scythed large blades into the animals. If they missed one they had long poles with hooks on the end to slam into the flesh and pull them back before plunging knives into their sleek, smooth bodies. The blood spurted into the water and high into the air.

Around the edge of the cove Suki watched a baby swim in terror, its small tail flapping a thousand beats per minute, trying to escape the horror. It was finally stopped by a fisherman with one of the poles. He plunged it into the baby's blowhole before yanking it back and clubbing it to death.

Suki couldn't move.

She wanted to run, to disappear, to die, but she was unable to. She was transfixed by the horror unfolding before her eyes.

The rain was harder now. The low rumbles of thunder that had been in the distance were coming closer.

And then if she thought it couldn't get any worse.

It did.

She watched as one of the men grabbed a dolphin by its tail, flipped it over and plunged a knife into its soft belly. He ripped a long, deep cut through the flesh. The squeaks and cries were piercing. And then, as a massive crack of thunder ripped through the air, the dolphin split open down its middle and a perfectly formed fetus spilled out into the red water. It floated there as its mother's head was severed from her body inches away.

At this point Suki's brain caught up with her body and her vocal cords started to function. Her screams could be heard even above the storm. A few of the men glanced up but then carried on as though she never existed—as though their actions were just another day at the office—which for them, they were.

But her screams carried further afield.

Suki never heard the noise behind as her father rushed up the slope. She never knew he had kicked down the fence, cutting his leg in the process, or even that he had scooped her up into his arms and pulled her face deep into his chest.

Her mind was so traumatized that she could make no sense of the actions she had seen; that human beings could do such things.

It was in that moment, though her little mind never understood it at the time, that she realized the evil of men, that some people were inherently bad—that they were programmed differently to others. It was in that moment that all love went out of her life. And the final disgrace was that she realized she was one of them—she was a human being, just like them.

And she hated herself for it.

Her father carried her down the slope to her mother.

Suki was shaking and staring straight ahead, hardly able

to breathe. He placed her down on the rug and her mother held her tight.

After ten minutes her breathing started to calm.

She glanced at her parents one at a time, but her expression was blank. It was as though she was far away, as though she was trying to leave this world.

When she did finally focus, her eyes came to rest on her shoes.

Her bright red shoes.

Her blood red shoes.

And something snapped inside.

She pulled at the straps, opening them up, tearing the shoes from her feet, as though they were burning into her. She threw them as far away as she could.

From that moment on she never owned or wore anything the color red ever again.

Some days later, after several visits to a doctor, who had given her some pills to help keep her calm, her father had taken her aside. He had tried to explain that not all people were bad. She had listened attentively, taken in everything he had said, but had never truly believed him. She knew now that it was the nature of Man to be evil, not good. Occasionally some of them found good in themselves, but it was they who were the exception.

Her mother had also spoken to her.

She had given her a small silver locket, emblazoned with a dolphin on each side. She had said that if Suki wore it, it would protect the dolphins, and they in turn would protect her. She had looked at it in her small palm for several minutes, as though deciding something, and then, without a word, had put it around her neck.

She had never taken it off.

Suki gripped the locket now.

The final clap of thunder had gone. The storm had rolled off into the distance. It took her a while to calm herself, but as she gripped the locket it gave her strength.

She wiped the tears from her eyes, climbed out of bed, and walked into the main living area of her home to get a glass of water.

She lived in a rather run-down shack with wooden walls and a corrugated iron roof that leaked when it rained. There were three rooms: a bedroom, a bathroom, and the living area. The side of the latter had a small kitchenette along one wall. The rest of the room was divided by a table to eat on and a sofa that looked at a small TV in a corner. There was a low window next to the TV and a door that opened out onto a narrow deck that ran the full length of the front. The walls were so thin it was as though they weren't there. She could hear every noise that came from the dense woodland around her. The only saving grace was that a small beach she loved was only fifty yards away.

The shack was situated at the end of a straggly group of buildings close to the village of Meyungs on a small island connected to the main island and the main town of Koror by a long causeway.

Once she'd drunk the water, she felt a little better.

She dressed quickly in her Lycra bodysuit and then grabbed her long free-diving fins and dive mask from the side of the small room. She also took her shark jaws Lycra hood —just in case—and then walked out into the early morning.

The dawn was just coming up. The sky had a bright, fresh feel about it.

While the storm may have been dramatic, it had departed as quickly as it had arrived.

She hauled her kayak down to the sand and paddled out into the calm water of the inlet.

Twenty minutes later she pulled the craft up onto the beach at the watersports center.

There was no one else up at this time. She wanted to be gone before anyone woke to stop her. She was occasionally allowed to use the Seabreachers, but today was a Saturday. The tourists would be out in numbers, so if she wanted to use one it would have to be now.

She walked up to the workshop and unlocked the door, easing herself inside, trying not to make the door creak in case anyone was around to hear. She reluctantly looked at the Suzuki outboard she was supposed to have repaired and then crossed over to a small cabinet on the wall. She opened it. Inside, hanging on a series of brass hooks, were a number of keys. She had wanted to take one of the single-seat Seabreachers, but she'd noticed the two single-seat versions were blocked in by other boats tied up at the long wooden jetty.

She didn't want to make a noise moving them.

She grabbed the keys for the sleek silver-gray two-seater that was at the end of the jetty. It had been designed to look like a dolphin, complete with large fins, tail, and a big painted smile on the nose.

She ran down to the jetty.

When she reached the craft she untied the bow and stern lines and carefully slid the canopy back, dropping her fins and mask onto the rear seat. She then climbed into the front, settling her legs either side of the T-shaped dashboard that had a GPS display in the middle. She located her feet on the pedals and then inserted the key.

She hit the engine start.

Behind her she heard the rumble as the 300hp Rotax water jet fired up.

She glanced back at the shore and saw a light come on in the main office. She could make out Matt staring down at the jetty. He seemed to look more closely and then walked outside.

He started to come over.

Suki revved the engine.

"Hey, Suki, you can't take that. We've got a booking for seven o'clock."

She glanced at him but didn't reply.

He was coming closer.

She gripped the arm levers that controlled the craft, one either side of her legs, and then squeezed the trigger throttle control on the right-hand lever. The machine eased itself away from the jetty as Matt ran toward her.

He was shouting now. "Hey, Suki, come back!"

She continued accelerating away, leaving a perfect widening wake behind her on the glasslike water. Matt stood at the end of the jetty, his hands on his hips.

"Goddamnit! You'd better not be long!" Then, as an afterthought, "And don't damage her!"

Then he turned and strode back to the office.

Suki loved this time of the day.

With the light brightening and the sky starting to turn blue, it almost made her believe it was a day in which good things could happen—almost.

She sped across the enclosed water of the bay, the open sea beckoning to her beyond.

As the wind streamed through her hair and filled her nostrils with the smell of the ocean, it helped her forget the horrors of the night and look forward to the encounter she was heading toward.

Once she reached the reef, she took a bearing from two islands she saw offshore and then headed south. She pulled the canopy closed above her head, sealing her in her own little cocoon. She was now completely enclosed. She squeezed the throttle all the way.

The small craft leaped through the water.

It was time to see what it could do.

She pushed both the arm levers forward. The Seabreacher nose dived below the surface. Not far, but enough for the water to speed over the canopy two feet above. The craft was doing about twenty-five miles per hour. The sense of speed was exhilarating. Suki raced along like this for a minute, weaving to and fro, just below the surface, then she yanked back on the controls and leaped clear of the water like an exuberant sea creature.

She sped on, ducking and diving like a playful animal—like her dolphins.

She plunged deeper and then headed straight for the surface, leaping fifteen feet vertically into the air, to crash down tail first.

Next, she went deeper still, and then at full power angled the craft up and out of the water. At the last second she pushed and pulled on the opposite arm levers. The effect was to barrel roll the machine through the air. She whooped with joy as she thumped back down before slowing to a steady pace as she reached the edge of the outer fringing reef.

Suki brought the craft to a halt and checked her position. She was now some way from the nearest land.

She wanted to make sure she didn't get lost.

She checked the fuel gauge, which was fine, and then

made sure the GPS display was working. There was a list of waypoints already in the system. You could set your current position so you could always return to where you were. She didn't need to do this, but she scrolled through the list of stored locations until she found one marked SANCTUARY.

She pressed the touch-screen.

A small dot appeared on the display ahead and to the right of her.

The distance said TWO MILES.

She took a final look around and then headed out into the open ocean.

Chapter Twenty-Five

Suki had been traveling for about ten minutes when she saw them.

At first there was just a disturbance below the surface. But then it became a ripple, and suddenly two dolphins leaped out of the water alongside the Seabreacher.

Her face wore a wide smile. Tears formed in her eyes, but these were tears of joy.

The dolphins raced with her further out into the wide expanse of blue ahead. And then suddenly two more joined the first two. It became a game as to who could come nearest and cross in front or beneath her. At one point, one even leaped over her head.

She dipped the Seabreacher below the surface and the dolphins came even closer, looking in at her through the thin canopy. She felt as though she was truly one of them.

She was a dolphin.

The game continued for another five minutes until she checked the GPS. She had arrived at the location called SANCTUARY.

She slowed the craft to a stop and shut off the engine. Then she slid the canopy back and sat there in the quiet, vast expanse of the ocean.

She could see nothing in any direction, except maybe the tips of a couple of the islands she had left behind on the horizon. She was alone, save for the wonderful creatures that surfaced around her and every now and then gave a release of breath from their blowholes like a contented sigh.

She had discovered this place after checking charts of the area. It was a deep seamount. When she had dived here before she had found it was somewhere dolphins collected in large numbers; for what, she had no idea, but if it allowed her to swim and be with her beloved animals, the reason didn't matter.

She pulled on her fins and mask and slipped into the water. She loved the feel of the liquid medium as it caressed her body. It was the one place she felt safe and secure, away from the trials and burden of the world above.

She reached over the lip of the cockpit and grabbed a small reel of fishing line. The reel itself had a positive recoil, which meant that when there wasn't any force pulling the line out it automatically kept it taut—when the force was released, it pulled the line back in. She attached one end to the Seabreacher using a karabiner on a small piece of rope. The other end, which was attached to a strip of Velcro about three inches wide, she wrapped around her right ankle. She didn't want to surface from the dive and find her ride home was nowhere to be found.

Next, she floated quietly at the side of the Seabreacher preparing herself.

She took the odd glance down into the depths into which she would soon be descending. Now, though, was all about getting her body ready for what was to come. The water was clear and blue but the depth was over two hundred feet. Even with the clarity she couldn't see the seabed.

All around her the sun's rays shone down from the surface, focusing deep below, like a cone of dancing light leading her into the depths.

She started by controlling her breathing.

She took long, slow breaths, completely expelling the air from her lungs when she breathed out. She needed to saturate as much of her bloodstream and tissues with oxygen as possible.

She continued for five minutes.

When she felt she was finally ready, she pushed gently away from the Seabreacher. She lifted the little silver locket around her neck, kissed it for luck, and then smoothly duck-dived down into the depths, her fins shooting high into the air above her.

A moment later she became a creature of the sea.

With her compact, lean figure, her body mass was such that she was neutral, to slightly negatively buoyant, in the water, and so she easily slipped into the deep with little work required from her fins. This would save oxygen and allow her to spend longer on the seabed.

Her record was six and a half minutes, and today she felt good. Her body was relaxed and she knew her friends were waiting for her below.

The first of them came up to inspect the new creature in their domain when she reached about forty feet. She had just finished clearing her ears for the second time, to relieve the increase in pressure, when he came into sight. He was a large male, and as he approached, Suki could hear the range-finding clicks that allowed the animal to see inside objects in three dimensions. It was their way of checking her out. She watched as he swam around, tail toward the surface, his inquisitive face bobbing in and out.

She smiled and headed deeper.

As she passed a hundred feet it was becoming darker and cooler. But it was so peaceful down there. It didn't scare her. She felt safe somehow. She felt she belonged.

A second animal joined the first. They escorted her deeper, like an honor guard.

At a hundred and fifty feet she could see the bottom way below. She couldn't make out the edges of the seamount, but she knew that not far away the water plunged to depths of thousands of feet on all sides.

And then she touched down.

There was very little there.

The seabed consisted mainly of a sandy substratum and the occasional rock. The light was dim, and as she stood there, a small life form in the midst of a huge ocean, she felt at one with the environment. The dolphins flitted in and out of her vision, still curious, but also accepting of her presence.

After a full minute, she gently finned off across the seabed. Her mind was clear. The trials and traumas of her life were far away in another world—the one above the surface.

After she had cleansed her thoughts and spirit for another three minutes her body told her it was time to go. She swam a lazy circle around an outcrop of rock and then reluctantly turned and headed up.

As she rose, so the water became brighter, and although she should have looked forward to the warmth and light the surface would bring, she always dreaded this time—returning to somewhere she felt far from relaxed and happy.

But return she had to do, and with a final rush she burst through the surface, gulping in the refreshing, life-giving air.

As she glanced around, she found she was about twenty feet from the Seabreacher. She swam over, the small reel attached to the craft spooling in the loose line as she went.

When she reached the side she hung on for a few minutes, replenishing the much-needed oxygen. She had gone deep, but she knew she could go far deeper if she needed to. These excursions to the seamount were merely exploratory dives. One day she would really push herself—see what she was capable of.

One day, maybe she wouldn't come back.

The thought almost sent a thrill through her body, but it quickly passed. She pulled off her fins and mask and threw them onto the rear seat before climbing into the front of the cockpit.

Once inside, she turned the key, gunned the engine, and drove in a wide arc ready to head back to the watersports center and the wrath from Matt that would no doubt follow.

She had just set the GPS, and was about to squeeze the throttle, when she noticed something way out on the horizon. She couldn't make out what it was, but it was red and something glinted off the top. It didn't look like it was moving, and although the color would normally make her turn the other way—anything out of the ordinary on the ocean required investigation.

She turned the craft around in the direction of the distant object and headed off across the water.

She kept her speed fairly slow as she approached.

Her natural instinct was flight rather than fight. She knew she could get away from any threat quickly in the

Seabreacher, but it looked as though that wouldn't be required.

She was approaching what looked like a small one-man life raft. It had black buoyancy tubes around its base, while the top was bright red. The reflection she had seen was from a transparent piece of plastic directly in front of the face of any occupant.

She made a wide pass around the raft, like a big cat cautiously circling its prey, then she moved in closer. As she approached, she could see the front was zipped tightly shut, but she could detect no movement from within. She bumped the Seabreacher up against the side and knocked the engine into neutral.

She kept it running, though—just in case.

She grabbed hold of the raft and leaned over to reach the zip that stretched all the way up the front. She slowly pulled the zipper down.

When she saw what was inside, she instinctively drew back.

A man lay in the cramped interior. He was in a sitting position as there was barely room for him inside. He was tall, had broad shoulders, and wore what looked like a bright red drysuit with a face section pulled away. She had never seen one like it before. His eyes were closed, and she couldn't tell whether he was alive or dead. She glanced around. There was a torch, a water bottle and some wrappers of what must have been emergency rations that looked like they'd been eaten recently.

But then her eyes focused on something else. Something she would have to lean in to reach.

Something she was reluctant to do.

What if he was alive and grabbed her?

But her urge was too great.

She reached back into the Seabreacher and pulled out her Lycra shark jaws hood. She slipped it over her head, and then, trying to create as little disturbance as possible, leaned into the raft and inched her hand along the side of the man's leg to where she saw the handle of an underwater housing.

She managed to reach it and curled her fingers around the hard black plastic. She started to pull, but it was wedged in tight between his leg and the buoyancy tube. She steadied her breathing and pulled harder. As it came free it rocked the small raft, moving the man's leg.

Once she had the housing free, she was about to turn and jump back into the Seabreacher when she glanced casually at his face.

And froze.

She found herself staring at the most piercing blue eyes she had ever seen. Although she was shocked, she didn't feel any menace from them. In fact, at this moment, the man's expression showed a mixture of confusion and curiosity rather than any malice.

Then she realized she had the hood on.

She started to lift the housing out of the raft when her arm was grabbed in a vice-like grip she couldn't believe came from someone in his condition. At the same time she saw his other hand reach up and grab her hood. She pulled back with a yelp and the hood came off. She was caught for a second, like a rabbit in headlights. But the man still had a grip on her arm.

And she noticed something in his eyes.

It was when he had seen her scar.

They had changed somehow. There was now a softness, a compassion that unnerved her—made her hesitate.

And then he spoke.

"You can't take that."

The voice was croaky and parched but there was strength to it. The words were simple, calm, direct and almost made her want to comply. But she was still recovering from the shock of seeing him alive.

She lurched back, away from him, managing to break his grip.

"There's something inside I need," he said. "Take the housing. Just give me what's inside."

Again the voice was calm, measured, not what she would have expected, but she was now in flight mode. Any amount of reasoning would have fallen on deaf ears. Also, if there was something important inside, that might be something she could sell.

She jumped back into the Seabreacher and gunned the engine. The man had her hood but that was too bad. There was nothing she could do about that now. In the back of her mind something said she was glad he was alive, and by the strength of his grip, he would be fine for a while. All she had to do was tell someone back at the center that a guy was in trouble out here and someone would go and get him—not her problem anymore.

That made her feel better.

As she turned the Seabreacher around she gave him one last look before speeding off across the water.

There was something about him she couldn't get out of her mind. Something about his manner that, even in the state and situation he was in, oozed calm and confidence—and kindness.

That was something she couldn't quite comprehend.

He was someone she would find very hard to forget.

Chapter Twenty-Six

The captain of *Blackfin* stabilized the controls.

The massive sub hung there in midwater about fifty feet below the surface. He clicked on the dynamic positioning system. Small water jets in the corners of the submarine fired off now and then to keep the vessel in a precise position.

The captain was in the control room along with Ivanov. They watched a screen displaying an image from an upward-looking camera. Ivanov was dressed in full combat gear, including a thin one-piece wetsuit, an oxygen rebreather and a compact waterproof automatic slung over his shoulder.

In the center of the screen was the underside of the life raft. They had watched as another craft had approached, circled the raft and then moved in close to it. They hadn't been able to see what had happened above the surface but it had been clear by the bobbing motion of both craft that an exchange of some sort, verbal or otherwise, had taken place between the person in the raft and the newcomer.

Ivanov had been particularly interested in the new craft. It was unlike anything he had seen before. He could make out large fins about a third of the way along the body—it almost looked like a mechanical dolphin.

As they watched, the second craft left the raft and headed away from the scene.

"Right, we go," said Ivanov. "We've no idea if the man in the raft has the drive or if he gave it to the person who has just left. He could have been in radio contact with someone ashore and they've come to pick it up."

"But why would they leave him?" asked the captain.

Ivanov thought for a moment. "No idea. We'll find out soon enough."

McCready was slumped back in the cramped confines of the raft.

He was physically exhausted and the strange encounter he had just had with the young woman confused him.

Why had she taken the housing?

What was she doing out here?

Why had she worn a hood?

She can't have been anything to do with the Russians—could she? None of it made any sense.

He reached above him and pulled the cowl of the raft down. He could now see where he was.

The storm had been bad.

He wasn't prone to seasickness, but being thrown around by massive forty foot waves in lashing rain had been enough to make him relieve his stomach on several occasions. But even through that he couldn't get the image of Craig Richards out of his mind. To be stranded in a submarine on the bottom of the sea with no hope of rescue must be unimaginable. He wouldn't wish it on anyone, least of all his best friend.

He looked around him.

The water was flat calm now. The sun was bright and high in the sky. He could see the wake created by the girl heading away. It didn't look like she was going fast. He could still make out the outline of the craft.

He was deciding what to do next, when about a hundred yards away there was a massive disruption to the surface of the water. Huge bubbles erupted out of the deep. It was as though part of the ocean had become a twenty-foot-wide jacuzzi. He watched in fascination as the bubbles increased. And then from out of the middle of the frothing surface emerged two black high-speed boats.

They rose, as though on an elevator, and then settled on the water while the area around them calmed.

There were three men in each boat, including the driver. They all wore black. As the boats bobbed in the water the men pulled dive masks from their faces and dropped small packs from their backs onto the decks. They looked like rebreathers, but they were the neatest ones McCready had ever seen. He could also see they were armed with automatic weapons. It didn't take much to realize their native tongue was likely to be Russian.

All he could do was wait for the inevitable, which didn't take long.

The boats turned and headed toward him.

One of the men in the closest boat appeared to be the leader. He glanced around, took a look at McCready, and then shot a glance at the retreating craft that was heading back to shore. It had, though, now stopped and was just sitting there about a quarter of a mile away. He barked an order that was definitely in Russian. The second boat headed off to investigate.

McCready watched as the man directed his boat to cross over to the raft.

As they approached, one of the men trained his weapon on McCready. He watched them come closer. There was nothing he could do.

When the boat bumped up against the side of the raft, the leader moved forward, his weapon slung behind his back. He looked down at McCready and around the interior of the raft.

"My name is Major Yuri Ivanov. I am looking for an item I believe you have in your possession."

He spoke good English but the accent was slurred with a Russian inflection. McCready could see this was a man with whom it would be hard to reason, but he had to at least go through the motions.

"I'm sorry. Who are you, and what right do you have to take anything from me?"

Ivanov smiled thinly. "I am an interested party. The gun my friend is pointing at you gives me all the rights I need. Now, are you going to give me what I want or am I going to have to take it?"

McCready looked straight at him. "I don't know what you're talking about. I'm the only survivor from a trawler that went down in the storm. I'm lucky to be alive."

"Maybe soon you will not feel that way," said Ivanov coldly.

He nodded at the man with the weapon. The man slung his gun and moved forward toward McCready.

When McCready objected, he slugged him in the face.

He then reached in and searched the small space around his body in the raft. He flung out the old rations packaging and other rubbish. All he found was the girl's hood, which he handed to Ivanov. Ivanov looked at it curiously. "What's this?" he asked McCready.

When McCready didn't answer, he indicated for the man to continue. He started to pat down McCready's body. He pulled out his iPhone and handed it to Ivanov. Ivanov looked at it and then threw it back in the raft. The man went to grab it.

"Leave it!" Ivanov ordered. "It can be tracked. Let it go down with him."

The man pulled back, disappointment on his face. "There's nothing else."

Ivanov turned to McCready. "So, you gave it to whoever came to see you. Who was that?"

"I have no idea," said McCready. "It was a fisherman who was heading home in a small boat. He couldn't fit me on board so he said he was going to get help to take me ashore. But now that you guys are here, maybe you could save them the time."

Ivanov stared at him with menace but said nothing. He turned to look at the second boat that was closing on the small craft in the distance. Then he spoke to his men in Russian.

The armed man sat down. The driver pushed off from the raft.

"Going so soon?" asked McCready.

"You'll wish you'd told me more," said Ivanov curtly.

As the boat was about to head away, he turned to McCready and, without any expression, lifted his gun and shot him.

He then fired two bullets into the buoyancy chambers of the raft. The air fizzed and bubbled as it rushed out.

The raft collapsed and started to sink, closing around McCready's body, dragging him below the surface.

Chapter Twenty-Seven

Suki had been traveling away from the raft, the face of the man etched into her brain, when suddenly she cut the throttle and stopped.

She sat there, her mind in conflict. She couldn't just leave him—could she?

She slowly turned the Seabreacher round to look back at the small raft in the distance. She pulled the canopy open and let the air flow in. But as she looked over the calm water she heard a strange noise. It sounded like a strong whooshing or frothing—something she couldn't quite place.

And then she saw a disturbance on the water.

It was churning and bubbling.

As she watched, two black boats rose above the surface. A few seconds later they headed toward the raft.

She reached below her seat and grabbed a pair of binoculars. She trained them on the boats. It looked like there were three men in each, all dressed in black—and they seemed to be armed.

It made no sense.

A moment later, she saw one of the boats peel away and head toward her.

She wasn't sure what to do.

Every bone in her body screamed GET OUT OF HERE, but she wanted to know what they were going to do to the man in the raft. Somehow she knew whatever it was wouldn't be good, and for some reason that really mattered to her.

She continued to watch, then she heard what sounded like three gunshots.

At first she didn't realize what they were, but any out of place sound always put her on alert, and, however unlikely, they had definitely sounded like gunshots.

She focused on the raft. To her horror she saw it had collapsed. It was starting to sink.

The second boat had also started to head toward her.

She panned the glasses to check on the other boat, but she didn't need them to see it was only a few hundred yards away, and coming fast.

Not for the first time in her life she had to make a quick decision. This time, though, she realized, as she made it, that it would be fight and not flight.

She dropped the glasses, tightened the safety harness around her chest, and then pulled the canopy shut. She gripped the arm levers firmly, checked her feet were securely on the pedals, and then squeezed the throttle—all the way.

The Seabreacher took off like a sprinter from the blocks —heading straight for the oncoming boat. She'd played chicken before, but this time she had a trick up her sleeve if the others didn't blink—she could go beneath them.

And she was counting on the fact that they didn't know.

The two boats approached each other at a closing speed of over a hundred miles per hour.

The guys in black started to look worried when the Seabreacher was fifty feet from them and not looking like it was going to move. It was like a big gray shark heading straight for them. At the last second the driver blinked, spinning the boat to the right, which was exactly what Suki had wanted. She dived just below the surface and turned slightly toward them.

As the Seabreacher sped beneath the boat, its tall fin struck the jet nozzle, smashing it beyond recognition. Without the ability to angle or control the jet of water that propelled it forward, the boat came to a halt, a mass of uncontrolled water gushing out of the rear. She also heard a crack as part of the fin broke off.

She was going to be in so much trouble when she got back.

One of the men aimed a rapid burst of fire at the Seabreacher, but by the time he could aim, Suki was almost out of range. She heard a bullet zing past the cockpit, but it was way off.

One down, one to go.

The second boat was heading her way.

It had not fully appreciated what had happened.

Ivanov had seen the two boats come close together. The dolphin boat had disappeared briefly but then reappeared, heading straight for them. At the same time the other boat had seemingly stalled in the water. He tried to contact them by radio but no one was replying. He ordered his men to fire at the approaching craft.

As the bullets zipped a path across the water ahead of her, Suki dipped the Seabreacher below the surface. She needed them to be disoriented enough so she could carry out her plan. It relied on them not knowing exactly where she was.

She had taken a mental bearing on their position and then turned in a wide arc underwater to approach from the side. She risked a slight peek above the surface, just bringing the craft up so the edge of the cockpit was clear of the water. The other fins could be seen but they would be virtually impossible to hit. Things were just as she wanted. The boat had stopped, not sure of her position. But then she saw one of the men aim his weapon. A hail of gunfire pitted the water in front of her.

She smiled.

The boat stayed at right angles to her so the men had a stable platform to shoot from.

A hundred feet out she took the Seabreacher back underwater. She went deeper this time, increasing speed. She hoped the men in the boat would assume she was going beneath them and would move to the other side to shoot at her as she came past. She calculated the boat's position and at the last moment pulled the controls back, heading the Seabreacher for the sky.

As she broke through the surface she briefly saw two of the men looking the other way, but one of them stood tall. He watched her come straight for him. At the last second, he realized his mistake. A look of fury crossed his face as he threw himself to the deck.

Suki was right on target.

The Seabreacher leaped out of the water fifteen feet from the boat. The arc of the jump took her across its low profile. She hit the central console that protruded in the middle and it spun the boat into a roll, throwing the men into the water and leaving the boat floating upside down.

Once she landed she didn't even look back, but instead, accelerated, heading out to where she could just see the final piece of the life raft disappearing below the surface.

It was the first time for many years she'd been happy to see the color red.

McCready had never been shot before. It was not an experience he wanted to repeat.

With the movement of the boat and the raft, Ivanov's aim must have been off, as the bullet had hit his shoulder. It had been painful enough, causing him to cry out, but it wasn't life-threatening. What compounded the problem were the two bullets that did find their mark. They destroyed any buoyancy the small raft had been able to provide.

When he realized what was happening, he zipped up the transparent cowl of the escape suit around his face. It would give him a small amount of air to breathe and would provide extra buoyancy. He had also thrust his phone into a pocket on the suit.

Fortunately, the men in the boat had turned their attention elsewhere, but as they'd left, McCready had felt himself sinking below the surface, the remnants of the raft wrapping around him like a lethal cocoon.

He scrambled to free himself, but his hand was trapped in a rope on the side and he was sinking fast now. Straining to see through the remnants of the raft, it looked like he was about thirty feet down and accelerating.

As he plunged deeper he became vaguely aware of a shadow passing over his head. The next thing he knew, something grabbed hold of his arm. He managed to extricate his hand from the raft, and the arm, along with the buoyancy in the suit, pulled him up.

As he hit the surface he saw the girl hanging onto him.

He was now even more confused.

She pulled his hand until he was holding onto the side of her strange vehicle. She then climbed in and reached down to help him. He patted the air, indicating he had to rest for a moment to get his breath back. The wound in his shoulder was starting to ache and he had to get the suit off, which was quickly filling with water through the hole created by the bullet.

"Hurry! Hurry! Bad men coming soon," the girl said.

"Okay, Okay. I have to get this off. Hang on a minute."

She glanced nervously around, back to where the boats had gone. McCready couldn't imagine why they weren't here, but he wasn't complaining.

He unzipped the suit, pulled the neck seal over his head, and wriggled out of the rest of it, leaving it floating on the surface. At the last second he remembered his phone and grabbed it from the pocket before the suit could drift away. He then climbed into the rear seat of the Seabreacher and slumped back with exhaustion.

"Thank you," he managed before creasing up with pain.

"What's your name?" the girl asked.

"McCready, Joh—"

She was watching the men in the boats.

"We have to go," she interrupted. "I am Suki."

And before he could say anything else, she'd pulled the streamlined canopy over their heads and turned to the front. A few seconds later the small craft shot off across the water.

As McCready looked out of the cockpit, he could see the Russian boats. One was stationary, some way away, seemingly drifting aimlessly, while the other was closer—but upside down.

He watched as two of the men climbed onto the hull. They each grabbed a line from under the boat, then walked backward using their weight to pull it over.

A few seconds later it was righted.

All the men climbed in. One of them, whom he could tell was Ivanov, picked up a walkie-talkie and spoke into it. He saw a man in the other boat look over and respond with a walkie-talkie at his end. After that, Ivanov's boat headed over and picked the man up.

It then turned and headed after the Seabreacher.

Suki had also seen the action in the other boats and that one of them was now chasing them.

Right now she was about a hundred yards ahead.

The Seabreacher was fast, of that she was confident, but the other boat looked impressive. The engine, she had noted, was under a cover and powered a water jet, which would make it maneuverable. And while the Seabreacher had its other skills, her greatest weapon was her knowledge of the rocks and reefs and where they were.

If things hadn't been so serious, she might have even enjoyed the contest—but they were.

She scanned ahead for a plan to lose the other boat. She had to get the man called McCready to a hospital without the men in the boat knowing where he was. That meant being a considerable distance ahead of them.

Once she was sure what she wanted to do, she turned the Seabreacher in a wide arc and headed toward the first of the nearby islands.

From his position next to the console in the RIB, Ivanov watched as the craft ahead of him turned to the right in a wide arc.

Inside he was furious.

The fact that the craft had damaged the other boat so easily and had capsized him and his men made his blood boil. He'd had no choice but to tell Kozlov in the other RIB to contact *Blackfin* and arrange for repairs. He'd then picked him up and could now concentrate on his prey without distraction. It was something the fire inside him relished. Now it was more than about successfully completing the mission.

As the strange craft had approached and leaped from the water, he had seen the driver. It was a girl who looked like she was still a teenager. From her looks she had an Asian lineage. As well as wanting to get even with her, his mind was planning many other things he would do to her when he caught her—and catch her he would, of that he had no doubt.

Suki glanced in the mirrors.

She could see that the boat was closer.

She checked her speed. They were doing over fifty miles per hour.

Her passenger hadn't said anything since they'd left, but an occasional glance in the rearview mirror told her he was in extreme pain, something only too evident from the grunts he made whenever the Seabreacher bounced over a small wave or leaped clear of the water and hit the surface hard.

She enjoyed the quick glances she took, but she had to concentrate on getting them out of there and getting him to medical care.

Deep Impact

She pulled up the GPS map and checked which would be the quickest route. It was some way to the hospital but she had no choice.

Satisfied, she made her way toward a reef she knew would buy her some time.

Behind, the men in the boat started to fire volleys of shots. Several flew past harmlessly but a couple hit the bodywork with loud thwacks. In the back, McCready kept as low as possible. At least he had the solid mass of the engine to protect him.

Suki checked her bearings.

Once she was happy, she concentrated on the color of water ahead. Deep blue was deep water, turquoise was shallow reef. Every now and then she dipped the nose below the surface to check she was on track.

She glanced back at McCready. "Hang on. This might hurt."

And with that she took the craft deeper.

McCready watched as the reef zipped past merely feet either side of the cockpit. The channel seemed to be becoming narrower and narrower. And then he saw what was ahead—a solid coral wall, and they were heading straight for it.

He braced for the impact.

"Really! Are you sure?"

But Suki didn't answer. Her concentration was complete. At the final moment she pulled back on the controls. The machine raced for the surface at an acute angle.

It burst through, still with massive forward momentum.

As McCready looked down he saw the craft fly over a section of reef that just broke the surface.

It would be impossible for a boat to follow.

They seemed to hang in the air forever before crashing down into a crystal clear stretch of water on the far side.

He cried out with the impact.

Once back on the surface, they sped on their way.

McCready thought he could hear a large exhalation of breath from the front seat, but he couldn't be sure.

"Remind me to never get in a car with you," he said.

In the front Suki smiled to herself and glanced in the mirror.

"No worry. I no drive."

Behind them, Ivanov saw the top of the reef at the last second. He yelled at the driver. The man managed to spin the boat just in time—the water jet turning it on a dime. It sat there bobbing in its own wake.

Ivanov watched as the Seabreacher disappeared into the distance. He glanced around and saw there was reef in all directions.

It could take them hours to find a way round.

But now he was even more determined than ever to find the drive—and the girl.

Chapter Twenty-Eight

Half an hour later Suki slowed the throttles. She pulled the Seabreacher up to the end of a long wooden jetty on the far side of the small island from where her house was located.

It was the back entrance to the Belau National Hospital and was McCready's only hope for treatment. The problem was that the jetty turned into a walkway that stretched across about four hundred yards of reef. There was no way she could get him over such a distance in his condition on her own.

She climbed onto the side, tied up the Seabreacher, and then looked down at him. He was either asleep or unconscious. He'd lost a lot of blood from the bullet wound and it was clear to see that the pain and exhaustion had taken its toll.

He wasn't going anywhere.

She checked out to sea to make sure there were no boats in sight and then ran up to the hospital.

Ten minutes later she returned with one of the staff and a gurney.

She glanced into the Seabreacher and then crouched down. She nudged him.

"Hey, McCready, you have to get up."

McCready woke slowly. He immediately felt the pain.

"Where are we?"

"Hospital," replied Suki. "You have to go now. But safe here."

He groaned, starting to ease himself up.

The hospital orderly helped him out of the craft and up onto the gurney.

McCready was about to lie down when he remembered the housing. "I need what's in the housing," he said weakly.

Suki glanced at it lying on the cockpit floor. "No, I saved your life. I take."

McCready shook his head. "Those men back there. You saw how serious they are. They're after what's inside. You won't be safe if you keep it."

Suki thought about this, but wasn't convinced. "I can look after myself. You stay good, McCready."

She gave a half-smile then jumped back in the Seabreacher and started the engine. She squeezed the throttle and moved slowly away from the jetty.

There was nothing McCready could do except watch her go. He waited until the small craft with the fascinating Japanese girl had disappeared around the end of a spit of land and then lay down, exhausted.

The orderly grabbed the end of the gurney and hurriedly pushed him up the jetty.

As he felt the rumbling of the wheels on the rough wooden planks he slipped blissfully into unconsciousness.

Suki checked the mirrors on the Seabreacher every few seconds until she was out of sight of the jetty.

She was experiencing feelings she hadn't felt in a long time.

But she knew men.

She knew their ways.

They always let her down.

Ultimately she knew she could never trust one ever again. All they had ever brought her was pain and suffering—except one, her father, and he was no longer with her.

The thought of him brought a tear to her eye. It was something she would never get over, would never forgive. And it brought her thoughts full circle to the man who had been responsible—Saito.

She stopped the Seabreacher, letting the craft float on the surface for a moment. She reached down to the housing and pulled it up into her lap.

She undid the latches and opened the back. It swung on hinges at the side and lay there like a patient awaiting an operation, the insides exposed. She didn't know what she expected to find. Its weight had told her there wasn't a camera in there—but then what? And what could be so important that armed men, appearing out of the water, could want it so badly?

She pulled out the bubble wrap and unrolled it. It revealed what looked like some sort of computer drive, and that was it.

She had no idea what it was for.

Maybe Saito would see some value and pay her well for it.

She was thoughtful as she wrapped it up and placed it back in the housing. She would be grateful for the money, but she didn't wish to see Saito again. She only suffered him because of her mother—her safety was the only thing that mattered. She would do whatever it took to keep her safe.

Beyond that, her own life was meaningless.

She had just started the engine and looked around to check which way to go, when her heart skipped a beat. Over to the right, growing larger by the second, was the unmistakable outline of the black speedboat.

It was coming straight for her.

She accelerated, heading closer to the island on her left. In her mirrors she could see the boat alter course to follow.

There were a number of islands in the area. As she closed in on the closest one, she hugged the side of it. It was dangerous. There could be small protrusions of rock that could catch her unawares, but if she kept the canopy half in, half out of the water she could see anything coming toward her underwater, as well as above.

The chasing boat was closer now.

In the cockpit Suki started to sweat.

She couldn't keep this up for much longer.

The rock was only inches from the cockpit and she was doing over forty miles per hour.

Suddenly, as she turned sharply round a corner to follow the wall, a large finger of rock stuck out straight in front of her.

She instinctively threw the controls to the right.

She just managed to avoid it, but her concentration had gone for a moment and the Seabreacher surfaced some way from the rocks.

At this, the other boat saw its chance. It closed in to race between the Seabreacher and the wall, giving Suki nowhere to go, except out into open water.

She turned, heading in a wide arc that would take her back to the island on her left. Behind it there was somewhere she knew they couldn't follow, though given how she had first encountered them, she wasn't so sure.

As she rounded the tip of land, she saw that the green vegetation extended right down to the water's edge. It was so close that, had the canopy been open, she could have picked leaves from the trees as she sped by.

Suddenly, a sightseeing boat appeared dead ahead, right in her path.

She again flung the controls to the right, narrowly avoiding a head-on collision. The violent maneuver sprayed the hapless tourists with a jet of water as she passed. Some of them whooped with excitement, others yelled in annoyance as the spray gave them an unwanted soaking.

But then she was past.

The bay she had entered was enclosed. There was no way out, but it had one of the most spectacular underwater locations on the islands. She was sure her pursuers would have no knowledge of it.

She spun the Seabreacher to the left, heading further into the bay, where there were numerous yachts and small boats at anchor.

She expertly weaved in and out of them, but the chasing boat wasn't far behind. It was like a game of cat and mouse, but one where the stakes were life and death.

When there was a clear shot the men in the chasing boat fired volleys at the Seabreacher. Most went wide, but several impacted the bodywork. One pierced the canopy.

Eventually Suki ran out of obstacles to hide behind or slow down her pursuers. She looked along the wall of the bay to her right, searching for the exact spot.

And she had to be exact. If she was even a few feet out she was looking at an early grave. The chase boat was gaining now they were clear of the other boats. In the mirrors Suki could see two of the men aim their weapons.

And then she had it.

She knew the small protrusion of rock about five feet above the surface of the water.

Without warning, she made a hard ninety degree turn to the right…

…and headed straight for the wall.

Behind her, the boat was taken off guard. It had to circle round to follow. When it did, Ivanov saw the dolphin-like craft increasing speed, heading straight for the rock. The driver was so concerned at not losing her, he followed blindly, assuming she couldn't possibly crash straight into the wall. But he'd forgotten the other skills the Seabreacher had.

About ten feet from the wall the craft suddenly dipped below the surface at full speed and disappeared.

Ivanov screamed at the driver.

The man spun the wheel at the last second, but it was too late. The boat smashed into the rock broadside. Kozlov and the second man were thrown into the water.

Ivanov looked around him as the driver helped them back into the boat.

What the hell just happened?

Where had she gone?

As the boat drifted away from the wall he peered into the water.

Below the surface, about ten feet down, he could make

out a large dark area in the rock. It was an area none of the sunlight falling on the rest of the wall illuminated.

He turned to the two men who were now back in the boat.

"Put on your gear. We have a rat to trap."

Chapter Twenty-Nine

Suki had almost closed her eyes as she'd pushed the controls forward to take the Seabreacher underwater.

The craft had shot below the surface, straight into the wide but shallow entrance to a cave.

It was one of the diving highlights of Palau.

The site was called Chandelier Cave and consisted of a number of chambers interlinked linearly by narrow tunnels. Each chamber had its own air pocket, and in some it was even possible to climb out of the water. All, though, had amazing stalactites hanging from the ceiling. There were also small side passages leading into the rock, and while it wasn't easy to stray far from the exit, for those that didn't know what was down there, it would be like a labyrinth.

Suki was banking on that.

She knew the men in the boat had underwater kit, but they didn't know the layout of the cave.

As soon as she'd entered she had aimed to go as deep as possible. The entrance sloped downward. She had to clear the rock that encroached from the roof.

She made it to about thirty feet before the engine died. It needed air to breathe and when it didn't get any, it said enough was enough.

She had wanted to go far enough in to reach the first air chamber but she hadn't quite made it.

Just before the engine gave out, Suki rolled the craft onto its back. The default state of the Seabreacher was positively buoyant, so it rose up to the top of the cave. The right way up, it could have trapped Suki in the cockpit against the rock. Upside down, it was easy for her to open the canopy. It also gave her an air pocket in which to breathe while deciding what to do. The divers would obviously check the Seabreacher, but when they found it empty they wouldn't know where to look.

She waited while the craft rose up to the roof and settled against the rock.

Once stationary, she looked down. The light from the entrance filtered through below. She didn't think it would be long before they followed her.

One problem she had was the water pouring in through the bullet hole in the canopy.

It was rising fast, starting to obscure her view.

She checked she had the camera housing and then pulled on her dive mask and had her fins ready. She took a series of deep breaths and then reached down to pull open the canopy.

It wouldn't move.

She tried again. It moved a quarter of an inch but then stuck fast.

More water poured in through the gap.

"Shit!"

Letting go of the housing, she grabbed the canopy release with both hands and tugged.

Nothing.

Just then she noticed the sweeping beams of torches below.

She froze.

If she made a noise and they saw her, it was over. But to hope they would swim past without looking up was wishful thinking. She glanced around the cockpit. It was difficult to see anything as she had no light.

But she had to get out.

She felt around the edge of the canopy to see if she could prize it open. She felt the gap; she just needed something to enlarge it.

Suki reached up to a small compartment in the footwell. She managed to open it and feel inside.

The cockpit was now half-full of water. She was having to twist her body to be able to keep her face above the surface to breathe.

Her fingers felt through the contents of the locker. Finally, she clasped what felt like a screwdriver. She pulled it out and almost cried with relief. She pushed the metal end into the gap, close to the bottom, then levered it back and forth, trying to ease the canopy open.

She felt it move slightly, but not much.

She was about to try again when the cockpit was engulfed in light. A torch from below had found her.

Her heart missed a beat.

She frantically put the screwdriver into the other side, desperate now.

The gap grew an inch.

Then another.

The torch beam had been joined by a second—then a third, flooding the cramped cockpit with light.

She dropped the screwdriver and grabbed both handles. She took a deep breath and pulled with all her might.

She almost shouted for joy as the canopy swept back. Water poured in, completely filling the cockpit.

Ironically, she could see more clearly now she was completely underwater.

Below her, two of the divers were about twenty feet away. The third had stayed on the cave floor, blocking the exit.

She quickly pulled on her fins and grabbed the housing. She then pushed off the bottom of the cockpit with all her strength, heading straight for the ascending divers.

As she approached them she saw they each had a large brutal-looking diver's knife in their hands. They also had small, compact rebreathers on their backs so there were no bubbles to give away their presence. She was still far more maneuverable, and with her long free-diving fins she would be able to move much faster.

As she swam aggressively down toward them they raised their hands to fend her off. At this, Suki made a fast turn to the left, heading up into the first chamber to get some badly needed air.

Above her, the roof of the cave turned upwards. She finned as fast as she could go, rising up into the air space. Once through the surface she gasped breathlessly.

But she wouldn't have long.

They would follow her up.

She managed to calm herself and then moved to the side of the chamber. It was rounded at one end but extended into the rock in a narrow tunnel-like section. The rock also had tall buttresses that she could hide behind. She crawled out of the water and behind one of the rock walls and waited, watching.

It didn't take long. She soon saw the wavering beam of a torch below. There was only one. That meant that one diver was likely guarding the cave entrance, and the other was waiting at the bottom of the chamber.

A minute later a head slowly rose above the surface. It was followed by a torch beam scanning the sides of the cave. At least there was only one light; most of the cave was in darkness, in which Suki could move.

The man in the water illuminated the cave systematically, checking the nooks and crannies created by the elaborate rock formations. When he was at one end of the small chamber Suki saw her chance. Having fully replenished her lungs she slipped into the water behind the man and slowly moved toward him.

She saw the large diver's knife that had now been sheathed on his calf. She swam down behind him and grabbed it..

Feeling this, he whirled round, but she was too quick.

She reached up, severing one of the twin rubber hoses that carried the rebreather's gas supply.

She was gone before he could grab hold of her.

She smiled to herself.

Again, one down, this time two to go.

There was no time for stealth now. She headed straight for the diver waiting below. She could see he had his knife drawn. As she approached him she saw a small side tunnel. She quickly diverted into it, but it was small, even for her. She was halfway through when she became lodged in the rock by her waist.

She twisted and wriggled, but she was stuck fast.

She felt something grab her foot.

She kicked and thrashed. The extra impetus managed

to loosen her body. With a final kick she shot out of the far side.

But once she was through she was disoriented.

It was dark.

She looked back. She had to get a torch. The danger was, she could wander into a tunnel with no exit and no air space.

She turned back, making her way slowly around the rock, via another route, to where the diver was. As she rounded the end she could see him still looking through where she had disappeared.

She approached slowly from behind, but at the last minute he must have sensed something. He spun toward her gripping his knife.

When he saw Suki he lunged.

The knife grazed the side of her leg, cutting the thin suit and drawing blood. But she would always have an advantage so long as she wasn't trapped. She didn't rely on a machine to keep her alive. She lunged forward herself, pulling the mask from his face, at the same time cutting the hose on the rebreather. The man reached up to his mouthpiece to try to restore the gas but it was impossible with a severed hose.

In panic he dropped the torch.

Suki grabbed the light as it sank and headed deeper into the cave.

She was now well into the tunnel system.

The entrance was barely a glimmer in the distance behind her. Two of the men were down but there was still the third guarding the way out. She needed to pause and think. She swam through and up into the second chamber that had an air space. She climbed up onto a small area above the water and checked her leg. There was a nasty gash, but nothing too serious. She lay back for a moment and relaxed, letting the air flow into her lungs.

After a few minutes she had a plan. She had a torch and a knife—so she had an edge. So long as she moved quickly, the man at the entrance wouldn't know what had happened to the other divers and wouldn't be expecting her to have a light.

She had the element of surprise.

If she approached shining the torch in his face, it would blind him until it was too late and she could slip past. Once she was clear, her superior speed would give her the advantage and she could escape.

She took a final few deep breaths and submerged smoothly below the surface, descending feet first in the clear water. When she was below the roof of the passage that led to the chamber, she started to swim steadily for the cave entrance. As she passed the first chamber she saw the body of one of the divers on the floor of the cave. He wasn't moving. She didn't feel any guilt. He would have killed her, of that she had no doubt. She felt no remorse. Maybe at one time she would have done, but not anymore.

She swam smoothly on.

Ahead, the glimmer of light from the entrance increased. She rose up to the cave roof, keeping herself hard against the rock. Far below she could see the third diver. He was about ten feet in from the bottom of the slope at the entrance of the cave. She moved across the cave roof until she was about twenty feet away.

Suddenly he glanced up.

Immediately, she turned on the light and shone it in his face. She could see this affected him as he put his hand up, indicating to move the light from his eyes. But she didn't. Instead she started to fin faster, heading straight for the gap between the man and the entrance. When she was right above him she dropped the torch.

She could see this confused him as his eyes followed the light.

As he reached up to grab it, she shot by just above. She felt his hand along her leg as he tried to grab her fin, but she was gone.

She shot out of the entrance like a cork from a bottle.

The sunlight was a welcome sight, and a shiver ran down her spine as she realized how lucky she'd been. Above, she could see the silhouette of the boat. She remembered four people had originally been in the boat, and she assumed the driver was still on board. She kept close to the coral wall until she had rounded a small outcrop of rock, and then, when she was out of sight, she surfaced and quietly gulped in the life-giving air.

She checked the housing was intact and then finned powerfully on toward a small beach a hundred yards further along the bay.

As she swam, a thought popped into her head—what the hell were they going to put on the insurance form for the Seabreacher?

When the girl had dropped the torch on top of him and shot past, Ivanov hadn't known what had happened. As soon as she'd gone, though, he put two and two together. The roar of fury he made through his mouthpiece could have been heard by anyone within a twenty-yard radius— even underwater.

He immediately swam further into the cave in search of his men.

Ten minutes later they were back on board the boat. Kozlov was dead. The other man was lucky to be alive.

Ivanov looked around the idyllic island paradise, at the palm trees, the blue water and the pleasure craft, but saw none of it. This was the third time he had been bested by this girl. He could barely bring himself to think it.

It had started out as a mission, and he was determined to bring it to a successful conclusion.

But now it was no longer just business.

Now it was personal.

Chapter Thirty

A few hours later Suki sat in her small bedroom contemplating what had happened.

The events of the day had been overwhelming. What had started out as a wonderful trip into the deep to see her dolphins had ended up in a battle of life and death.

And staring her in the face, right in the middle of it all, was the man called McCready.

However much she fought it, however much she tried to push it from her mind, she found herself feeling something for this man that she had never thought she would feel for anyone.

They had barely said a word to each other, but still she had felt compelled to risk her life for him. She didn't know what to think. She'd tried to analyze it but had come up blank. Maybe it was true what they said about your feelings for someone at first sight. Maybe it had been the way he'd looked at her when she'd taken the housing from him, that of curious puzzlement—not anger. There had been no threat, and men had always been a threat to her.

Or maybe it was just physical. She'd seen his body when he'd removed the strange suit he'd been wearing. He did have a certain rugged look about him after all. And there were those piercing blue eyes she'd just loved looking into.

Her own eyes came to rest on the housing, which was lying on the floor. It jolted her back to reality.

After escaping from the cave she'd returned to the watersports center, but she'd been unable to tell Matt what had actually happened. For a start he would never have believed her. Instead, she'd made up some story about trying out some moves with the Seabreacher in the secluded bay and that the craft had gone out of control and ended up in the cave. He had listened to her incredulously and then quietly said he would send some divers to take a look. He had then spoken very calmly but firmly and said, in no uncertain terms, that she was fired. While she was a great mechanic, and they really needed one, she'd been away for hours, telling no one where she'd gone, and had now apparently destroyed a $120,000 machine, which was a vital asset in the tourist season. As a result he could no longer trust her.

She'd been left distraught, but she'd accepted his decision.

What she didn't want to do was mention McCready. He was clearly involved in something beyond her understanding. It would be up to him to talk to the people he needed to talk to. Something, though, in the back of her mind, said she owed him nothing. In fact, it was because of him she was in this position—and she had saved his life. But however bizarre, for some reason she felt a loyalty to him— one she would protect, whatever it took.

What all this meant for her future she didn't know, but she knew she could not go on as she had been. Maybe the housing and its contents would make a difference. Maybe Saito would let her go. Now she no longer worked at the center maybe she was of no further use to him. She knew these were false hopes, but she had to have something to hold onto.

She slowly stood up from the bed, pulled on some jeans and a T-shirt and then bundled the housing into a bag.

She had left a message for Saito to meet her at the usual place at 7pm.

Somehow, though, she felt she was at a turning point. Something was coming, and one way or another everything would be different after tonight. And she thought her feelings for McCready had something to do with it. They gave her a confidence she'd never known she had.

She picked up the housing and walked out of the shack.

It was nearly dark when she pulled her kayak up onto the gently shelving beach close to the watersports center.

She could see Matt and a couple of the staff closing up for the night. She kept her approach away from any lights that might alert them to her presence.

She waited until they left and then made her way around the back of the workshop to the small shed behind. She paused at the door, dreading the man she would find inside. He always made her skin crawl, but tonight, after what she'd been through, she thought she could handle just about anything.

She was wrong.

She turned the handle firmly and walked inside. It was dark, and there were no lights. The only way she could make out anything was from the moonlight spilling in through the clear plastic corrugated roof.

There, at the end, Saito waited.

She could hear the rasp of his breathing from the doorway. She quickly closed the door and walked over to him. After carefully unwrapping the housing, she held it out to him. He took it and laid it on a shelf to inspect.

"You have not been very busy," he said. "I need more from you, girl."

"The... the storm," she stuttered. "It was not possible. No one was in the water."

"Excuses," said Saito without even looking at her.

"Inside, there is something that might be worth a lot. A man had it. It was valuable to him."

Saito glanced at her dubiously and then opened the catches on the housing and took out the bubble wrap. He glared at Suki. "No camera. That's not good."

Suki said nothing.

Saito unwrapped the bubble wrap and looked at the drive. He took out a small penlight torch and inspected it. He had no idea what it was. "This is worthless," he said eventually. "You will need to do more or else your mother will suffer."

Suki stood dead still. She was at breaking point. But did she have the courage? She didn't reply at first.

"Well, what do you say?"

Very quietly and very deliberately Suki raised her head and spoke one word.

"No."

Saito looked at her. "Excuse me?"

"No."

"You do not say 'no' to me, little girl. There will be consequences," said Saito evenly and without raising his voice. It sent a chill through her body, but she took a deep breath and continued.

"I do not believe you will do anything to my mother. I have had enough. I will leave."

Saito grabbed her arm, and even his frail, wasted form had surprising strength. He pulled her close to him, spinning her round so his arm was across her chest and she was pulled back against the front of his body. "I will tell you when you can leave. I will tell you what you can do. Or else!"

"Or else what?" Suki didn't care anymore. She just wanted to be free of the clammy grasp of this hideous man.

"Or else this!"

Saito pulled a photograph out of his pocket. He thrust it in front of her face. She took it and he released his grip. She sprang forward, straining to see the content of the photo in the dim light. But as she moved to a brighter pool of moonlight, a very bad feeling started in the pit of her stomach.

She stared at the photo.

And as she held it in the light her world collapsed. It showed a picture of a woman lying on the ground, her throat cut. Blood pooled around her neck. She looked like she'd died horribly.

It was her mother.

Suki let out a wail and fell to the floor. The tears rolled down her face, her body wracked with pain.

Saito walked past, carrying the housing and the drive. He flung a ten-dollar bill on the floor. Once at the door he turned and spat at Suki.

"More cameras, or that is you!"

He slammed the door behind him and disappeared into the night.

When he had gone Suki backed into a corner of the small shed and tried to disappear into the darkness. She clutched her knees tightly to her and the photograph of her mother to her chest. The tears wouldn't stop pouring down her delicate cheeks. She had never known you could feel like this. Never known this sort of pain existed. There was nothing to live for anymore.

She stayed like that for half an hour.

But as the tears slowly ran out and the shock started to subside, something inside her found a thought to cling on to. Maybe there was one thing. It was like a lifeline in a sea of despair. It was ridiculous. It was crazy.

But when you're drowning, you grabbed hold of anything you can find.

After all, what did she have to lose?

Chapter Thirty-One

Duffy Jenkins drove the high-powered Jag up to the security gate at Number 85 Albert Embankment at Vauxhall Cross.

The building was the headquarters of the Secret Intelligence Service, otherwise known as MI6, and was situated on the South Bank of the Thames. It was a light sandy color with dark green aspects and was laid out in descending layered blocks on the river side, leading to its colloquial name of 'the wedding cake.' However, it was more like an iceberg. There were far more levels and facilities under the ground than there were above it.

Steel had always wondered at the concept of one of the world's most secret organizations having such an auspicious building, but at least it announced the organization's presence and helped to maybe solidify the myth. It also looked great in movies. At least, that was, until they'd gone and blown it up in one of them. Fortunately this was real life, and she was still there safe and sound.

The security system had already flagged up the number plate of the Jag to the armed officer in the small room next to the metal gate. He glanced into the car. As the two occupants looked back, facial recognition cameras confirmed their identities and security clearance, along with their expected presence at the building. He gave a respectful wave and pressed a button. The gate moved smoothly to one side and Jenkins drove down into the underground car park.

He pulled up at the small lobby entrance where the elevators were located.

"I'll be about half an hour or so, Duffy. Shouldn't be much longer," said Steel.

"No worries, sir. Got the latest Jack Reacher. Take as long as you like."

Steel smiled and climbed out of the car, while Jenkins drove off to park.

As Steel headed for the entrance, a man exited the door in front of him carrying a large kit bag over his shoulder. He was dressed in a stylish dark blue suit, but the tie had been pulled loose from the collar. He was above medium height, had short-cropped hair and looked powerful in a catlike sort of way. He reminded Steel of an older version of the guy out of *Layer Cake*.

"Hi, Jim, how's it going?" said Steel, knowing the name would wind him up.

The man turned to look at him. The ice-blue eyes narrowed, revealing a hint of the danger that lurked behind the calm exterior. "All good, thank you, sir." He kept on walking.

Steel nodded at the kit bag. "Going somewhere?"

The man glanced round. "Thought I'd do a spot of climbing in Norway." There was no further elaboration.

"Anything I should know about?"

The man stopped and looked directly at Steel. "I'm sure, sir, if you should know about it you already would."

There was a half-smile on the inscrutable face as he turned and walked to his car.

Arrogant bastard! thought Steel. He carried on toward the entrance to the elevators when he heard the door-lock blippers. He turned and saw the man pull a heavy-duty charging cable out of the rear side panel of the car.

"How's that going?"

The man looked up, a touch of annoyance on his face.

"Not exactly the image, is it?"

Steel smiled. He was about to turn, when he had a thought.

"By the way, how many cupholders?"

The man was about to open the door, but he stopped and glanced over, a puzzled expression on his face, which turned to a thoughtful one. "None. They always take them out when they install all the other crap. Bloody nightmare!"

Steel smiled. "Stay safe."

"Always do," the man replied, before climbing into the silver Aston Martin Rapide E.

Steel walked in through the glass revolving doors and over to the elevator bay at the far end.

He didn't have long to wait. Once inside, the car traveled quickly up to the fifth floor.

He walked out into a workspace that was smartly decorated but in a restrained style.

Halfway down the open-plan walkway he reached an assistant's desk. He remembered her name as Melanie, a bright, young twenty-something who smiled up as he stopped in front of her. "Morning, Mr. Steel," she said in a friendly but no-nonsense tone. "He's on a call but said to go straight through."

"Thanks, Melanie," said Steel.

He walked down the short corridor to the end office that

looked out over the Thames and was separated from the rest of the space by a solid wooden wall.

He knocked and walked in.

Robert Cooper was indeed on the phone. He was standing, talking into the handset, looking out over the river. As Steel entered, he gestured for him to sit in a chair opposite at the large oak-paneled desk.

Steel nodded and sat down. Cooper spoke for another couple of minutes before putting the phone down and walking over to Steel.

"Morning, Martin. Thanks for coming." They shook hands.

Cooper returned to his side of the desk and sat down.

"I was intrigued by your call," said Steel. "Something to do with our current operation in the Pacific, I understand."

Cooper looked at him for a couple of moments before speaking. When he did so he had an inscrutable expression on his face.

"Yes, sort of. I never question your methods, or your loyalty, Martin, and I know you and the Prime Minister have a certain way of working, but I like to try and stay on top of things. Make sure our paths don't cross unintentionally, shall I say."

Steel nodded, wondering where this was going.

"It's really a follow-up," continued Cooper, "re the information leak to the Russians." He glanced at Steel. "Certain things have happened that could only have occurred if certain parties had certain information that was highly classified. I can see no alternative to there being a leak, and at the highest level."

"Any idea who?" asked Steel.

"Maybe," said Cooper, revealing nothing. "I just wanted to see if you had any theories."

Steel looked at him for a moment.

"No one specific, though there are individuals on the radar."

"Such as?"

"Carol Baxter, for one. I know she's chief of staff, but I was never quite sure how she managed to get there, and believe me I've looked."

"You two don't get along, do you?"

"You could say we have our differences," said Steel carefully. "But that's no—"

Cooper waved his hand, dismissing that line of thought. "No need to go there. We've been getting a lot of chatter out of Moscow for a while now. Our bureau has had dealings with various persons of interest. There's nothing definite, but they've raised some interesting questions we've followed up back here."

Steel sat forward slightly. "Okay," he said with interest.

Cooper picked up a manila folder from his desk. He dropped it in front of Steel.

"We found this."

Steel picked up the folder and opened the cover.

Cooper watched him closely.

Staring at him from within the folder was a large black and white photograph of Stephanie Caine. Steel was very good at hiding emotion and surprise and the only giveaway was a slight grinding of his teeth.

"You're not seriously suggesting the Foreign Secretary is a traitor?" said Steel.

"Go on," said Cooper, indicating the folder.

Steel turned the pages. More photographs were revealed. They were all shots taken at night in what looked like a well-to-do residential part of London. In one of them Steel noticed the Russian ambassador's residence in Kensington Palace Gardens. The big giveaway, though, was the chief aide to the Russian ambassador, Andrei Stepanov, who was also in the picture. He had his arm wrapped tightly round Stephanie Caine. As Steel flicked through the rest of the photographs the connection became even closer, with the two of them engaged in an intimate embrace where their mouths were locked together in what could only be described as the ultimate in détente.

However much he might not like it, the evidence was there: Stephanie Caine was involved with a member of the Russian Embassy's staff. He wasn't sure if it was the situation that rankled him the most or the twinge of jealousy he refused to accept.

"There is a second folder," said Cooper, nodding at it sitting on his desk.

"Do I want to know what's in it?" asked Steel.

"Not unless you really have no interest in Ms. Caine in anything other than a professional capacity," said Cooper evenly. "She's very athletic. But then again, you probably already knew that."

Cooper's words were not meant in any way to gloat and were not said with any animosity. They were just an assessment of the facts based on the information available. Steel knew that in his position he would have been, and probably still was, under the eye of the intelligence services. It came with the territory. He was quiet for a few moments, then looked directly at Cooper.

"I can't believe in any way that she's betraying her country."

"Because you had a relationship with her? Spent a few nights with her? Come on, Martin. We both know that means nothing in this world."

"I know. But like I said, Stephanie Caine is not selling secrets to the Russians."

Cooper raised his eyes dubiously. "Okay, duly noted, but we're still going to watch her."

He took the file back from Steel then leaned back in his chair. "So, how are things going... with the operation?"

Steel's expression turned hard. "Not good. The plane went down in a storm. The last thing we heard, the sub was in the air, but there had been a problem with the parachutes. We've no idea if they even made it to the water safely, let alone down to *Resilient*."

"That's not good," said Cooper. "What's the contingency?"

"We have to assume the worst. The *Queen Elizabeth* will be in the Palau region in the next few days. They have divers on board and an ROV. We'll see if they can get down and see what happened. There's not a lot else we can do right now."

Cooper thought for a moment and then gave Steel an unreadable expression.

"Tricky times."

Chapter Thirty-Two

"Oh… my… God!" said Jade as she pushed open the wide glass panel that made up the front door into Clare's new house at the top of Laurel Canyon in the Hollywood Hills.

She looked around her at the large, wide vestibule that fed through to an all-white open-plan living room, and then beyond to what looked like an outdoor area and pool. Everywhere there were boxes and packing cases, much of which had come from the storage company where Clare had kept her things while staying with Jade.

Clare ran over and hugged her. "So whadaya think?"

"It's amazing," said Jade, still slightly speechless at what she saw around her. "Hey girl, I'm moving in with you. To hell with Malibu!"

"I really hope you're joking," said Clare apprehensively. She loved Jade to bits and was eternally grateful when she had put her up for the last few months following her separation from her ex, but the thought of a long-term arrangement was somewhat worrying. For one thing, there were her racks of dubious plants she grew on the balcony in Malibu.

Deep Impact

And the last thing she wanted was Jade's new 'friend' coming round. She'd have to check the china every time she left.

They walked through into the breezy living room. There were high ceilings throughout and much of the space was taken up with a large, low U-shaped couch with scatter cushions across it. Off to the right, through an archway, was a modern kitchen with all the appliances you could ask for. Above a central workstation was a hanging rack for pots and pans, and on the wall by the massive fridge freezer was a cool cabinet for wine. It was currently empty but it wouldn't take long to fill it up.

"So, all went through, no problem?" asked Jade.

"Yep, sure did," said Clare, smiling. "There were just a few last-minute details regarding the mortgage, but you're looking at one proud new homeowner."

Jade smiled, but then stopped and looked at her for a moment. "Hey, you really are happy right now, aren't you? And it ain't just the house." She looked at her closely. "No, I know you, girl. There's more than that." She thought for a second. "You heard back from him, didn't you?" Her face cracked into a wide smile. "Gotta be it. Always the men with you, like a barometer to your mood. So predictable. So come on, what did he say?" Jade grinned, an expectant expression on her face.

Clare looked a bit sheepish all of a sudden. "Well, it wasn't him actually."

Jade's eyes widened even more. "Girl, now you really have to tell all!"

They walked toward the wide glass panels that had been pulled back to expose the full width of the house. As they did, Max ran up to greet Jade. He'd been playing in the garden and was getting used to his new home. He let her fuss over him for a while and then dashed back outside to explore some more.

The outside was just as spectacular as the inside. It was built out on stilts and was about the size of two basketball courts. The boundary curved round in a wide arc. At its edge was a three-foot-high glass surround, beyond which was a spectacular view across Los Angeles from the vantage point close to the top of the hill where the property was located. A large part was taken up by an oval swimming pool whose turquoise tiles reflected the sun in a dazzling display. Around the pool, the garden consisted of short-cropped grass with strategically placed arrangements of plants, as well as a number of rock features. At the side boundaries tall palms swayed in the breeze, giving a tropical feel to things.

On the house side of the pool, four large recliners with yellow cushions were laid out with low glass tables and sun umbrellas at the side of each.

The girls walked over to the recliners and sat down. Jade was eager to hear all of Clare's news.

"Okay," said Clare. "It's all about the job interview. When I got there the guy interviewing me turned out to be someone I knew in college. We dated for a while and had a great time together, but he'd wanted more. Back then, as you know, I was all about changing the world, and we split up. I knew he never forgave me. We didn't see each other after, but apparently he'd been checking I was okay all these years and what I was up to. He set up the interview. It's a real job and everything, but he just wanted to see me. Isn't that sweet?"

Jade was looking somewhat skeptical. "Or creepy."

"No, it's not like that. I know Brad. Anyway, I ended up

staying down there and we had a great evening... dinner at this hotel, and then..."

"And then what...?" said Jade, her eyes expectant.

Clare's expression turned whimsical for a moment. "And then he escorted me to my room and... we said goodnight."

"You mean nothing happened?"

"Nothing happened."

"But you wish it had?"

"I don't know." Clare looked at Jade. "Yes. Maybe. It's all a bit confusing."

"You mean, 'the hero.'"

Clare smiled. "Yeah, 'the hero.'"

"Well, you guys are quits. He saved your life. You saved his. You don't owe him nothin', girl."

"I know, but it's not about that. There was something between us, I'm sure."

"And this Brad?"

"Different things." Clare looked out across the pool to the view beyond, as if the answer would be out there somewhere.

"Okay," said Jade. "What you gonna do?"

"I wish I knew."

"You heard back from him yet?"

"That's the thing. No. I thought he was different, but I've called loads of times. It just goes to voicemail. I've given up leaving messages. I wouldn't know what to say. I don't even know where he is."

"So, I guess if he ain't on your Find Friends app then you two were never destined to be."

Clare was still looking out over LA, when she suddenly had a thought. "What did you say?"

"If he ain't on Find Friends..."

"Brilliant!" said Clare, jumping up and walking back into the house.

"Huh?" said Jade, following her inside.

Clare suddenly looked intensely focused. "He's not on Find Friends. But..." She grabbed a large box marked OFFICE STUFF and rummaged around inside. She pulled out a box file, and among paper clips, rubber bands and some old receipts was a folded, well-creased piece of office stationery. She lifted it out and opened it up. At the top was the company logo for London Water, and scribbled across the main body of the paper, was a web address and a series of numbers and letters.

"Bingo!" exclaimed Clare.

"And that is?" asked Jade.

"This, my dear, is Find Friends without them finding you!"

Jade looked confused.

But Clare was reaching for her laptop. "The last time I needed to track him down..."

"Do I sense a pattern here?"

Clare gave her a look.

"...a friend at work knew a guy who set me up on this website that, with a specific code, could track cell phone locations. Worked last time. No reason to think it won't work this time."

Jade moved in closer so she could see the screen.

Clare clicked on the browser and entered the details into the website. She hesitated before clicking the SEARCH button, then made up her mind and tapped the trackpad.

A map of the world appeared on the page, centered on the United States, along with a small spinning circle and the word SEARCHING.

After a few seconds the map shifted, moving across the

Western Pacific, to end up covering an area showing the Philippines and the archipelago of Palau.

Jade looked skeptical. "You sure this is right?"

Clare was also not sure. "Well, it worked last time."

"Maybe he sold his phone. Had it stolen?"

Clare put two fingers on the trackpad and spread them apart to enlarge the map. She zoomed in until they could see the flashing blip that indicated the phone was on a small island in Palau just to the north-west of the capital, Koror. She zoomed further and Clare's breath caught in her throat.

She glanced at Jade who also now looked concerned.

Right next to the flashing blip were the words BELAU NATIONAL HOSPITAL.

Clare threw her hand to her mouth.

"Oh no," she said under her breath.

Jade put her hand on her shoulder. "It don't mean nothing. He could be visiting someone. Staying nearby. Any number of reasons." But her expression didn't share the confidence of her words.

Clare suddenly looked very intense. "I have to go to him."

"Whoa, slow up, girl."

"Can't you see? That's why he hasn't been in touch. Something's happened. I just know it has."

"Okay, let's think this through, shall we? Why not call the hospital first, before traveling thousands of miles around the world, huh?"

Clare paused. "Okay, yeah, right. Good idea."

She returned to the screen and typed in a search for the Belau National Hospital. It took a couple of seconds for the results to come up. When they did she scrolled down past the address to the phone number. She then grabbed her phone and dialed. She hadn't had time to work out the time diffcrence, but it was a hospital, there would always be someone on duty.

After what seemed like forever listening to an unfamiliar ringing tone, it was answered by the prim but relaxed voice a of a woman. "Hello, Belau National Hospital."

"Yes, hello," said Clare almost breathlessly. "Could you tell me if a John McCready has been admitted recently?"

"Okay, ma'am, one second."

Clare could hear the clicking of a keyboard, then, "McCready, you say? There's no one in the system yet, but we are a bit behind. Just hang on a sec." Clare listened as she heard the woman shout to someone away from the phone. "Hey, Paulo, know of anyone called McCready been admitted?" Clare could hear words being replied, but she couldn't make them out. After about a minute the woman was back on the line. "We have a guy who was brought in with a gunshot wound. We were told his name was McCready. Not sure of the first name. Apparently he had no ID, just a phone we couldn't access. We charged it up, but we're not allowed to use any of his biometrics to open it. Guess we'll just have to wait till he wakes up after surgery."

Clare's heart caught in her mouth. "Surgery? Will he be okay?"

"As far as I know it was a shoulder injury, but he lost a lot of blood."

"Okay, thanks for your help."

"No problem."

Clare put the phone down slowly, her mind racing.

"So, was it him?" asked Jade.

Clare looked at her, a tear in her eye. "There is someone there called McCready. They don't know his first name. But he's been shot. He's had surgery. Lost a lot of blood."

Jade put her hand on her friend's shoulder.

Clare looked straight at her. "It has to be him. I have to go. There's no need for me to be here right now. I've said I'll get back in the next couple of weeks re the job, and you could take Max, couldn't you?" Her eyes were pleading.

"And what about Brad?"

Clare looked distant for a moment. "Yeah. Give me time to think about that too."

Chapter Thirty-Three

McCready felt like he was floating.

Not the kind of experience you have when you're underwater, more a gentle, carefree drift through space. He felt weightless, as though he could be blown by a small breeze through the air. He also saw colors. Numerous bright, flickering colors. They added to the surreal nature of his being. It was unlike anywhere he had been before. Then slowly it started to fade. Noises intruded in the distance. They started to come closer. At first they were musical in nature, but then they became more defined, more focused. Above him the colors seemed to coalesce into shapes that moved around him, and then suddenly the noise was clearer but still the vision was not.

He could hear people talking, but he couldn't make out what they were saying. The shapes continued to move around him. There were two of them. One was on his right, the other on his left. The one on the left suddenly came very close. He felt his right eyelid being held open. A bright light entered his brain.

He groaned.

The same thing happened with the left eye.

And then one of the voices was crystal clear.

"Mr. McCready. Hello, Mr. McCready. Can you hear me?"

Then his vision became clearer and he could see a man standing over him looking concerned. He had dark skin, a lean oval face and short black curly hair. He must have been in his early thirties. He wore a white lab coat and thick black-rimmed glasses were perched on his nose. He held a small pencil torch in his hand.

"Hello, Mr. McCready, I'm Doctor Jansen. Can you hear me?"

McCready flicked his eyes around as he began to see things more clearly. He was lying on a comfortable bed in a small airy room. The walls were a pale yellow and the ceiling white. To his left, behind Jansen, was a window that let in bright sunlight. It was open. A refreshing breeze blew in, ruffling a colorful drape that was secured at the side. Otherwise it was hot. To his right, a young but efficient-looking nurse was attending to a monitor on a square metal trolley. As he looked at his arm he could see a narrow plastic tube ending in a needle that entered his skin.

He suddenly felt woozy. The clear image swam before his eyes for a moment, before sharpening up again. His gaze came to rest on the doctor.

"Yes, I can hear you."

Jansen smiled. "That's good. Could you tell me your first name, Mr. McCready? We only have your last."

McCready thought for a moment, as though trying to focus, jump-start his memory.

"John, it's John McCready."

"That's good," said the doctor, a smile on his face.

"Where am I?" asked McCready.

"You're in a hospital in Palau. You were found floating in a raft offshore. You've suffered a gunshot wound. Can you remember what happened?"

McCready thought for a moment, and then suddenly everything came flooding back like a tidal wave of comprehension—but not a good one. The storm, the plane, the Russians, the girl, the submarine, and then the most horrific image of all—Craig Richards marooned on the seabed, alone, running out of air.

He took a gasp of breath and started to sit up.

The doctor, alarmed, moved forward to steady him.

"No, John, you're too weak," said Jansen. "You've had surgery to your shoulder and you've lost a lot of blood. You have to rest."

"But... but..." said McCready desperately. "No time... my friend... he's dying... on the seabed... not much air."

"Steady, John. Steady. What are you talking about?"

Suddenly McCready focused intently. He looked straight at Jansen. He managed to grip his arm with a strength that seemed to surprise the doctor.

"How long have I been here?"

Jansen eased him back onto the pillows. "You came in yesterday afternoon. You were found floating in the raft yesterday morning. How long you were at sea, I have no idea."

McCready looked up at the ceiling and shut his eyes. The doctor looked at him, concern on his face. Then McCready opened them again. "You have to get me a phone. I need one now."

Jansen nodded at the nurse, who left the room.

"You had one on you when you were found. We've

taken the liberty of charging it. Nurse Willow has gone to get it. But what's so urgent?"

"My friend. He's in a submersible. It's damaged. He's running... he may have run out of air by now. I have to get help to him."

The doctor looked slightly dubious, as though he thought McCready was delirious. He was quiet for a moment, then said. "Given the nature of the way you were found, there's a policeman waiting who would like to speak to you. Also, as you had no ID, we need to know if you have insurance or how you intend to cover the care you receive here. I understand this is not the right time for the question, but to be honest, there never really is a right time." Jansen looked genuinely apologetic.

McCready took a deep breath. He was about to answer when the nurse returned with his phone. She passed it to McCready. He thanked her and then glanced at Jansen. "I'm going to talk to someone who'll be able to answer your questions and cover any expenses."

McCready looked at the screen and the facial recognition opened up the phone. He saw there were a number of missed calls but went straight to the speed dial section. He scrolled down the list and found the person he was looking for.

He pressed the button and listened to the ringing tone.

After about ten seconds it was answered.

"Martin Steel."

"You son of a bitch!"

Jansen glanced at McCready, somewhat shocked at the tone of the words. He ushered the nurse out of the room, before closing the door behind them.

"John?" The voice sounded surprised, but also McCready could detect what sounded like genuine relief.

"Yes, John. Why the hell didn't you tell us what was going on?"

There was silence from the line for a moment. "Okay, back up a bit. Where are you? What happened?"

"Right now I'm in a hospital in Palau. I've been shot by some crazy Russian. *Resilient's* crew are dead. Craig is still down there. You have to send help. I don't know how much time he has left."

"So you entered the sub? You have the drive?"

"Jesus! Did you hear what I said?"

"Yes, I heard, John, but I have to look at the bigger picture. How long has he been down there?"

McCready tried to think, to work out days, hours, minutes, but it wasn't coming to him. "Two, maybe three days."

"And how much air does he have?"

"I don't know. Not a lot."

"I wish it were possible, but I don't think we can get to him in time. The *Queen Elizabeth* is steaming your way. She'll have equipment on board, but she was delayed by the storm. She won't be there for a day or so." He paused before continuing. "What happened down there? The last we heard was a transmission from the plane saying she'd been hit by lightning and was going down, but that the sub, and you, and if I heard this correctly, had left the aircraft—separately?"

"We made it to *Resilient* but the crew were dead—murdered. She was lying over at an angle like you said. But the crew had been gassed. The Russians got there before us. But why do I somehow think you already knew that?"

"It's complicated. For operational reasons I couldn't tell you anything. I needed you to go, and if I'd told you, you might not have gone."

"Well maybe you should have had enough faith to realize that other people can think there are some things worth dying for."

McCready heard a pause and a deep breath over the phone. When Steel continued, there was a different tone to his voice. Somewhere in there, there was respect and a certain puzzlement.

"Maybe I misjudged you, in which case, I apologize. But I couldn't take that risk. There's more at stake here than you can possibly know."

"Then enlighten me."

"I can't do that."

"My friend's down there because of the Russians. No, actually, he's down there because of you! If we'd been prepared, maybe we could have done something. At least we'd have had a chance."

"You may be right." He paused and then continued. "And the drive?"

McCready sighed. "I found the drive. Got it back to the sub and then we were attacked by a Russian drone. There was only one escape suit. Craig insisted I use it. I made it to the surface in the middle of the typhoon and must have blacked out. The next thing I know, I was rescued by this girl who was in the area. But then the Russians found us. How she got me to the hospital I will never know. I owe her my life." At this, a thought struck him. "She's still out there. She's in danger. She took the drive from me. The Russians won't stop. They'll be back to find me or her, and when they do it won't be pretty. I have to get out of here."

"Can you get it back?"

"I don't know," said McCready genuinely. "Maybe."

"We need that drive, John. What can I do to help?"

McCready took a deep breath. "There are some people

here who'd like someone to tell them who the hell I am. I have no ID and no funds. The police are waiting to talk to me and I have no way of covering the medical costs."

"Okay, no problem. I'll make some calls."

"Thank you."

"Anything else?"

"Yeah, what the hell's on this drive you'd risk so many lives for? Is it really worth it?"

"I can't tell you, you know that. And is it worth it? Oh yes, it's worth it."

Outside the room Jansen was watching through a glass panel. He opened the door and came in.

"Look, I have to go," said McCready. "Make sure those things are taken care of."

"I will. And John, I'm coming down there. If there's anything you can do to recover the drive, do it. But stay in touch. Understood?"

McCready hung up and turned to Jansen. "Someone will call you and talk to the police to explain everything and take care of the costs. Right now I have to get out of here. The girl who brought me here is in great danger."

He started to get up but the doctor moved forward quickly. He checked the meds in the drip and adjusted a dial on the monitor. "No, I'm sorry, but you're not going anywhere. You need to rest. Get your strength back. You need sleep. Nurse Willow will check on you later."

McCready was about to protest, but then he slumped back as the pain kicked in.

Before he left the room Jansen switched McCready's phone to SILENT to make sure he wasn't disturbed.

As McCready saw Jansen close the door behind him, and despite his best efforts, he found himself slowly slipping away. He felt almost as though he were being swallowed by the soft mattress.

He'd done everything he could. He did need the rest, but as the medication started to take effect and he fell into unconsciousness, he couldn't get the image of the Japanese girl with the terrible scar out of his mind.

She had risked her life for him.

It was a debt he wanted to make sure he could repay.

Chapter Thirty-Four

McCready awoke a few hours later.

But this awakening was more relaxed.

There was none of the disorientation of before. He still felt fairly groggy, but his mind was working and he was up to speed with where he was and what had happened.

When she had seen he was awake, Nurse Willow had brought him some food—nothing too much, just some soup and bread to eat and some water to drink. But with every bite of the bread and every swallow of the cool water slipping down his throat, he felt his strength starting to return.

His left shoulder was the problem though. They'd had to remove the bullet and he'd had to have a blood transfusion. The shoulder was sore, and the surgery, while neat, would leave a permanent scar.

He thought back to what Steel had said.

McCready was a pragmatic man, and while he took on board the situation and understood there was nothing he could do for Craig, at the back of his mind he would never give up on his old friend until his death had been confirmed.

The one thing he could do something about, though, was the girl. He could still see her delicate face with the violent disfigurement staring at him in the raft. Her features had, on one level, been so pure and innocent, yet she had somehow suffered terribly at the hands of others. And if he didn't do something soon, that experience was going to be repeated at the hands of the Russians, who he was sure would already be on the islands trying to track them down.

He had to do something.

When the nurse had brought him a drink an hour later, he was still awake. She had put the glass of juice down on the small table at the side of the bed and asked how he was feeling. After he had said he was fine, considering, he'd asked her if she knew the name of the orderly who'd brought him up to the hospital. She'd replied it had been a man called Patrick. McCready had asked if he could talk to him.

The man was now standing at the door looking in through the glass pane. He knocked gently, almost as though not wanting to disturb the patient.

"Come in," said McCready.

Patrick entered the small room. He was in his early twenties, thin as a rake, and had a toothy grin that looked out of place on a serious face. He was clearly a local and had thick black hair that was longer than probably the hospital would like.

"Yes, boss, what can I do?" he asked politely.

"Thank you for helping me yesterday, Patrick."

"No problem, boss. Just doing my job."

"I need to get in touch with the girl who brought me here. The Japanese girl."

"That would be Suki, boss. But…" he continued hesitantly, "she said not to say nothing about her. I don't think she wants to see you."

This was half what McCready had expected. Given she'd taken the housing from him, he could understand. He thought for a moment.

"Do you know her well?"

Patrick looked even more hesitant. "Quite well, boss. She real pretty. Except for the scar, of course."

McCready looked at him for a second, thoughtful.

"You know something, Patrick, that scar is part of her. It makes her special. Makes her like no one else on Earth. Ever think of that?"

Patrick looked uncertain. "Not really, boss."

"Well maybe you should."

Patrick looked like he was thinking really hard, like the cogs were turning. Eventually his expression changed, as though he had suddenly come to a realization. McCready smiled to himself before continuing.

"I understand your loyalty to her, and I know what she said, but she's in real danger. You may know I was shot. The people who did that to me could want to harm Suki. I only want to help her. You have my word."

McCready could see Patrick was wrestling with his conscience. After a long while he seemed to come to a decision. His face turned even more serious—as though he was deciding whether to send a country to war.

"Okay, boss. Only because you want to help her. I don't know where she live, but she works at the watersports center. Go over the causeway. Turn right on Main Street, then over two more causeways and ask for Palau Watersport Adventures. You should find her there."

"Thank you, Patrick. I promise I only want to help."

"Okay, boss." He looked like he almost wished he hadn't said anything, but it was too late now. He left rather sheepishly. Once the door was closed, McCready could see him hurrying away as though he'd just committed a crime.

McCready let out a sigh and started to sit up. The pain immediately hit his shoulder. He grimaced, gritting his teeth.

But he had to leave.

There was a small button on the side of the bed. He pressed it twice.

A minute later, through the glass of the door, he could see the figure of Doctor Jansen coming toward him. He opened the door and stepped into the room. He was carrying a small backpack in his hand, which he placed on the floor.

"Ah, you're awake, John. How are you feeling?"

"I've been better, but thank you for all you've done."

"That's no problem. We heard from your contact. All your expenses have been covered for as long as is necessary. The policeman has also gone. I'm not sure what your friend said to him, but it seems he couldn't get out of here fast enough."

McCready smiled at the thought of Steel putting the fear of god into the local constabulary.

Jansen's face then turned serious. "I was told to give you this." He handed McCready a small envelope. McCready opened it and flicked through the dollar bills. The total added up to a thousand. At the back there was a scan of his passport that he could use in an emergency.

"I was also asked to let you leave without any pressure, should you decide to do so. I must stress you're still very weak, and need time to rest. I would say another two days at the minimum."

"I'm sorry, Doc, but I have to go now. I appreciate your concern but there're some things I have to do."

"I thought you might say that," said Jansen, "so, I brought you these." He indicated the backpack. "Change of clothes. Few bits and pieces."

"Thanks."

"Jansen pulled out a couple of small tinted plastic bottles from his coat pocket. These are painkillers and antibiotics. Take them as described on the labels. They should help keep you going for a while. If there's anything else you need, you know where we are."

McCready looked at him and smiled. "I really appreciate it. Thank you again."

"You're welcome." And with that Jansen turned and left the room.

McCready watched him go and then started to ease himself out of bed. He got halfway and wondered whether this was really such a good idea. The pain shooting through his shoulder was agony. But then he thought of Suki, and Ivanov, and of what might be riding on him recovering the drive.

He struggled on.

Forty-five minutes later the cab McCready had ordered from the hospital turned off Main Street and headed down a narrow pothole-ridden tarmac track between a line of ramshackle buildings.

The trip from the hospital had only taken ten minutes, but there was no way he'd been up to walking the distance. It was also the first time he'd had a chance to see where he actually was and to get a feel for the place. He was dressed in a pair of tan slacks and a loose-fitting pale blue short-sleeved shirt that he'd found in the backpack the doctor had given him.

After leaving the hospital the road had reached out across a long causeway over a shallow lagoon. From the car McCready had seen a number of local fishing boats heading out to sea. In the distance, a group of tourists in kayaks had made their way around the edge of the island's green vegetation that stretched down to the water's edge. It brought back memories of his own adventures on the water back home in Scotland, though those were somewhat cooler.

Once the car had made it onto land again, they'd driven through a small hamlet and then turned onto Main Street. This had led out over a shorter causeway, across a small tree-covered island, before another causeway took them to the island where they were now. After rolling past a wide-open wharf on the left with a small marina beyond, and what looked like a large hotel, the car had turned left down the track.

A couple of turns later and the taxi bumped over some deep potholes to deposit McCready in a small car park. Out of the window he could see the words PALAU WATER-SPORT ADVENTURES above a wide covered area through which he could see more water beyond. To one side was an office, and on the other, a shop selling all types of watersports equipment and clothing.

He paid the driver and climbed out stiffly, slinging the small backpack over his right shoulder—the other was still too fragile.

As the taxi drove away, he stretched his body, twisting at the waist to try and loosen his muscles and joints a little. It was good to be out in the fresh air.

He then headed through the undercover area to the water and beach on the far side.

He emerged in front of a wide slipway used for launching boats. Beyond, a long, enclosed bay stretched away from him. To his right, was a curving, fine sand beach with a number of paddle boards and Jet Skis drawn up on it. To his left, various boats and other watercraft were tied up to a number of small jetties.

He noticed a couple of Seabreachers.

But what was of most interest was at the head of the slipway. A small mobile crane had one of the craft suspended from its jib. It was hanging there, swaying gently in the light breeze.

As he moved closer he could see it had suffered considerable damage. The main dorsal fin had been partly broken off. The cockpit canopy and the bodywork had a number of holes in them, which must have come from the Russian bullets. He had no idea what had happened to Suki, but he had to check she was okay and warn her about the danger. But it didn't look good.

He walked over to the office.

Inside, a tall blonde-haired man was trying to deal with a family and four kids. He seemed to be in some sort of disagreement with the father, while the youngsters ran around the office making a nuisance of themselves. He looked like he'd walked off the set off *Baywatch*. He was tall, well-muscled and had wavy blonde hair that touched his shoulders. McCready could also tell he wanted to throttle the kids, given the chance. He seemed to placate the father, who was now looking at a timetable on a noticeboard, and then he looked over at McCready.

"Yes, mate. Name's Matt. How can I help?" The accent

was broad Australian. The expression was friendly but harassed.

"I can see you're pretty busy right now," said McCready. "I'm just trying to contact Suki. Japanese girl. I understand she works here."

"Used to, you mean. She's a great mechanic, but a real pain in the butt. Damaged one of my Seabreachers. Came up with some cock and bull story about what happened to it. She's screwed up my week, not to mention the season, with it out of action. Had no choice but to fire her."

"Any idea where I can find her?" asked McCready.

Matt took more of an interest. "What do you want her for?"

"I'm an old friend of the family. Was in the area. Just wanted to catch up."

Matt looked at him as though trying to judge him.

"Hey, you!" said the man with the kids, who'd been looking at the noticeboard. "There's no trip to Blue Corner for Thursday. You said there would be."

Matt looked over at him. "Are you looking at the revised timetable? Like I said, mate, it's on the board next to the window."

"Huh?" The man looked over to the window. "Ah, right. Should make it more obvious."

Matt shook his head and then looked back at McCready, just as one of the kids knocked over a scuba tank next to the door. It crashed to the ground before starting to roll across the floor.

"Jesus!" exclaimed Matt. McCready was closer and rescued the tank. He laid it down in a corner with a dive weight up against it so it wouldn't move and no one could knock it over.

"Thanks," said Matt. "Always crazy this time of year.

Look, Suki lives over near Meyungs. Same island as the hospital. You go past the hospital, then follow the road round to the left. Just keep bearing left and eventually you'll come to a small jetty. She lives in one of the shacks in the woods just behind it. Or, if you want to hang on here, there's a water taxi that does the rounds. Should be in"—he checked his watch—"fifteen to twenty minutes."

"Thanks. Water taxi sounds great."

"If you see her, tell her she's a good kid, but I got a business to run." He looked genuinely sorry.

"Will do," said McCready before exiting the office.

Once outside, he walked over to a small bar in the center of the covered area. He knew he probably shouldn't drink with all the medication he was on, but the thought of a cool beer was too tempting. He ordered a bottle of Becks and sat in the sun watching the tourists go about their day, all completely oblivious to the drama playing out around them.

The water taxi turned up twenty-five minutes later. It was a small, open boat with a tiller at the rear. McCready hopped on with a few locals and a couple of tourists. One of the locals had a large petrol can, the fumes from which spread out across the boat. While the tourists gabbled excitedly about the islands and the amazing diving, a mangy dog, which looked like it was on its last legs, also jumped on board. It promptly lay down and went to sleep as they chugged away from the jetty.

McCready was almost beginning to relax and enjoy the tropical sun and the clear, calm waters swishing past a couple of feet from where he was sitting, when he looked back across the small bay.

On the far side, heading toward the watersports center, he could make out a large black **RIB** weaving its way between the collection of moored yachts and day cruisers.

There were three men on board. One was standing at the front, scanning the area.

It was Ivanov.

When the Russian spotted the Seabreacher hanging from the crane, he pointed for the driver to take the boat in to shore.

McCready turned his back.

He hoped it wasn't too late to find Suki.

Chapter Thirty-Five

After about twenty minutes the boat dropped McCready at a small dock on the island. Two of the other passengers also got off, and the dog, which the driver clearly knew lived there, had to be woken from its slumbers before begrudgingly climbing out of the boat with a loud sigh.

Once on land McCready looked around him.

There were a number of other boats moored up. At the end of the dock was a small car park with a couple of vehicles waiting for passengers from the water taxi. One was a dark brown pickup that had seen better days, the other a small hatchback with a damaged bumper.

As he looked along the shore the vegetation was thick, but he could make out some small wooden buildings spread out in clearings between the trees. To one side of the car park was a shop that sold groceries and other basic amenities. McCready walked over and stepped inside.

There wasn't a whole lot of choice, but they had the usual necessities: milk, bread, vegetables, cans of food. A rickety fan twirled in the ceiling providing a welcome flow of air. There were no other customers but there was an elderly woman behind the counter. She must have been in her late seventies. As McCready walked along the single aisle she looked up at him.

"Can I help you?"

He smiled and crossed over to the counter.

"I hope so. I'm looking for a friend of mine. She lives in one of the houses round her. Her name's Suki. Japanese girl."

"Ah, Suki," said the old lady. "Very nice girl. She live in the blue house just along a bit. Got a small wooden deck and a kayak pulled up outside most the time. Don' know if she there now, though."

McCready grabbed a bottle of water from a fridge, which, from the sound of the constant rattle from its motor, was working overtime to keep its contents cool. He placed it on the counter. "Thanks, that's very kind of you. I'll take one of these."

The lady rang up the till. McCready paid her and walked back outside.

The heat was even more intense now. He could feel the sweat building down his back making his new shirt cling to him. He unscrewed the top of the bottle and took a swig of water. For all the effort the fridge had been making, it had been in vain.

He glanced beyond the dock and saw a path that ran along the water's edge close to the trees.

As he made his way over to it, the sounds and smells of the island hit him. It really was a beautiful place, the sort of place he would love to visit under different circumstances.

He'd gone about a hundred yards, and passed a couple of buildings, when he saw a small blue-painted shack set back in the undergrowth. It had a corrugated roof and a deck at the front. Just peeking out from behind the left-hand wall was the bow of a kayak.

McCready turned away from the water and walked over. He wasn't quite sure how to approach this. He knew Suki wouldn't be expecting him and she would be on edge from what had happened before. At the same time, he didn't want to alert her and have her run away. He wouldn't be able to catch her in his condition. She would also know the area and would be able to vanish in seconds, probably never to be seen again.

He approached the building quietly. As he came closer he could hear noise from within. There was a scraping of something being moved around and also the creaking of floorboards as someone walked across them. He made his way round to the door at the side. When he reached it, he grabbed the handle and turned it as carefully as he could. Even so, there was a loud squeak as he did. A second later all noise from the house ceased. He pushed the door slowly open. Again, there was a squeak from the hinges. But he was past the point of no return and stepped inside.

He was in a room that seemed to double up as an eating, cooking and living area. A TV was in one corner but it wasn't on. Ahead of him were two doors. He assumed the left-hand one to be a bedroom, as there was more wall associated with it than the one on the right, which was presumably a bathroom. Here the wall was barely wider than the door itself.

He moved slowly toward the bedroom.

There was still no noise.

He reached out for the handle and turned it. He pushed the door open and moved quickly inside. There was no light in the room. The drapes were closed, making the interior gloomy and dark. Before he was even fully through the door something swung out of the gloom and hit him squarely in the face.

He saw stars briefly before collapsing to the floor.

When he came to, Suki was crouched over him, a concerned look on her face.

He started to raise himself up but groaned with the pain. She reached out to help him by pulling on his injured shoulder. He cried out. She let go in fright. He fell back, banging his head on the floor.

As he looked at her, he could see she was sorry but didn't know what to say. There was also fear on her face, as though she expected a violent response. Instead, he looked at her with a lopsided grin.

"Thanks, that really helps!"

She didn't know quite what to do.

"I am sorry," she said, hesitantly. "I didn't know who you were."

McCready eased himself up to a sitting position. She then helped him to stand, making sure she didn't go anywhere near his shoulder.

"How are you?" she asked tentatively.

"Well I was doing great," said McCready. At this she looked pained, but before she could say anything he smiled at her again. "You did the right thing. I could have been anybody, and right now, 'anybody' could be someone bad."

She helped him out of the bedroom and sat him down on the small sofa in the living area.

"Can I get you a drink?" she asked.

"Some water would be great, thanks. Cold, if you have it."

She filled a glass from a jug in the fridge and then

brought it over to him and sat down on a chair opposite. He raised the glass, almost draining it in one go.

She just sat there watching him.

Now she realized McCready wasn't a threat, all the fight had gone out of her. Her expression showed one of such loss and despair that McCready desperately wanted to know what had happened to this girl to make her this way.

"I know why you are here," Suki said somewhat apprehensively. "I took something from you. I know it was wrong, but I thought it would help me. I am in very bad situation." She hung her head.

McCready thought for a moment.

"Suki, I am here for a number of reasons. The first is to thank you for saving my life. If you hadn't been there I would probably be dead. You not only helped me but risked your own life to do so, so anything else you may have done means nothing compared to that, okay."

She raised her head slightly, a glimmer of hope in her eyes.

McCready continued. "The second thing is that what you took from me is very valuable to me—not in a financial way, but in ways you couldn't possibly know. I need it back, and we can talk about that in a minute. But the third thing, and the one that is most important right now, is that you are in danger from those men in the boats. I saw them at the watersports center not long ago. If I can find you, they can find you, and they will not rest until they have the item that was in the housing. So, what we need to do is firstly get away from here, and secondly, I need you to give me what was inside the housing."

He looked pointedly at her.

Deep Impact

She realized what she had done. It had done her no good and she had been bad to the man in front of her, who she found, minute by minute, was having an effect on her she thought no man could ever have. He was the first man to ever show her kindness—and after she had stolen from him.

"I do not have it," she said eventually.

McCready looked at her hard, concern on his face.

"I gave it to a man I have to supply with housings and cameras."

"But why did you do this?"

She thought long and hard and then looked up at him. He was listening, and had that curious, interested expression she had seen before, one that carried no accusation, no hostility, just interest.

Then, over the next half hour, she relayed the story of her life.

She had never told anyone these things before. She had never thought anyone would listen or even care. But once she had started, she couldn't stop. It all came out. It was as though she were throwing a final lifeline in the hope someone would catch it and understand her life, why she was as she was.

It was, in a completely desperate way, a cry for help.

Her last chance.

Do or die.

She spoke dispassionately, without emotion, almost like an automaton. She told him how her father had been killed in front of her. The time in the brothels. The way she had scarred herself to make herself unattractive. How she had run away. Being found by Saito. And the final blow: the photo of her mother's body.

McCready listened as though he were in a dream, but it was more like a living nightmare. How could anyone do these things to someone, let alone a vulnerable young girl? It wrenched his insides apart and sent such feelings of rage and violence to his brain as to what he wanted to do to the people who had done this to her that he had to take a deep breath. Once, though, when he had those thoughts under control, he found himself looking at her with such an all-enveloping love that in that moment he knew he would die to protect her.

Finally, after she had taken a deep breath, she looked at him. "If you want to get the item back, I can arrange to meet this man tonight. Maybe he still has it. But he is bad man. Very bad man."

"Okay," said McCready, still barely being able to contain his anger, "I would very much like to meet this Saito."

Chapter Thirty-Six

When they arrived at the storeroom at the back of the watersports center it was pitch-black.

Suki had called the number she had for Saito and said she wanted to meet. She wanted to make up for the way she had behaved. She had something really special for him. It was to do with the item she had given him last time and he must bring it with him. There had been a heated discussion, but he had eventually agreed to meet her. He would see her there at 9pm.

As they approached the entrance to the shed, all was quiet. The center was closed up. Even the bar, which had shut early for stocktaking, was silent.

It was unlikely they would be disturbed.

Suki pushed the door open. It creaked on its rusty hinges.

She walked in.

As ever, it was dark inside, with only some dim moonlight struggling through the corrugated plastic roof. It had been decided McCready would stay outside and only come in if Suki had any problems. He'd been reluctant to agree to this, but she'd been clear: she wanted to do this herself. So, right now, McCready was just outside the door listening to whatever transpired inside.

Suki could make out the figure in the corner. Again, she could hear the rasp of his breathing. She had to prevent the bile from rising in her throat as she moved closer to him.

"What have you got for me?" said Saito, in his emotionless voice.

"I need to see the item I gave you," said Suki. "It fits into something I have."

Saito pulled the drive out of a pocket in his coat and brought it into the dim light.

"What is it for?" asked Saito.

Suki didn't know what to say. "It's for a special computer. I have the name of the owner who would pay highly to get it back."

"I don't think so," said Saito, a sneer in his voice. "I don't think you're any use to me anymore."

He moved forward surprisingly quickly and grabbed Suki around the throat. She cried out, trying to fight him off.

From outside, McCready heard the cry. He needed no further bidding. He crashed through the door and crossed the space to where Saito was holding Suki before the man had even registered what was happening.

McCready punched Saito in the face. The man cried out and let go of Suki, blood pouring from his nose. He dropped the drive and it fell to the floor. McCready picked it up and checked it briefly before putting it into his pocket. He then turned to check on Suki. She nodded that she was okay, holding her throat, her breathing slightly ragged. She looked at Saito and spat in his face. The old man smiled evilly up at her, goading her. She lunged at him ready to kill him, but McCready held her gently, but firmly, back.

"It'll do no good. You'll regret it."

She looked up at him, and for the first time he saw real fire in her eyes.

"But it will do me good," she said. "He took everything from me."

McCready's attention was on her. His back to Saito.

Saito slid his right hand under his coat and slowly pulled out a large knife. He moved his arm back, lining up on McCready, when a beam of moonlight reflected off the blade.

It caught Suki's eye.

As Saito hurled the knife with all the force he could muster, Suki screamed, pushing McCready to one side.

But it wasn't enough. The knife hit him in the leg.

He went down.

At this, something flipped inside Suki.

Her focus and attention was complete. To her, things seemed to be happening in slow motion. She glanced to her right. There was a speargun leaning against a row of dive cylinders. She picked it up, and in a single motion she pulled the bungie cord that armed it.

She spun around, aiming at Saito.

The old man's expression was now one of fear. Gone was the arrogant bully. He fell to his knees, pleading with her.

She stared at him for a second, finally seeing him for

what he was, a pathetic coward who'd had control over her for too long.

He was nothing.

She didn't even think twice as she pulled the trigger.

The spear flew fast and true to its target. It passed through Saito's left eye and out of the back of his skull, nailing him to a wooden pallet that had been leaning against the wall behind. An anguished scream followed by a whimpering wail came from his mouth before he was quiet.

Suki was still standing, looking at him, when McCready turned around. He had pulled the knife from his leg. It hadn't penetrated too far.

He crossed over to her and slowly took the speargun from her hand. He let it drop to the floor and then held her to him. She closed her eyes and clung to his strong, warm body. He lifted her up. She clung on tighter, as though she never wanted to leave the protection of his arms.

For the first time in many, many years she felt safe. It was a feeling she hardly understood. It was one she was reluctant to succumb to in case it was only an illusion.

She felt no joy at Saito's death. No jubilation. No victory. Just an understanding that justice had finally been done. And along with that, she realized she was free of him forever, but also that she had no past to go back to.

Nowhere to go.

The only thing in her life that made sense was the man she was currently clinging to.

It was all she had.

McCready carried Suki from the shed without a backward glance at Saito.

He made his way along the darkened roads, over the

causeway to the island, and back through the trees to Suki's home.

It took forty-five minutes.

In the whole time they never said a word to each other, but the grip of the girl in his arms never lessened for a second. She was like a frightened animal clinging to him for life. The only indication she was even alive was the rapid beating of her heart against his and the constant stream of tears rolling down her cheeks onto his chest as she hugged herself to him.

She was a broken girl, lost and desolate, and as he walked, he realized she was a human being completely on the edge. It was a raw, cathartic experience, born out of pain and suffering that created an emotional bond between them that would last until the end.

When they reached the little wooden shack, McCready pushed the door open and walked inside. Despite Suki being as light as a feather, McCready's shoulder was starting to feel the strain. Also, the cut to his leg was deeper than he had thought and blood was seeping down his slacks.

Suki's tears had all but dried up and her heart rate had returned to a resting beat. McCready carried her and laid her on the bed. They really needed to leave here, but he wasn't going to do that with her in this condition. They could wait until the morning. He'd take the chance.

When he turned to look at her she was looking straight back at him. There was a calmness in her eyes he hadn't seen before. There was also an eternal gratitude that he found hard to look at. He had barely done anything, whereas she had been through so much.

"Would you like something to drink?" he asked.

She nodded. He went to fix some water and brought it back to her. She propped herself up on one elbow and shakily drank it down. It seemed to give her some strength, because when she looked at McCready some life had come back into her eyes.

"Thank you," she said simply.

He just smiled.

She noticed him looking at the dolphin locket around her neck.

She peered down at it, and then, for the first time in her life since her mother had given it to her when she was five years old, she took it off. It almost felt like a transformative moment, as though she were passing her protection, her love, from one human being to another. She gave it to McCready. The gravity of the moment must have shown in her face as he looked at her strangely.

"You okay?"

She smiled at him.

"Yes," she said. "I am."

McCready turned the locket over. It had a dolphin engraved on the front and the back. On one side the animal was leaping out of the water. On the other, it was sticking its head above the surface, its mouth open, as though smiling. He indicated whether he could open it.

She nodded.

He carefully put his nails between the two sides and prized them apart. Inside there was space for two photographs, one either side. On the left was a picture of a woman in her twenties who looked a lot like Suki only with longer hair. The man on the right was smiling confidently and had a kindly, weather-beaten face.

"My parents," she said. "My mamma gave it to me to protect me."

Suki then explained about that life-changing day at Taiji. Her body shuddered as she relived the experience.

McCready found it hard to comprehend how so much hurt and pain could be heaped on one so innocent.

When she had finished she looked at it sadly. "This is the first time I have ever taken it off," she said, looking at him.

He smiled at her, not wanting her to see the feelings that were running through him right now. He gently closed the locket and started to give it back to her.

"No," she said. "I want you to have it."

It was McCready who was now hesitant. "Suki, I can't. It's so precious to you."

He looked at her and she knew she was in love for the first time in her life.

She had never been with any man she had wanted to be with. She thought she never would. She slowly and very deliberately took the locket from him and placed it on the table at the side of the bed. She then reached up and put her arms around his neck and pulled him down on top of her, but she felt him resist.

"Suki, I can't. We shouldn't. You've been through too much."

He pulled gently away and sat on the side of the bed.

She looked up at him. She could see the torment in his eyes.

He looked at the floor for a moment, breathing deeply, before turning to her.

"I care about you more than you could possibly know. I would do anything in my power to protect you... but I can't do this. Not now."

The look he gave her of such love and affection melted her heart, and as much as she desperately wanted to sleep with him, she respected him more than ever for the way he was acting. She had never known anyone like him.

He started to stand.

"I'll go and sleep on the sofa."

At this, she jumped up, holding onto his arm.

"No, I will go. You are injured. You need to rest."

She could see he was about to protest, but she could also see he knew he needed to sleep. He hesitated for a moment and then slowly lay back on the bed. She pulled the thin sheet up around him and kissed him on the forehead.

"Sleep McCready."

She walked to the door. When she reached it, she turned briefly. There were three words she wanted to say to him, but his eyes were already closed.

She smiled a contented smile before turning away.

Suki made her way to the main room and lay down on the sofa. It was hot and she didn't need any covering to sleep. But her mind was so full of emotions and feelings she probably wouldn't have been able to anyway. All she could think about was McCready.

This man who was so assured, so in control. A man who wasn't cruel or rough, but gentle and tender, and at the same time, confident and strong.

She had never known she could feel like this.

After a few minutes she knew she couldn't be alone that night. She got up off the sofa and crept silently back to the bedroom. She watched him from the door for several minutes before crossing over to the bed and climbing in next to him.

Deep Impact

As Suki lay there, her arm around McCready, listening to his deep breathing and feeling her heart beat in time with his, she dared to dream. A dream that a life was possible, maybe with this man, maybe not. But a life free of pain and heartbreak.

Free of abuse and violence.

A normal life.

For once she felt truly at peace.

She had known love.

Chapter Thirty-Seven

Getting to Palau had been a long haul.

Clare had, of course, heard of the islands but had never actually considered where they were, and certainly not how you got there.

In the end it had involved three flights.

The first had taken her from LAX to Honolulu in Hawaii. Following a brief stop and change of plane, she had flown to Guam in the Western Pacific. The final flight would land at Palau's Roman Tmetuchi International Airport twenty hours after she had left Los Angeles.

The traveling, though, had given her time to think through many of the issues going on in her life right now.

On the job front, the potential was really interesting. She actually felt a thrill of excitement when she thought of the possibilities. Sometimes in life you needed a change and a new direction. You never knew what sort of opportunities could open up for you or where they might lead.

Along with the professional side of things, though, there

was her personal life to consider, and more specifically, Brad.

Everything she'd done with McCready had been incredible, certainly not your standard date experience. But had it been too much of a whirlwind? No time to catch her breath and think things through. She'd been so swept off her feet by what they'd been through together that she'd never really sat down to think about any long-term considerations. She did know, though, that he was a man of his word and a good soul, who only wanted to do the right thing. He was someone she could rely on.

But there was the dilemma.

She'd known Brad far longer and knew him more as a person than she did McCready. True, they were older, and in some ways different people now, but they were also wiser, had more life experience, and, given all that, she found herself being drawn back to him. The differences she saw as a positive. It would make it all the more interesting discovering each other again.

But, still, something nagged at her.

With McCready, she felt things would always be fresh and exciting. With Brad, she felt that while he would always love her and do right by her, maybe after the honeymoon period it could fall into more of a routine relationship. Not that there was necessarily anything wrong with that. In the end, neither was right or wrong, it was all about chemistry and how two human beings fitted together in the game called life.

As the cabin attendant made the announcement of their imminent arrival at Palau, she glanced out of the window and looked down onto an amazing landscape. It was starting to go dark, but the distinctive islands and lagoons of clear water were discernible from the plane.

She started to get butterflies in her stomach. She wasn't sure if it was because it was a new land, a new adventure, or if it was because of McCready. Either way, she didn't worry. All she had to do now was think of what she would say to him when she saw him. She smiled at the thought. She was sure he'd be pretty shocked to see her.

She just hoped it would be a good shock.

There'd been a slight delay before they could land. The pilot had said they had to abort the approach as some official VIP flight had been given priority. He'd sounded pretty annoyed, as though this had never happened before.

When they had finally touched down and were taxiing the short distance to the terminal, Clare had seen a medium-sized aircraft parked away from the main building. It was too big for a private jet but also wasn't a standard commercial aircraft. It had four engines slung beneath a top wing. It was white and the only distinctive marking was a Union Jack flag on the tail fin.

Parked next to it was a large gray military-looking helicopter. Its rotors were spinning at full speed. As her plane had pulled to a stop, she had seen the steps of the white plane drop to the ground. A man dressed in a dark suit, with a large backpack slung over his shoulder, had hurried over to the waiting chopper. He hadn't even looked around him, just made his way confidently to the side door of the helicopter. Once he was inside, in what seemed like only moments later, there had been a massive increase in engine noise and the giant machine had lifted off, heading away from the airport, out over the water to the south.

Once she'd disembarked, she'd quickly made her way through customs and collected her bag from baggage reclaim. It had taken another half hour to sort out the car hire, but then she'd sat in the car park with her phone. The first thing she'd done was check the website that showed McCready's position.

As the small dot had appeared on the map, she'd breathed a sigh of relief. At least the phone was no longer at the hospital. In fact, it wasn't far away on the same island, close to the water on the other side. She still didn't know if this would actually be McCready. She'd almost pressed the button to dial his number but hadn't wanted the awkwardness of speaking on the phone. Anyway, he might not have even answered. It was late after all.

No, she would do this face to face and have it out with him one way or another.

Now, as she approached the wooden door of the small shack among the trees, she wondered if she'd made the right decision. What could he be doing here?

But she had come this far.

She was about to knock on the door when she saw it was slightly ajar. She took a deep breath, pushed it slowly open, and walked inside.

"Hello?" she called out tentatively.

There was no response.

She moved into the room beyond the doorway. Glancing round, she noticed how small it was. There wasn't much furniture. There were two doorways on the wall facing her, which was illuminated by the moonlight coming in from the undraped windows at the front of the house. The right-hand door was closed. The one on the left was half open.

She walked toward it, stopped, and then after a moment of indecision, pushed it open further.

It squeaked as she did so.

Suki had slept better than she had in many years.

She had also dreamed.

She'd been living on a tropical island with a man she deeply cared about. They'd been using all its resources to survive. They weren't disturbed by anyone from the outside world and they were hopelessly in love with each other. Every day she would swim in a lagoon of turquoise water where a family of dolphins would come to her. They would spend the afternoon frolicking in the water before she would be joined by her man. They would make love in the water and then he would carry her back to their hut at the edge of the beach where he would hold her in his arms until she fell blissfully asleep. When she awoke she would look up into those piercing blue eyes and know that all was right in the world.

She was protected.

She was loved.

It was while she was luxuriating in his gaze that she heard a noise that didn't belong. It was a squeak, followed by a large intake of breath and a small cry.

Suki couldn't work out how these noises had got to the island, but her autonomic nervous system told her they needed investigating. Her internal system clicked into gear, did its job, and made her open her eyes.

She was brought back down to earth with a crash.

She lay on the bed, naked, her arm wrapped tightly around McCready. It was still hot, even for the middle of the night, and the single sheet was thrown back, lying half on the floor.

Standing in front of her, in the moonlight, was a

woman. She was dressed in lightweight shorts and a white polo shirt with a red collar. She was currently staring at Suki, her hand over her mouth.

Suki quickly pulled the discarded sheet over herself and McCready.

"Who are you?" she said angrily.

The woman just stood there, seemingly in shock.

"I... I've made a terrible mistake."

Suki saw that she couldn't take her eyes off McCready's sleeping form.

Suki shook McCready's shoulder. "McCready! McCready! Wake up!"

McCready groaned and rolled over. He lifted his head from the pillow and propped himself up on one elbow. For a second he was startled to see Suki was in bed with him, but was then more concerned as to why's she had woken him.

"What is it?" he asked. "You okay?"

Suki didn't take her eyes of the woman. "Look!" she said.

McCready squinted and rubbed some sleep from his eyes. He then glanced up and saw the woman. His mouth literally fell open.

"Clare?"

Suki looked at him. "You know her?" she said, incredulously.

McCready ignored her. "What... what are you doing here?"

Suki pulled the sheet around her. She was looking between the two, a horrified expression on her face.

McCready eased himself up and pulled on some shorts.

"I came to find you," Clare said eventually. The shock was starting to wear off to be rapidly replaced by a growing mixture of confusion and anger. "You never returned my calls, my messages. I didn't know if something had happened to you. I found out you were in a hospital and came to see if I could help. But"—she glanced at the girl—"it seems you have all the help you need."

At this, she turned and strode from the room.

"What is this? Who is she?" asked Suki nervously.

"Stay here!" said McCready.

He ran into the living room, but Clare was already out of the front door.

McCready raced outside.

Clare was at the car door.

"Clare! Clare, wait! I can explain." He realized as soon as he said it that it was a stupid thing to say. It was what all guys said when there was clearly no satisfactory explanation. He ran forward and tripped on a loose plank. He cursed, hobbling toward the car.

Clare was inside now.

She'd started the engine.

The lights flicked on. The engine overrevved as she tried to get it into gear. McCready had to jump back as she finally hit first and the car leaped forward, the rear tires spinning in the loose earth. She just managed to turn the wheel in time to miss one of the trees at the edge of the clearing.

As the car shot past, he had time to see her turn and look at him. Their eyes locked briefly. He could see there were tears in hers. And then she was gone, the bright red glow of the taillights illuminating him as she disappeared into the night.

He stood there for a moment, shock written across his face. He wasn't sure what to do. He couldn't go after her—

he had no idea where she'd gone—and he had to try and explain things to Suki. He turned back to the shack.

Once inside, he took a deep breath and walked into the bedroom.

Suki was sitting on the bed, her arms wrapped tightly around her knees. She watched him as he came over and sat on the bed next to her. Her eyes were moist. She looked frightened and lost again.

He took one look at her and put his arms around her, holding her close. He soothingly rubbed her back and stroked her hair. Then he sat back and looked straight into her eyes.

"Who was that?" she said, the words barely making it from her lips. "Was that your woman?"

McCready took a deep breath.

"She is a friend. We have shared things, yes, but, no, I would not say that she was 'my woman.'"

At this, a flicker of hope crossed Suki's face, but it was gone almost as quickly. "I have been bad," she said, her head dropping to avert his gaze. "I have brought you trouble."

McCready gently reached for her chin and raised her head so she was looking straight into his eyes.

"You've done nothing wrong," he said simply.

As she looked at him, she could see he was telling the truth. With any other man she wouldn't have believed him, but here, now, with McCready, whatever else happened, somehow she knew that to be true.

"I have a complicated relationship with her," said McCready eventually. "We have been through a lot together, but sometimes that isn't enough. Sometimes that doesn't mean it will work out. I will explain to her. Maybe she will understand. Maybe she will not. But right now, here with you is where I want to be. Okay?"

Suki nodded slowly. She put her arms around him and they lay down together.

She wished she could be back on the island.

But there were dreams and then there was reality.

Chapter Thirty-Eight

After she'd left the shack in the trees, Clare's head had been spinning.

She'd barely been able to concentrate on the road or where she was going. The hotel she'd booked was back on the larger island not far from the airport. She almost missed the turn but then noticed a sign at the last second, screeching tires as she skidded across the road.

Once she reached the hotel she sat in the car for ten whole minutes trying to compose herself.

This wasn't what she'd expected to find when she'd embarked on the trip.

She took deep breaths, trying to steady her nerves, get herself under control. She looked at her hands.

They still gripped the wheel.

They were shaking.

Out of all the scenarios that had run through her mind as to how she would find him and what he'd been doing, this had never even been on the radar.

She simply didn't know what to do.

The sensible thing would be to try to talk to him. Try to understand this. In her heart she had thought he was a decent person. Someone who would not, without good reason, behave in the way he appeared to be behaving. One of the things that had drawn her to him was his almost pathological need to always do the right thing, regardless of the consequences. Now, though, she didn't know what to think. It was as though she didn't know him at all.

Slowly, her mind started to function again.

Bottom line—whatever he was doing, he hadn't seen fit to talk to her. He hadn't replied to any of her messages, and she could not, for the life of her, think of any rational explanation he might have that would satisfy her. And to think she'd forgone letting things develop with Brad because something at the back of her mind had made her think in some way that she was being disloyal to McCready.

Fuck him!

She didn't owe him anything.

With that, and the thought of a strong brandy from the hotel minibar, she climbed out of the car, grabbed her bag and made her way to the reception.

The sun would be up in a couple of hours. She needed to get some sleep before deciding what to do next.

Martin Steel looked out over the short runway from the control tower as the first light of dawn sent fingers of light crawling across the sky.

He'd barely slept in the last twenty-four hours, keeping going on caffeine and adrenaline. He lived for moments like this, when the pressure was on and the decisions he made could have life-changing consequences for millions of people. Every day the balance could tip: in your favor—not in your favor. It was a tightrope he walked between success and failure, where the outcome wasn't a lost business deal or a failed interview, but the fate of a nation.

He never felt more alive than at times like these.

He took another sip of coffee and looked out of the stormproof windows that surrounded the control tower. Below him he could see the giant gray Merlin helicopter that had brought him here the previous evening. Its massive rotors were now swept back in line, facing the rear of the machine. She was parked at the side of the runway. As he looked over to his left he could see an F-35 Lightning II readying for takeoff. It was a training sortie, coupled with a show of force for those who might be watching.

A couple of seconds later the engine noise changed in pitch. A man standing to the side of the jet made some specific signals to the pilot, and after a sweep of his arm, the engine pitch ratcheted up a notch further and the plane tore off down the runway. As it reached the end it shot up the colloquially known ski jump that would give it the airspeed to make it off the flight deck of the massive aircraft carrier.

The ski-jump at the front of the flight deck enabled HMS *Queen Elizabeth*, the United Kingdom's latest carrier, to launch vertical takeoff aircraft in a way that conserved fuel by giving them a boost up into the sky to create air speed and the necessary lift to get them into the air. It meant the carrier didn't have to have the complicated machinery of catapults and arresters to launch and recover aircraft, thereby saving cost, weight and repair issues when things went wrong.

She had been commissioned in 2017 at a cost of over three billion pounds to the British taxpayer. She was one of two; her sister ship HMS *Prince of Wales* was launched in

December 2017 and commissioned in 2020. They would form the backbone of the Royal Navy for decades to come.

The carrier was over 900 feet long, with a beam of 240 feet. As well as the distinctive ski jump at the bow, it was unique in that it had two 'islands,' or control towers, from which the operations of the ship were run. One was concerned with navigation and piloting, the second was responsible for the aerial and defense capability.

And this was formidable.

She carried 36 STOVL F-35B Lightning II jets, the vertical takeoff variant of the F-35. Built in America by Lockheed Martin, they had the latest stealth technology and could fly at over 1200 miles per hour. Along with this awesome firepower, the *Queen Elizabeth* also carried a number of Merlin and Wildcat helicopters, as well as numerous small watercraft she could put to sea when required.

"Beautiful sight," said Captain Paul Hargreaves.

"She certainly is," replied Steel, not taking his eyes off the flight deck. He watched as a second F35 lined up for takeoff.

Hargreaves waited until the jet had sped down the runway and into the air before turning to Steel.

"So, what's the plan?"

Steel glanced at him.

Hargreaves was just as he had imagined after seeing him on the video screen at the Cobra meeting: tall, weather-beaten and with a crown of neat white hair. A man of experience. A man with morals, and above all, a man who liked to get things done. He was currently wearing navy-issue summer fatigues consisting of a short-sleeved white shirt and long shorts. He had forgone the captain's hat and would never wear a baseball cap, as was so prevalent among American captains.

"Firstly," said Steel, "I'm sorry for the loss of the crew of *Resilient*. This whole operation has got out of hand. It was always going to be risky with the Russians, and while I'm not at liberty to explain all the details, I would never have believed they would take such action. It's effectively an act of war, but one that has to be handled behind the scenes, not going off on some public knee-jerk reaction. You do that, you end up involving every protest group and nutjob that objects to anything. They all come out of the woodwork. Those days have long gone. We handle things the right way now, behind closed doors, minimal publicity."

"I couldn't agree with you more," said Hargreaves.

"Before we can do anything…" continued Steel, "we need to debrief McCready. Hopefully that'll happen later today. We need to know exactly what happened. He's also supposed to be recovering the drive." He paused. "At least there's some good news. That emergency beacon you investigated—nice work."

"Thanks," said Hargreaves, smiling thinly.

Steel knew it wouldn't make up for the loss of the crew of a nuclear submarine but every positive was a win in these sorts of situations.

Chapter Thirty-Nine

When McCready and Suki awoke there was an awkwardness between them.

The events and emotion of the previous night had drained even McCready, so he could only imagine how Suki must be feeling.

They got up and dressed with barely a word spoken.

He had wanted to leave early, put some distance between them and the house, in case Ivanov found them, but as no one had turned up yet, he thought there was at least time for breakfast.

As McCready wolfed down some fresh fruit, toast and jam, Suki took a shower.

He used the opportunity to call Clare. He had no idea what he would say to her to explain things. It might even be better to leave it until everything was over and he was back in the UK, when she would have had time to get over the emotions she would currently be feeling. The problem with that, was it would also give her time to draw her own conclusions about any future they might have had together.

Deep Impact

Something that right now was non-existent. A fact confirmed when any attempt to call her phone received a BLOCKED message.

He put the phone back on the sideboard next to the drive that had caused so much trouble. He noticed Suki's locket lying there. He picked it up and looked at the dolphin motifs on either side. He knew how much it meant to her and that it was something she would never willingly part with. He looked between the drive and the locket and came to a decision. It revolved around a piece of equipment Craig had given him on the Globemaster—his idea to give them an edge over Steel. He knew the decision might get him into trouble down the line, but that was the future, and they had to get there first. Right now, he cared a whole lot more about Suki than he did about the drive.

He went to his backpack and put the drive inside. He then picked up his phone and removed a small square piece of plastic from a pocket in the case. It was half an inch by half an inch, embedded with electronics, and about as thick as a coin. It was also very light and had a thin sliver of metal on one side that was magnetic.

Next, he went to the sideboard and picked up the locket.

Five minutes later Suki emerged from the shower looking fresh and revived. There was a sparkle of life in her that he hadn't seen earlier. Maybe she too had been thinking about things. She came over to him, a towel wrapped around her body, her shoulders and hair glistening with droplets of water. She put her arms around him and hugged him tightly. She then took his face in her hands and kissed him. Not a long, deep kiss, but one that showed love and affection.

Before she disappeared into the bedroom, McCready picked up the locket from the sideboard.

"You know, your mother was right. You should always wear this. It will protect you."

"But I gave it to you."

"And now I'm giving it back." His tone was fatherly and his expression showed he wouldn't take no for an answer.

She pouted, glanced at the leaping dolphin, and then looked deep into his eyes, as though realizing the symbolism of this. She then offered him the back of her neck, inviting him to attach it for her. McCready did so, squeezing her shoulder when it was secure. She turned around and smiled. "I have to get dressed," she said, but there was a touch of sadness in her eyes. She then disappeared into the bedroom, closing the door behind.

"Don't be long. We have to leave," he shouted after her.

McCready returned to his breakfast. He needed some more jam for his toast. He stood up, walked over to the small cupboard above the sink, grabbed the jar, and then sat back down at the table. He was just unscrewing the lid when there was a massive CRASH from behind.

He spun round.

The front door had been torn from its hinges. Standing in the doorway was Major Yuri Ivanov.

Before McCready could move, Ivanov had entered the room with two other men, all dressed in black.

There was no escape.

Ivanov had his weapon drawn. McCready could see neat revolvers in holsters around the waists of the other two. One of them checked the bathroom and then the bedroom. He emerged dragging a screaming Suki behind him. She was hurriedly pulling on a T-shirt. Once in the room, the man held her in a firm grip in front of him. She stared at McCready, trembling. Fear in her eyes. He looked back at her with such a relaxed and confident expression that it went some way to calming her down.

Ivanov scanned the room. His gaze ended on Suki. "Well, what do we have here? I take it you were the girl in the watercraft?"

She said nothing.

"Never mind." He turned to McCready, glancing at the bandaged shoulder. "Bad shot. Sorry, I'm not normally so sloppy."

"What do you want?" asked McCready.

"You know what I want. Where is it?"

"I don't know what you're talking about?"

Ivanov sighed. "You can play games if you want, but I will find the answer one way or another. I don't know how much pain you can stand, or what training you've had, but I will break you."

"I've had no training, but I don't know what you want."

At this, Ivanov raised an eyebrow. "So which branch of the military are you?"

"Not military," said McCready. "Just a civilian."

Ivanov seemed to find this curious. He nodded at one of his men. The man moved behind McCready. He grabbed his arms, pinning them behind his back. McCready struggled, but it was useless.

Ivanov moved forward, fixing McCready in his stare. "As I'm sure you realize, there are two ways we can do this."

McCready returned the stare evenly.

Ivanov reached forward and took hold of McCready's injured shoulder. As he squeezed, McCready gritted his teeth, a sharp release of breath issuing from his mouth. Suki strained at her captor's grip. A cry came from her lips.

"This can get much worse," said Ivanov. "Just tell me where the drive is and we need go no further."

McCready looked at him. "Like I said, I've no idea what you're talking about. I was on a ship. It capsized in the typhoon. As far as I know all the crew were lost. I managed to make it to the raft. That's where the girl found me. It's as simple as that."

Ivanov looked at him condescendingly. "Wearing a submarine escape suit?"

He glanced away and then spun back, hurling a fist into McCready's stomach. McCready gasped from the impact. He fought to try to get a breath. Ivanov followed up with three more equally vicious punches. McCready cried out and fell to the floor.

"McCready!" cried Suki, trying to run to him, but she was held fast.

Ivanov looked at Suki. He walked over to her. She tried to squirm away but the hold the man had on her was solid.

Ivanov gripped her jaw in his hand, forcing her to look at him. She cringed, trying to avert her eyes, but he slapped her hard across the face. He traced his finger along the length of her scar. "Good, you know what pain is like. You will feel more, much more."

Suki tried to struggle. A tear fell down her cheek.

"You bastard!" said McCready.

Ivanov ripped her T-shirt down the front, leaving her chest naked and exposed. She tried to turn away but was unable.

The Russian glanced round the room until his gaze fell on a large kitchen knife by the sink. He picked it up and returned to Suki. "I think there should be a matching scar on your chest, don't you agree? Just to even things up."

Suki whimpered as the steel tip of the knife touched the middle of her chest between her breasts.

"Leave her alone," said McCready, without raising his voice. "Or I promise you, you *will* regret it."

Ivanov glanced at him, vague amusement on his face.

"She knows nothing of this," continued McCready. "She's innocent. Let her go."

"I don't think so," said Ivanov. "She was responsible for the death of one of my men. I think she and I are going to spend some quality time together before this is over."

The look he gave Suki made the hairs on the back of McCready's neck stand on end.

"First though," said Ivanov, "I need the drive." The point of the knife was still on Suki's chest. A small dribble of blood made its way from the contact point down her smooth skin. "You do what I want or else this knife goes on a painful journey around this beautiful body."

To make his point he applied pressure to the blade, drawing it a couple of inches down Suki's chest. The blood flowed more strongly now.

She cried out in pain and looked imploringly at McCready.

He had to make a decision. The stakes were huge. If it had been only him, he could have handled it. But it wasn't, and he knew he really didn't have a choice.

His jaw tightened. "Okay, you win."

Ivanov nodded at the man holding McCready and he loosened his grip. McCready staggered forward. He crossed over to his backpack and pulled out the small enclosure holding the drive and gave it to Ivanov.

Ivanov looked at it. He then nodded to himself and put it in a small bag he produced from his pocket. He turned to the man holding Suki.

"Take her!"

The man hustled Suki from the room. She screamed,

kicking her legs in the air, trying anything to break free, but it was no good. The man clamped his hand over her mouth to lessen the noise.

As she was dragged from the room, the last thing McCready focused on was the small, precious locket around her neck. And then the door was closed and all he could hear were her muffled cries as she was taken away.

The other man grabbed McCready again. He found himself back in the vice-like grip.

"So, what, you just kill me now?"

Ivanov looked at him. "Oh no. You will not be so lucky."

"What then?"

Ivanov smiled, moving close to McCready's ear. "Be in no doubt that I know how to treat girls like that. I know what to do to them to make them give me pleasure. She will know pain like she has never felt before. It will not be quick. It will not even be slow. It will take days until I tire of her, and then, when I have, she will die slowly. I will enjoy every moment of it. But you know what I will enjoy even more? Knowing that when you wake up you will know what is going to happen to her and you will know there is nothing you can do about it. You will live with that knowledge for the rest of your life. And the worst thing will be that you will know it was all your fault."

He nodded to the man holding McCready. The man took his gun from a holster and smashed McCready across the back of the skull.

His world went black before he even hit the floor.

Chapter Forty

When John McCready came to, it was to a world of pain, despair, and the sound of a ringing phone.

He was lying on the floor. At first he had no idea where he was. All he knew was that he had a blistering headache and his shoulder felt like someone was ramming a nail into it. He glanced briefly down and saw blood oozing onto his shirt.

He slowly managed to sit up, but even that caused him pain. He looked around and it all started to come back. And along with the memory came a feeling he'd never felt in his life before: a blinding overwhelming tidal wave of shame and disgust at what he had allowed to happen. It was a feeling of such extreme helplessness that he didn't recognize the man he appeared to be.

Seared into his mind was the image of Suki being dragged from the building screaming and kicking, a look of sheer terror on her face.

He had let her down in the most horrible way imaginable.

And then there was Clare.

Her expression as she had driven away—one of confusion, shock, and, above all, complete disappointment in him—only added to the pain.

It was this that jolted him properly awake. He pushed himself off the floor and grabbed the phone before the caller rang off.

He hit ANSWER.

"Clare! Clare!"

There was silence for a moment, and then the slightly puzzled, but calm, voice of Martin Steel came over the line.

"Not when I last checked. John, how are you? We need to talk."

McCready stared out of the small, oval window in the side of the Merlin helicopter as they swept over the reefs that bordered the south of the islands.

As he looked down it was as though onto another world—one of fun, recreation, beauty, things that were currently absent from his life, and, as far as he felt right now, would be so for as long as he lived.

Steel had told him not to explain anything over the phone. He'd asked him where he was and had said he would send a helicopter for him. They'd agreed a pickup point: the flat concrete dock where he had disembarked from the water taxi had seemed as good as any. Half an hour later he had been waiting as the giant machine had come in to land. The rotor wash had sent dust flying and loose rubbish scurrying into the air.

He had climbed aboard and was now heading out to sea.

Before he'd gone to the dock he'd searched in vain

around the vicinity of the shack in case there was any sign of Suki, but he knew in his heart she was gone, lost to the monster that was Major Yuri Ivanov. He knew in no uncertain terms that the man would do exactly what he said he was going to do, and there was no way he could stop him. He had been right: McCready would think about this for the rest of his life. He would never know peace. He had always thought there was nothing in life that could break him, no problem he couldn't solve if he applied himself.

But this... this was something he'd never imagined.

And just as he tried to reassure himself that things couldn't get any worse, his thoughts turned to Craig Richards.

He realized he was at the lowest point he had ever been in his life. He was starting a slow descent into a hell of his own making and there was no way he could ever see to possibly claw his way back out.

John McCready was a man who didn't cry, but right now tears formed in his eyes and started to run down his face.

Fifteen minutes later, as he tried to wipe the thoughts from his mind, McCready saw an object appear in the distance on the ocean. It was joined by a number of others, all ships. Behind these, a larger object appeared. It was standing proud of the water and was huge. As they drew closer it slowly came into focus. He found himself staring at one of the most impressive ships he had ever seen.

A couple of minutes later the Merlin came in to land on the massive flight deck.

McCready jumped down at the bidding of a young naval rating on the deck. The noise of the rotors screamed down from above. He ducked low as he was escorted to the second of the two islands on the starboard side of the ship.

Once inside, the noise quietened as the door closed behind him.

"If you could follow me, please, sir," said the rating who had met him on the deck.

It was the first time anyone had called McCready 'sir' in a long time.

He followed the man down into the ship, through a labyrinthine network of passages and steep metal stairs, until they came to a door at the end of a corridor. The rating opened it and ushered McCready inside.

"If you could just wait here, please, sir."

"Thanks," said McCready as the rating turned and left.

He looked around him.

He was in a small meeting room. Judging by the route they'd taken they were at least three decks below the flight deck. There were no portholes, but given the angle of one of the walls, they must be up against the side of the ship. The far wall was covered with shelves, which had books and charts stacked on them. At one end was a serviceable sofa. A long table filled most of the center of the room. Six chairs were arranged around it. It looked as though the room had been in recent use as the chairs were scattered in a haphazard fashion, not neatly aligned against the table.

A couple of minutes later the door opened. McCready turned and saw Martin Steel standing there. He carried a compact laptop. He entered the room and offered his hand.

McCready didn't take it.

"Like I said before, you son of a bitch!"

Steel moved to the far side and sat down, putting the laptop on the table.

"Sit down, John."

He pulled up a chair. They sat watching each other for a few moments.

"Okay, I deserved that," said Steel after a while. "But I make no apologies. As I've said before, I'll do whatever it takes to protect the country. Sometimes that means making unpalatable decisions. I don't expect you to understand, but that's the reality of the world we live in today. Now, we need to go through what happened. And I need that drive. I hope you have it."

"You cost my friend his life, not to mention many other things that have happened since." McCready's stare was unwavering. "Why should I give you anything?"

Steel sighed and looked at McCready, weighing up what to do.

"Okay," he said. "This might go better if you come with me." He noticed McCready's shoulder. The blood staining his shirt. "Looks like you could do with some attention for that as well."

"Where are we going?"

"Medical. Follow me."

Steel led him from the small room and out into the corridor.

Five minutes later, during which time McCready had become hopelessly lost, Steel showed him into what could only be described as a mini hospital, complete with consultation and treatment rooms, resuscitation and theater facilities, even a dental surgery.

There were also twelve bed spaces.

They walked into the ward from the reception area. None of the beds were occupied, that McCready could see, but there was a screen drawn around a bed in the far corner.

"At the end," said Steel, pointing. "I'll wait here."

McCready glanced at him curiously, hesitant.

"Go on," said Steel.

McCready slowly walked down the room, past the empty beds and up to the sectioned-off area. He finally reached it and with a glance back at Steel, walked around the screen.

The sight that greeted him stopped him in his tracks.

Chapter Forty-One

The area was small.

In it was a single bed, next to which was a monitor with a screen displaying heart rate and other medical information. On the far side was a small table. There was a glass of orange juice sitting on it, as well as a number of bottles and pills.

A nurse, wearing the standard dark blue pants and short-sleeved tunic of the Royal Navy, tended to the patient in the bed. He was sitting up but was connected to the monitoring equipment and had a drip in his arm. He was currently about to take a mouthful of what looked like chicken soup from a bowl on a tray across his knees.

As McCready walked in, the patient looked up.

"What the hell are you doing here?" said McCready.

He stood there, staring at Craig Richards, unable to believe his eyes.

"Well," said Richards. "When you get left on the bottom of the ocean, with no hope of rescue, you have to make your own arrangements!" He grinned at McCready.

McCready was lost for words, but then he moved forward to sit on the end of the bed. "How? What? What the hell happened?"

The nurse picked up an empty cup from the tray and spoke to Richards. "Now, Craig, don't forget to take your pills after your soup. I'll come back to check on you later. If you feel up to it you can go for a walk, okay?" She smiled at him before turning to leave, nodding at McCready as she went.

"Thanks, Cindy," said Richards. "I'll look forward to it," he called after her.

"Oh God, don't tell me we're going to have a sub called 'Cindy' next?" said McCready.

Richards put on an inscrutable expression.

"Craig, how the hell did you get out of there? If there had been anything I could have done, you know…"

Richards just looked at his friend. "You couldn't. There was nothing you could have done. And I'm fine with that. The escape suits should have been checked earlier. But it doesn't matter now."

"But how?" persisted McCready.

"Well," started Richards, "I had a bit of time on my hands." McCready rolled his eyes. "And I got to thinking. As well as the one-man raft you took up with the suit, we had the other two on the outside of the sub for *Resilient's* crew." McCready was listening intently. "I managed to get enough power for the manipulators to bring the rafts round in front of the dome and attach them to the main frame. It was then just a matter of pulling the inflation cords. There was enough buoyancy to get off the bottom, and then, of course, they expanded on the way up.

"From then it was easy. On the surface I set off the emergency beacon and waited. At least I was protected in the sub from the storm. Not exactly pleasant. Never been so sick in my life, but after a while there's nothing more to come out. It was just a matter of waiting to see if anyone picked up the signal. Must admit, didn't expect the whole sodding navy to turn up, but beggars can't be choosers."

McCready could hardly believe it. As he leaned forward to hug his old friend his eyes became moist again. He needed some good news right now.

"God, it's good to see you."

"So, how'd it go your end? You still have the drive, yeah?"

McCready was silent for a moment.

"A lot's happened, Craig. We'll talk later. Right now I have to go through things with Steel... God damn it's good to see you!"

And with that he left and walked out of the ward.

For the first time that day a brief glimmer of hope for his salvation crept into his soul.

Half an hour later, after one of the doctors had attended to McCready's shoulder and dressed the knife wound in his leg, he was back in the small meeting room opposite Steel.

"Better now?" asked Steel.

McCready looked at him, a sense of relief in his eyes.

"Yes, thanks."

"Okay, take it from the top."

When McCready had finished, Steel eased himself back in his chair, deep in thought. Eventually he looked up. "I'm aware of Major Ivanov. His prints are all over this with the use of the gas. That's gone far beyond normal encounters with the Russians and will not go unpunished. The boats that followed and attacked you will almost certainly have come from one of their new special forces' submersibles—most likely their latest called *Blackfin*. It has a cavitation drive that allows unprecedented speed while submerged. If that's the case, he'll be long gone by now. There'll be no way to get the drive back." He paused, thinking. "Okay, that concludes your involvement in the operation. I know it hasn't gone as you expected. And you may not believe this, but I am grateful for your efforts." He then looked straight at McCready. "For the record, John, would you have gone if you knew about the Russians?"

There was a slight pause.

"I guess we'll never know."

Steel nodded slowly, a wry smile on his face.

He stood up, about to leave. McCready remained seated.

"What about the girl?" he asked.

"What about the girl?"

"We can't just abandon her. She saved my life."

"She also stole the drive from you. If it hadn't been for her, we'd probably have it in our possession." He hesitated slightly as he said this. McCready didn't think anything of it.

"I have to find her," he said.

Steel stopped and turned to him. "And just how do you plan on doing that?"

"There might be a way, but I would need your help."

Steel sighed. "John, go home. Your work here is done. Forget the girl. You'll never find her, and if you do she'll probably be dead. This is a military operation now."

"I can't let it go."

"If you try and do something, you may make a critical situation even worse. You don't know what you're dealing with. I can't allow it. In fact, if you persist with this we may have to rethink our arrangement with regard to that wall you have at the rear of your house."

Steel's tone had changed. McCready could tell that any slack he'd been accorded for his and Richards' help was fast evaporating.

He thought for a moment, then said, resignedly, "Okay, I'll leave it alone. Can you arrange for a ride back to the island?"

Steel looked at him thoughtfully. "One hour on the flight deck."

And with that, Steel left the room.

The hangar deck of HMS *Queen Elizabeth* was vast. It occupied the size of two football pitches. It was where the aircraft were kept during bad weather and where they were serviced and repaired. Right now, McCready, and a still rather weak Craig Richards, were leaning against a railing at the edge of the massive forward lift that took aircraft from the hangar up to the flight deck. Further along the hangar, the battered hull of *Emily* was parked against the side.

"I still can't believe you made it," said McCready.

"It was touch and go," agreed Richards. "Better not be that close next time."

McCready gave him a look, but then his face turned serious. "I lost the drive, Craig, but more importantly, I let a girl, who saved my life, be taken by one of the most evil men I've ever met. He's going to torture and kill her."

Richards remained quiet, letting his friend say everything he needed to say.

"I have a million to one shot of doing something about this."

Richards looked up at him.

"On the sub I never had time to put the tracker you gave me in the drive. When I knew there was the possibility of the Russians finding us, I had to make a decision, one based on everything I believed to be right at the time." Richards watched him carefully. "I put the tracker in a locket the girl wears around her neck. I need you to tell me how to track it. Range, signal strength, frequency, any equipment I need. Anything you can."

Richards said nothing. He was thinking.

"This is the most important thing I've ever asked of you," said McCready.

When Richards looked into McCready's eyes, he knew he wasn't lying. He had never seen him like this. Something had changed in his friend, and it wasn't for the better. That carefree, fix-anything side of him appeared to have gone. In its place was a colder, harder man who seemed to have lost something. He was worried for him. He knew if he helped him it might mean the end of his life. He knew McCready would go to the ends of the Earth to find the girl. What would happen if he found her was anyone's guess. But it wouldn't end well.

Richards took a deep breath. McCready wouldn't like what he had to say, but he wasn't the only one who tried to do the right thing.

"John," he started, "you'll never find her. And if you do, what could you do? If she isn't already dead she'll be with this man, and if he's as bad as you say he is, what chance would you have?"

McCready didn't answer. He just stared at the water passing below the ship as it frothed and foamed with the passage of the hull.

"If I tell you how to track it you'll end up dead. It's as

simple as that. This girl is gone. You can't save her. Why not live for something you can save. Call Clare. Go back to your life."

"I can't call Clare."

"Why not?"

"She was here. She's probably over there somewhere." He nodded at the islands in the distance. Richards was confused. "She came to see how I was. She found the girl in bed with me."

Richards was shocked.

"It's not what you think. The girl's position was so helpless. She was in such despair…"

"So you had to sleep with her?" Richards said incredulously. There was a tinge of anger in his voice.

"Nothing happened. Really. Nothing happened. It's impossible to explain. But you know me Craig. I had my reasons."

"Maybe I don't know you anymore," Richards said quietly.

"So will you help me?" McCready said, rather too sharply.

Richards glanced at him. "I can't, John. Not this time. That sub crew died. I nearly died. If you do this, you will die. I can't have that on my conscience. How many more have to die before enough is enough."

McCready stared straight at him.

"Just one."

With that he turned and walked over to meet the rating who was heading their way.

Richards watched him go. As he did, he shook his head. Why were things always so complicated with McCready?

He stared at the water for a while, his mind wrestling with a decision. It was one he didn't want to make, but somewhere deep inside, despite his objections, he'd always known he would.

He had, at least, had to try.

He pulled out his phone. He typed a brief text message, then put it back in his pocket—out of sight, out of mind.

He wondered if it was the last time he would ever see his friend.

It had been difficult, but Clare had been able to come to only one decision, and that was, that right now she couldn't deal with everything. Maybe in a few days, a few weeks, she didn't know, but now all she wanted to do was get the hell out of there.

After sleeping late she'd told the hotel to cancel her three-day reservation; she had to return to the States for a family emergency. She had then called the airline and managed to get a flight out the same day.

Now, as she sat in her first-class seat—she needed something to comfort her—she leaned back as the Boeing 787 Dreamliner thundered down the runway.

As the plane rose into the air, the lush green vegetation of the island dropped away, and they were soon out over the azure sea.

She wished she'd been able to stay longer, but it wasn't to be.

As they banked round to line up on the flightpath for Guam, she noticed the gray military helicopter she'd seen on the runway the night before heading back to the island. Ahead, she could make out a number of naval ships in formation. A large aircraft carrier was in the center of the group. She saw it had a strange design with two large towers on its starboard side. She thought it was unusual, but then turned her attention to the in-flight entertainment.

She needed something to take her mind off the events of the last twelve hours.

The Merlin helicopter was about to come in to land on the small dock when McCready's phone pinged, telling him he had an incoming text. He clicked on the notification, opening the app.

He read the message. There was little more than a small line of information. But it was the most critical information he had ever received.

It was the listening frequency for the tracker around Suki's neck. Other than that, the only words in the message were—GOOD LUCK, C.

Thank you, Craig, McCready said to himself as he jumped down from the chopper onto the concrete. He waved to the crew. The helicopter immediately lifted off, heading back out to sea.

Before he left the dock, he reopened the message app, selected another number, and typed a brief yet succinct message.

PLAN B - GO.

Six thousand miles away, in the Aberdeen Royal Infirmary, a nurse made her way along a corridor to the private room at the end.

She was in more control of herself now, as the two men behind the door had seemed to have calmed down somewhat. She thought it must have been the actions of the man who had come to see them a few days previously. However, since then, she'd detected a slight rise in tension, particularly when the Englishman had been told he would be there for another few weeks and the Scotsman had been told he could leave in a few days.

So there were, at least, a few more days of bickering. She was sure she would be able to cope, though. She had three children, after all, who, while aged between four and ten, and undoubtedly had higher IQs than the men in the room, were still a handful.

She opened the door prepared for anything she might see…

…except for what she did see.

The Englishman was sitting up in bed reading a newspaper, a big smile on his face.

The other bed was completely empty.

She rather pointlessly checked behind the door and under the bed and then glanced at the Englishman.

"Where is he?"

At this the Englishman carried on reading, and with a superior tone, which was quite difficult in an East End accent, said cheerily, "He's gone."

"But he can't leave until he has the all clear."

The Englishman was still reading. "Ah, but what did I tell you, never trust a Scotsman. Unreliable, that's what I always said, but no one listened."

"I'll have you know, Mr. Porter, that I'm Scottish and proud of it."

At this, Porter dropped one corner of the newspaper to glance at her. "Yes, luv, but you're a Scottish *woman*. Whole different ballgame."

"Well thank you. At least that's something."

"Whole different set of problems," said Porter from behind the paper.

The nurse glared at him.

"Did he say anything?"

"Well, it's always difficult to understand a word he says, but he got this text, then, quick as you like, packed his things and left. He may have uttered a 'bye,' but I couldn't be sure."

"I'll have to report this," said the nurse.

"Probably a good idea," said Porter.

Once the nurse had closed the door behind her, Porter dropped the paper and leaned back on the bed. He put his arms behind his head. The smile grew even wider.

"Peace at last."

McCready took a deep breath, looked around the dock, and then slung the small backpack across his good shoulder.

He could feel a sense of his soul returning. Never again would he allow himself to fall to such a low, but never again would he allow himself to screw up so badly.

There was maybe one way out of this, but it would involve doing something he'd promised himself he would never do.

He glanced down at the Breitling watch around his wrist.

There was no other choice.

Chapter Forty-Two

Since the opening of the Suez Canal, linking the Mediterranean to the Red Sea, in 1869, the 120-mile-long waterway had become a vital artery in the road map of international shipping routes. Cutting the distance from the North Atlantic to the Indian Ocean by over 3,700 miles, it had seen its usage grow from its inauguration year, where less than five hundred ships made the journey, to the present day, where nearly twenty thousand ships used the canal.

In all that time, more than a few of the ships traveling through the Red Sea never made it beyond its desert borders. They were unfortunate victims, confined to the bottom of the clear waters through acts of war, errors of navigation, or at the hands of merciless storms. These gales, which sprang up out of nowhere, swept the hapless vessels onto dangerous reefs, whose jagged clutches lay just below the surface like rows of malevolent teeth lying in wait.

One such wreck was the *SS Aurelia*, a 250-foot steam sailing ship. She had been commissioned by King Alfonso XIII of Spain and had been returning from the Far East, laden with treasure and gifts for the monarch. Unfortunately, as far as people could tell, she had been boarded by pirates off the coast of Eritrea. At the same time, she had encountered one of the fiercest storms in living memory. It had blown the ship northward. She had ultimately foundered on a reef that wasn't shown on any chart.

She went down with all hands.

As she had been in the hands of pirates at the time, no position of the loss had ever been recorded. However, a memo found in a pile of documents from the ship's insurers, bought at auction in 1998 by an American treasure hunter, Red Stanmore, threatened to throw some light on things. It documented witnesses from the shore, stating that a ship, matching a description of the *Aurelia*, had sunk off the coast of Saudi Arabia around that time.

Stanmore had immediately put together a team to survey the southern Red Sea. He had searched the area for over a year with no success.

As the search had continued, and his funds dwindled, he had turned to a contact in the Saudi royal family to inject some much-needed cash. Prince Khalid Amir Yassin was known to indulge in exciting and unusual adventures, much to the chagrin and disapproval of his family. He had agreed to come on board under condition of complete discretion.

Eventually, a target that matched the approximate length of the *Aurelia*, and in the approximate area where she could have sunk, was found in around six hundred feet of water. The only problem was that she was in Egyptian waters. Stanmore knew if he declared the wreck to the authorities then anything brought up would be reclaimed by Egypt. The last thing he wanted was to deal with a never-ending line of corrupt officials who would ensure he only ever saw a tiny percentage of the potential find. He therefore lied about the position, saying it was in Saudi waters. He told the truth to the prince and that any recovery operation had to be done in secrecy to protect the find. This cloak and dagger approach appealed to the prince, who underwrote the whole operation, fully understanding that if the shit hit the fan, it really would, and he would be in very choppy diplomatic waters with both his family and the Egyptian government.

He had insisted the best divers and crew were brought on board.

Stanmore had contacted a company he had worked with before called Deep Sea Explorations Inc based in Florida.

And so it was that an experienced, no-nonsense commercial diver was introduced to a Saudi prince on the deck of the salvage vessel *Deep Challenger*. It was the first time John McCready had ever met royalty, and he wasn't particularly impressed.

The relationship was to prove to be one of confrontation.

The main problem was that the prince expected everyone around him to do exactly what he said, when he said, regardless of the need and the accuracy of what was being asked. McCready wasn't having any of this and had decided to treat the prince like a deckhand, telling him exactly what he thought of him when he was trying to do something that was either wrong or dangerous, particularly when it came to diving operations and the safety of McCready and the other divers.

However, rather than becoming mad at McCready and demanding he be fired, the prince actually looked on him as an experiment—like a rare creature you found and didn't quite understand but wanted to know more about. No one had ever treated him this way. He found it fascinating—intriguing almost.

McCready had also seen the prince as a strange and interesting figure, but from another point of view: he was a royal pain in the butt. Over time, though, they had met in the middle and a grudging mutual respect had grown between them, to the point where they could coexist.

The prince almost took the insults and corrections McCready constantly threw at him as some form of therapy or cleansing of his life. The fact he was prepared to take this on board did not go unnoticed by McCready. In fact, to McCready, it almost seemed as though the prince was constantly trying to impress him—that his approval mattered. Maybe he had family issues. It was a state of affairs he could have easily taken advantage of, but never did. This, in turn, was something the prince eventually realized, and his respect for McCready grew even more.

The whole situation, though, had come to a head when someone had been caught with Red Stanmore's wife. Stanmore hadn't known who it was. The man had legged it out of the cabin window before he could see, and his wife had refused to say. Judging by the argument that had ensued, the general disagreement seemed to center around the use and general condition of Stanmore's 'equipment,' which seemed quite reasonable to the crew—he was thirty years older than she was. That she should be open to offers from males more in their prime was completely understandable.

Stanmore had banned his wife from ever coming on board again. A divorce had followed shortly thereafter.

Rumors had started to circulate that the prince had been the one in the cabin. If proven, this would have been a disgrace for the prince, his family, and Saudi Arabia.

So why—and McCready could never quite remember,

but a bottle of Remy Martin the prince had plied him with probably had something to do with it—McCready had taken the blame and admitted it had been him in the cabin, he would never fully understand.

He had been duly fired, not only from the job, but from Deep Sea Explorations as well. Also, as word had found its way to the Saudi royal family, it was considered that disgrace could have been brought to the family by association, so McCready had been banned from ever setting foot on Saudi soil. Not that he had any plans to do so, but the principle was not conducive to McCready's way of thinking, given he had nothing to do with the incident.

This had left the prince deeply embarrassed.

Ultimately, the prince had saved face, his family had never had to deal with the disgrace, and when McCready had left the ship the prince had taken him aside and told him that if he ever needed anything he only had to ask. McCready had said little, other than that he really hoped this was the last time they ever met. As McCready had walked off the gangplank, the prince had whispered in his ear that he really didn't mean that, and for some reason McCready had found himself smiling.

A month later, he had managed to secure a new job at a company called Global Salvage, and after returning from his first contract for them in the North Sea, he had found a package waiting for him at home.

When he had unwrapped it, he had found it was from Yassin. How he had got his address he had never known, but the package contained two antique gold pistols and a Breitling watch. With them came a note reiterating that if he ever needed anything, whatever it was, he only had to press the buttons on the watch in a predetermined sequence and he would receive assistance.

Deep Impact

The final words on the note were, A DEBT IS ALWAYS PAID.

The watch had lain in the drawer at McCready's house, unused, until now.

As he looked at it in the bright sun of Palau, he hesitated. He had wanted to put that episode of his life behind him.

But then he thought of Suki.

And of Ivanov.

And of what the man was capable of.

It made him tremble with rage.

As he thought of what he would do to Ivanov if he ever found him, he realized he was having thoughts he didn't know were within him. It frightened him. He also realized he was at a point of no return. To go beyond this point would mean going to places he had never been before—physically, mentally and emotionally.

He took a deep breath, closed his eyes and pressed the buttons on the watch.

Top right once.

Bottom left once.

Top right twice.

Bottom right three times.

Once the sequence was complete, he opened his eyes and stared down at the face.

Around the circumference, a series of red lights, which he'd never noticed before, pulsed in a circular fashion. As he watched, a small LCD panel appeared in the center behind the hands.

A second later, a string of Arabic writing that he couldn't understand, scrolled quickly across the screen. This was accompanied by a series of beeps.

Finally, the words MESSAGE SENT appeared.

Followed by STAND BY.

McCready sat down on a rock. He looked out over to an island across the bay.

A shoal of small fish jumped out of the water, frightened by some unseen predator. They splashed back down, dappling the surface like some sort of localized rain shower. A bird swooped down to grab an unexpected meal as it passed.

As he watched the world go on around him, oblivious to his personal drama, there was one overriding thought going through his mind.

What had he started?

Chapter Forty-Three

The deserts of Saudi Arabia covered an area of over five hundred thousand square miles. It was from beneath these rolling waves of sand that the country's extreme wealth had emerged in the form of oil. When it ran out, and it would, the power of the nation and its standing in the world would be inexorably diminished. It was a situation Dubai had transitioned through over a number of years, and which had been circumvented by concentrating on building a brand for the country where tourism, financial services and investment could flourish, not to mention a city that was an architectural marvel. The definition of 'superlative' on every level. Whether Saudi Arabia could pull off the same trick, only time would tell.

Five hundred feet above the sand in the west of the country, a falcon soared on the heat rising from the desert below. It was a magnificent animal. Although not quite the ultimate bird of prey—that distinction fell to the eagle—the falcon was a superfast and agile jet fighter to the eagle's fighter bomber.

The falcon spread its feathers on the thermals. It could minutely adjust them to allow it to move in any direction in an instant.

Far below, it could see a man standing at the top of a sand dune. He was dressed in the standard white Arab thawb and headdress, which flowed as the wind clutched at its fabric. On his right hand he wore a thick leather glove. The falcon could see him watching the bird's flight through the air.

Suddenly the man thrust his hand upward, as though reaching for the sky.

The falcon's immaculate vision, which was quite capable of detecting prey over two miles away, had no problem seeing the small mouse grasped between the fingers of the glove.

Immediately, the bird made a hard bank to the right, lining up on the glove. It dived down at a speed of over eighty miles per hour. Just when it looked like it would crash into the steep side of the dune, it flared its wings, bringing its body upright, rushing in to land expertly, but gently, on the man's hand.

As the sharp talons clutched the leather of the glove, the falcon's fearsome beak jabbed down to grab the mouse. Using one of its talons to hold onto the animal, it ripped the head clean from the body and then slowly ate the rest of the rodent piece by piece.

When it had finished, it lifted its head and looked straight into the eyes of its master.

"Excellent!" shouted Prince Khalid Amir Yassin, triumphantly.

He kissed the bird on the head before covering it with a small leather hood to obscure its view and keep it calm.

Yassin cut a dashing figure.

Deep Impact

He was nearly six foot tall, with a strong, lean physique. He had a neat mustache and short black beard. His face was weather-beaten from many hours in the sun, traveling around the world on numerous outdoor pursuits. When you had unlimited funds at your disposal, your only limitation was your imagination. While many of his compatriots spent much of their time in their own country, he had sought out the world's great adventures. He was totally signed up to the *with great power and wealth comes great do-what-the-fuck-you-like* philosophy.

He pulled a small walkie-talkie from his pocket and clicked the transmit button, looking up high across the dunes as he did so. "Did you get that?"

A crackly reply came back. "Yes, Khalid. Perfect." The voice was almost drowned out by the roar of a helicopter's rotors.

A second later the Bell Agusta sped low above Yassin. A man waved from the open doorway, a Nikon DSLR with a 500mm telephoto lens held in his hand.

The helicopter banked round, coming in to hover at the crest of the dune. The top was almost like a Himalayan peak, with steep sides slipping away to the desert floor below.

There was nowhere to land.

The pilot expertly juggled the controls. Without even deploying the landing gear, he brought the open doorway level with Yassin. The prince stepped across the gap into the helicopter, as though entering a car.

Once inside, he passed the falcon to one of the two men sitting in the rear. When he was free of the bird, he turned to the photographer.

"Let me see."

The man turned the camera round and clicked through

the shots on the large LCD screen on the back. Each one held a perfect, tightly focused image of Yassin holding his hand in the air like some ancient ruler, the falcon diving down to meet him and land on his glove.

Yassin beamed, patting the photographer on his back. "Well done, Yousef. They're great."

Yousef beamed back.

"Now, what shall we do for the rest of the day?" said Yassin, smiling.

He was about to turn to click the mike to talk to the pilot when he felt the phone in his pocket vibrate. He pulled out his gold-plated iPhone and glanced at the screen...

...and his heart almost stopped.

He stared at it in disbelief. He had to hold it closer to make sure there was no mistake. An app had activated with the incoming message. On it was a map of the world with the words MCCREADY HELP written across it. Next to the words was a REPLY option in Arabic.

Yassin had often thought of the diver over the years, but, out of respect, had never contacted him. He knew this was what McCready had wanted. In fact, although he would never admit it, and certainly not to McCready's face, he probably respected him more than any man alive.

He stared at the screen for a second longer, as though in a trance, then he became very focused, very serious, very quickly.

He pressed down on the REPLY button.

Immediately the map enlarged to show the position from where the transmission had come. He looked at it for a moment, typed a short message, and then changed to the main phone mode. He dialed and spoke urgently in Arabic to someone on the other end.

He then picked up the mike and spoke to the pilot.

Deep Impact

A few seconds later, the door had been pulled to, shutting out the scream of the rotors, and the Agusta had banked round in a tight turn.

It headed off at full speed across the desert toward the glistening buildings of a distant city that sparkled like a mirage in the blistering heat.

Over six thousand miles away McCready walked along the beach at the watersports center.

He hadn't spoken to anyone.

He could think of only one thing.

He didn't even know if Yassin would get back to him, or if he even remembered him. He thought he probably would, but memories could fade. He had always seemed like a man of honor, though. McCready felt he would get in touch, but when that would be, he had no idea.

Whether he would even be able to help, he had no idea.

But he'd had no choice but to ask.

This was it.

His only option.

He knew he was up against virtually insurmountable odds. If you were going against that you had to have an edge. Yassin's power, wealth and contacts were that edge—coupled with the man's thirst for adventure and a devil-may-care attitude.

But maybe this was too big even for him.

And then his watch beeped. He glanced at the display.

There was a simple message.

IS YOUR LIFE IN DANGER?
YES—TOP RIGHT 1
NO—BOTTOM RIGHT 2

He pressed the bottom right button twice.
Ten minutes later another message came through.

PALAU AIRPORT. TOMORROW. 19.00. YOUR FRIEND, KHALID.

He shook his head slowly, and this time he did smile.
The man had not forgotten.

Chapter Forty-Four

When Clare touched down at LAX she was drained, exhausted, and a feeling of deep depression had settled over her.

The fact that dark clouds and a light drizzle blanketed the city only added to her mood.

Long flights were normally a time to relax and rest, but she'd barely slept a wink the entire time. Couple that with the jet lag and the fact that her bag was the second to last one to flop onto the baggage claim conveyer belt and she wasn't in a fit state to do much at all.

An hour later her cab had fought through rush-hour traffic and deposited her at her house in Laurel Canyon. This was at least somewhere she could finally relax, though the house was cold and dark.

Many of her things were still in boxes and there was no sound of the pattering of feet to welcome her home as Max was still with Jade. She hadn't even had the energy to call her friend telling her she would be home early.

She just wanted to have a shower and curl up alone.

The events of the last couple of days had made her see some things more clearly, which, though, had only ended up making things worse. She now realized how much she had wanted to be with McCready. All her other thoughts had merely been 'in the moment,' however much she might have enjoyed seeing Brad again.

But having understood that, she could now also not see how McCready could be an option.

She just couldn't get the image of him and the girl out of her mind; that he would do something like that. And while she hadn't given him time to explain—what was there to explain? How could he justify his actions?

She dropped her bag in the open area by the kitchen and flicked the kettle on to make some hot chocolate—her comfort drink.

Once it had boiled, she filled a large mug and then went to sit on one of the expansive sofas that looked out from the main living area over the pool. In the distance lightning flashed across the LA skyline. The drizzle had increased to a light, but persistent, smattering of drops on the glass.

She drew her feet up under herself on the deep cushions and closed her eyes.

And she found they were full of tears.

How could she have got him so wrong?

She awoke an hour later.

It was nighttime.

The rain was a consistent driving force now, but she didn't close the drapes. Being inside looking out made it feel cozy, protected from the elements.

She rubbed her bleary eyes and glanced at the still full mug of chocolate—now, not so hot.

Deep Impact

She eased herself stiffly off the sofa, every muscle seemingly aching as she did so. Somehow she made it to the bathroom on autopilot, and after a steaming shower, which helped her relax, she wrapped a thick white toweling robe around herself and walked back into the living room.

Some of the emotion had gone now. She'd had some rest, but her brain was still on Palau time, and she had that thick, slightly out of this world feeling that jet lag gave you.

She crossed over to a small dresser set against the wall and picked up her phone. She hit the first number under FAVORITES and went to sit back down on the sofa.

On the third ring she heard Jade's voice and smiled. How many times had she rung her friend in times of need and been cheered up?

"Hey, girl, how's it going?" Clare could hear the smile and happiness in the voice.

"Not so well actually."

There was a pause on the line, followed by, "I know that tone. Come on, tell all… Also, you're really clear by the way. Sounds like you're just down the road."

"I am just down the road."

"Huh?"

"I'm home."

There was another pause.

"Wait right there, I'm coming over."

And with that the phone went dead.

Clare smiled weakly. There were few people you could count on in this life, but she knew Jade was, and always would be, one of them.

Forty-five minutes later she saw the lighthouse-like sweep of headlights across the front of the house.

She walked over to the entrance lobby and opened the wide glass panel that formed the front door. She could see Jade grabbing a carrier bag from the rear of the car when a small bundle of fur came racing toward her.

She smiled again, lifted Max up into her arms, and almost drowned with the licking her face received. His fluffy tail wagged like crazy, and the licks came thick and fast between attempts at barking and excited whimpers. Eventually she had to drop him down as Jade walked up. He ran off into the house.

Jade stopped in front of her. She could clearly see Clare had been crying, and that, along with the tired, weary look she wore, made her wrap her arms around her, giving her a bear-like hug and a warm kiss on the cheek.

"Come on girl, let's talk."

Once inside, Jade pulled a bottle of wine from her carrier bag and went into the kitchen to pour a couple of large glasses. They then sat on the sofa as the rain continued its relentless assault on the glass at the rear of the house.

Jade didn't say anything, knowing Clare needed time to collect her thoughts and explain what had happened.

When she did, it all poured out. She went through everything. From initially thinking things were good because McCready wasn't in the hospital. To finding the small shack in the woods. To going inside and seeing him in bed with another girl. To the shock and realization as to how she really felt about him, and that how, now, it had all been completely destroyed.

When she had finished, Jade looked at her with a serious expression. "Men! They're all the same. Hairy, smelly things." Clare smiled at her, happy she was there.

"I don't really know how to process this," said Clare eventually.

"Maybe you don't want to," said Jade. "I mean, you never gave him a chance to say anything. To explain."

"Would you have?"

"I don't know. Probably not at the time. Maybe later…"

Clare took a sip of wine and let the alcohol seep into her.

"Maybe it's time to move on," she said. "There are opportunities here now. Maybe I need to buckle down and bring some calm into my life. Maybe McCready was just a diversion after the split from my ex. Some excitement. It was a unique situation and maybe I was just caught up in it all." She stared out at the rain that was falling more heavily now.

"Maybe," said Jade. "But maybe you're also trying to justify your actions."

Clare shot her a look.

"Just saying," said Jade.

Clare remained silent, her thoughts far away. She wiped a tear that had formed in the corner of her eye and sat back into the cushions.

"I have to think of the future, and I think that's here," she said eventually.

As if in agreement, Max came trotting in after checking everything in the house was still where he had left it. He ran up to Clare, and, as if sensing her sadness, hopped up into her lap and contentedly curled up in a ball. She glanced down at him, stroking his soft fur.

She looked at Jade and nodded to herself.

A certain strength was starting to return.

A life-changing decision was coming.

Chapter Forty-Five

John McCready climbed out of the taxi and looked around him.

He was at the Roman Tmetuchi International Airport and he was an hour earlier than the message had suggested.

The airport was relatively small, with just the one main public terminal, shaped in the form of a T. It was modern and attractive and had a high steepled red roof and a large car park at the front.

The only baggage McCready had was the small backpack the doctor had given him. He had no idea what would happen next or where he might be headed. He assumed someone would meet him and give him an airline ticket to a destination Yassin had specified. Since he'd been unable to speak to anyone he assumed Yassin was just going through the motions.

It had been fifteen years after all.

The air was still muggy, even though the sun had gone down and it was now early evening. The sweat from the day was barely drying on his clothes. One thing he intended to do, once inside the terminal, was check to see if there were any showers. If he was out of luck, anyone sitting next to him on the plane would be unable to say they'd had a pleasant flight when they landed at their destination.

He entered the terminal and walked over to an information desk. The girl behind the counter was dressed in official, smart, island attire, which consisted of a flowery blouse and a dark skirt. She smiled warmly and pointed him toward the rest room at the rear of the main building.

As he made his way over, he couldn't help but notice the mass of smiling faces around him. Some would be meeting loved ones from whom they had been apart for too long; some were arriving for the adventure of a lifetime; others were just glad to be here and wore the relief and exhaustion that accompanied the end of a long flight.

He walked on and passed a shop selling clothing and tourist memorabilia.

He emerged a few minutes later with a black short-sleeved shirt and khaki pants that could be unzipped halfway down, turning them into shorts.

Twenty minutes later he left the rest room a refreshed man. He was dressed in the new clothes, the others having been resigned to a waste bin in the block behind him. He was freshly shaven, washed, and felt somewhat more awake, though it didn't change the brooding feelings of shame and rage that were eating him up inside.

As he had no ticket he couldn't go through to departures. He had to stay in the main entrance to the terminal. While he waited, he grabbed a copy of the UK *Times* from a rack of international newspapers in a bookstore and flicked through the pages.

Every now and then he would glance at his watch and

check the terminal for anyone who might be looking for him.

At exactly 7pm, as he was reading through the sports section, he noticed a pair of immaculately polished shoes appear on the floor below the paper. They were black and had a glimmering shine that almost seemed out of place in the tropical environment.

McCready lowered the paper and looked up. In front of him was a man who looked like he was some sort of official. He was short, slightly portly, and, as well as the shoes, was dressed in a dark-colored suit, striped tie, and a white shirt. His face was tanned from the climate. He had friendly but slightly weary eyes. He was in his forties and there was an efficient air about him.

"Mr. McCready?"

McCready folded the paper. "Yes."

The man held out his hand. McCready stood to shake it.

"I am Mr. Andreas. I am the manager of the airport."

McCready looked at him, slightly puzzled. "It's nice to meet you."

Andreas continued. "I have received an instruction that I am to extend you every courtesy while in the airport and I am to escort you to your flight."

"I hope you haven't been put to too much trouble."

"Oh, no trouble," said Andreas sincerely, smiling. "If you could just show me some ID; I need to make sure." He looked apologetic.

"Of course," said McCready. He reached into his backpack and pulled out the temporary passport Steel had arranged for him.

Andreas checked it quickly and then handed it back.

"Wonderful. Everything is in order. If you will just follow me."

With that, he turned on his heel and walked toward a door at the side of the building—away from the departure gates. McCready followed.

When they reached the door, Andreas held it for McCready. Outside, a black SUV waited near the curb. Andreas again held the door and McCready climbed in.

The car drove around the side of the terminal and through a security gate that led to the airside part of the airport. There was a brief stop at the gate, where Andreas showed his pass, and they were waved quickly through.

Five minutes later they had driven round to a secluded area where there was a compact private terminal building. They drove straight past and out onto a small concrete apron. When they pulled to a stop McCready had to smile and shake his head. Sitting on the apron in front of him was a Bombardier Global 6000 private jet.

The sleek white machine glistened in the airport lights.

The steps were lowered at the front, and as McCready climbed out of the SUV, a tall man in Arab dress walked down onto the tarmac.

Andreas turned to McCready. He again held out his hand. "Thank you for using our airport, Mr. McCready. I hope you have a pleasant flight, and if you ever come back, please let me know if there is anything I can do."

McCready stood there, slightly speechless, and watched as Andreas climbed back into the SUV and was driven swiftly away.

The tall Arab reached McCready and bowed slightly. "Mr. McCready, my name is Rashid. I am honored to meet you. Prince Yassin sends his regards and apologizes for sending the small jet, but it was very short notice."

McCready again found himself shaking his head. "Please tell the prince, apology accepted."

At this, the Arab smiled knowingly. "I will indeed, sir. Now if you will follow me, I am at your disposal."

McCready followed Rashid up the steps into another world. It was the first time he had been on an aircraft where turning right was very much okay.

The interior was luxurious but not ostentatious.

He walked through into the main cabin past a small galley. The interior of the jet was over forty feet long and around eight feet wide. Just past the galley was a small, formal seating area with wide leather seats and fold-down tables. Beyond this, a couple of sofas lay against the cabin sides. At the far end, a door led through to what looked like toilet and washing facilities and a sleeping quarters.

Standing in the center of the plane, though, was a strikingly beautiful woman.

As McCready made his way into the main cabin, she came forward with a genuine but alluring smile. She was of medium height, dark-skinned, with long black hair, and an exotic face that oozed sophistication and grace. She was dressed in an Arab-inspired dress with Western inflections that merely added to her mystique.

"This is Nylah," said Rashid. "She will be looking after you during the flight. If there is anything you need, you only have to ask."

Nylah walked forward and gave a small, polite bow.

"Nylah, it's very nice to meet you," said McCready. "I could use a drink."

"Of course, sir. I can get you one once we're in the air. What would you like?"

"Whisky. Thank you."

Nylah disappeared toward the galley. McCready turned to Rashid.

"If you speak to Prince Yassin, please tell him his hospitality is overwhelming."

"Of course, sir."

McCready thought for a moment. "Where, exactly, are we going?"

"Ah," said Rashid. "His Highness has the use of a small place in Dubai. He thought it more convenient to meet there than back home."

McCready smiled. Yeah, way more convenient, given he'd been banned from Saudi Arabia.

"Thank you, Rashid."

Rashid smiled. "If you could strap in for takeoff, sir. We have clearance from the tower. We should be airborne in around fifteen minutes."

McCready sat down in one of the four cream-colored leather seats and eased himself back into the luxury the chair provided. He started to relax for the first time in many days. Some of the stress and pressure of recent events seemed to drain away and he managed to try and ease the tension that had been building up within him. He almost thought of asking Nylah if she would give him a massage, but quickly dismissed the idea.

He was in enough trouble already.

He leaned back in his seat and closed his eyes.

He was instantly asleep.

It was several hours later when McCready awoke. He yawned, stretched his legs and for a second didn't remember where he was.

In the background was the constant drone of the engines. The sun was starting to rise, sending shafts of light through the rectangular windows along the length of the cabin.

As he started to straighten himself in his seat, he noticed Nylah approach from the galley.

"Would you like that drink now, sir?"

McCready focused on the woman and smiled.

"Yes, thank you, and please, call me, John."

Nylah smiled demurely. "I'll just get it for you now, sir."

McCready let it go. He settled back in the seat and looked out at the approaching dawn.

When his drink arrived, he sipped the welcome whisky, letting the alcohol relax him some more. He needed to think through what he was going to say to Yassin when he saw him. Despite the man's promise to help, what he was going to ask of him could be too much. It wasn't so much repaying a debt, it was asking him to do the impossible. He didn't even know if he would be able to find out what McCready needed to know. He knew Yassin had access to many things and many people, but the murky world of espionage and Russian military assets was maybe going to be a step too far.

A while later, Rashid entered the cabin and explained that he was also Prince Yassin's personal physician, and he had been instructed to make sure McCready was fit and well.

McCready let him check over the wound in his shoulder and the gash from the knife in his leg. Rashid had looked at him disapprovingly, changed the dressing on his leg, and given him some more painkillers.

When he had finished, McCready drifted in and out of sleep. He had no concept of the passage of time as he struggled with his thoughts.

Deep Impact

At some point Nylah brought him a delicious meal of traditional Arab food, which he devoured with relish. Coupled with several glasses of a smooth Château Margaux, he was feeling more than relaxed when Rashid entered the cabin to inform him they would shortly be landing.

McCready buckled his seatbelt and looked out of the window. The sun was high in the sky now and there wasn't a cloud to be seen. He stared down at the Earth below. They were flying over a series of high mountain peaks that gave way to barren desert beyond.

What seemed like moments later the plane descended sharply. He found himself having to pop his ears to cope with the increase in pressure. It looked like they were going to make a direct final approach into the airport with none of the stacking as was common with most commercial flights.

As the plane dropped lower, McCready could see the phalanx of tall buildings that made up the linear city of Dubai. In the center of these was the jewel of the desert—the Burj Khalifa: a needle-like glass-walled tower that was the tallest building in the world. He already had to look up to see the top; the plane was well below the antenna that sent the total height to over 2,700 feet.

He could also see they were not landing at Dubai International Airport, but at a smaller facility to the north of the city.

Moments later the wheels touched down with barely a bump, followed shortly after by the roar of the reverse thrust. The plane taxied to a private terminal at the side of the runway. The steps were lowered, and even before McCready had reached the exit the extreme heat found its way into the air-conditioned cabin.

Nylah thanked him and smiled as he left, still insisting on calling him, 'sir.'

Rashid led him down the steps and over to a waiting white Airbus AS365 helicopter around fifty yards away. He opened the nearside door, allowing McCready to climb in, before walking round to the far side to also climb in the back. Once they were both seated he indicated for McCready to put on the headset. Rashid then instructed the pilot in Arabic. Seconds later the machine lifted off smoothly into the hot, thick air and banked around toward the sea.

Once over the water they turned south, tracking along the shoreline. They were not particularly high, about the height of most of the skyscrapers along Dubai's waterfront, but they were still way below the towering height of the Burj. He stared in awe at the architectural marvel as it passed to his left.

Looking out of the window to his right, on the seaward side, he watched as they passed over 'The World' development. Further down the coast he could make out the two 'Palm' developments, all of which had been reclaimed from the sea. They could be seen from space, and were now home to many wealthy celebrities and individuals from around the world who wanted their own piece of this amazing land.

As he remembered, though, from a previous trip, Dubai was a great place to visit, but he wouldn't want to live here. It would be like living in a massive theme park.

As they cleared 'The World' the pilot dropped altitude and banked round, slowing their forward motion. McCready could see they were approaching the top of an exotic-looking building. It had been built at the end of a small man-made peninsula that stretched out into the blue waters of the Gulf from a sandy beach.

"The Burj al Arab," said Rashid over the headset. "Prince Yassin will greet you here."

McCready nodded and looked down at the amazing structure they were fast approaching.

It looked like a huge white sail billowing in the desert wind.

On the roof, if you could call it that, just behind the 'mast' of the sail, was a round green helipad, suspended out over the side of the hotel.

It was breathtaking.

As the helicopter came in to land, McCready could see a tall figure in flowing white robes standing with his hands on his hips looking up at the approaching helicopter.

McCready was in no doubt who he was looking at.

Chapter Forty-Six

Once they had landed, Rashid said this was where they parted ways.

McCready thanked him for all his help and opened the door. Immediately the wash from the rotors buffeted him as he made his way under the spinning blades to the side of the helipad. A moment later the machine picked itself up and effortlessly banked away over the water.

As the noise faded, he turned from watching the departing helicopter.

McCready found himself staring into the face of Prince Khalid Amir Yassin. The Arab looked at him carefully, his expression neutral. He stepped forward. A smile appeared on his face.

"John, it is good to see you again."

McCready looked into his eyes, still not sure how he felt about the man. He held out his hand, trying to suppress a smile.

Yassin looked at the hand with disapproval and moved closer. "My friend, did you not know it is 'Hug an Arab' day today? All part of community integration!" The smile broadened and he moved closer so he could throw his arms around McCready.

McCready had little choice but to reciprocate.

"You bastard!" he said, but there was a smile in the tone.

They broke the embrace and Yassin looked him up and down. "You look good, John. But I see the years have not been kind. The hair is too short. Perhaps losing some?" he said with a twinkle in his eye. "And there is stress and weariness in the demeanor. That is not good. And Rashid tells me you have been collecting bullet and knife wounds. Now this is also not good. It is clear we have much to discuss. Come!"

And with that he led McCready from the helipad. They made their way down a set of white metal steps and into the main hotel. As they crossed to the elevator McCready spoke.

"It's good to see you, Khalid. Thank you for the plane."

Yassin brushed it away. "Ah, it is nothing. But I am thinking that things must be very serious for you to have called on me... am I right?"

"You would be right."

Yassin thought on this for a moment. "First we must have refreshment and then you must tell me all that has happened over the years. And then we will talk about this thing. I am intrigued, John. Very intrigued."

Once in the elevator Rashid pressed his palm against a scanner to the side of the buttons. An electronic voice said, "Penthouse floor. Clearance approved."

With that, the elevator descended a couple of floors. The doors slid smoothly open, accompanied by the voice announcing their arrival at the penthouse.

McCready had seen pictures of the hotel on TV before.

It was certainly opulent. In fact, 'pretty garish' would have been his description, but, as ever, as they entered Yassin's penthouse, there was style and class as well.

Yassin pushed the door open and walked through. McCready followed. "I persuaded the hotel to combine two of their suites. I keep it for when I am in Dubai, which is not for much of the year, but the hotel is quite happy to have a paying guest who is never here."

"You always were the frugal one!" said McCready with a shake of the head. He would have to stop doing that. Nearly every action Yassin took required a similar head movement.

The inside of the penthouse was spectacular, and not only because of the view. McCready walked through a reception area to the main living space, which looked out onto the Gulf through floor-to-ceiling glass and then further along the coast, past Dubai, to the sands in the distance. Far below, a number of kite-surfers were making good use of the winds blowing in off the water. The room itself was luxuriously furnished with two sofas arranged facing each other, close enough to the windows to be able to enjoy the view.

Two of Yassin's staff were in the room; one a tall, powerfully built man, who was clearly something to do with security, the other, a woman in her early twenties who approached when Yassin beckoned her over.

"What would you like to drink, John? I remember whisky was your preference."

"No thanks. Just a beer for now. Maybe later."

"Aliya, two beers," said Yassin to the young woman. She gave a slight bow and disappeared into the kitchen area.

"Please sit," said Yassin.

Deep Impact

McCready sat.

And over numerous beers, McCready and Yassin caught up on fifteen years of each other's lives.

By the end, McCready had started to relax and realize just how much he had missed the man seated before him. Any of the unease he had previously felt about calling Yassin had gone. He still had that devil-may-care attitude, but it had been tempered by a maturity that had clearly grown over the years.

McCready had ended with a description of the events that had led to his current situation.

For his part, Yassin had listened with interest, smiling, and occasionally showing expressions of shock where appropriate. He had particularly liked McCready's account of the incident with the gold in London.

"My friend, you are finally thinking like me," he said with a broad grin and a laugh, slapping McCready on the back.

McCready smiled.

But then Yassin's expression turned serious.

"But you did not contact me to chat about old times. Please tell me how I can help."

The look on Yassin's face was sincere, but there was also a tinge of worry to the expression. McCready wasn't sure if it was because he might have to turn his friend down when he discovered what it was McCready wanted, or that he wouldn't be able to help in any way; something McCready felt would leave the prince feeling in some way inadequate.

And so he told him everything that had happened: from the phone call with Martin Steel—at the name, he thought he detected a flicker of recognition on Yassin's face, but then it was gone—right up to when he had used the watch to contact Yassin. He left nothing out; what would be the point? If Yassin was going to help him, he needed to know exactly what he was getting himself into, and also, what the implications were for him and the potential repercussions should things go wrong.

When he had finished, McCready leaned back in the comfort of the sofa and waited for a response.

Yassin steepled his fingers together and rested his chin on them. After a few seconds he looked straight at McCready. "And what is it that you need from me, John?"

This was going to be the hard bit.

McCready took a deep breath. "I need to find where the Russian has taken the girl. I know it's possible she's already dead, but from the way he looked at her, I think he has far worse things in mind than death. The drive I don't care about. But the girl saved my life. It's a debt I have to repay. You, of all people, must understand that."

Yassin nodded. "Do you know the name of this Russian?

"Major Yuri Ivanov."

"And what else do you have to go on?"

McCready pulled out his phone. He brought up the text Richards had sent him. He showed it to Yassin. "This is the frequency of the transmitter in the locket around the girl's neck."

"Which could, of course, no longer be there."

McCready dipped his head in recognition of this. "But assuming it is, I need to find out where it is now."

"Where do you think it is?"

"I have no idea. The Russians appeared out of the water. They'd attacked the British submarine and were operating underwater drones. There must be a larger sub of some description that it was all coordinated from. I assume, now they have the drive they'd head back to their base, or a rendezvous somewhere, so they could off-load it to their government or higher up the military ladder."

Yassin looked straight at McCready, his face serious. "This is very difficult, John. It is also very delicate. It could get me into a lot of trouble with my family and my country."

"I know I am asking a lot, too much, but…"

"But I love it!" A smile crossed Yassin's face, though there was little humor in it. "This Ivanov must pay for what he has done. I cannot promise anything, my friend, but I will make some calls. This will be a very big adventure."

"Yassin, I just need information. You don't need to get involved beyond that."

Yassin looked at him pitifully. "John, I am disappointed. I give you the information, what can you do? What facilities, equipment do you have? No. You want my help, you have all of it."

McCready didn't know what to say. They said a trouble shared was a trouble halved. It wasn't quite half, but even a fifth taken off his shoulders seemed like a massive weight lifted from him.

"Thank you," was all he could manage.

Yassin suddenly looked very focused. He grabbed a cell phone from somewhere beneath his robes and hit a number. "Get some rest. I have things to do."

And with that, he strode toward the door accompanied by the large bodyguard. As he went he turned back. "My home is your home. Make use of all its facilities," he said with a wink.

The last thing he said as he strode from the room was to

call out Aliya's name. As the door closed behind him, she came hurrying into the room. She looked around expectantly. When she saw Yassin was not there, she turned to McCready.

"Sir, is there anything I can do for you?"

McCready again found himself shaking his head.

Chapter Forty-Seven

When McCready awoke, he again had trouble working out where he was.

It didn't take long, though, as the sheer luxury he was surrounded by, from the satin sheets to the numerous soft pillows scattered around the king-size bed, helped him remember.

He eased himself up onto one elbow, glanced around the room, and then reached for a button on a side table that operated the drapes. A quick click and the wall of fabric across the full-length windows swept back to reveal the dramatic view of the blue Gulf waters beyond.

He glanced at his watch: 7am.

He climbed out of bed and walked into the bathroom. He checked his shoulder in the mirror. The scar was still there, but the work Rashid had done on the plane had tidied it up. There was no blood seepage but the pain was still present. He grabbed the small bottle of painkillers Rashid had given him and quickly swallowed two with a swig of water. He then climbed into the shower and allowed the all-over body jets to ease his other aching muscles.

When he came out of the bathroom some new clothes had mysteriously appeared on the bed. There was a loose-fitting white round-necked shirt and some white pants, again loose-fitting, all of the highest-quality cotton, that would allow freedom of movement and be cool in the heat he knew would soon be raging only inches beyond the protective glass of the windows.

Now refreshed, he walked out of the bedroom, down a short corridor, and over to the dining table beyond the living area. Yassin was nowhere to be seen, but as soon as McCready entered the room, Aliya appeared, as if from nowhere, and asked him what he would like for breakfast.

He was just finishing up a spread of fresh fruit, coffee, orange juice and toast when the door to the apartment opened and Yassin entered. He looked tired and, from the state of his clothes, McCready could see he had probably been up all night. He also wore a serious expression on his face. There was no quip, no small talk. He simply beckoned McCready over to the sofas by the widow. He laid a laptop on the glass table and sat down.

"We need to talk."

McCready walked over and sat next to Yassin so he could see the screen.

"You look like you haven't slept."

"You would be right."

Yassin opened the computer, clicked some keys, and pulled up a map of the world.

"I take it you found something," said McCready.

"You could say that, but it does not look good, John."

McCready prepared himself for what the prince had to say.

"I have been in touch with the GID in Riyadh, the General Intelligence Directorate. As you know, we have close ties with the Americans, and some strings have been pulled to get this information. You have got yourself involved with some very nasty people."

McCready didn't say anything and didn't need to be told that. He knew, though, that the Saudi security services, the GID, were very thorough, and, as Yassin had said, had close ties with the Americans, therefore access to some of the most sophisticated monitoring and intelligence-gathering systems and equipment in the world.

If they couldn't help, no one could.

Before Yassin continued, he glanced over at the kitchen. "Aliya, some water."

A moment later Aliya came over carrying a jug of iced water and two glasses. McCready thanked her, while Yassin zoomed in the map on the computer to show the distinctive outline of Palau. He then moved a finger across the trackpad and the map enlarged to show the island where Suki's shack was located. He clicked a button. The map view changed to a satellite view, showing the world from above in pristine detail and clarity. People thought Google Earth was good, but this was on a whole other level.

"It was possible to track the frequency you gave us for a short period of time," said Yassin. "The NSA monitors all signal traffic in the atmosphere. They record this data for a period of a month—at least that's what they say, it could be longer, of course." McCready was watching the screen closely. "They factored back to the time point you gave me."

He clicked a key on the laptop.

A blip appeared at the location of Suki's shack.

McCready checked the time/date stamp and nodded. That would have been the morning he placed the tracker in Suki's locket.

And then something happened that left McCready completely dumbstruck.

Yassin glanced at McCready. He clicked another button and the image started moving. As McCready realized what he was looking at his jaw literally fell open.

"How? What…?"

"This is classified, John. You cannot tell anyone you saw this."

"So, what are we watching?" he said slowly.

"You're seeing the recorded trace of the tracker combined with recorded real-time satellite video of the geographic location."

McCready had to process this for a second. "Hang on a minute. So, you're telling me they just happened to have a satellite overhead at the exact time I asked you for?"

Yassin paused for a moment before continuing. "Not exactly. All that drama you see in movies and TV shows where they can't monitor something because they have to retask a satellite…" He shook his head. "Not quite like that anymore. They have real-time video surveillance of the whole planet twenty-four seven, three sixty-five days a year. And this is recorded for way more than a month."

McCready was speechless. He didn't know what to say. But at the same time, he felt a surge of hope. This could be a game changer.

"The signal was quite strong to begin with," Yassin continued, moving the pointer on screen and clicking a GO button. Immediately, a linear yellow track started to move from the point of origin.

The two men watched as the yellow line moved slowly

across the screen. Initially it was over a small group of trees, but as it crossed onto open ground McCready could actually make out small figures moving. And for a heart-stopping moment he found himself fighting for air as he realized he was watching Suki being taken away to whatever fate awaited her.

They continued to watch as the group made its way the short distance to the small dock where McCready had come ashore when he had been looking for Suki. At the dock was the outline of a boat. Seen from above it was difficult to make out, but McCready was sure it was the same fast black craft that had chased them several days earlier.

The figures climbed into the boat. A few moments later it started moving. It turned a full one-eighty away from the dock and sped out from the shore, its position made even clearer by the giveaway wake spreading out behind.

McCready watched in silence as the boat moved past the islands and out into open water to a point in the ocean about two miles offshore. He felt a part of him was being ripped out and there was nothing he could do about it.

The boat stopped. Yassin hit a fast-forward control. "It's stationary for about fifteen minutes." He moved the recording forward, then let the image play.

The boat was still on the surface, but suddenly, without warning, it started to disappear. At first McCready couldn't understand. What was happening to it? It was as though it was dissolving into the water. But then he got it. It was slowly sinking below the surface, like an elevator descending beneath the waves.

And then it was gone, vanished as though it had never been. Along with it, the blip of the tracker disappeared from the screen.

McCready slumped back into the cushions. He glanced at Yassin.

His friend's face was serious, but a moment later he continued. "They were obviously rendezvousing with a submarine. And, as you can see, the tracker can't be detected underwater."

"So we've lost them." It was a statement, not a question.

Yassin let McCready suffer a little longer. "Maybe not."

McCready glanced at him.

"The area shows no further signal from the tracker. That's clear. But the Americans have some pretty sophisticated kit, and this whole episode was beginning to interest them. From what my sources say, they knew nothing from the British about the operation, so they were quite keen to see what was going on.

"Normally, tracking a submarine from space is not practical, except under certain circumstances. There have been incidences where phosphorescence created by the wake has been able to be detected, but it's not reliable. The normal way is using the IUSS system."

McCready knew about this. It was the Integrated Undersea Surveillance System. It relied on listening devices on the seabed around the world, as well as remote drones that could be submerged for years at a time, to listen for submarine activity.

Yassin continued. "However, that can be a bit hit and miss and doesn't cover a hundred percent of the oceans. What did come up, though, was an anomaly detected by an American satellite that measures sea level height and profile. This is only likely to work in calm conditions, but they picked up something interesting."

McCready moved forward in his seat.

"About half an hour after the disappearance of the

tracker they detected a surface anomaly that indicated a fast-moving object deep below. It's known the Russians have been working on a cavitation drive, which allows a thin layer of air to be pumped over the surface of a submarine's hull, thereby reducing drag through the water. The predicted speeds of this are in excess of a hundred miles per hour, which is pretty crazy."

McCready was thinking ahead. "So the speed would send a pressure wave up through the water, displacing the surface slightly, even from a couple of hundred feet down, which could then be detected by a satellite?"

"Exactly."

"Wow. And that's what they think they have?"

"It's very likely. The thing is, the track continued for a couple of days and then they lost it." McCready looked despondent. "That could be due to a number of reasons. The most likely is they turned off the cavitation drive and proceeded at conventional speeds."

"Why would they do that?"

"Anyone's guess. The Americans think the drive may only be a prototype and they didn't want to strain it, or that something went wrong and they had no choice but to use an alternate system."

"So that leaves us back at square one. I mean they could have gone anywhere," said McCready, dejectedly.

"Again, maybe not," said Yassin, a slight gleam in his eye. "Look at this."

He made some movements on the trackpad and clicked a button on a window that appeared on the screen. The window hid itself and a new track appeared from the point in the ocean where Suki's tracker had disappeared. "This is a track of the surface level change they think was caused by the sub when using the cavitation drive," said Yassin.

The line was red this time. It extended north from its start point until it had cleared the northern reaches of Palau. It then made an angled turn to the north-east. The track continued until it stopped at a point due south of the most eastern reaches of Japan. "This is where they lost the data," said Yassin. "Now watch this." He clicked another button. A dotted line continued on from the end of the track, again in red. "If you extrapolate the direction of travel you reach this point here." The track had now arrived at the Kamchatka Peninsular in Eastern Russia.

"How accurate is that?"

"Well, the extrapolation is obviously just that, but the sub doesn't have to follow any sea lanes. It's not restricted on its movements, so there's no reason to go in any direction other than where you want to go. Also, if for some reason the cavitation drive had a problem, there could be other issues with the sub that might mean it had to get back to base by the most direct route."

"So where do they think it's headed?"

Yassin turned to the screen and clicked another button. The track moved along the peninsula and turned directly into it at a point on the southern coast around a hundred and fifty miles from its most western tip.

"Here…" said Yassin, "is a suspected Russian submarine base. The Americans don't have any details, but there's a facility they're concerned about. The area surrounding it is fenced off. There are security gates everywhere. There's definitely something going on there; they're just not sure what. All they can see is a lake at the top of some cliffs, some buildings, a car park, nothing else. They could be wrong, but they've followed previous tracks to the region and have observed large heat blooms coming from the rock of the mountain behind that are at odds with what you would expect. It was filed under 'to be investigated,' but nothing was ever done."

McCready looked at the screen for a moment, imagining what Suki must be going through and wondering where along the track on the screen she might be, if indeed anywhere.

Eventually he sat back and looked at Yassin.

"I don't know how to thank you. That's amazing."

"Don't thank me yet. We only think that's where the sub has gone. If it is, it's in the middle of a secret Russian base. No way in. No way out if you get in."

McCready smiled.

"Someone once told me that about $100 million worth of gold."

Yassin looked at him dubiously.

Chapter Forty-Eight

The two halves of the large circular door at the entrance to the underwater tunnel moved smoothly apart.

A few minutes later *Blackfin* made her way carefully through the narrow passage. Once inside, the sub aligned to a precise position, controlled by lasers, and settled onto the metal cradle on the track on the tunnel floor. Large hydraulic clamps moved into place to secure the massive machine. The whole cradle, with sub attached, then made its way along the track.

Once it reached the end, it moved through the inner door and guides at the side of the cradle extended out to connect to the track on the vertical shaft and clamp it into place. When all the recognition lights in the control room flashed green, telling the technician all was well, he pushed a small button. The cradle rose up the shaft to bring the submarine to the surface of the artificial lake.

Twenty minutes later it was safely moored back in its dock under the protective canopy of rock.

The main hatch opened.

It fell back on the deck with a resounding metallic clang.

First out of the confines of the hull was Ivanov. He carried the same compact kit bag he'd had when he entered the vessel several weeks before. He was followed by two men who led a small, frail figure between them.

Suki had a black bag over her head. She stumbled as she was ushered across the curving hull to the gangplank that led to the dockside. Once on dry land she was handed over to two armed men who were waiting for her.

"Take her to holding. I will question her later," said Ivanov. "And make sure she gives you no trouble. She is responsible for the death of one of my men."

The guards led Suki away.

A figure watched from the large window of the base commander's office above the massive tank.

Ivanov spoke to a couple of men on the side of the dock and then strode over to the elevators. Behind him, technicians and engineers started to crawl over *Blackfin*, checking her over and making her ready for any return to sea.

Ivanov entered the elevator. He pressed the button for the control center. A few seconds later the door opened. He walked quickly through to the base commander's office.

When he entered, Admiral Vladimir Cherenko looked up.

"Major. Congratulations. I hear your mission was a success."

Ivanov placed the drive on Cherenko's desk, but his expression was not one of pleasure.

"In one way, yes. But the propulsion system failed again. We would have been back days ago if the cavitation drive had not broken."

"It's an experimental system," Cherenko explained. "These things are to be expected."

"And what if we had needed the speed? What if we were pursued or under attack? What then?"

Cherenko just looked at him. "You know as well as I do, Major, everything we do has variables. Outcomes cannot be known. We must deal with problems as they arise."

"Then I suggest you deal with the designers. They need to be punished."

Cherenko picked up the drive on the desk. "So, this is what all the fuss is about."

Ivanov glanced at it. "It would appear so. The British went to extreme lengths to secure it. Its value must be immense. What will happen to it?"

Cherenko looked at him. "It is to be sent to Moscow when our technicians have inspected it to make sure it is genuine, and to see if there is any technology we can learn from. Then, when in Moscow, the information will be accessed by the GRU."

Neither spoke for a few moments.

"There is one other thing," Cherenko said eventually, his face turning hard. Ivanov looked at him. "I am not happy that you brought the girl here. Your transmissions were vague. I can see no justification for it. She was no threat. I know why you did it, and it has nothing to do with security. It is a risk bringing her here."

Ivanov turned on Cherenko.

"May I remind you that I am in command of this operation. The mission has been successful." He indicated the drive on the desk in front of them. "I do not think Moscow will worry too much about an insignificant little bitch that got in the way, do you?"

Cherenko stared at him in disgust.

"Anyway, she won't be leaving, so you have nothing to worry about."

Suki was terrified. She found it difficult to walk with the bag over her head, even with the two men guiding her either side.

She had no idea where she was.

She heard noises that were new to her. Banging and clanking. The sounds echoed, indicating they were in a large space of some sort, maybe a hangar, or even a cave.

She was then led inside a more confined area, where the noise quietened. There was a constant humming in the background. It was as though they were on a ship, but the ground beneath her feet was stable, so she couldn't be afloat.

She then felt herself moving upward at speed. An elevator. And then marched down a corridor.

She was amazed how much she could discern. It was true when people said that if you were deprived of one of your senses the others became more acute. That said, she had no idea where she was. The only clue came from the voices, which all spoke in Russian, and of which she couldn't understand a word.

Suddenly, a hand on her shoulder forced her to stop. She was held stationary for a minute and then walked slowly forward. A second later she was made to sit down on a padded surface about the height of a chair. The bag over her face was removed. She squinted against the bright light that flooded into her eyes.

When she had regained her sight, she looked around. Two men in uniform were standing over her. They were both armed. One leaned down. There was no threat or, indeed, any emotion at all on his face. He spoke in faltering English.

"You stay here. Someone will come for later."

"Where am I?" she asked, more in hope than expectation.

"You are nowhere," the man said before leaving, but she noticed a pitiful look on the second man's face. The door closed with a loud bang, sealing her in. What worried her more, though, was that the expression on the man's face was tinged with dread.

Suki looked around the room. It was small, about ten feet by fifteen. There were no windows and the walls were light gray in color. There was the bunk she was sitting on, with a barely adequate mattress and bedding material. In one corner was a toilet and basin. A chair and table were further along the wall. Apart from a sealed light in the middle of the ceiling, and what looked like a security camera behind toughened glass in the corner, that was it.

She sat on the bed and pulled her knees up to her chest, wrapping her arms tightly around them—her default comfort position.

Since she'd been dragged from the shack in Palau and seen McCready knocked to the floor, her mind had been in turmoil. She'd had little time to think until she'd been taken aboard the submarine. To get there she'd been given breathing equipment, which she was comfortable using, though, to be honest she could have easily free dived to the massive vessel that hovered at a depth of about eighty feet. The underwater boat had entered through a large open cowl just behind the conning tower. Once inside, the water had drained out fast. She'd been taken to a small storeroom deep in the bowels of the sub. She had never been on a submarine before and had felt quite claustrophobic. Hardly anyone she saw spoke English. The only one who could, fluently, was the one called Ivanov, and he terrified her. There was something wrong with him. He looked at her with an evil lust that made her shudder.

She'd been locked in the storeroom for the duration of the voyage. One thing, though, she still had the locket around her neck. At least they hadn't taken that away from her. Whenever she felt she was about to lose control, she clutched it, remembering everything it stood for, and also that McCready had held it not long before.

She had thought about him a lot during the days in the sub.

How could this have happened to her?

Just when it looked as though her life was over, she had met someone who had been kind to her. All her life she had been used and abused in some way. She had never known that people, men in particular, could be like that—so gentle, so understanding.

But he had been.

She knew she couldn't say that he had been hers—the arrival of the woman in the middle of the night had seen to that. And that was what affected her most. She'd clearly caused trouble between them and that was the last thing she had wanted to do—bring him pain.

It brought tears to her eyes.

And now she would never see him again.

Now there really was no hope.

She had been here many times before, but this time, somehow, seemed different—more final.

She turned onto her side, curled into an even tighter ball, and tried to go to sleep.

Ivanov entered his room and threw his bag on the bed. He then stripped off the jumpsuit he'd worn in the sub.

Before he went for a shower he clicked a button on the TV remote and pressed a sequence of numbers. The picture changed from the news channel to the security camera in Suki's cell. He saw her curled up on the bed, her body shaking every now and then. A cruel smile spread across his lips. To him, she wasn't a frightened young woman, she wasn't even a human being—she was a pastime, a pleasure he would take, whenever and however he liked.

He walked into the shower room. His smile broadened at the thought of what he was going to do to her, the education she was going to receive.

Cherenko was checking through his schedule for the week when his intercom buzzed. He clicked the answer button.

"Alex Vasiliev from tech is here to see you, sir," said a voice over the speaker.

"Send him in."

A moment later there was a knock at the door. A small man in his thirties entered. He was dressed more casually than the military types that made up most of the personnel at the base. His hair was unkempt and he wore a T-shirt and jeans, not the usual military uniform.

Cherenko looked up and grimaced slightly. He disapproved of the man's attitude, but he did quite like him, and he was a very good technician.

Vasiliev crossed over to the colonel's desk. He nodded a greeting at him. His gaze fell to the small box-like device on the desk.

"Is this it?"

Cherenko leaned back in his chair, also looking at the small box on the desk.

"Yes."

Vasiliev picked it up almost reverently and turned it over in his hands.

"How long will it take to check?" asked Cherenko.

Vasiliev was still marveling at the device. "Couple of days. The radiation tests will determine if it's been in orbit. Make sure it's for real."

"Get on with it then. That will be all."

Vasiliev nodded at the colonel, not taking his eyes off the device. He was still looking at it when he exited the room.

As he left, the phone on the desk rang. Cherenko picked it up. "Yes."

"Sir, this is Lieutenant Volkov in the security center. We have a target on the radar that's been making a number of passes along the coast. It's now sitting about a mile offshore."

"What is it?" asked Cherenko.

"From what we can tell it's a Japanese whaling ship. We don't have a visual, due to the fog, but from the electronic ID she appears to be the *Nippon Maru* out of Kesennuma."

Cherenko thought for a few moments. "It's probably nothing, but keep an eye on her. See if you can contact the captain. Find out what she's doing. Tell them it's a restricted area. Report anything out of the ordinary."

"Yes, sir."

Cherenko replaced the receiver thoughtfully. It was probably nothing, and, anyway, he had far more important things to be dealing with.

Chapter Forty-Nine

The four-hundred-foot Japanese whaler factory ship *Nippon Maru*, moved slowly through the water around a mile offshore from the Kamchatka Peninsula.

She had a black hull and a dark green deck, while the superstructure was white. The bridge was located toward the front of the ship. The mid and rear sections were taken up with equipment and areas for processing the whale meat that came from the carcasses of whales dragged up the enclosed slipway at the rear of the vessel. Two large A-frames arched high over the rear half of the ship.

At present the sea conditions were fair. There was a light but increasing swell and the winds were low, something that had contributed to the dense fog that hung over the region. But while the wind might not have been strong, it was still cold out in the open.

The captain checked the radar plot on the bridge, making sure they were keeping a good distance from the coast. He had made two tracks past a point he had been asked to focus on. He was now holding station about a mile out from the location when the radio crackled to life. The voice spoke in English but with a strong Russian accent.

"*Nippon Maru*, this is a transmission from the Russian military. Please respond, over?"

The captain picked up a mike and clicked the transmit button. "This is the *Nippon Maru*. Over."

There was a moment of silence filled with radio static then the Russian voice continued. "*Nippon Maru*, you are in a restricted area. Please move to a radius ten miles from the shore."

The captain looked at the two men standing next to him.

In turn, McCready glanced at Yassin.

"At least we know we're in the right place," said McCready.

"What would you like me to say?" asked the captain.

Yassin thought for a moment. "Tell him what we agreed."

The captain clicked the mike again. "Russian military, this is *Nippon Maru*. We are a civilian ship making our way through your waters en route to the Arctic. We have encountered engine problems and are attempting to repair. We cannot move at the present time."

There was a pause.

More static.

"*Nippon Maru*. Stand by."

The captain glanced at the two men while they waited for a response.

A minute later it came.

"Okay, *Nippon Maru*. Please expedite repairs as soon as possible. Keep us advised. Out."

The captain replaced the mike and turned to Yassin.

"They know we're here. We will have limited time. You'd better get ready."

Yassin and McCready exited the bridge. They made their way down to the large indoor area where the whale meat was processed. It was currently empty, but the vast, hollow space wreaked of death. The smell was overpowering.

McCready had not been happy when Yassin had told him of the plan.

After they had gone over the route of the Russian sub and agreed the Kamchatka Peninsula was the probable destination, the problem had then been coming up with what to do.

From the information they had, that particular region of Russia was desolate and unforgiving. The coastline consisted of high cliffs, with mountains beyond. It seemed an odd location for a submarine base; there was no way in.

But McCready thought there was more to it than met the eye.

Either there was some way around through a local inlet or river that led to the base from another direction, or else there had to be some sort of underwater access that wasn't identifiable from the surface. Submarines didn't just jump up hundred-foot cliffs.

To check this, they would need underwater surveillance equipment. McCready wished he'd been able to bring Craig Richards on board, but he knew his friend disapproved of what he was doing and would refuse to help, if only to try to prevent McCready from doing what he felt he had to do.

That had left Yassin and his contacts.

The prince had been up the following night... again, and a plan had formulated. His family had contacts within the Japanese government. They would make sure they had access to a vessel to take them to Russia. The equipment Yassin would then acquire, along with a number of men to accompany them. McCready had given him a list of what was needed.

The wheels had been put in motion.

McCready had been amazed at what Yassin had been able to pull together at such short notice, but the Arab had merely smiled an inscrutable smile, saying that McCready would be surprised at the contacts he had. The statement had been loaded but McCready hadn't really picked up on it; he had too much on his mind.

The part McCready had not been happy about was when they were standing on the dockside in Kesennuma, in the north-east of Japan. It brought back traumatic memories from his childhood. His mother had been killed by a Japanese whaling ship when he had been fifteen.

He had never forgiven the country for that.

As he'd walked along the dockside, he'd looked for the ship that had committed the crime, but he couldn't find it. If it had been there he didn't know what he might have done.

He had told Yassin of the events and that he had half wished the ship had been there. He had also thought it would have been good if a friend of his by the name of Porter, who could make things go bang in interesting ways, had also been there. He had then had a rueful grin and explained that Porter had enough trouble with Scotsmen in 'skirts,' so had he been there, he would probably have had a hard time with Arabs in 'dresses.' He'd then spluttered with laughter when Yassin had suggested he could have given him a thawb and headdress to wear to help him fit in.

Once McCready had worked through his feelings, they had been met by three of Yassin's men. They were from his personal protection squad. Their background was in Saudi Arabia's special forces. Yassin knew them personally and trusted them with his life. He had introduced them and told them that McCready was like a brother to him. They were to protect him at all costs. The men, who were called Ahmed, Omar and Jamil, had bowed slightly and then quietly gone about their business checking and preparing the equipment.

The equipment included a small underwater drone they could use for surveillance. It could send pictures and audio back to the ship from up to two miles away. There was a fast RIB to get them in and out of any situation, along with sets of rebreathers to allow them to infiltrate underwater without being seen. There were also diver propulsion vehicles to allow them to travel long distances without expending energy. The list was completed by the addition of explosives and weapons.

They also had to think about what they would do if the operation was successful. They had to be able to get Suki out, and jumping off a hundred-foot cliff was not an option. They had to have gear to be able to evac her underwater if necessary. They still didn't know how they were going to gain access to the base, but all options had to be considered.

So now, sitting a mile offshore, McCready was as prepared as he was ever going to be.

The five days it had taken to reach the location had allowed them to go over all the scenarios that might arise, check over their gear to make sure it was working, and for McCready to get to know Yassin's men. They were attentive, dedicated and calm. There was no bravado, no showboating, just quiet, simple focus.

He was in good hands and he was thankful.

The other thing that had energized him was that several

hours previously the signal from Suki's locket had been picked up. And while it didn't mean she had it on her, or even that she was still alive, it gave him hope: hope of finding her and hope of some chance of redemption, however small.

When they were in Dubai, Yassin had arranged for an app to be loaded onto McCready's phone that allowed him to monitor the signal from the locket. If they made it to where they were heading, knowing precisely where she was would be vital, not only in finding her, but finding her quickly. It might be the difference between success or failure.

Life or death.

Four hours later they were ready.

It was starting to go dark.

There had been no more transmissions from the Russians, so at least they were being tolerant for now. Time might change that, but McCready was hoping they wouldn't need much more time.

The first task was to work out access. Climbing the cliffs was an option, but not ideal. The preferred choice was to see if there was an entry point beneath the surface. If there was, it would be a more stealthy route into the facility.

The small drone was released into the water from a crane at the side of the ship. It disappeared into the depths, heading for the coast. It would take around five minutes to get there.

McCready, Yassin and his men were in one corner of the meat processing shed. They watched the operator at a remote monitor housed in a large metal transport case. On the screen they could see the water sweeping past either side of the drone. It was murky, and every now and then large accumulations of plankton shot past like snowflakes in a blizzard. The lights on the drone were turned off in case there were guards on the clifftop, but given the fog, it would have been unlikely the drone would have been spotted. The camera also had infrared and thermal imaging capability, so a significant amount of information could be received whatever the conditions.

After a while, the image on the monitor showed an area of darkness ahead. It was the vertical rock wall appearing out of the gloom.

The operator stopped the drone.

On a laptop next to him was a readout of the exact position in relation to the signal being received from the transponder in Suki's locket. At present they were almost vertically aligned. The problem now was to locate any underwater entrance, if indeed there was one.

It took an hour, but after a stressful sixty minutes the camera showed a section of rock wall that was clearly manmade. As the drone moved through the water it showed a circular area about fifty feet in diameter.

It could only be some sort of entrance to a tunnel.

McCready watched the screen with anticipation. Now, they just had to work out a way to get through.

Over the next hour they went through the options.

Yassin's men were confident the explosives they had would do the job. Again, McCready found himself wishing Porter was there, but given his aversion to water, they were probably better off with people who could, at least, swim.

More discussions followed.

A plan was formulated.

All was agreed.

It was finally time to go.

McCready went through his equipment methodically and started to kit up.

First, he dressed in a Thinsulate undersuit to keep warm. Over this he pulled on an O'Three crushed neoprene drysuit. This would add to the warmth and was the layer that kept the water out. Next, he conducted the pre-dive checks on his rebreather. This involved ensuring the nitrox and oxygen cylinders were at the required pressure and the breathing loop was open and working. He switched on the computer control system and went through the checklist on the small screen that would attach to his wrist underwater.

Finally he was ready.

McCready glanced over at Yassin. He was deep in conversation with his men. Once he had finished talking to them they walked quickly away to their gear. Yassin crossed over to McCready. He looked him straight in the eye with a serious expression.

"John, my friend. Do not do this. My men can go into the base."

"No way," said McCready. "It's my mess. I'll clean it up. And it has to be me that saves Suki. I'm responsible for her being there."

Yassin looked down briefly. "Yes, I understand. But you know it is likely to be a one-way trip."

McCready was silent for a second. He knew this, but he wasn't quite ready to accept it.

"I guess we'll see what we will see."

Yassin grabbed hold of his shoulders and pulled him toward him, hugging him. He then kissed him on both cheeks.

"So I cannot talk you out of this?"

"No, and you should also tell your men not to come further than the entrance. If they get me in, I can go the rest of the way. As I said—my problem."

Yassin shook his head. "Now it is my turn to say no. They have orders to protect you with their lives. And they will do this."

"Khalid, no. I…"

"I will hear no more of it. You had better get going if you are to do this stupid thing." And with that he walked away and out of the cavernous expanse of the processing room.

McCready carried his gear out to the deck at the rear of the ship. He dropped it down next to the RIB, which was already loaded with the DPVs and explosives and was being prepared by Jamil. Harsh arc lights shone down, illuminating the scene.

Ahmed and Omar were kitted up at the side of the RIB. It sat on a small wheeled cradle, which in turn was attached to a cable on a winch at the top of the slipway at the back of the ship.

It wasn't lost on McCready that this was where the dead whales were brought out of the water. The image of one of the greatest animals on Earth, bleeding, possibly still alive, being hauled up into this area, could not leave his mind.

He pulled the heavy rebreather onto his back and grabbed his fins. He was using a full face mask, which had built-in comms so he could talk to the other divers. He also carried a throat mike and earpiece to be worn above water that could communicate with Yassin on the ship.

He took a final look around to check he had everything. He made sure the gear for Suki was in its waterproof bag, along with Ahmed and Omar's weapons. There were also

Russian uniforms for them to change into when they were inside the base. He then threw it all into the boat and climbed in. He nodded to Jamil, who was driving.

He was ready.

It was now pitch-black, except for the bright work lights that shone down from the A-frame.

The boat slid slowly backward down the ramp in its cradle, finally coming to a stop at the water's edge. As the cable was let out further, the RIB floated on the water in the domain it was designed for. Jamil turned the ignition and the engine came to life. It coughed and spluttered and then settled down to a powerful and purposeful crackle and hum. At the bow, Omar untied the line connecting them to the cradle. The RIB slowly reversed out of the docking bay and turned away from the ship. Jamil gunned the engine. The boat sped off into the night.

The wind had increased slightly, so it wouldn't be long before the tops of the swells turned into rolling waves with whitecaps breaking across their surface.

Things were going to get interesting.

From high on the ship a lone figure stood, leaning against a railing, and watched them go.

Yassin said a short prayer in Arabic and then whispered into the night.

"I hope to see you again, my friend. May Allah protect your journey and those who travel with you."

Chapter Fifty

The RIB sped away from the *Nippon Maru*.

It was dark and they couldn't use any lights for risk of being seen.

All McCready could make out was the steadily increasing swell and scurrying clouds above from the snatches of moonlight that occasionally made it through. Other than that, his only sensory feeling was the wind on his face and the occasional splash of spray as the boat rose out of the water for a moment and then thumped down as it raced across the surface.

He knew what he was doing was probably the riskiest thing he had ever done in his life.

But he had no choice.

He had endangered Suki's life because of the situation he had put her in. She had been an innocent bystander, and when she hadn't stood by, it had been to save his life. That was a debt he was prepared to do anything to repay, whatever the cost.

When he thought of her, it brought out a deep rage

from within, which he never knew he had. What she had suffered in her short life no human being should have to go through. And while he knew it was going to be difficult to explain things to Clare, he hoped one day she would understand.

"Two minutes," said Ahmed, bringing him back to the present.

Ahead now, they could hear the crash of surf against the massive cliffs. It was accompanied by the occasional eruption of spray reflected in the moonlight as the waves smashed into the impenetrable rock face.

A few moments later Jamil slowed the boat.

Ahmed and Omar immediately started to make final checks on their equipment. McCready pulled the full-face mask over his head, ensured it was securely over the hood seal on the drysuit, and then did final breathing checks on the rebreather and the computer display.

He then glanced over at Ahmed and Omar.

They gave him a thumbs up, and at a signal from Jamil, they rolled over the side into the cold and unforgiving water.

Jamil handed the DPVs to each of them, and the bag with Suki's gear to McCready. He clipped it securely to his harness with a karabiner. He then vented air from his buoyancy compensator and slipped below the surface.

There was some light in the water from the moon, but it was gloomy and dark. McCready checked the DPV worked by flicking the trigger control. The small propeller at the back of the torpedo-shaped device spun up to speed. It jerked him forward through the water—all good. Satisfied, he clipped the small line on the top of the machine to a D-ring on a belt on the rebreather. This would allow the strain of the pull through the water to be spread across his body rather than being taken by his arms, which would have become tiring after a while.

When he looked up he saw the outlines of Omar and Ahmed hanging in the water ten feet away. "All okay?" asked Omar over the comms. McCready acknowledged. Omar indicated for him to follow them. The three men set off through the water like wraiths of the sea heading for the rock wall.

They reached it five minutes later.

The rock itself was sheer, and disappeared into the depths below. How far down it plummeted they could only guess. All they needed to do was find the location of the door.

They had homed in on a beacon from the drone. As they approached the wall, Omar indicated, 'down,' and they started to descend.

After a few minutes they could make out the drone in the dim light waiting for them below. Its position indicated the location of the entrance on the wall. The data from the drone said it would be at around fifty feet. As they approached, the depth checked out. It was about thirty feet to the top of the smooth area that was the entrance. Descending further, they came to a depth of fifty-five feet dead center.

The two Arabs moved to the side of what looked like a massive door that was split horizontally across the middle. They started to prepare the explosives from the work bags strapped at their sides. McCready took the opportunity to look around at where they were.

The light was increasing slightly as the dawn came up, but it was still dark. The temperature was equally fitting. He was glad of the warmth provided by the drysuit. Hopefully they would soon be out of the water and undercover inside the base.

He was taking a closer look at the construction of the door when a loud groaning came from behind the massive, flat surface.

"What's that?" said Omar, looking over at McCready.

"No idea," he replied, but he moved closer to the other two. They all glanced at each other. The groaning turned into the more mechanical sound of cogs engaging. A minute later the surface of the door started to split in two from the center point. The top part moving up. The bottom half moving down.

They quickly swam to the side of the rapidly emerging tunnel entrance and watched and waited.

The huge sections continued to move apart until both had disappeared into the rock, leaving a massive fifty-foot diameter hole in the wall. As it was revealed, eddies and currents exchanged water between the two masses, swirling and twisting plankton into strange and ethereal spirals.

McCready edged to the side. He was about to put his head around the entrance, when what appeared to be a thirty-foot-high black wall moved past him. The pressure wave knocked him backward. He was grabbed by Ahmed, who steadied him. He nodded his thanks. All three hung there, watching in awe as the submarine made its way out of the tunnel.

It took three minutes for the massive machine to clear the entrance. They were so dumbstruck they almost missed the golden opportunity. As the sections of the door started to rumble closed, they finned quickly inside.

McCready had a wry smile; stand by a locked door long enough, eventually someone will come through and open it for you.

Once the door had clanked shut behind them they found themselves in a massive tunnel. It was pitch-black, so they switched on their torches.

On the floor, a large cradle sat on a metal track that disappeared into the blackness ahead. It must have been used to carry the submarine through the tunnel. As they looked around, there was a mechanical clanking sound.

The cradle started to move.

"Let's go," said Omar over the comms. McCready didn't need any second bidding. They swam quickly down to the cradle and grabbed hold. It would be far easier to hitch a ride to wherever the tunnel led rather than swim. It would also conserve the DPV batteries, which they would likely have to use later to escape with.

As they moved off, McCready had a thought.

While it had been lucky a sub had come through and inadvertently let them into the tunnel, if they now wanted to leave this way, they'd have to blow their way out—something that might take a considerable time when they might not have any.

It gave him an uneasy feeling.

They hung on tightly to the cradle, marveling at the feat of engineering the tunnel represented.

Twenty minutes later the cradle came to a halt with a loud clunk at a second door. It took around two minutes, but eventually the door opened and the cradle moved through.

It butted up against the end of a vertical shaft. McCready estimated they must have traveled around a quarter of a mile in that time.

A minute later the door rumbled closed behind them, sealing them in.

It was lighter here so they clicked their torches off.

McCready checked his computer. It registered a depth of a hundred feet. He glanced above him and realized where they were. The shaft disappeared upward to what was, no doubt, the lake in front of the mountain.

Omar indicated to move up, keeping to the sides in case anyone was looking down. They had no bubbles to give them away, but any movement might be noticed by an observant guard looking into the water, particularly when they got closer to the surface, where it would be lighter.

Alexie Orlov was in a hurry.

Today was his twentieth wedding anniversary and he had a two-hour drive to get to the surprise party he had arranged for his wife. He was already going to be an hour late if he left right now. But the delay in the launch of the sub—for technical reasons, whatever that might mean—meant he was going to be in real trouble when he got there. At this rate he was worried whether there would be a twenty-first for him to go to the following year.

He hurriedly reset the controls to their default position in the small control room on the concrete dock in the middle of the artificial lake.

There was a rigorous checklist he had to go through. He might not be on shift the next time a sub was put to sea or recovered through the tunnel, so everything had to be left just right, else he would get a severe talking to. He might even forfeit some pay, which he certainly couldn't afford.

He had checked the indicator light confirming the outer door had closed.

He had checked the inner door confirmation light.

He had checked the cradle was back in its bay at the base of the shaft.

But the one thing he hadn't checked were the CCTV cameras in the shaft. Why would he? The sub had gone. He'd flicked them off at the beginning in case he'd forgotten later.

If he had left them on he would have seen three shapes moving around the bottom of the shaft.

But he hadn't.

Orlov hurriedly threw things into his small backpack.

He was going to be in so much trouble.

McCready, Omar and Ahmed made it to just below the surface without being seen.

The computer control systems on the rebreathers had provided them with the perfect mix of oxygen and nitrogen to mitigate any decompression they might have had, so they could surface without any risk.

McCready was the first to poke his head above the water. He could see they were in an area the same size as the shaft. It was surrounded by a concrete wall on three sides: one short, two long—the shape of a submarine. The other short side was open. Looking through it, across the surface, he could see a large area of water that stretched a few hundred yards to the mountain beyond. It seemed to disappear into some sort of cave in the rock.

On the dock was what looked like a small control room with a light on inside. There was a speedboat moored up close by. A man was in the building, visible through a window. He was packing things into a small backpack.

They needed the boat.

Omar signaled silently for them to follow him to the dock directly beneath the control room. There was a metal ladder leading out of the water.

They swam over.

Omar silently removed his rebreather and fins and started up the short ladder that led onto the dock.

The man in the control room was still packing.

Omar reached the top of the ladder and froze as the man glanced out of the window for a second, as though checking the boat was still there. When he turned back, Omar moved forward like a cat.

He was inside the room before the man knew what was happening. He wrapped his huge arm around the man's throat and squeezed, exerting enough pressure to knock him out but not kill him. They didn't want blood on their hands unless absolutely necessary. He then eased the body to the floor.

He immediately turned out the light in case anyone was watching from the mountain.

The other two climbed out to join him.

They quickly unstrapped their gear, hiding it under an old tarpaulin that had been lying over some oil drums further down the dock. They then pulled out the Russian naval uniforms and changed quickly.

Five minutes later they climbed into the small speedboat.

McCready and Ahmed lay down so they wouldn't be seen. Omar started the engine and drove slowly away from the dock out onto the main body of water.

They found themselves in the middle of a large lake extending out from the mountain. Currently, the furthest point disappeared into the fog. It was cold enough for a few sections to be frozen, but any ice was minimal. Most of the surface was clear.

Ahead of them was the mountain. To go there would

invite trouble. They wanted to remain as covert as possible for as long as possible.

Omar checked the sides of the lake. Over to the right, between the swirls of fog, he could make out a building of some sort butting up against the rock behind. There was a car park to its right.

He turned the boat in that direction and made his way over toward it.

Major Yuri Ivanov lay on his bed staring straight at the ceiling.

He had slowly come down from the adrenaline high of the mission. The objectives had been achieved as usual.

But he was not satisfied.

He had not brought all his men home safe, and that was something that angered him. Also, the fact that the reason for this was a woman—no, a girl—made him even more furious. The good thing was, that problem would soon be avenged.

He felt a strange thrill course through his body. He was incredibly skilled in causing pain. Pain for the other person, which was inevitably pleasure for him. And when that involved sexual torture, the pleasure was even more intense. He somehow felt that with this girl he was going to feel things he had never felt before.

The thought made him shudder with anticipation.

He rolled over on the bed and picked up a handset from a side table. He then pressed a single digit on the phone. It rang twice and was answered. After the person had asked him what he wanted, he replied in a cold, emotionless voice.

"Bring the girl to me."

Chapter Fifty-One

Suki sat on the bed, hardly moving.

She had calmed down from when she'd been brought in and was now in an almost stupor-like state. It was something she had trained herself to do over the years: to blank out whatever terrible experience she was going through. It allowed her to separate herself from the real world; to pretend she was just watching what was happening to her, while the 'real' her was somewhere else, detached and safe. It didn't always work, but she'd had to try something to survive the situations she had been in.

She was in this state when she heard footsteps outside the room. They stopped. Keys were inserted in the lock. She clearly hadn't managed to get herself totally in the zone, for as soon as the door started to open, all the fears and terror came rushing back.

She pushed herself hard against the wall, knees to her chest, arms wrapped tightly around, as though it would somehow protect her, make her invisible.

As the door opened, a man stood there in a naval

uniform. He wasn't one of the men who had brought her earlier. There was something different about him. His expression wasn't hard, as the others had been. Somewhere in there she thought she saw compassion, a conflict almost, like he didn't want to be there.

"My name is Pasha," he said gently.

She just looked at him. He didn't rush forward and drag her to her feet. He just stayed where he was by the door.

"What is your name?" he asked in a soft tone, heavily accented.

She looked at him for a moment. Then, in a small voice, said, "Suki."

"That's a pretty name, and that's a pretty locket you have there," he said, nodding at the dolphin around her neck. She gave him a weak smile. Maybe things were going to be alright.

But then his face turned serious, and he said gently, "You have to come with me."

The small boat reached the side of the lake.

McCready, Omar and Ahmed climbed out onto the surround. It was still dark, but the light was increasing, and although there was no one up and about to see them, they looked around cautiously before heading for a door into the building at the side of the mountain.

Omar and Ahmed made sure their weapons were close at hand. If anyone saw them there was no reason for suspicion as they had the appropriate uniforms. The problem would be if anyone spoke to them. None of them could speak much, if any, Russian.

As they approached the door, they had to walk past a small carpark. There were few vehicles, but McCready

Deep Impact

noticed an old Lada that had seen better days. It looked like it should be on a scrapheap. Clearly they believed in getting value for money from their products in Russia.

They reached the door, noticing that lights were on inside. Omar was about to open it when they saw someone approaching from the other side. He pulled the door open. An old lady, wrapped in a thick woolen coat, scarf and hat, looked up and walked through. She carried a bag full of cleaning materials and glanced at the men.

"*Spasibo*," she said as she passed. Omar and Ahmed simply looked at each other. In case the old woman thought more of it, McCready quickly answered.

"*Spasibo*," he said, glad that he was fluent in 'thank you' in over six different languages.

He smiled at the old woman as she walked past and headed toward the battered Lada.

The men made their way inside. Once through the door they breathed a sigh of relief. They were halfway there.

Now they just had to find Suki.

Outside in the cold, Irina Lazarev glanced back at the closed door. She had never seen those men before. There was something different about them, something she couldn't quite put her finger on. But who was she to reason why? She shrugged and climbed into the old car. She turned the ignition. It took four attempts to start. When it did she crossed herself three times and touched the crucifix hanging from the rearview mirror before driving off.

Inside the building, McCready pulled out his phone and opened the app. While it couldn't give any form of layout of where they were, it could give a fix on the locket and where it was in relation to where they were.

The blip appeared on a grid. It showed the locket was about a hundred feet from them. Also, what it couldn't show was vertical height. In other words, given they were in a building, it couldn't show what floor the locket was on, only which direction.

The other thing he noticed as he watched the blip on the screen... was that it was moving.

Lieutenant Pasha Sokolov walked down the corridor from the cell with Suki at his side.

He had persuaded her to come without a fight, but he could tell she was scared. He hated this job. He knew what Ivanov was and what he was capable of. But he also knew how powerful he was, and to cross him would mean the end of his career, maybe even his life. And he couldn't leave his wife Yulia to bring up their daughter Dominika on her own. He would have to see it through.

Without even knowing it, he found himself reaching for and squeezing the hand of the terrified Japanese girl at his side. He glanced down and saw her wide, frightened eyes looking up at him. He could see the pleading in them—a forlorn hope that she could trust him.

He hated himself.

They rounded a corner in the corridor. In front of them a new corridor ended thirty feet ahead. There was only one door, on the right-hand side toward the end. He slowly walked forward, and as if the girl had picked up on his thoughts, she started to hang back from him, pulling at his arm. He could hear a slight whimper come from her lips, but he kept his head forward, one thought on his mind.

Yulia and Dominika.

Yulia and Dominika.

They reached the door.

He took a deep breath and knocked.

"Enter!"

Sokolov opened the door and walked inside. Suki followed him, but when she saw who was there, she cried out and turned, trying to run.

Sokolov held onto her.

Ivanov walked over to them. He grabbed Suki from Sokolov's hand and wrenched her over to him. Suki turned and stared at Sokolov in shock. Her eyes showed his betrayal, and something died inside him. All he could see were the eyes of his wife and daughter accusing him.

"Leave!" ordered Ivanov.

Sokolov stood still, unable to move.

Conflicted.

Torn apart.

When he didn't move. Ivanov walked over until he was right in front of him. Their faces were inches apart. Their eyes dead level. But when Sokolov looked into those eyes, he backed away in fear. There was a crazed madness in them, something he had never seen in a man before.

"Leave now, or you will be going home in pieces," said Ivanov slowly. The voice was calm, but the tone was undeniable.

Sokolov backed toward the door. He hardly dared look at Suki. But he couldn't leave without a final glance. When he did, her expression told him everything he needed to know.

How could he live with himself after this?

As he pulled the door to, he heard her cry out in desperation. But then the door was shut. He heard the lock click fast.

There was nothing he could do now.

Suki stared in terror at the man in front of her.

He had barely spoken to her on the submarine but she had seen what he had done to McCready, how evil he was. She suddenly knew that whatever she had endured over the years at the hands of men would be nothing compared to what was about to happen. She found herself shaking uncontrollably, fear taking over her whole being.

Ivanov walked over to her.

"You have caused me trouble. I do not like that. You were responsible for the death of one of my men. I do not like that. What is going to happen to you now, you will not like."

With that, he smashed a backhanded slap across her face sending her sprawling onto the bed, blood oozing from a gash on her cheek.

She was crying now.

He crossed over to a drawer at the side of the room. He pulled out a whip, a large knife with a curved blade, and two sets of handcuffs.

Suki could hardly speak. She was hyperventilating. She had pushed herself back against the headboard of the bed as far as she could go, but she knew there was nowhere to hide.

Ivanov grabbed her, as though she weighed nothing. He knelt on top of her, pinning her arms to the bed, and then he ripped open her jumpsuit, revealing her body beneath.

He picked up the knife and ran the blade around the

curve of her breasts. Blood started to ooze from the thin line left by its track.

She screamed.

He then pulled the jumpsuit completely from her, leaving her naked and exposed. He threw the knife on the floor and grabbed the handcuffs. He pulled Suki's right arm and clamped the metal bracelet over her wrist. He then dragged her to the side of the bed where a rope loop was concealed behind the headboard. He pulled this out and clipped the cuffs to the rope. She was now secured to the bed by one hand.

She spat in his face, clawing for his eyes with her nails.

His response was to again slap her hard across the face.

"Oh, you're going to regret that!"

McCready and Yassin's men had reached a small atrium.

So far, anyone they had encountered had paid little attention. No one had talked to them.

McCready checked the display on the phone. The blip had stopped but it seemed to be close by, almost back the way they had come. That meant the locket was probably on another level.

He indicated the elevators at the side of the atrium.

They walked over and pressed the CALL button.

A few moments later a car arrived and the doors slid open. A tall man wearing a naval uniform walked out and they walked in. As they did, he turned to look at them. Clearly something had attracted his attention, but before he could say anything, the doors had closed. McCready looked at the floor options. Everything was written in Russian. He couldn't understand any of it. They would just have to go floor by floor.

He pressed the button for the next one up.

They reached it and exited the elevator but quickly turned back. There were people everywhere, hurrying about their business. It looked like the main control facilities of the base were on this level. It would be too risky.

Back in the elevator, McCready pressed the next button up.

When the doors opened it was quieter, so they carefully exited the car.

They seemed to be in some sort of living quarters area. It almost looked like the inside of a cheap hotel. Corridors led off in different directions with doors at regular intervals along the narrow passages. McCready again checked the blip on the app. He nodded at Omar and Ahmed and they set off down a passageway lined with rows of doors.

As they approached the end they saw it turned to the right. The two Arabs pulled their weapons and stepped around the corner. The passage ahead extended for about thirty feet, and there was only one door.

It was at the end on the right.

Outside the door stood a man in a naval uniform. McCready checked the phone.

"Down here," he said. "The door at the end."

They started walking down the corridor. As they approached, the man looked up. He appeared wary, nervous almost. When they reached him, he turned to block the passage.

"Who are you?" he asked in Russian.

McCready glanced at the other two and nodded.

They both raised their guns, aiming at the man. He looked as though he was going for his sidearm, but the clear intent of the men in front of him made him stop before he got halfway.

"Do you speak English?" asked McCready.

The man looked at him in astonishment. "Yes, a little," he said.

At that moment a scream came from behind the door.

McCready looked at Omar, then turned to the man.

"You need to let us in there right now."

The man didn't seem to know what to do.

"All we want is the girl," said McCready.

Again the man looked at him in astonishment.

"What you want with her?" he asked in faltering English.

"To take her out of here. Far away," said McCready.

The man seemed to be thinking.

"Okay," he said eventually. "There is very dangerous man in there. But he has locked the door. I cannot let you in. But I will not stop you."

McCready wasn't sure, but there was something about the sincerity in his eyes that made him believe him.

"Okay," he said. "Thank you." He then turned to Ahmed. "We need to open the door."

Ahmed moved forward and pulled some small strips of plastic explosive from a pocket in his uniform.

Again, screams and cries came from the room.

"Hurry!" said McCready.

Ahmed didn't acknowledge him, but he kept on working methodically. He spread the Plasticine-like material in a strip down both sides of the door. He then connected the two strips with wires to a small detonator, then indicated for everyone to step back down the corridor. They moved off, along with the Russian. When Ahmed was sure they were safe, he flicked a button on a small remote.

There was a loud explosion and the door blew off its hinges into the room.

Ahmed and Omar ran in first. McCready was right behind.

Ivanov had wiped the blood from his face where Suki's nails had scratched down his cheek. He had clipped the second handcuff round her other wrist. As she had screamed, he'd slapped her even harder, knocking her unconscious.

He was reaching for the rope loop on the other side of the bed when the door blew in.

The explosion sent shards of wood flying across the room and the door landed on the floor on the far side.

Ivanov rolled off the bed and reached for a gun he kept underneath. The explosion had been a shock but he trained and survived on instinct. The triggers that had entered his brain had been automatic, no thought process required.

Ivanov's first shot hit Ahmed in the chest, sending him down. At the same time, Omar was in the room with McCready behind. Omar raised his gun and fired, the shot grazing Ivanov in the arm, but he was still able to fire back. The bullet hit Omar's gun, sending it spinning from his hand.

Ivanov was about to fire again.

"Drop it!"

The order had come from the door. Ivanov turned to see Sokolov standing there, his weapon aimed at Ivanov's chest.

"What are you doing?" said Ivanov.

"Throw the gun over there." Sokolov indicated the door to the bathroom. Ivanov held onto it, a cruel smile reaching the corner of his mouth.

"You will not fire. You do not have it in you."

The shot startled everyone.

It hit Ivanov in the shoulder of his gun arm. He dropped the weapon, grunting with pain.

Omar picked up his gun and brought it to bear on Ivanov. He was going to pull the trigger.

"No!" said Sokolov. "I will let you take the girl, but I cannot allow you to kill him."

Omar looked like he was going to shoot anyway, but McCready touched him gently on the shoulder and shook his head. The Arab had a hard time controlling himself, but nodded imperceptibly.

McCready immediately ran to the bed. Suki was still dazed and semiconscious from Ivanov's assault.

"Where's the key?" asked McCready, looking at Ivanov.

Ivanov just stared at him, a thin smile on his face.

McCready didn't have time for this. He pulled a knife from a pocket in his uniform and cut the rope at the side of the bed. He grabbed Suki's jumpsuit and lifted her gently into his arms, the handcuffs dangling from her wrists. There would be time for those later.

Before McCready left with his precious cargo, he glanced at the Russian who had helped them. "Thank you."

The man nodded.

McCready walked out of the door and along the passage. Omar followed. There was no way they could retrieve Ahmed's body and have any chance of escape.

Sokolov watched them go.

When they were clear he turned back to Ivanov…

…and his face turned to horror.

Ivanov was kneeling at the side of the bed, a large

curved knife in his hand. Before Sokolov could bring the gun to bear, Ivanov leaped forward, slashing the knife across his throat. As Sokolov sank to the ground, blood spurting from his neck, all he could hear was the word 'traitor' hissed in his ear.

Ivanov picked his gun up from the floor and grabbed an automatic from a cupboard by the door.

He then lifted a phone handset and spoke quickly.

"Control, this is Major Ivanov. There are intruders on the base. Two men and a girl. One of them is of Arab origin. Find them and terminate the men with extreme prejudice. They are armed and dangerous. Anyone touches the girl will answer to me."

He slammed the handset down and ran out of the room.

From the floor Sokolov watched him leave. The last thing he heard was the sound of alarms echoing through the base.

The last thing he thought before slipping into eternal blackness was of Yulia and Dominika and how he had failed them.

And then he was still and at peace forever.

Chapter Fifty-Two

Admiral Vladimir Cherenko looked up from his desk as the alarms sounded in the background.

He immediately picked up his phone and rang through to the security center.

"Lieutenant Volkov, what is going on?" he asked.

"There are intruders in the base, Admiral," came the reply from a clearly harassed Volkov.

"Where did they come from?" asked Cherenko.

"No idea, sir, but Major Ivanov informed us."

Cherenko gritted his teeth. "Okay, keep me up to date with any developments."

"Yes, sir... And there's something else."

"What is it?" asked Cherenko.

"We have not been able to raise that whaling ship in the last half hour."

"Can you still see its location?"

"No, sir," said Volkov, slightly uncomfortably. "That's the thing, there's some interference with the radar. All our screens are down."

They were halfway along the corridor when Suki started to wake up.

She struggled initially and then opened her eyes, looking shocked as she had no idea where she was. She looked up and saw McCready. Her mouth fell open and her eyes went wide.

They had to hurry, but McCready also had to give Suki a minute; she was still naked. He indicated for Omar to wait a second. He nodded and checked behind them, his weapon at the ready. All around they could hear the alarms. It wouldn't take long for someone to find them.

McCready set Suki down on her feet. She stood, slightly unsteadily, and trembled as she tried to cover her nakedness. But as she looked at McCready, the look of sheer happiness on her face was impossible to ignore.

"Suki, we have to get out of here, okay."

She nodded vigorously. "How? Where?" she managed.

"That doesn't matter now. Here put this on." He passed her the jumpsuit. "There'll be time for answers later, but we have to move. This is Omar. He's a friend." Omar nodded at her. She smiled back at him as she pulled on the jumpsuit, overwhelmed by events. "Now, stay close to us. This is going to be difficult."

All Suki could do was smile up at McCready and throw her arms around his neck, hugging him tightly. He gave her a second and then they had to leave.

They reached the end of the corridor and made their way back toward the elevators. There would be more people here, but they had to get down to the Tank Level and somehow back to the water.

As they approached the atrium, they noticed that people were moving around quickly. Someone spotted them and called out, but most stayed back when Omar leveled the gun.

Then came the sound of automatic fire from behind. They ducked as they saw Ivanov charging down the corridor toward them.

They had to move fast.

At that moment the elevator 'binged.' A man walked out and two women stayed inside.

McCready and the others ran into the car as Ivanov reached the atrium. The mere presence of Omar's gun caused the women to run out, but one of them wasn't fast enough. She caught the full force of Ivanov's bullets as he fired into the elevator on full auto. Omar returned fire, while McCready shielded Suki.

The doors closed before Ivanov could reach them.

The women in the elevator had clearly been going up, as the car ascended once the doors had shut. They had no idea of the layout of the complex, but Ivanov would probably assume they would head for the tank. But he could also see where the elevator went.

When the doors opened two floors up, they exited cautiously.

They found themselves on a quieter level. There was again an atrium, but this wasn't a residential floor. Here they saw a single corridor lead off down a passageway. It looked like there were a number of scientific labs set out one beyond the other.

They made their way along the passage. Some of the labs had large windows, others just a small round window in the door, like a porthole on a ship.

At that moment a scientist emerged from a lab ahead. The trio managed to squeeze themselves into a wide alcove, a storage space for trollies, set back from the main corridor. A second scientist joined the first. They were chatting in Russian in the middle of the passage. The discussion became heated. There was nowhere for McCready and the others to go. They had to sit it out. McCready's gaze turned to the lab opposite.

As he looked through the wide glass window at the equipment inside, he saw a series of large computer towers at the back of the room. In front of these were several long tables with equipment set up on them. He looked along the tables, stopped, did a double take, and then returned to an object that was clamped in a small frame. It had wires leading from it to the computer array behind.

It was now his turn for his mouth to fall open. He was staring at the drive from the satellite. There was no choice. He had to get it.

He peered around the corner. The scientists were still arguing. A moment later they both walked back into the lab at the end of the corridor.

This was his chance.

There was no one in the lab where the drive was. He ran across the corridor and pushed the door open, moving swiftly to the table where the drive was located. He looked at it for a moment, wondering how to disconnect the tangle of cables that had been plugged into it. After realizing he didn't have a clue, and hoping no damage would be done, he pulled them out as fast as he could. Then he grabbed the drive and shoved it deep into a pocket and ran for the door.

He emerged just as there was a muted BING from the elevator down the corridor.

A second later, Ivanov turned toward them, his automatic held out in front of him.

McCready only just made it back to the alcove.

They cowered as bullets flew around them. Omar

crouched down and slid out into the corridor returning fire. They heard a cry and a thud as Ivanov fell to the floor.

McCready looked the other way down the corridor and could see a sign high on the wall at the far end, next to a door. He couldn't read Russian, but the universal sign for 'stairs' was unequivocal. He pulled Suki to her feet and turned to Omar.

"Come on, we have to go."

They ran down the passage, Omar firing covering bursts back up the corridor. They reached the door, but not before another burst from Ivanov raked the walls around them. As they rushed through the doorway, Omar let out a shout and fell forward. He glanced down at the blood oozing through his shirt from a wound in his arm.

Suki cried out.

Saudi special forces were tough, though. He winked at her. "Just a scratch."

They headed on down the stairs.

Behind them, Ivanov picked himself up off the floor. One of the rounds had hit his leg, sending him down. He grabbed a radio from his belt and spoke quickly.

"They're heading for the tank. Do not let them leave." Then he headed down the passageway after them.

The stairs led all the way to the bottom of the complex.

They reached the Tank Level and approached the door cautiously, McCready looking through the window in it. On the other side were the massive dry docks with the water beyond. He could see all the way outside to the daylight, which was getting brighter by the minute.

He turned to Omar. "You okay?"

The big man grinned through gritted teeth. "Never better."

McCready looked at Suki. Again the same question. "You okay?"

She smiled a little nervously, but McCready could tell in her eyes that there was nowhere else on Earth she would rather be right now. Anywhere was better than where she had been only minutes earlier. He gave her shoulder a squeeze and then pushed the door open.

They walked out onto the dock surround. The door was partially hidden by a small truck that gave them a token amount of cover while they worked out what to do.

McCready turned to Suki.

"We're going to have to go underwater to get out of here. We brought some gear, but it's out on the dock in the middle of the lake. You ok with diving gear?"

"No problem," said Suki.

McCready looked around again, then at Omar.

"Okay, you see those boats in the dry dock with the sub?" Omar glanced round the side of the truck. There were four small speedboats moored up in one of the flooded dry docks that also had a large nuclear submarine filling most of the rest of it. On the other side of the concrete, next to the full dry dock, was an empty one. It lay there like a massive hole in the water. Omar nodded his acknowledgment.

"Okay," continued McCready. "If we can get to one of those and try to disable the others, maybe we can buy us some time to get to the shaft in the lake. But we'll have to move fast."

He looked back across the tank surround. There were a number of armed men walking around the side. They were clearly on alert. One pair was heading straight toward them.

McCready nodded at Suki. "Okay, it's now or never. Let's go!"

And with that they raced from the shelter of the truck and ran for the boats.

Omar was in the lead. As the armed men saw them, he opened fire. Impacts from bullets exploded the concrete at their feet, driving them back. They dived for cover behind some supplies.

A second later, gunfire came from behind them as Ivanov burst out of the doorway at the bottom of the stairs.

They ran on, keeping low. It was only another fifty yards. Eventually they reached the concrete section splitting the two docks. The boats were ten yards away. Suddenly, a man appeared from a small hut on the dock. He turned toward them, a gun in his hand. Omar barged straight into him, sending him spinning backward into the empty dock. His scream carried all the way to the bottom before ending in a sickening THUD as his body impacted the concrete fifty feet below.

And then they were at the boats.

McCready leaped into the first RIB with Suki right behind. She moved to untie the bow line while Omar acted as rear gunner to deter any followers. When he heard the engine splutter to life he jumped in. McCready hit the throttle and the boat leaped away from the side. As they left, Omar strafed the other boats in the hope of rendering them useless.

More gunfire came from behind them.

Omar returned fire just in time to see Ivanov slide to the ground on the dock and jump into one of the remaining boats. Two of them had slowly started to sink but one was still afloat.

McCready powered forward. They were heading down the narrow piece of water between the dockside and the massive hull of the submarine. They'd just drawn level with the conning tower when a fast boat appeared from behind the bow of the sub ahead, heading straight for them.

A man stood up in the boat and fired.

There was nowhere for them to go.

McCready had to think fast. There was only one option. He accelerated toward the boat, the two now closing at over eighty miles per hour.

There was going to be a collision.

At the last second McCready yanked the wheel to the left sending the boat skidding up the smooth metallic hull of the sub. They shot over the top, sliding down into the water on the other side.

Behind them they heard an almighty crash. An explosion of water erupted from the far side of the sub. The only thing McCready could think was that Ivanov had crashed into the other boat.

He pushed the throttles forward, heading for the end of the dock. And then he realized he'd made a terrible mistake. The sub must have been in for repair as the dock was being slowly drained. At the end was a solid gate, which kept the water out beyond. There was already a six-foot wall, and it was getting higher by the second.

He looked behind him. Suki was clinging to the side of the boat for dear life. Omar was watching for any pursuit. McCready looked ahead. He saw what he had to do. He glanced back.

"Get down and hold on!"

Deep Impact

They looked at him with alarm and then hunkered down on the floor, holding onto anything they could find.

McCready looked forward and pushed the throttles as far as they would go. Ahead of him was the massive control hydroplane of the submarine. It was a ten-foot-wide movable plane that was used to dive and surface the sub. Right now it was in a resting position, but that was at a slightly elevated angle.

It was the perfect ramp.

He clutched the wheel as though his life depended on it and aimed for the center of the vane. He hit it perfectly, the smooth metal aiming the boat into the air. It shot off the end of the makeshift ramp and flew thirty feet, crashing down on the other side of the gate.

It was now clear water all the way to the dock in the middle of the lake.

They were almost home free.

McCready looked around. The water was flat. There were no obstructions. Behind them he could see people rushing around the dockside, but, so far, no boat followed them.

They continued for about a minute without incident.

It was only when they were fifty feet from the dock in the middle of the lake that the deadly whine of a bullet whistled past McCready's head. He crouched down and looked back. He could see a boat some way away, but closing.

He pulled in fast to the dock and drew up next to where they'd left the gear earlier. As soon as they were against the concrete wall Omar jumped out. He helped Suki up onto the side. McCready secured the boat to a bollard and then ran over to the dive gear. He was pulling off the tarpaulin when a hail of bullets splintered the wooden walls of the control room behind them.

Omar spun to return fire. He got off a volley, but then, with a massive cry, was hit in the chest. He fell to the ground, blood oozing from beneath his uniform. Suki cried out and ran to him but McCready pulled her back.

"We have to go," he said.

"But Omar?" she replied tearfully.

"I know. Get ready. I'll do what I can for him."

McCready gave Suki her suit and gear. He laid out the small dive cylinder for her and also the weight belts they would need to compensate for the buoyancy of the suits. He pulled on his own suit and was just about to lift the rebreather onto his back when another hail of bullets crashed into the windows of the control room.

He turned to see Ivanov pull up in the boat. The Russian had his gun trained on Suki.

"Don't move," he said, a triumphant sneer across his face.

Suki stopped what she was doing. She hadn't even had time to put on the suit. The boat bumped gently against the concrete side of the dock. Ivanov stepped up onto the side.

McCready could see he was wounded in the leg and arm, but it didn't seem to be slowing him down.

The gun was rock steady. His eyes were like ice as he looked at both of them.

Chapter Fifty-Three

McCready stood just beyond Suki. On the ground, Omar groaned in pain.

"Please," said McCready, "he needs help."

Ivanov walked forward. He looked at McCready and then glanced down at the Arab. He lowered his weapon and shot him through the head. He looked up at McCready.

"Not anymore."

Suki cried out.

Ivanov took a step toward her and backhanded her across the face, sending her sprawling to the ground with a cry.

McCready was about to jump at him but Ivanov brought the gun to bear.

"Ah... Ah. Stay there!"

McCready stopped.

"I'll deal with her later. I don't think she needs to see what the grown-ups are going to discuss, but then again, maybe it would be good for her to watch what happens to people who cause me problems, and you, Mr. McCready, have caused me so many problems."

"What kind of sick excuse for a man tortures young women?"

Ivanov smiled. "You don't know the half of it. I was just getting started. Something I will happily continue when I've disposed of you."

Suki was starting to come round on the ground. She eased herself up and looked in shock at Ivanov and McCready.

"Ah, looks like she'll be able to watch after all," said Ivanov. He pointed the gun at Suki. "If you move, he will suffer even more."

Suki said nothing. Her eyes were full of fear as she looked up at McCready. He smiled at her, but he was trying to work out an angle, some way he could distract Ivanov so he could bring him down. But he was all out of options.

"In fact, I have a better idea," said Ivanov. "Just to make it interesting." He walked over to Suki. She retreated against the oil drums but Ivanov grabbed her by the hair, pulling her over to a railing at the side of the dock. He snapped the open handcuff round the railing, then took the key from his pocket and put it on one of the drums at the side between himself and McCready.

"You get that, you can take her."

Ivanov put the gun down on top of the drum next to the key. He then turned to McCready and came at him.

McCready was ready, but he wasn't prepared for the physical onslaught that hit him. The man must have had fists of iron. The first hit him in the gut. He managed to dodge the second, replying with a punch of his own, but the third smashed into his face, sending him spinning to the ground, seeing stars.

Suki could only watch in despair. There was nothing she could do.

McCready was a big, strong man. He was quite capable of looking after himself in most situations, if provoked, but this was something else. He wasn't combat trained. He realized pretty quickly there was little he could do against Ivanov. It was a matter of trying to protect himself and hoping luck would give him a break. Give him something he could use as an edge.

Ivanov backed off to give him some space.

"Come on, McCready. This is too easy. You don't want to look weak and pathetic to your little girlfriend here. She'll be begging for a real man when I've finished with you!"

McCready started to raise himself to his knees. He was trying to get his breath back when Ivanov moved forward and kicked him in the ribs. He felt one of them crack as he rolled back over onto the ground.

"Jesus, this isn't even a workout!"

Suki watched from her position at the railing. She could see the key on the top of the drum and also the gun. If there was only a way she could get to them she could help McCready. She strained as far as she could go, but she was still many feet away when her wrist came up sharply against the metal of the cuffs that dug into her flesh.

She was helpless.

McCready again started to lift himself up. Before he had even reached his knees Ivanov kicked him in the head.

This time he was down and out. He felt the blackness of unconsciousness creeping up on him. He felt bile and nausea fill his body. He started to slip away, but as he did, he realized Suki's hopes would be gone too. Somewhere, something deep inside him made him fight back. He couldn't leave her again, whatever the cost.

Slowly, his thoughts started to return. He managed to focus through the pain, through the splitting head, through the damaged rib. He somehow found the strength to push himself onto his knees. He was breathing heavily, head down. But as he started to stand he heard Suki cry out.

"No! No!"

Ivanov held his gun rock steady. There was a thin smile on his face.

He fired, hitting the ground inches from McCready, splintering the concrete.

Suki screamed.

Ivanov put the gun in his waistband, crossed over to the drum, and picked up the key. He then unlocked Suki's handcuffs, put the key back on the drum, and dragged her over to McCready.

"She can watch up close. Give her a final memory of you."

McCready could do nothing but wait for the inevitable. This was how he was going to die. All he could think about, though, was how he had failed Suki again.

Ivanov's gaze was on McCready. He pulled the gun from his waist and aimed it at his head. It didn't waver. His peripheral vision told him Suki was at his side.

She was no threat.

He was in complete control.

While Ivanov was focused on McCready, Suki looked desperately around.

Deep Impact

There had to be something.

Anything.

It couldn't end like this.

And suddenly there was.

She thought about it for a split second. And knew what she had to do.

Keeping an eye on Ivanov, she inched forward until she could reach the weight belts on the dock just behind the Russian. Carefully, she dragged two of them toward her, wrapping them around her waist. She then quietly started to breathe deeply in and out, saturating her tissues with oxygen.

Then slowly she moved her left hand toward Ivanov's right foot.

Ivanov cocked the gun. The metallic click had a certain finality about it. He let out a contented sigh.

"Goodbye, McCready."

He tightened his finger around the trigger and started to squeeze.

Before he could apply the final pressure that would end McCready's life, he heard another metallic click.

This one came from his right foot.

He eased the pressure from the trigger and stared down. He hadn't quite registered what had happened when Suki leaped for the water two feet away. As she moved, the handcuff, now attached to Ivanov's ankle, yanked him off his feet.

Suki rolled over the edge dragging Ivanov with her.

They hit the water with a loud splash.

"Suki... Nooooo!" cried out McCready.

He managed to hobble to the side as they disappeared below the surface.

He turned, desperate. He had to do something.

He grabbed the one remaining weight belt and slung it round his waist. There was no time to get the rebreather ready. He reached up for the key to the handcuffs on the oil drum and slid it inside the cuff of his drysuit. He then grabbed the small lightweight cylinder and regulator he had brought for Suki and pulled on her mask. Once he had them in place, he hauled himself the short distance to the edge of the dock, rammed the mouthpiece into his mouth, and fell into the water.

A moment later he had stabilized himself, gasping at the pain from his injuries.

He looked down.

He could just make out the two figures below.

They were receding quickly, now barely visible, their fates intertwined as they were dragged inexorably down to the bottom of the shaft a hundred feet below.

And neither of them had any air.

Chapter Fifty-Four

When Suki hit the water, she knew she was probably going to die.

But it didn't matter. She had to save McCready.

As she fell beneath the surface her immediate thought was that it wasn't such a great idea. The cold stabbed at her like knives piercing her skin. She had known it would be cold, but she'd never felt anything quite like this before. It undid a lot of her attempt to saturate her blood with oxygen, as the shock of the temperature made her gasp, losing much of the air she would desperately need. Also, with Ivanov's weight on her wrist, the metal of the handcuff had dug into her skin, drawing blood.

But that was the least of her worries.

The weights around her waist were pulling her down fast.

Not only that, she wasn't attached to an inert object. Ivanov was desperately trying to swim upward. The kicking action of his legs tore her wrist from side to side, deepening the cut. But even Ivanov's formidable strength couldn't overcome the laws of physics and the pull of gravity.

They sank deeper and deeper, all the while the water around them becoming darker and more desolate.

Finally they reached the bottom, a hundred feet down.

Initially she didn't feel too bad, apart from the cold. She'd been to these depths many times, but this time she had no mask, so although she could make out shapes, she couldn't see detail. She could see enough, though, to realize a fist was rapidly coming toward her face.

Underwater, movement is dampened and slowed by the mass of water, but even so, the fist approached at an alarming rate. She managed to reel back before the next one came at her. It was like a slow-motion boxing match where all the punches were thrown from one side.

After a couple of missed blows, Ivanov lunged at her waist, trying to reach the belts that were holding them on the bottom. But the buckles had slipped around to the back and he couldn't locate them.

Next, though, he did something that did concern her. She vaguely saw him reach into his jacket and pull something out. When a glint of light reflected off the blade of a knife, Suki knew she was in trouble.

Ivanov bent down and started to hack at Suki's wrist. She let out a scream, losing more valuable air. She kicked him in the face, trying to retreat—but wherever she went, he was pulled after her. Her kicks landed on his face, but again, the energy was absorbed by the water. They barely registered. Ivanov merely deflected them like an animal swatting a fly with its tail.

And then he came forward again, the knife firmly in his grip.

McCready could make out the two figures below him as he descended.

He swam down as fast as could. The pain increased in his eardrums due to the speed of descent. He tried to clear them, but one wouldn't go. He felt a piercing stab, like a needle being driven into the side of his head, and he knew one of the eardrums had burst, but he had to go on. Once the pain had subsided he felt nauseous. A deep cold seeped into his skull, but he had to fight through the feeling to concentrate on what he had to do.

Below him the two figures moved around each other. Suki was trying to fight off Ivanov. What brought a chill to his veins was the knife he could see in Ivanov's hand.

He swam faster.

Suki was fading fast.

She knew what it was like when you were about to black out. She'd been close on a number of occasions but had never fully succumbed. This time there was no easy way out. The pain she felt in her wrist from the knife had faded into the background, helped by the numbing cold.

She knew when she controlled her breathing before a deep dive and when she plunged her face into the water that her heart rate slowed down, allowing her to stay longer in the depths. This was one benefit of the cold; it slowed her heart rate even more.

But now she felt she was close to the end.

She barely made out the new shape that arrived behind Ivanov. She saw, rather than felt, the cutting motion stop on her hand, and then she felt something shoved toward her mouth. It was bubbling and was small and black but she couldn't work out what to do with it. She reached for it but then almost immediately dropped it. The shape in front of her picked it up, took it away briefly, then pushed it back toward her.

She didn't know what to do.

The blackness was increasing.

The first thing McCready did when he reached them was pull Ivanov off Suki. He gripped the Russian's arm and wrenched it backward, making him drop the knife.

Next, while trying to contain Ivanov, he took his mouthpiece out of his mouth and passed it to Suki. There was very little air in the small tank but it should be enough to get them to the surface if he could get her to breathe from it.

But try as he might, she wouldn't take the mouthpiece. He looked into her eyes and saw that she didn't have long.

Ivanov was still struggling.

It left him with no option.

McCready reached down to the floor of the shaft and picked up the knife. He had never killed a man before but he had no choice. He knew it was the only thing he could do if he wanted to save Suki.

He pulled his arm back as far as it would go and plunged the knife down into Ivanov's chest. Immediately a smooth red smear oozed out from his body, like a thin red mist in the clear water. Ivanov grunted out a mouthful of air as the blade went in. He convulsed several times. But the struggles slowed and finally stopped altogether.

He lay still.

McCready put his fingers under his drysuit cuff seal, reaching for the key to the handcuffs.

But it was gone. It must have fallen out in the struggle.

He glanced at Suki. Her eyes were barely open. There

was only one thing for it. He grabbed hold of Ivanov's leg, close to the handcuffs. He then purposefully, and with no emotion, took the knife and sawed at his foot. It wasn't easy. The bone was hard. He had to crack the ankle joint across his knee and work the knife between the bones, but eventually the foot detached from the leg and he could pull the handcuffs free.

He looked at Suki, ready to head for the surface. Her eyes were still, but they were locked onto his. He could see her lips move slowly…

… and he thought he could make something out.

Three… simple… words.

He stood motionless for a second, unable to move.

Suki felt the weight of Ivanov disappear from her wrist. There was now a lightness to her arm she found comforting. She could see McCready right in front of her. He was reaching to grab hold of her.

She could also feel herself slipping away.

But there was something she had to do before she went. It was really important to her, and she was really frustrated. She couldn't make her lips move. Such a simple thing, but they wouldn't move.

Then with one final effort she managed it. She put every atom of her being into moving her lips. Everything else in her body had gone, shut down.

This was it.

They moved imperceptibly…

I

Keep trying. It was really hard but she managed to get the second one out…

LOVE

Only one to go, and then she was done…

YOU

She knew the message had been received when the figure in front of her stopped moving.

She smiled to herself.

She felt the world receding into the distance, like light disappearing at the end of a tunnel, and she saw them all around her.

Her dolphins.

She could swim freely with them now.

No one could stop her.

No one could hurt her ever again.

She was at peace.

And with that her heart stopped beating and she died.

Chapter Fifty-Five

McCready stood on the bottom of the shaft, completely still.

He was in total shock.

He couldn't believe it.

Then something at the back of his brain told him to wake up. Told him to sort the situation. Told him to pull himself together. And as if a switch had been pulled he clicked into gear.

There was no way they could get out through the tunnel now. And he couldn't leave Suki here whatever happened. There was one chance and one chance only.

She wasn't wearing any protective clothing and the water was close to freezing. Her heart rate would have slowed from the temperature.

He clicked the stopwatch on his watch.

He knew of people who had been revived twelve minutes after their heart had stopped in cold water. He had also heard stories of far greater times, but that hadn't helped his brother when he had died in his arms at the bottom of the North Sea. He would go with what he knew. He had twelve minutes to get her to the surface and revive her. If they were captured by the Russians, so be it.

He grabbed her inert body, dropped the weight belts, and headed up.

A new purpose. A new hope.

When he broke through the surface he checked his watch.

2 minutes.

He swam to the side of the dock and grabbed hold of the ladder. He literally dragged Suki up after him. She weighed little, and there was no time to stand on grace. He looked around him. There was no one there.

No one to help.

He was alone.

He threw off his gear, then laid her gently on the concrete. He compressed her chest thirty times. He then extended her neck and breathed twice into her lungs, watching her chest rise and fall. He then repeated the cycle. He knew the procedure could work, but what he really needed was a defibrillator. If he couldn't revive her within a couple of minutes he would take her back to the base and seek help from the Russians. This had its risks; what if they just shot them both?

He was continuing the compressions when he heard a crackle in his ear.

"John, this is Khalid. Do you copy?"

He pressed the throat mike on the collar around his neck.

"Khalid, go ahead."

"What's your status?"

"Not good. Omar and Ahmed are down. We found the girl but she's stopped breathing. I'm trying to revive her, but

Deep Impact

I may have no option but to surrender to the Russians and see if they can help."

There was a pause on the line. When Yassin replied, his voice was deadly serious.

"John, there is another way. Listen to me very carefully."

After Yassin had spoken, McCready almost stopped giving the compressions. He couldn't believe what he had heard. He had to force himself to continue trying to revive Suki. When the prince spoke again there was even more urgency in his voice.

"John, you have to decide now. We have a surveillance drone in the air. They're coming for you."

At that moment McCready looked back toward the base. He could hear and then see the small, fast boats heading his way. They were filled with armed men.

He had no choice.

Again Yassin came over the comms.

"John, trust me. I... will... catch... you."

And then he decided.

He picked Suki up and staggered over to the RIB at the side of the dock, ignoring the pain in his body. He climbed in and laid Suki on the floor. There was no time to continue the cycle. But if he didn't act on Yassin's information there would be no hope at all.

He hit the starter and the engine spluttered to life. He heard a buzzing sound and glanced up. He could just make out a small surveillance drone hovering fifty feet above.

He glanced back toward the base. The boats were a hundred yards from the end of the dock and closing fast.

He checked his watch.

5 minutes.

He pushed the throttle forward, turning the boat away

from the side. He had to briefly head toward the base to get around the dock that surrounded the shaft.

By the time he had cleared it, the chasing boats were close enough that he could see the faces of the men. There were five boats in all. As he turned to head away from them they fanned out to block any escape behind them.

A second later, bullets rained down around him. Several hit the dock behind his head, sending splinters of concrete into the air, but then he was gone.

Ahead of him was nearly a quarter of a mile of water and the cliffs beyond.

"*I will catch you*," Yassin had said. McCready still didn't believe him, but despite everything he did trust the man. That trust was going to be put to the test.

He pushed the throttle all the way forward. The boat raced along, the smooth water skimming past below the black fiberglass hull. There was still some fog ahead but it was beginning to clear above and the sun was threatening to break through.

More bullets hit the water around him, one striking the left-hand buoyancy chamber. It exploded, the sound eclipsing the roar of the engine.

They were halfway to the end of the lake, and McCready was beginning to think they were going to make it, when the engine coughed and spluttered.

He looked back, but it coughed again and then died.

The speed dropped off and the boat eased down, gliding to a smooth stop. The boats behind were now closing at a terrifying rate.

McCready moved to the rear.

There were two fuel cans on the floor. One was plugged into the outboard motor. He lifted it.

Empty.

The second one was full. He quickly unplugged the fuel line from the first and plugged it into the second. More bullets zipped past. One ricocheted off the engine cover causing a shiver of plastic to embed itself in his arm. He swore and then started to pump the small balloon-like pump in the fuel line to feed the fuel to the engine.

He moved back quickly to the controls and hit the engine start.

First time no go.

Second time no go.

Third time a charm.

The engine spluttered to life. He rammed the throttle forward and they shot off across the water. Just as they did, another bullet blasted into the remaining buoyancy chamber.

It burst like a gunshot.

The boat was now only staying afloat on speed alone. If he stopped it would sink below the surface.

9 minutes.

He looked ahead. All he could see was the end of the lake approaching fast. The water lapped against a small, sloping grass verge. Beyond that was a narrow track and then the vertical cliff face and the jagged rocks a hundred feet below.

I will catch you.

Well, he was about to find out.

More gunfire ripped into the boat, this time grazing his arm. He glanced back. His pursuers were still fanned out. Two either side, one directly behind.

He suddenly heard a piercing roar coming from in front of him. It was like a mechanical hurricane, a screaming maelstrom. A noise like he had never heard before. He looked forward and was met by an incredible sight.

About forty feet either side, and a hundred feet ahead, two F35 Lightning jets rose vertically above the fast approaching cliff edge. A second later their canons fired simultaneously, spewing thousands of rounds a minute down the lake. He glanced behind and McCready saw four of the boats disintegrate as they were blown into the air. It was as though they were hurled skyward in slow motion to turn and crash down into the water below.

There was one boat left.

It was now so close the jets couldn't fire for risk of hitting McCready. He took his faith in his hands and looked ahead. He eased himself as low into the boat as possible and made sure Suki was close to him.

And then he shot out over the hundred-foot cliff into thin air.

For several seconds he thought he was going to die.

The fog hid what lay ahead. All he could see were the churning waves a hundred feet below. But as the boat flew out over the void something else came into view and he could hardly believe his eyes.

Right ahead, eighty feet from the edge of the cliff, was the steep metallic slope of the ski jump at the bow of HMS *Queen Elizabeth*.

He only had a second to process this before the boat crashed down onto the sloping takeoff ramp, skidding uncontrollably. As it hit, he held Suki's inert body close to him and grabbed hold of anything he could find.

And prayed.

The boat skidded down the slope. As it reached the bottom, the now redundant propeller caught on a metal strip, sending the boat cartwheeling sideways in an uncontrollable spin. It rolled over and over down the flight deck.

Behind it, the remaining Russian boat had followed

McCready out over the cliff. It remained upright as it hit the ramp, shooting down onto the deck of the carrier, only to slowly grind to a halt as it lost all momentum.

It was immediately surrounded by armed men. The startled driver and his compatriot couldn't believe their eyes. They looked around in bewilderment. The man with the gun dropped his weapon and they both slowly raised their hands.

McCready had held Suki close to him to prevent her from being thrown from the boat. When they finally came to a stop he relaxed his grip.

But there was no time to rest.

He checked his watch.

13 minutes.

Chapter Fifty-Six

McCready scrambled out of the boat, ignoring the pain shooting through his body.

He could see people running toward him, including Yassin, but more importantly, a gurney was being rushed across the deck with medical staff in attendance. He picked himself up, wincing in agony, and quickly lifted Suki's small, fragile body up from where she lay.

As the gurney arrived he placed her on it.

One of the doctors turned to him with a reassuring sense of urgency.

"What's her condition?"

"She stopped breathing over thirteen minutes ago. But she was in cold water... Please save her," pleaded McCready. "You have to save her."

"We'll do all we can," said the doctor before she was wheeled away at speed, two of the orderlies carrying out CPR as she left.

Once McCready could see there was nothing else he

could do, he fell to his knees, finally allowing the pain of his injuries to enter his consciousness.

He felt himself becoming nauseous. The world was swimming before him and he collapsed to the deck. The last thing he saw was Yassin's worried face calling for a medic.

When McCready awoke he had no idea where he was.

It seemed to be a state he had been in a lot recently. Almost every awakening had been under duress, or else extreme stress, and nearly always accompanied by a huge amount of pain.

As his eyes flickered open this time, though, there was a friendly face looking down.

Yassin's expression was one of concern, relief, and sadness.

McCready tried to ease himself up but fell back onto the pillow with the pain that seemed to be registering from every part of his body.

"Rest, my friend. You have been through quite the ordeal," said Yassin.

But McCready suddenly felt panicked.

"Suki, how is Suki?"

"They are still working on her, John. But she is in good hands. She has a chance."

McCready slumped back, worry etched on his face. Then he looked at Yassin.

"I don't understand. How... where did all this come from?"

Yassin's expression took on a conspiratorial air. "Ah, well now, that goes back a long way. When we were planning everything, I knew our little expedition had little chance of succeeding on its own, so I had to have a backup—a Plan B as you Brits are so fond of calling it.

"When I was at Oxford—your godforsaken country does at least have some benefits—I bumped into a certain Martin Steel. We were rivals. I respected him, but I would never say we were actual friends. So I made a couple of calls. I told him that if the British government wanted those billion-pound arms deals his Prime Minister was so grateful for, I needed a little help. He was quite obstreperous to begin with, but I think he came round." He spread his arms, indicating where they were.

McCready again found himself shaking his head.

"By the way, where is that son of a bitch?"

"He is very busy dealing with the Russians." Yassin's face took on a sad expression. "He is ensuring the return of Omar and Ahmed's bodies to us. A straight swap for their two men who landed on the ship. Under the circumstances I don't think the Russians have much choice. We managed to get the carrier and the fleet in close by jamming their radar, and the firepower at Mr. Steel's disposal is somewhat overwhelming. I think he is just itching for a fight as payback for the crew of *Resilient*."

"Thank you, Khalid. Thank you for everything."

Yassin bowed gently and then looked straight at McCready.

"You need to rest now, my friend. We will talk later."

And with that, Yassin left.

McCready watched him go. He had never really doubted him, but the man had repaid the debt, in full... and then some.

He dozed for around half an hour and then found himself focusing on something in his mind, something Yassin had said.

Plan B.

With everything that had been going on, he felt he'd been out of control for much of the time, a situation he didn't like to be put in. There was one thing, though, he needed to check on, that he felt he was very much in control of.

He clicked a call button at the side of the bed. A minute later one of the nurses came over to him. He was in his early thirties, dressed in the standard naval uniform, and with an efficient air about him.

"Are you okay, Mr. McCready? Anything I can get you?"

"Yes, do you know where the things are that I had on me when I… er… came aboard?"

"They're in a box in the cupboard by the side of your bed. Shall I get them for you?"

"If you could, thanks."

The man went around the side of the bed and reached into a small cupboard built into the unit. He pulled out a box the size of a laptop and around six inches deep. He then pressed a control that raised the back of the bed so McCready was in more of a sitting position and placed the box in his lap.

"Is there anything else?"

"Yes. Do you know the condition of the girl who was with me?"

At this the nurse's expression turned serious. "I'm afraid I'm not sure. One of the doctors will be along shortly to talk to you."

And with that, he left, but McCready couldn't help noticing a bad feeling starting to grow in the pit of his stomach. He tried to push the thought from his mind and turned to the box.

He opened the lid and looked inside.

The first thing he saw was his phone, which he needed, and he took it out. He switched it on and put it on the side table. The only other thing in the box was the drive assembly. Clearly no one had known what it was or anything about it and had just put it in with his things. He wondered what the look on Steel's face would be like when he produced it. At least from Steel's point of view the outcome would have been a success. It remained to be seen, when McCready heard about Suki, whether it would be from his.

He picked up the phone and tapped on the message app. He selected MAC LOGAN from the list of names and typed the simple message:

PLAN B?

He wondered how long it would take to get a reply, but he had barely put the phone back on the side when he heard the familiar 'ping' indicating a message had come in. He looked at the screen and frowned. What the hell did that mean?

PLAN B ALL DONE. IF THEY COME, THEY'D BETTER NOT LOOK AT THEIR FEET.

He was still frowning when he saw the shadow of someone approaching. He almost had a smile on his face as he tried to work out what Logan had meant, when he looked up and saw a doctor standing there. He was of medium build, around fifty years old. He clearly had experience, but he was wearing an expression you never wanted to see on a doctor's face.

McCready knew before he could even utter a word.

"I'm terribly sorry, Mr. McCready, but we couldn't save your friend."

McCready just stared at him, not wanting to believe the words he was hearing.

After everything they'd been through. After the pain of her life. After the joy he had seen on her face.

For it to end like this.

"We managed to get a weak pulse, but it didn't last. We tried for several hours, but she had been gone for too long. I'm so sorry. If there's anything you need, please don't hesitate to ask." He paused for a moment. "Do you know if she had any family, relatives? Anyone who should be contacted?"

McCready was still lost for words. Slowly, he managed to focus on what the doctor had asked.

"No, no. There was no one. She was quite alone."

He thought for a moment how desperately sad that was. And as he did, he knew what he had to do. He looked up at the doctor.

"Can I ask for one thing?"

The doctor looked at him. "Of course," he said gently.

"She... She should be buried at sea. She loved the ocean, the animals in it. They were her family. It's where she would want to be."

The doctor thought for a moment and then came to a decision. "I'll talk to the captain, but I'm sure that can be arranged... when you're fit enough to attend."

"Thank you."

The doctor was about to leave then seemed to remember something. He reached into his pocket. "I almost forgot. She was wearing this. I'm sure she would have wanted you to have it." He pulled out the dolphin locket and handed it to McCready.

As he took it he could feel himself choking up. He nodded at the doctor but couldn't form any words.

"I'll leave you alone. If there's anything you need…"

And then he left.

Once he had gone McCready took a deep breath.

He felt close to tears.

He held the locket by the delicate chain and lifted it up. The dolphin seemed to be smiling at him. He managed a weak smile as the memories of her came tumbling back. And as they did, an idea formed in his mind. It grew from the things she had told him about her childhood, the things that had started her on a life of sadness and despair, and he knew what he was going to do. He had to act for her in some way. It was his promise to her, to her friends from the ocean where she had been happiest.

He opened the locket and the tracker fell out. He had almost forgotten it had been in there. He glanced briefly at the small pictures of her parents looking out from either side and made a promise to them that he would do something for their daughter.

He then closed the locket and picked up the tracker.

He glanced at the drive sitting on the side table and an idea came to him.

This thing that had caused so much pain and death; he needed to have an edge.

Chapter Fifty-Seven

The wind blew across the flight deck of HMS *Queen Elizabeth*.

It tugged at clothing and sent the white ensign fluttering at its position halfway up the mast.

McCready had been recovering for the last two days, and the doctor had finally given him permission to leave the ward. His rib was cracked, but it wasn't broken. His eardrum was perforated, but with time it should heal, though he would have to be careful on descents when diving in the future, and he might have trouble with hearing certain frequencies going forward. Overall, he would just have to take things easy for a while, but with rest he would be able to make a full recovery.

He still felt battered and bruised though.

The full ship's company, save those on duty in essential positions, were lined up in rows on the deck in uniform. At the side of the ship, a black platform, around eight feet long by four feet wide, had been erected. On the top of it lay a shape, the size of a small woman, hidden beneath a Japanese flag.

McCready had been to see her before she had been enclosed in the burial wrap. She had looked so sweet and innocent just lying there. It was hard to believe what she had been through in her short life. In one way he was glad she was now finally at peace. Nothing could ever harm her again. He had kissed her gently on the forehead and whispered a few words in her ear before leaving. No one in attendance had heard what he had said.

As the wind calmed a little, the ship's chaplain said a few words of introduction and then asked McCready to step forward.

He looked around at the men and women on the deck, to Yassin, the chaplain, the captain, and also to Steel, whom he had noticed at the rear of the group. It was the first time he had seen him since coming aboard.

He took a deep breath.

"I didn't know Suki for very long, but in the short time that I did, I came to love a free spirit. Sadly, it was one that had been shackled by the life she had been given, forcing her to live in fear for too many years and hiding a truly lovely and beautiful soul. My hope is she will now be free for all eternity, and may she forgive me for not protecting her as I should. May she rest in peace."

He stepped back and the chaplain stepped forward.

As the chaplain read a short prayer McCready found his eyes welling up. How could life be so unfair, so unkind? He found himself focusing intently on the small form on the platform.

When the chaplain's words came to an end, one of the ratings stationed at the head of the platform pulled a lever at the side. The platform tilted up, allowing Suki's body to slide out from under the flag. She was tightly wrapped in blue cotton sheets, which completely covered her head and body.

She slipped off the end of the platform, and then there was the long drop to the waiting ocean below.

McCready watched until the final bubbles of the impact had disappeared and she had been taken by the waves forever.

As the crew filed solemnly back to their posts, he turned and looked out to the horizon. It was the end of the day. The sun was slipping below the thin line at the edge of the world and the sky was alight with crimson and orange.

It was a fitting farewell.

He was lost in thought when he felt a presence behind him.

"I'm truly sorry, John."

McCready turned to find himself face to face with Martin Steel.

The man looked at him evenly. His expression was neutral, but McCready could tell his words were genuine; at least, they seemed that way.

"I'm only sorry we couldn't have done more."

"Thank you for coming," McCready managed eventually. "I probably wouldn't be here if it wasn't for you." And then added, "In more ways than one."

There was an awkward silence between them.

"What happened to Craig?" asked McCready.

"The doctors said he was fit to travel, and he wanted to return to Scotland. He flew back a few days ago. He seemed fine considering what he went through."

McCready nodded, watching a seagull wing its way on the late afternoon wind blowing across the sea. He reached into his jacket pocket.

"Here, this is for you."

McCready pulled the drive out of his pocket and watched Steel closely as he presented it to him. What he saw was not what he had expected. Initially there was shock, which was understandable, and then a brief moment of anger, which was confusing.

Steel took the drive. He turned it over several times in his hands and then looked at McCready. Something about his expression had changed. There was none of the empathy that had been there moments before. He suddenly seemed somewhat tense—on edge.

McCready looked at him curiously. "Thought you'd have been pleased. It's what this was all about, after all. The number of people who've died…"

Steel composed himself. "I am. It was just a surprise seeing it here." But McCready wasn't convinced.

"So what will you do now, John? We can make arrangements to fly you back to the UK."

"No, thanks," said McCready. He glanced at the platform where Suki had been lying only minutes before. "I'll go back with Khalid to Japan on the whaler. There's something I need to do for someone."

"Okay," said Steel. He paused, looking out over the ocean for a moment. Then he turned to McCready. "Look, I have things to do. I'm sure we'll talk back in London."

And with that he headed briskly away toward the rear of the two islands at the side of the ship.

McCready watched him go and then pulled out his phone. He scanned through the contacts and clicked on one. After a few rings it was answered. He spoke quickly.

"Hi, it's John."

He listened briefly.

"How's the recovery going?"

He smiled at the reply.

"Okay, can you meet me? I need your help with something. I'll send you a ticket, all the details."

A minute later he ended the call and looked back out over the water to where the wind was increasing and whitecaps were forming on the tops of the waves.

He had a purpose.

He had a plan.

And he felt something returning that had been absent from his soul for quite some time.

In a hospital corridor at the Aberdeen Royal Infirmary, the nurse was just starting her night shift. There was now only one man in the private room from hell, and for that there were small mercies. But she still had to endure the constant nagging and complaining. She had thought it would get better with only one of them, but sadly, now there *was* only one, everything had come her way.

She picked up his medication and set off toward the door at the end of the corridor.

The man had, in fact, been healing quicker than the surgeons had expected. The cast on his leg had been reduced in size, and while the scars would remain for some time, some of them forever, if he took care of himself he'd be right as rain. He'd be walking around on crutches within a couple of days but would still be here for at least another two weeks.

As she reached the end of the corridor she took a deep breath and pushed open the door…

…and froze.

Both beds were empty.

All the man's belongings, his clothes, bath robe, radio,

had gone. In the center of the bed was what was left of the cast, split neatly down the middle, lying there like a big white slug.

She again checked pointlessly under the bed and behind the door, as she had when the other one had disappeared.

But he was gone.

A slight smile spread across her lips.

What was that saying? *To lose one may be regarded as a misfortune, to lose both is…*

…fortuitous?

Chapter Fifty-Eight

Three days later, McCready stood in the arrivals zone at Kansai International Airport in Japan. The airport was a triumph of engineering, having been built on an artificial island in the middle of Osaka Bay.

The place was crowded and, like everywhere in Japan, everyone seemed to be in a hurry, heads down, racing through life with no time to stop.

As the new arrivals streamed out of the customs hall, McCready could make out the distinctive shape of Eugene Porter making his way through the throng.

As he approached, the Englishman wore his usual annoyed expression. He had no trolley and his only baggage was slung across his back, but he was making heavy weather of pushing through the mass of people on his crutches.

As he reached McCready, there was no great welcome, merely a scowl followed by, "Only trouble with going abroad is all the bloody foreigners!"

McCready had to smile. Porter had his issues, but he was good at his job and he needed his expertise. A typically harassed traveler brushed past, knocking one of Porter's crutches to the ground. He muttered a hasty apology in Japanese as he hurried on.

"Oi, you! Johnny Jappo!" shouted Porter, but the man was gone.

Porter shook his head and then looked at McCready, who had bent to pick up his crutch. "Sorry, guv, but you'd have thought they'd at least learned to speak bloody English."

"It is their country, Eugene."

Porter thought about this for a minute and then shrugged. "Yeah, guess so. Still bloody inconsiderate!" He looked at McCready.

"Now, what was it you wanted demolished?"

It took them over an hour to get out of the car park in the white Toyota Land Cruiser McCready had rented. Piled high in the back, kept well undercover, was the equipment Porter had said he would need. Some of this included unused explosives from the operation at the Russian base that had been left on the whaler. The rest were specific items Porter had requested.

McCready had had a long conversation with Yassin. The prince had wanted to come with McCready on what he was planning. McCready had declined, saying he had already done enough and he didn't want to be responsible for a diplomatic incident between Japan and Saudi Arabia. Yassin had seen the wisdom of this but had used his contacts to arrange the equipment. It wasn't as though you could just fly in with it through customs, after all.

So McCready was now driving south from the airport on a promise he had made to Suki, one he had told her about as she had lain at peace in the morgue aboard HMS *Queen Elizabeth*.

It was about ninety miles to their destination.

At least they didn't have to navigate the bustling streets of Osaka, being well to the south of the main city. They were soon through any built-up area and out into the open green mountains and valleys of the southern region of Kansai.

As he drove, McCready explained to Porter why they were there; how he had got involved with Suki; her traumatized life; and why this was so important to him.

Porter had listened intently, and while McCready had thought he would take it with his usual grumpy, flippant attitude, he noticed, with the odd sideways glance, that the man was incredibly subdued. He couldn't be sure, but he thought he had even seen him wipe a tear from his eye at one point; not that Porter would ever have admitted it. When McCready had been about to say something, he had quickly complained about getting dust in his eye. McCready had smiled, realizing he was seeing the man in a new light.

When he had finished, Porter had sat there quietly for several minutes before saying, almost under his breath, "Okay, guv, let's teach these bastards a lesson!"

Three hours later they hit the coast at Shingu and turned south for the ten-mile drive to Taiji. The roads were good and McCready could smell the saltwater in the air. There was a light breeze blowing in off the sea, the air was fresh and clear, but as they reached their destination he couldn't help feeling a deep depression settle over him.

The town itself was a pleasant little fishing community, which, from the outside, seemed like any other in the world.

There was the bustling harbor with a constant stream of boats coming and going. There were the fishermen with nets strewn up on the dockside, some drying, some being repaired. There was even a tourist vibe to the town, with a whale museum, advertised boat trips promoting the local coastline, and numerous fish restaurants touting for business, each claiming they had the best catch in town.

But McCready knew there was a dark side.

It was here where hundreds of dolphins were slaughtered every year in a small cove to the north of the town. It was this that McCready had flown Porter halfway round the world to help destroy. True, there were other coves that could take over the gruesome activity, but it would be a symbol of resistance and a statement that the practice had no place in the twenty-first century.

They drove past the harbor, through the town, and entered a short tunnel beneath a tree-covered hill. They emerged into daylight. On their left was a parking area; on their right, a small bay hidden by a mound of earth.

McCready drove into the parking area.

They climbed out of the car, stretched their tired limbs, and then walked across the road and up onto the raised bank of earth by the water.

The bay was quite small, and it looked innocent enough from here. The water was calm and blue and it was like any other small bay you could find on numerous coastlines. But behind the rock wall on the right-hand side there was a second, concealed inlet: a hidden, secluded cove where the fishermen could go about their deadly slaughter undisturbed and unseen.

Even from back here, he could imagine the horror.

They surveyed the bay for around ten minutes and then walked back to the car.

One thing he'd noticed while driving around was that, following publicity about the actions of the fishermen—there was even a documentary, entitled *The Cove*—the authorities were particularly nervous about strangers. The area had become a magnet for environmentalists and protesters and a high police presence was in evidence.

They were going to have to be careful.

One thing was for sure, it wouldn't be possible to carry out what they needed to do from the car park; it was just too public.

Before he had left for Japan, McCready had researched the location.

They drove back through the tunnel and made an immediate left down a small road. This led to the sea on the far side of the land that bordered the right-hand side of the hidden cove.

They found a place to park next to some houses. It was fairly quiet and they didn't think they'd be disturbed.

Porter immediately set to work preparing his gear. Given he was restricted by his lack of mobility and dislike of water, it would be down to McCready to place the charges. Porter would instruct him where to put them, set up the remotes, and cover the technical side of things.

While Porter prepared the explosives, McCready checked through his gear. He unpacked a wetsuit, a small oxygen rebreather he could wear on his chest, his fins and mask, and an underwater drill that was air powered from a small cylinder.

He wouldn't be going deep, but he did need to be stealthy. If there were bubbles, they could be seen by anyone on the surface. He didn't particularly want to be caught by any angry fishermen with steel-hooked poles and ferociously sharp knives.

An hour later, as night started to fall, they were ready.

Porter went over the procedure with McCready.

The charges had to be drilled into the cliff walls precisely six feet below the surface, to a depth of a foot into the rock. The smaller charges, to break the nets lying across the entrance, had to be wrapped around the top of the main cable holding them in place. These should be set on the cable against the wall at either side of the cove. While he was doing this Porter would be at the top of the cliff preparing the control systems. McCready should join him there once he had set the charges. From the vantage point they'd be able to set off diversionary explosives to scare any fishermen from the water. They didn't actually want to kill anyone. Then he would detonate the main charges.

McCready grabbed his kit and walked down to the water's edge.

He eased himself into the water. It was cool, but not cold, and was refreshing on any skin that was still exposed. He headed along the rocks, keeping close to the side.

Ten minutes later he rounded the entrance to the cove and swam to the line of nets held in place by the cable screwed into the cliff face on either side.

Although it was close to the end of the killing season, there were dolphins in the water. He could hear their squeaks and cries of anguish. He could also make out a misty fog in the water. As it was now dusk the color wasn't clear, but he was in no doubt that if there had been light he would have been swimming through a sea of red. It gave him extra impetus as he swam around to the nets.

Once there, he reached into the bag he'd attached to the rebreather harness and pulled out the first of the two shaped charges.

When the first one was securely in place he descended

to the bottom of the cove. He swam across to the far side to repeat the process. They needed to get any animals out of the area before bringing the cliffs down.

Once the second charge was in place on the net cable, he dropped down to a depth of six feet on the rock wall. He pulled out the drill, checked the air cylinder was turned on, and drilled four precise one-foot holes at the specific intervals Porter had instructed. He then inserted the long, thin tubes of explosives into the holes.

At one point he saw torchlight above the surface. A beam swept his way. He crouched in close to the rock, the darkness concealing him. The light swept further on along the cliff.

Once complete, he swam around to the far side of the rock promontory that divided the secret cove from the rest of the bay. Here, he repeated the procedure with the charges without incident. He then returned to the exit point where he had entered the water. He carried the gear back to the Land Cruiser and made his way up the hill to join Porter at the top of the cliff.

As he approached, he could see the explosives expert with an array of switches and remote control boxes laid out beside him. He was currently lying prone on his stomach, his head over the edge, watching proceedings below. He was muttering to himself.

McCready joined him and lay down on the grass.

"Bastards! Utter bastards!" said Porter as quietly as he could manage.

"It's why we're here," said McCready.

"All good?" asked Porter, without taking his eyes off the water below.

"Guess we'll find out soon enough."

Porter eased himself back from the edge. "Okay, we blow the nets first. Then you lob these over the side."

McCready looked at what appeared to be a number of small oval objects that looked a lot like hand grenades. He glanced worryingly at Porter.

"Don't worry, guv, they won't kill anyone; they'll just go off with a ruddy great bang and scare the shit out of 'em!"

He was trying to suppress a grin.

"Once the nets are down, hopefully the dolphins will escape. But to make sure, if you lob the rest of the, er, grenades into the water near the shore, that should flush 'em out. When we're sure they're all gone, we blow the main charges. They're staged to go off in sequence. It'll send a ripple through the rock. Gives more impact for a given charge."

McCready glanced around the cliff top. He noticed Porter had a series of wires leading over the edge of the cliff in front of them.

"What's that for?" he asked.

Porter glanced back innocently. "Oh that, no need to worry about that," he said, turning his attention back to his boxes.

A couple of minutes later, he glanced at McCready.

"Okay, ready?"

"Ready."

They looked down over the edge again. McCready held the small grenades in his hands.

Porter hit the remotes for the net charges.

Below, there were two small explosions. Spray erupted from the cable holding the nets either side of the bay.

Immediately the fishermen looked up as the nets sank to the bottom. There was instant shouting and gesticulating.

Torches and high-beam lights were directed at where the nets had been.

A second later McCready threw the small grenades over the edge. He flung them in a pattern across the cove, making sure several landed in the water close to shore.

As the explosions went off there was panic.

They were as loud as flash bangs used by special forces. The noise was deafening. The fishermen cried out and started shouting at each other. More lights came on, but the explosions had the desired effect.

Everyone ran from the water.

At the same time, McCready could see flashes beneath the surface. The dolphins that were still able were fleeing the deadly waters, rushing to the safety of the open sea beyond the entrance of the cove.

Porter then brought out two remotes. He flicked the protective covers up, and then, with a glance at McCready, jabbed down simultaneously on the two red buttons.

What followed was a series of muffled blasts that seemed almost subdued compared to the flash bangs, but which sent a tremor through the ground beneath their feet. It was followed by a slow rumble that built in intensity until it became a roar.

They watched in awe as thousands of tons of rock that made up the promontory that hid the cove crumpled into the water revealing the bay beyond.

A moment later, Porter pulled another remote from his pocket and pushed down on that. Again there was an explosion, but this was even more muted. It came from just over the cliff edge in front of them, where the set of wires McCready had noticed, disappeared. McCready glanced at Porter, but he wasn't watching. In fact, McCready could see a slight smile on his face as he hummed away to himself.

In front of them a massive pall of smoke hung over the cove like a shroud.

As the smoke cleared, McCready and Porter crawled cautiously forward.

They looked down into the cove and at a whole new landscape.

The rock promontory had totally collapsed, blocking the entrance. No amount of digging would make a difference. And even if the rock could be moved, there was now a clear view across to the bay beyond. Nothing would be secret ever again.

The cove was gone.

The fishermen were gathered on the beach looking at the fallen wall, unable to believe their eyes. But gradually, as the situation dawned on them, there were a series of angry shouts in Japanese. This only intensified, with seemingly one group blaming another. This escalated until there were fights breaking out across the small beach and the police had to intervene.

McCready and Porter looked down with no sense of victory, just a grim satisfaction of what they had done.

"Come on, we'd better get out of here," said McCready.

He was about to stand up to leave when he noticed something on the rock just below the top of the cliff, visible in the glow from the lights below. There were three letters, etched in the rock. From where he stood, they were upside down. He craned his neck to read them.

P - W - E.

"Porter."

"Yes, guv."

"What's this?"

Porter walked over to peer down the cliff, then turned to

McCready, a smug look on his face. "Every great artist signs his work."

"P - W - E. What the hell is PWE?"

Porter looked at him as though he was stupid. "Porter Was 'Ere. Isn't it obvious?"

McCready looked at him incredulously. "But where's the H?"

"What 'H'?"

"In 'here'?"

Porter again looked confused. "There's no 'H' in 'ere, guv." He turned to pick up his gear. "And I thought you was an educated man."

McCready shook his head, smiling. He then stopped and glanced back down at the water below the cliff. He turned to Porter. "Go ahead, I'll be with you in a minute."

"Okay, guv."

McCready walked back to the edge of the cliff.

The shouting below had subsided as realization hit the fishermen their cove was no more. The breeze was becoming a stronger wind now. Clouds were starting to move in off the ocean.

McCready reached into his pocket and pulled out Suki's locket. He kissed it once and then looked at it for a full minute before taking a deep breath.

"Go and be with them. Go and be free!"

And with that, he threw the locket far out into the water.

A moment later, he turned and walked into the night, following Porter back to the car.

Chapter Fifty-Nine

McCready stepped out of a cab on Whitehall and stared up at the imposing black gates at the entrance to Downing Street. He'd flown back to Heathrow with Porter, whom he'd thanked for his help and said would see him soon. Porter had had to fly on up north, while McCready had been asked to Number 10 at the Prime Minister's request. It had come through Martin Steel. McCready wasn't quite sure how he would feel when he saw the man again, but at the end of the day he couldn't turn down an invitation from the PM.

It was a beautiful day and there was a light breeze. The sun was out, but there was still a slight nip in the air. The downside of the visit, though, was that McCready had persuaded himself he had to wear a tie, something that was particularly alien to him. He loosened it a fraction and tried to stretch the all too tight collar as he approached the gates.

After passing through security—he was on the list—he walked into the street he had seen so many times on television. It somehow seemed smaller, more confining, in real life. There were none of the banks of photographers and journalists that normally lined the left-hand side in times of crisis or major news events. Instead, there were a couple of cars parked just beyond the famous black door and that was it.

As he approached the entrance, a tall, striking black woman walked out. He recognized her as the Foreign Secretary. He managed to make it through before the door was closed again.

Once inside, he was met by a PA who took him through the corridors and up a set of stairs to a drawing room on the first floor. The PA knocked and then entered.

McCready followed the man into the room, where he saw the Prime Minister and Martin Steel seated in conversation in front of a fireplace. They both looked up at his arrival and stood.

"Mr. McCready," said Carter, "thank you for coming."

"Hello, John," said Steel.

McCready walked forward and shook both their hands. "Thank you, sir. It's an honor." He nodded at Steel.

"The honor's all mine," said Carter. "Please sit. Can I get you a drink?"

McCready noticed both men had stylish, chunky glasses in their hands. "Yes, thank you. Whisky would be great," he said as he sat on one of the large sofas.

Carter fixed the drink, handed it to McCready and then sat down on the sofa opposite.

"How are you, John?" asked Steel.

McCready hesitated. "Okay, thanks. I've been better, but a lot happened out there; a lot of people lost their lives."

Carter and Steel exchanged glances. The Prime Minister fixed McCready with a friendly but firm expression.

"John, I know you lost someone you cared about, and I know you were not given all the information before the operation. For that I am truly sorry." He paused. "We're fighting a war here that has no rules, as I am sure Martin has told you. We have to be ruthless to try and stay ahead of the game. We have to think outside the box if we're to have any chance of containing the threats that face us out there. The way this all unfolded was not as we would have wished. I can't give you all the details, for reasons of national security, but I can tell you the way you acted is greatly appreciated. You did what you thought was right in an impossible situation, and I want to thank you for that from the bottom of my heart."

McCready looked at the man. He seemed genuine, but at the end of the day he was a politician; how genuine could he be? He thought for a moment and then sighed. He would have to give him the benefit of the doubt.

"Thank you, sir. I appreciate that."

Carter stood up. "Now, I have a meeting I have to attend. If you'll excuse me, Martin here has some things he'd like to go over with you."

Carter left.

Steel and McCready found themselves staring at each other.

Finally, Steel spoke.

"He really means it, you know. He is very grateful… I'm very grateful."

"So what happens now?"

Steel didn't answer for a moment, as though thinking how to broach the next subject. Finally, he looked up.

"Now, I'm afraid, John, we have a little problem."

McCready stiffened.

"We're going to have to do something about that gold."

He looked pointedly at McCready.

"Given what transpired in Russia these past few weeks, in so much as you went expressly against my wishes and what you said you would do, I'm going to have to ask you to hand it over."

McCready just stared at him.

"You said if we helped you we could keep the gold."

"I know. Circumstances change."

McCready was quiet for a moment. "And what if I say you can't have it?"

He watched Steel carefully.

"I did anticipate that response, but I'm afraid it's too late for that. It's one of the reasons you were asked here today. My men are at your house as we speak. Don't worry, when you get back you'll have a perfectly sound wall at the side of your games room."

He paused.

"It just won't be worth quite so much."

McCready could feel his anger growing, but there was one thought that kept him calm.

"I guess that means I can never really trust you again," he said.

"I would understand if that was the position you took," replied Steel.

McCready stood up. "I don't think we have anything else to talk about, do we?"

Steel also stood. "John, I know it's a cliché, but it's nothing personal. I'm amazed at what you achieved and, believe it or not, I'm glad I asked for your help. No one else could have done what you and Richards managed to pull off. I would have no hesitation asking you again if I felt you could be of service to the country. I can quite understand why you might not agree, but, as I told you at the beginning,

I would do anything to protect this country." And then he added, "Even if it meant my own life."

McCready stood watching the man for a moment, and the anger that had been present minutes before started to subside.

He actually believed him.

He held out his hand. Steel took it and they shook—to say warmly would be too much; firmly was probably a better description.

"I can see myself out," said McCready.

And with that, he turned and walked from the room.

As he left, Steel was thoughtful. There had been something in McCready's eyes. A confidence that should not have been there.

He'd taken the information about the gold far better than he'd expected.

When he exited the gates of Downing Street McCready decided to take a walk. He was booked on the 5pm flight back to Aberdeen so he had plenty of time. It was also such a glorious day he thought he would take advantage of the weather. He very rarely made it down to London, and while he was someone who loved the country and wild open spaces, the odd excursion into the capital was occasionally interesting, though his previous visit had been somewhat more eventful than interesting.

He set off up Whitehall toward Trafalgar Square.

The conversation with Steel had been disappointing but, in some ways, not entirely unexpected. He'd always learned that whatever situation you were in it was best to try and be ahead of the game. In the Pacific that hadn't been the case, but if you tried to plan for all eventualities it did at least give you a chance when things went sideways; and going sideways was very much where they had gone in relation to the gold.

He'd been fully expecting to have to give it back when he had first had the call from Steel, but since the man had said they could keep it, he'd thought there might have been a chance to use the funds to make big changes with Ocean Oil moving forward. The fact that Steel had gone back on his word actually irked him more than his statement that men were at his house to demolish the wall and take back the gold.

As he walked into Trafalgar Square he marveled at the 170-foot-tall column with the statue of Nelson standing proud on the top. It was quite clean now many of the famous pigeons that used to frequent the area were no longer there. Beyond it, on the far side, the imposing columns and dome of the National Gallery looked down onto the square below.

He checked the traffic and took his life in his hands to dash between a black cab and a Deliveroo cyclist to make it to the pedestrianized area in the center.

With the sunshine many tourists were out in force. The place was like a melting pot of nations. Everywhere you looked there were people from the four corners of the Earth, all nationalities getting along just fine. It was a microcosm of what the world should look like, but it was more a pipe dream of hope rather than any form of reality.

He grabbed a coffee from a vendor selling hot drinks and snacks, and then walked over to sit on one of the low stone surrounds that encircled the two ornate fountains.

He took a sip of coffee and put the cardboard cup down

next to him, careful not to let it fall into the water. He took out his phone and pulled up the security app for his house. It notified him if any alarms went off, but it also allowed him to control and monitor the CCTV cameras he had located around the property.

The screen currently showed a series of still frames from the various camera positions.

He clicked on the one that showed the rear patio of the house. The image immediately went full screen and turned into high-quality video. He could see a couple of men in work overalls. One of them was carrying a Kango hammer, another was pushing a wheelbarrow. He moved a small digital joystick on the phone. The camera panned slowly around. It was hidden behind a neat weatherproof glass dome so there would be no chance of anyone seeing the movement.

There was no audio, but he could see a man, probably the foreman, talking to someone off camera. The man with the Kango walked over to the center of the wall and placed the hammer against the 'bricks.'

He started it up.

Dust and masonry flew into the air.

After a few seconds he stopped, moved up to the wall, peered closely at it and then tried again a few feet to the right. After a similar result he called the foreman over. The man approached the wall, looked at it, and then indicated he should try other areas.

After about ten minutes there were small holes of broken brickwork in an even spread across the wall. The man with the hammer turned to the foreman and shrugged. He stepped back and wobbled slightly on a loose flagstone. He steadied himself as the foreman pulled a phone from his pocket.

What followed was a heated discussion. He put the phone down, while the other man packed the tools into one of the wheelbarrows and left the shot.

Before everything went quiet, the foreman walked back into frame and stood looking at the wall. As he did so, he stepped on the wobbly flagstone, leaving it tilted at a slight angle.

McCready had a sudden thought and his heart skipped a beat.

He toggled the pan and zoom of the camera to move in on the corner of the flagstone.

Plan B all done. If they come, they'd better not look at their feet.

The light wasn't in quite the right place, but there was no mistaking the golden gleam coming from beneath the flagstone.

When the call came in, Steel was standing in an office he used as his own on the first floor of Downing Street.

He'd been expecting it, but not the information the caller relayed to him.

"You've definitely checked the whole wall?" he said.

"Yes, sir. It's just bricks. Regular, common as muck, house bricks."

"Son of a bitch!" He thought for a moment. "Okay, come on home."

"Yes, sir."

He clicked the phone off.

His face initially showed anger, but then slowly his expression turned to a wry smile. It wasn't the first time he'd underestimated McCready. The respect he had for him grew even more. He would let it go for now. And despite what the man might be currently feeling, he somehow knew their paths would cross again in the future.

He turned back to his desk and looked at an object sitting on the corner.

He sighed deeply.

There was something he still had to do.

Chapter Sixty

Once McCready had seen the man walk off the patio, there'd been no more activity for several minutes. He assumed they wouldn't be back.

Everything would be okay.

He owed Logan one. But considering part of the gold was his, he was sure he'd been glad to have the opportunity to help.

He wondered what Steel would be thinking, and he smiled to himself. But then his expression turned serious.

He looked down at the phone in his hand.

There was something he had put off for far too long. But with everything that had happened he'd shut it out of his mind, thinking it could be taken care of later. But you could only do that for so long.

He had to call Clare.

He really didn't know what he was going to say. She deserved an explanation, and he knew he wanted to see her again. It just wasn't the thing to do long distance; these things never were. But with her on one side of the planet and him on the other, there wasn't much choice.

He clicked the speed dial for her number and listened while the phone rang. At least it wasn't blocked anymore. That had to be a good sign.

Finally it was answered.

"Hi, this is Clare. I can't be reached at the moment. Leave a message at the beep."

BEEEEEP.

He spoke for over a minute. He wasn't sure he made any sense but he had to say something. When he hung up he wasn't relieved, or even happy with himself. He had no idea what she would think or say. He just knew they had had something special, and now that recent events were over, he had come to the conclusion that he needed her far more than he'd previously been prepared to admit.

He just hoped she'd see it the same way and at least give him a chance to explain.

He was about to put the phone away when he noticed one of the app icons he'd almost forgotten about.

It was the one Yassin had put on his phone so he could monitor the tracker in Suki's locket. The tracker he had transferred to the drive that had caused so much trouble.

Out of curiosity he clicked on it.

When it opened, it initially showed a signal strength reading. He hadn't known what would happen as he had no idea where the device had been taken. It was probably at GCHQ, Government Communications Headquarters, in Cheltenham, or some other such location. He was surprised then to see a figure of ninety-eight percent signal strength.

He was even more surprised when the map opened up.

As the last destination had been in Russia, it took a couple of seconds to realign itself. When it had, a red dot, indicating the position of the tracker, appeared on a large-scale map of the UK.

It was in London.

He zoomed in.

As he did, the detail of the map grew greater and greater. When it reached the highest resolution, he stared at the screen, dumbstruck.

The blip indicated the tracker was a few hundred yards away—and it was moving.

He watched as it moved up Horse Guards' Road and along the side of Horse Guards Parade, the large parade ground where the Trooping the Colour ceremony was held in celebration of the monarch's birthday every year.

He jumped up, barely able to take his eyes off the screen.

He headed west through Admiralty Arch and entered The Mall, the wide red tarmac-covered boulevard, lined with trees, that led down to Buckingham Palace at the far end.

The screen showed the tracker moving west from Horse Guards Parade into St James's Park, which bordered the southern side of The Mall.

McCready walked along the edge of the park, keeping station with the position of the tracker. He could see it was now moving along the side of the picturesque lake in the center.

He entered the park halfway down The Mall.

The large, grassy expanses were intersected by gravel paths. He walked down one that led to the lake about four hundred feet in front of him. All around, couples and office workers were out enjoying the sunshine, some lying on the grass, some concentrating on laptops, some just sleeping.

But McCready saw none of them. He was purely focused on the little red dot on the screen of his phone.

The tracker slowed.

It wasn't far away.

He glanced up, wondering who might be carrying it, but his view was obscured by some trees that backed onto the lake. The tracker was just beyond the trees.

He moved closer.

There were a series of benches along the path around the lake. He could see a man in a dark jacket sitting on one of them. He was in his late sixties and had thin graying hair. He was reading a newspaper, occasionally stopping to look at the ducks on the water in front of him.

As McCready watched, he could see another man in a light-colored windbreaker walking along the side of the lake. He wore a hat, which obscured his face, but from the phone screen it would appear that he was the person carrying the tracker.

McCready turned on the camera app and started recording. He checked he had a 5G signal and was comforted with the thought that the footage would already be winging its way up into the cloud.

The man walked up to the bench and sat down.

McCready moved in closer, using the trees for cover. He was about eight feet behind the bench, hidden in the foliage but with a clear view, when he heard the men speak. He couldn't understand what was said, because, as had been proven recently, the only Russian word he knew was for 'thank you.'

A few minutes later the elderly man stood up, patted the other man on the shoulder and walked off in the opposite direction along the path around the lake.

The man in the light-colored windbreaker sat there for a

further minute. McCready stopped recording and flipped back to the tracker app. It showed the tracker moving off down the side of the lake. He switched back to the camera and focused on the man on the bench.

He didn't know what to make of it.

But a second later his whole world fell apart.

Up became down.

Right became wrong.

The man took out a phone and called a number. McCready couldn't hear who answered, but he heard the words the man uttered.

"Yes, Prime Minister, it's done."

And with that, Martin Steel stood up from the bench, glanced around briefly, and then headed back toward Horse Guards Parade.

Chapter Sixty-One

Steel had walked about twenty yards when he slowed. It was as though he had sensed something behind him.

He continued walking, but then glanced casually back. When he saw who it was, he stopped dead.

He turned to face McCready.

The two men stood there, neither speaking.

Finally McCready lifted the phone, showing Steel the screen. It played back the meeting on the bench.

McCready watched him closely.

"It's all in the cloud, so if you plan on doing anything stupid, I'd be careful," said McCready.

Steel looked at him. His expression was as hard as McCready had ever seen it. He knew he was on thin ice, but what was the guy going to do in broad daylight with people all around?

He heard them before he saw them, but by then it was too late. He turned to see two armed men in plain clothes approach from behind. They grabbed his arms and frog-marched him to the nearest bench. At the same time, one of them jabbed a small needle into his neck. The last thing he remembered was being eased down onto the bench and seeing a black Range Rover driving across the grass.

Then everything went dark.

When he came to, he found himself in a small nondescript room.

It was square. There were no windows and the walls were a pale gray. He was sitting at a bland, functional table, about six feet by four feet. There were two chairs, one either side. Both were secured to the floor, as was the table. There was no other furniture. There was also no large black panel on any of the walls signifying a one-way piece of glass, but there were cameras in all four corners of the room. Each one had a little red light beneath. He was in no doubt whatsoever that every moment was being watched and recorded.

He wasn't secured to the chair in any way, but the way his head felt, it would not have been a good idea to stand up —and anyway, where would he go?

Five minutes later the door opened.

Martin Steel walked into the room.

He crossed over to the table and stood watching McCready for a moment. He then shook his head, slowly.

"John, what am I going to do with you?" He sat down on the chair. "Like some water?"

McCready stared at him for a moment, as though resisting any response, but then realized the futility. He nodded slowly.

Steel asked for some water to be brought in—just speaking into the air.

Yes, they were listening.

A moment later a man dressed casually in jeans and a T-shirt brought a tray with a jug of water and two glasses. He placed them on the table and left.

Steel poured the water. He pushed one of the glasses over to McCready.

McCready picked it up and took a long drink. It felt good. When he put it down, Steel leaned back in the chair and fixed him in his gaze.

"That wasn't very clever, what you did back there."

"I had to protect myself," said McCready.

"You don't know what you're protecting yourself from, John. We're the good guys."

McCready gave him an incredulous look. "Really? Giving the drive to a Russian. After all that's happened. The people who've died. All your words about protecting the country. Give me a break!"

Steel stood up and walked behind the chair. He seemed to be thinking how much he should say. He finally stopped and looked straight at McCready.

"My instinct is not to tell you this, but if I do, I hope you'll realize the sacrifices that have been made and understand the decisions I had to make. I also hope you'll realize the lengths I'd be prepared to go to to keep this quiet."

McCready watched him carefully.

Steel continued. "The alternative is that you never see the light of day again."

McCready could tell he wasn't joking. He felt a slight perspiration on his brow.

"Go on," he said slowly.

After a short pause Steel continued.

"I'm sure you're familiar with the concept of the Trojan Horse—Greeks, Trojans, all that. Been great fodder for movies over the years and with good reason: it's a great story—worked pretty well. But you may not know of another tale of deception. One from the Second World War. *Operation Mincemeat*."

McCready was listening.

"The body of a tramp, one Glyndwr Michael, who'd died from eating rat poison, was dressed up as a captain in the Royal Marines. He was given false ID papers, as well as bogus documents, indicating the Allies planned to invade Greece and Sardinia rather than the main objective, which was Sicily.

"The body was released from a submarine off the coast of southern Spain. It drifted with the currents and tide and was picked up by Spanish fishermen. When the documents were handed over to the authorities, the supposedly neutral Spanish promptly showed them to the Germans.

"The information was deemed so important it was sent straight to Berlin. Because of the nature of the way the information was found—so realistic, so believable—no one questioned its authenticity.

"As a result, Axis forces were moved to Greece and Sardinia, allowing a relatively easy ride for the real invasion in Sicily, which was liberated with little loss."

You could have heard a pin drop.

Steel paced some more, as if thinking whether he really wanted to go further.

"Which brings us to our little operation. The Russians were led to believe the computer drive contained information that would give away a major part of our intelligence-gathering capability. Also, that on the drive was a backup of this data. While we do have this capability, the backup wasn't on the drive—merely some made-up information. In fact, the satellite that crashed was one that had been put up a year ago as part of the operation. It was brought down to make the Russians believe the credibility of the information that was being fed to them.

"After that, things went a bit awry. We thought they would get on site far quicker than they did. The hope was for them to reach the satellite and recover the drive just as we were getting there. There would be some sort of standoff and they would prevail.

"However, they had some problems with their sub. To cover this, they put drones in the water to monitor the site. When we turned up we couldn't just wait around for them to get down there. We had to go through the motions of recovering the drive. We then left with the drones following.

"We then had to think on our feet and come up with a plan for them to still get to the sub and recover the drive. They were given information that *Resilient* was experiencing mechanical difficulties. The initial information they received downplayed the severity. But then, through back channels, we made it clear the sub was more crippled than at first thought—again, to add credibility. It was supposedly losing propulsion and unable to surface. Its final position was given as the location off Palau and that part of the fleet was heading there at full speed to assist.

"Where everything went wrong was when Ivanov decided to poison the crew. That was not the plan. They were supposed to just threaten *Resilient*. The captain would then give up the drive to prevent an attack on the sub risking his crew. The Russians would have the drive, we could send in a 'rescue' ship for the sub and all would be fine. What actually happened, was that after Ivanov poisoned the crew, their minisub accidentally hit *Resilient*.

This caused her to roll over, putting the escape hatch at ninety degrees and creating the situation where we required your involvement to access the sub to recover the drive."

McCready was listening incredulously.

"So what would have happened when we had the drive?"

"Again, a meeting would have been engineered where the Russians found you, threatened you, and you would have given them the drive. You weren't military—you'd have been told to hand it over. No one would have thought any more of it."

"You were taking a hell of a risk with our lives," said McCready.

"Yes, but we didn't count on Ivanov behaving the way he did, or indeed, you, when you went off on your little rescue mission."

McCready was trying to process everything he'd heard.

"Okay, say I believe you, and you didn't want any of this to play out as it did. Why do you want the Russians to have the drive so badly?"

Steel looked at McCready. He stood stock still, legs slightly apart.

"I can't tell you that, John."

"Who was the man in the park?"

"A Russian contact. Let's just leave it at that."

McCready thought about this for a moment.

Steel continued. "You have to delete the video you uploaded. This can't get out."

McCready looked up at him. "I want to believe you. I really do. But how do I know you're not just playing me—just some other cog in your elaborate plan?"

"I guess you don't..." He paused. "Maybe you should

use your instinct... Right now, that's all you have to keep you alive."

McCready looked at him sharply.

He had a decision to make.

Finally, he made it.

"Okay, I'll delete the video if you tell me why it's so important the Russians have the drive."

Steel looked at him.

McCready's expression was set.

Steel maintained his gaze for a few more seconds and then spoke to the room again.

"Turn off the cameras and mikes."

McCready stared at him with alarm. He watched as the four red lights below the cameras flicked off one by one.

Steel moved forward and leaned toward McCready, his hands on the table.

"There are only two people in the world who know what I'm going to tell you. Not the MOD, not MI6—just the Prime Minister and me. If this comes out, I will know where it came from. Am I clear?"

The implication of Steel's words was crystal.

McCready nodded.

Steel took a deep breath and stood upright.

"The drive contains a computer Trojan. When it's plugged into the Russian network, which it will need to be to break the encryption, it'll provide an undetectable back door into their system even Mr Kaspersky couldn't detect. It'll allow us unfettered access to everything from command and control protocols and troop movements to war game scenarios and political strategies. We'll even be able to block launch commands to their nuclear missiles. It'll be the greatest intelligence coup in history. It'll change the game forever."

Deep Impact

McCready listened, stunned at what he was hearing.

Suddenly everything made sense.

He understood.

He couldn't talk for a full minute.

Then he looked at Steel. "You got my phone?"

Steel pulled it from his pocket and slid it across the table.

McCready picked it up, tapped the screen several times, waited for an affirmative response, and then looked up at Steel.

"Done."

"I hope so, John. For your sake."

"So, what happens now?"

Steel looked at him closely.

"You're free to go."

McCready looked at him, not quite believing what he was hearing.

"Really? Just like that?"

"Just like that."

"Why?"

Steel thought for a moment.

"I think we have an understanding, you and me."

McCready nodded slowly. He started to get up, still not sure if someone would rush in and restrain him.

He headed for the door.

Steel stepped back to let him pass.

He was almost at the door.

"By the way," said Steel, "where's the gold?"

McCready stopped and turned. He thought for a second and a smile crossed his lips.

"Wouldn't you like to know."

And with that he turned and left the room.

Martin Steel watched him go.

Yep, they had an understanding.

Chapter Sixty-Two

Clare carried the groceries in from the car and dropped the bags on the kitchen floor.

The removal men had finally finished, but that just meant she was surrounded by piles of even more boxes that had to be gone though. She then had to find places for all her things around the house. That was supposed to be the fun part. It certainly didn't feel like it at the moment.

A second later, though, she smiled as Max raced in, skidded on the marble tiles and bumped up against her legs with a disgruntled woof. He licked her feet, and then, as was his habit recently, nipped at her with his small needle-sharp teeth. She yelped and picked him up to give him a cuddle before he could do anymore damage.

"You gorgeous, naughty bundle of fur, you!" She kissed him and then dropped him back down. He had a quick check round in case anyone else was there, and when he realized it was safe, he walked over to his bowl for a drink of water before heading back out through the rear of the house that led to the pool.

Clare looked over at her phone she'd left on the central island in the kitchen. She noticed there were a couple of messages. She clicked the play button and started to unpack the shopping. The first was from her dad, saying he missed her and she should come back up to Montana to see him soon. She smiled at the sound of his voice. They'd wasted too much time apart. She would phone him later to arrange some dates.

It then moved onto the second message.

"Hi Clare, it's John."

This was followed by a pause.

She stopped what she was doing and looked at the phone.

As McCready continued, she walked over and sat on a stool next to it so she could listen.

"I can't imagine what you must have thought last time we met. There is no easy answer, so I will not try to explain in any great detail now, but there is an answer, and an answer, not an excuse." Again a pause. *"I've been involved in some things I couldn't talk about and needed my full attention, which is why I never called you. I realize now that was a mistake. I never saw it from your side. I was stupid. But things have changed. The woman you saw me with died a week ago. I knew her for very little time, but her story is one that needs to be heard to be understood or believed. I would really like the opportunity to tell you about it sometime. In the time I've been away, Craig Richards was nearly killed, I have a number of bullet and knife wounds in my body, and I believe I'm lucky to be alive. I'm not saying this to garner any sympathy or sorrow from you, but to help explain that I haven't just been lying around in the sun, and also that I realize now how much you mean to me, something that maybe I didn't quite understand before. All I ask is you give me the chance to explain in person."* Another pause. *"I'll be thinking of you. I really care about you."* Again, a pause. *"Bye."*

Deep Impact

Clare sat there for several minutes thinking through everything he'd said. She wanted to hate him, for him to have no good explanation. It would make things so much easier.

She crossed over to the fridge, pulled out a carton of apple juice, poured a large, tall glass, and then picked up her phone and walked out onto the surround by the pool. She sat down on one of the padded recliners, put the phone on the low glass table, and then looked up at the sky, letting the sun warm her face.

On the table next to the recliner, she'd left the contract papers for the job at the conference center.

She really liked the idea of the change. She needed something to move forward in her life. But she knew if she took the job it would mean working with Brad, and she knew if she was working with Brad they would become involved. There was just no way round it. She knew he wanted that, and if she didn't, then the position would be untenable. There would just be too much tension. Too many awkward moments. No, if she took the job, she was taking on Brad as well.

She sighed deeply.

But then there was McCready.

She lay back on the recliner and closed her eyes. She had to make a decision.

After five minutes she leaned forward and looked out over the city.

It was a big wide world out there.

It hadn't seemed long since she'd been doing this with Jade on her small balcony in the cramped apartment in Malibu.

But things changed.

The world moved on.

Life moved on.

She watched Max as he ran around the garden, stopping at a tennis ball that lay on the grass. He looked at it and then at a black cat that had suddenly appeared on the top of the neighbor's fence. He couldn't work out which was more important.

Even animals had to make decisions.

She picked up her phone.

Tapped **FAVORITES**.

A small list popped up on the bright OLED display.

She looked at two of the names for more than a minute, her finger hovering above the screen.

Sensible/reliable—exciting/passionate: the eternal female dilemma.

She then focused her eyes on one of them and pushed her finger down.

The phone rang four times and was picked up.

She heard the familiar voice at the other end.

She took a deep breath.

"Hi, it's me."

Next in the John McCready Series

vinci-books.com/deep-hostage

Save the one you love… or save the world.

When terrorists take two of the most powerful people on Earth hostage, for John McCready, a rescue mission turns into a race against time to a backdrop of global disaster.

As events spiral out of control, he faces an impossible decision with the fate of millions in his hands.

Turn the page for a free preview…

Deep Hostage: Chapter One

Eight months ago

With the mercury hitting a hundred and ten degrees Fahrenheit, and humidity at ninety-eight percent, the Paco district of Manila at midday was not a place for the overweight.

But despite the all-encompassing heat, the conditions were not on the mind of Manny Pincher as he eased himself out of the burdened rickshaw. Weighing over four hundred pounds in his boxers, his huge bulk made the average sumo wrestler look anorexic, but his mind was elsewhere as he subconsciously mopped his glistening brow with an already dripping handkerchief.

Mr. Chin, the rickshaw driver, heaved a sigh of relief, wiping away an equal amount of sweat as he watched the kaftan-adorned Pincher lumber across the road.

Chin was in his sixties, thin as a rake, and used to students and tourists, even backpackers with huge rucksacks, but the American was something else. He had paid well—

too well really for the short ride from the Sheraton Manila Bay hotel. The tip had been a week's wages. Even so, it hadn't been worth it.

He arched his back in pain, trying to ease the strain from the half-mile run, and then glanced over as Pincher miraculously made it to the far side of the road without a single collision with any of the numerous bicycles and rickshaws that swerved and veered around the moveable chicane, their little bells tinkling in protest.

Mr. Chin watched as Pincher headed for a side street. He hoped he'd never see the man again. There was something about him that wasn't quite right, and it had nothing to do with his weight.

As Pincher reached the far side of the road he glanced at the rickety array of abandoned, half-built houses that lay in an uneven row down the street ahead. A couple of them had bamboo scaffolding supporting the outside walls. Seemingly the builders had clearly been on half pay when they had constructed them. They were built from wood, and none of the upper floors were aligned with any of the others.

He pulled a piece of paper from his pocket and checked an address.

Number six.

The details on the paper matched the number on a wooden post leaning against the wall of the third house along on the right-hand side.

He walked toward it, his garish yellow flip-flops sliding across the dirt of the road, sending up a trail of dust in his wake.

He shoved the paper back into his pocket and pulled out

a Snickers bar. He tore off the top of the wrapper, dropping it on the ground, and took a bite of the chocolate.

As he did so, a mangy mongrel emerged from under a wooden deck at the front of one of the houses. It walked over to the wrapper and sniffed it. Pincher glanced down at the pitiful beast. Most of its fur was scabby. One of its ears had been half bitten off, and it had a slight limp in its front left paw.

Pincher held the chocolate down so the dog could smell it. The dog approached slowly, cautiously. It had almost reached the bar when Pincher pulled it away and kicked the mutt in the ribs. It yelped in pain, hobbling over to cower behind an overflowing trash can next to the closest building.

Pincher laughed, stuffed the remains of the bar into his mouth, and threw the rest of the wrapper onto the ground. He then walked over to number six and pushed open the door.

It creaked and groaned on its hinges.

It was dark inside.

The door hadn't been locked. He could tell by the state of the place that it had been used by anyone who had chosen to gain entrance. There was a strong smell of urine and rotting waste. He wrinkled his nose at the stench. Why couldn't his clients choose a civilized location for once? But they were paying the big bucks, and his was not to reason why.

He had been told he had to proceed upstairs. He took one look at the narrow, uneven set of wooden steps and wondered if he'd survive the exertion.

Five minutes later he emerged at the top, wheezing hard.

He found himself in a large room.

The whole level of the house was open. There were no internal walls, and there was only one window at the far end, which was covered with a bamboo blind.

The sole illumination came through the uneven joins in the walls that let narrow shafts of light stab across the room. But for what Pincher needed to do, he didn't need a whole lot of light.

In the center was a table and chair, and, as he had known there would be, on the table was an open laptop, its screen emitting a bright glow, like a beacon drawing him forward. There was a USB stick protruding from the side. The laptop was sitting on a raised box about two inches high. It had the same dimensions as the computer.

The only other object in the room was a small high-impact case, about six inches square, sitting on a narrow shelf beneath the window.

Pincher crossed over to the table and sat down on a chair he was sure wouldn't survive his visit. He glanced at the laptop.

The screen was blank except for two document icons in the lower right-hand corner.

As he sat down, a messaging app opened.

He immediately glanced around the room. In one of the far corners, in the shadows, he could just make out a small blinking red light. He couldn't see the camera he knew it would be attached to, but they were watching, of that he could be sure.

He turned his attention back to the screen.

A message had appeared telling him to open the first document on the desktop.

He did so.

Contained within it was a description of information his

client wanted him to access. Once the files were downloaded they were to be put on the USB stick plugged into the computer.

Pincher read through the instructions again.

He smiled.

This would be easy.

Normally there was something that might challenge him, but for one of the premier hackers on the planet, retrieving the security protocols, original blueprints, and details of the senior personnel of a building was child's play —but hey, it was their money.

He rolled his shoulders and started to work.

His fingers flew over the keys. As they did, screens opened within screens, accessing controls and corners of the web few knew existed. It took him all of ten minutes to retrieve the files that had been requested and transfer them to the USB stick.

He had no idea what they were. It was none of his business. He never wanted to involve himself in his client's requests; that could get him into a whole lot of trouble. But he had briefly caught a glimpse of the schematics he had downloaded. As the plans had streamed onto the screen he'd noticed high-tech elevators, secure, pressurized rooms, even a tunnel carved out of rock. It looked impressive.

Once the files were securely on the USB stick, he clicked on a COMPLETE button within the messaging app. A return message confirmed his $100,000 fee was ready to transfer.

He sat back, a smile on his face.

But there was the second document on the desktop.

He clicked on it.

The file also contained instructions. As he read through,

an even broader smile spread across his face, particularly when he saw his fee.

This was more like it.

A challenge…

…with a price to match.

He interlinked his fingers, stretching his palms outward, like a conductor about to control an orchestra, which, in essence, was what he was about to do.

He concentrated on the screen, thought for a moment, and then let his fingers play across the keys. He would have to go far deeper into the web to find the tools to hack into the Pentagon.

As he worked, he felt a thrill spread through his body that was better than sex.

While Manny Pincher was not adept in the physical world, he was a supreme athlete in the digital one. There may well be people who could run faster, jump higher, swim further than him, but there were few who had the dexterity, ability or talent to go where he was going now.

It took longer this time.

Twenty minutes.

But when he had finished, he had the complete schedule for the US Navy's covert vessels research and development program.

He transferred the documents onto the USB stick and clicked COMPLETE.

A return message confirmed his fee had grown by $500,000 to a total of $600,000 and was now ready to transfer.

But then another message beeped.

It instructed him to take the USB stick and put it in the case by the window.

That was strange.

What could be the purpose of that?

But again, his was not to reason why.

Anyway, his head was filled with the thoughts of what he was going to spend the money on. There was a red, second hand Ferrari Testarossa at the dealership in Mandaluyong that had his name on it.

He ejected the stick, pulled it from the side of the computer, and shambled over to the window. He opened the highly protective case, placed the USB stick inside, and closed the top securely.

When he returned to the computer, there was a message instructing him to place his eye close to the laptop camera to confirm the transfer of funds.

He sat down and moved forward to look into the tiny lens at the top of the screen.

As soon as his corneal pattern had been confirmed, there was a beep.

It was the last thing Manny Pincher ever heard.

The explosives in the box beneath the laptop detonated, blowing off half the American's head, totally destroying the laptop.

The blast wasn't enough to damage the room. In fact, more damage was done by Pincher sliding off the chair and crashing to the floor, splintering a number of the floorboards.

He would never see the young girl, who, ten minutes later, ran into the room, picked up the case by the window, retrieved the camera from the corner, and ran out again without a glance at the massive hulk lying on the floor.

It also meant he would never hear the faltering patter of tiny feet as the mangy dog hobbled up the steps and into the room.

Deep Impact

If Pincher had been alive he would no doubt have felt a warm sensation in his left foot, one that would have turned into a sharp pain, as the starving mongrel, first started to lick his foot, and then chewed and gnawed ravenously through the bones in his toes.

Deep Hostage: Chapter Two

Six months ago

The tiny bubble started its desperate bid for freedom from around a hundred feet underwater. Along with countless other small silver spheres, it headed up toward the pale moonlight that was imperceptibly breaking through the surface somewhere above.

When it reached a depth of thirty-three feet the water pressure had reduced by half, allowing the bubble to expand to twice its size. It had now become dome-shaped, resembling a quivering spaceship as it hurtled ever upward. With its increase in size came an increase in buoyancy and therefore speed.

When it finally broke the surface, it was traveling far faster than the fifty feet per minute at its birth, and it had again doubled in size, this time between thirty-three feet and the surface—a perfect demonstration of the physics of Boyle's law.

With a small pop, it expelled its gas into the atmosphere

in a joyous gasp, now free from the constraints and tethers of the inky black depths below.

The makeup of the gas was eighty percent nitrogen, sixteen percent oxygen and four percent carbon dioxide. The exact composition of exhaled human breath.

The surface began to froth with the now constant release of gas from the regular stream of bubbles rising from the depths. Between the shimmering silver balls on their upward charge, a flickering, dancing light could be seen, growing brighter by the second. It was an erratic, haphazard light that seemed to represent a panic all of its own. Within seconds it was flashing across the surface, heralding the arrival of something greater. As if in support of the imminent event, the bubbles joined as one in a frothing mass of incandescent light sparkling in the water.

Suddenly, the neoprene-clad hand of a fully equipped scuba diver broke through the surface. Droplets of water cascaded in all directions, backlit by the moon like some sort of surreal special effect.

As the diver rose up, the momentum of the high-speed ascent sent his upper body three feet out of the water.

With a gasp, Ilya Kozak ripped the Oceanic Omega demand-valve from his mouth, sucking in the life-giving air. As his body settled back, he jabbed the direct-feed control on his buoyancy compensator, injecting air to provide lift and keep him on the surface without struggling. Pushing the dive mask to his forehead, he looked around desperately in all directions. Even in the moonlight, his young East European features were evident, almost beautiful, despite the harrowed, anguished expression he currently wore. All around, the sea was an oily calm, the moonlight sending an uninterrupted ribbon of glistening silver to the horizon.

He stared in all directions, flashing the dive-light across

the surface as if looking for someone, but he was alone. As he turned, he spotted land in the distance. Trying to focus, he made out a harbor at the base of a cluster of lights. It looked like there were buildings, and movement—yes, a vehicle's headlights, people walking around, and the muffled hum of a generator drifting on the night air. He finned madly out of the water, waving his arms and yelling at the top of his voice, but no one heard him.

The sound of the generator hid his plight.

He shouted again, but to no avail. In desperation, he took another look round, then struck out for the harbor. It was a harried, frantic, overarm stroke, his fins beating the water in an undisciplined effort to propel him toward safety.

Grab your copy...
vinci-books.com/deep-hostage

About the Author

Throughout my life I have always tried to seek out adventure, whether real or imaginary. Much of this has taken place in, on, or under the water.

My love of diving has allowed me to explore the oceans of the world and also work extensively in the film and TV industry.

This spirit has filtered through to my creative writing, which includes the John McCready thrillers – a smart, fast paced action/adventure series with twists and turns right up to the end.

In the real world, LIGHTS! CAMERA! SUB ACTION! takes you behind the scenes of underwater projects in the film and TV industry.

But the one thing all the books have in common, is a sense of excitement and the unknown; whether journeying with a hero battling the odds on thrilling and dangerous adventures, or diving sunken shipwrecks and coral reefs in the company of sharks, manta rays and other creatures of the deep.

Lights! Camera! Sub Action!

A behind-the-scenes look at working on underwater projects in the film and TV industry.

LIGHTS! CAMERA! SUB ACTION!